Michael M. Naydan

SEVEN SIGNS OF THE LION

A NOVEL

GLAGOSLAV PUBLICATIONS

SEVEN SIGNS OF THE LION

by Michael M. Naydan

Publishers Maxim Hodak & Max Mendor

© 2016, Glagoslav Publications, United Kingdom

Glagoslav Publications Ltd
88-90 Hatton Garden
EC1N 8PN London
United Kingdom

www.glagoslav.com

ISBN: 978-1-911414-17-9

A catalogue record for this book is available
from the British Library.

Michael M. Naydan

SEVEN SIGNS OF THE LION

A NOVEL

DISCLAIMER

If you see yourself or anyone you think you know as one of the characters in this work of pure fiction and unadulterated authorial imagination, you are sorely mistaken. It is definitely not you or the person you think you might know and you may have a problem distinguishing fantasy from reality. This book, however, might actually be for people like you, though there are certain dangers in associating yourself with characters of fiction. Real place names and real names of certain public figures are used for the sake of establishing setting. All scenes are fictional! None of this ever happened, though you might think it did, and who could blame you for that? Thinking is always allowed. Any similarities in the pages that follow to real living or deceased individuals would be purely coincidental.

ACKNOWLEDGEMENTS

An excerpt from the novel "The Seer of Specters" appeared in issue No. 20 of the journal ElevenEleven. An excerpt of the first three sections of the novel appeared in Larysa Bobrova's Ukrainian translation in the Internet literary portal Zakhid-skhid.

For the best of Muses – Yaroslava, Myroslava and Kalyna

*HIS*STORY

Stories all must start somewhere, so this one starts right here or maybe just before or right after. Where it will end not even the author knows sometimes. Some authors follow a well-designed plan with everything laid out in exquisite logical order, others just follow a path or a road, and no matter how much it zigzags or winds, goes uphill or down, it always *must* take you somewhere or back to where you came from. So if you follow it, you will end up wherever it takes us both, to a somewhere, because this author is not the kind who can ever lay out everything in advance like crooked cobblestones on a seemingly perfectly straight road. One should add, though, that tales could often come to a crossroads with a significant choice of three paths to take. At those crossroads a raven usually caws and speaks. He might tell you, in whatever language you speak, that one road may lead to great riches, another to happiness and love, and the third possibly to death. But, of course, heroes sometimes never know the true meaning of the raven's riddle. Riches can lead to ruin, happiness and love can end up in boredom, and the path of death can lead to a great quest, a spiritual awakening, and untold rewards. Or, then again, it might be none or a combination of the above…. I'm not sure what the raven would caw here if he would speak in his hoarse gravely raven voice, since there is no raven to riddle us with the meanings of the choices about to be made.

WHERE DREAMS HAPPEN, JOURNEYS FOLLOW

This story begins with a dream. The dream of Nicholas Bilanchuk to be more precise. It was a murky, dark dream, one that left him brooding. It was a call, an invitation to take a journey to seek out something. One of those lucid dreams that makes you shudder when you wake up because it appears so real that you're not sure if it is, or whether you're waking up in the dream or in your reality. It's one of those dreams that make you question whether you even know what reality is sometimes. Even though the dream was lucid, Nicholas had waited too long before writing it all down, so he was left just with the patchy outlines of his fragmented memory.

It was a dark, misty night in the old downtown of a city with winding well-worn cobblestone streets. It looked centuries old, but there were slow-moving dark green tramcars screeching on tracks and people dressed in fairly modern clothes. So it couldn't have been that long ago, and it could have even been right now or tomorrow. There were older, heavyset women wearing scarves selling some kind of blackish beans in paper cups and scruffy beggars sitting in doorways in scratchy dark brown wool pants with matching oversized suit coats that seemed to be as old and dusty as the beggars were. There was a balding, bearded man dressed in a colorful bowtie and black tuxedo, who seemingly had come to life after having stepped down from a statue on one of the buildings in the city square. He was telling Nicholas he had something to show him, even though Nicholas could not speak the language that the statue-turned-into-a-man was speaking. The more he listened, the more Nicholas understood the language. Something about keys to unlock locks. The doors of tomorrow. Equilibrium. Universe. Powerful energy fields rising from beneath the earth. All over the city. The eye in the triangle. Following every step. Dangerous passage. Restless spirits. Wandering. Steps to a cavernous cavern and an underground river where two worlds meet, or two sides of the same world, a line that was both a barrier and an interface. Something about signs. Signs of the lion. Seven of them. The signs needed to be found. Order needed to be restored. Order out of chaos. Out of the order – disintegration. Two worlds along the fault line of quotidian and non-quotidian time.

The man in the tuxedo and red plaid tie smiled and pointed at Nicholas. "You're the one," he seemed to be saying. "You're the one." Nicholas heard the thoughts even though he didn't understand the language. And Nicholas felt a tug at his heart and mind. "Come to the city, the city of lions. All the answers lie there if you make the journey." Nicholas looked up on top of a building and saw the head of the statue motionless and back in place on the roof. How it came down to speak with him he didn't know.

Snippets, just patches of words quilted together. Nicholas wished he could have remembered more. In those moments right after lucid awakening, everything is clear. Just a short time later the dream memory like a stained glass window broken by a thrown brick and fallen to the ground was now shattered in shards and losing its narrative. You could see parts of it in individual pieces, but its wholeness was gone. Perhaps the wholeness of it would have made more sense to him. But then again, it was now a mystery. Mysteries leave a trail to follow to solve and a pressing need to solve and resolve them. And Nicholas needed to find the glue to reconstruct the shattered stained glass narrative for himself.

HEROES

What should a hero be? Joseph Campbell says he can be of a thousand faces. A hero can be pure of heart, pure of spirit, a man of suffering, a man of forgiveness, a man of wildness tamed. Or a woman of all the above, since heroes are not just of one gender. There are all different kinds of heroes. Some show feats of strength. Some show feats of mind and mental acuity. Some stumble their way into situations backward. Some try too hard. Some don't try enough. Some who want to be heroes just can't be, some who think they can't be turn out to be the best of them. All heroes have doubts and failures because all heroes are human. It could be a random teenage girl with a calling to lead the armies of France, or Davids tossing stones at Goliaths, or a paralyzed Ilya of Murom who drinks the water of life to gain his strength back to defeat the evil Tartars threatening his homeland. Throughout all of recorded and unrecorded time one person has always had the capacity to make history turn, though most people may not believe that. All heroes must begin their journey with the first page. This is already the fourth.

SLIGHTLY REMEMBERED ANCESTORS

It was a journey he planned to the roots of the homeland of not particularly remembered ancestors, one that was foreign to him, since he grew up in the environs of the melting pot of the New York City area. Those ancestors simply weren't remembered by him in his own living memory, so he had to learn about them in other ways, and if such a thing exists, perhaps it was some kind of a genetic memory of them that he somehow still retained as well as bits and pieces of familial oral history. He was also forced to learn about them in the dreaded Ukrainian Saturday schools where he had to memorize poems by Taras Shevchenko, Ivan Franko and Lesya Ukrainka and where he was taught by laxative-intolerant refugee men and women in their seventies. In that way he learned about the language and country of what had become fossilized in their fading memory from the years 1943-1945 when these refugees were forced into Nazi work camps. They were later to be named with the more elegant euphemism – displaced persons. Nicholas's grandfather and father used to call them dependable people. His grandfather learned the trade of a mason even though he was a schoolteacher back in the old country. His university degree and education meant nothing in a land where he needed to learn English just to survive, much less find the money to return to school for more degrees even to approximate his previous social status. His first job was as a janitor, then a night watchman, and then an apprentice mason's assistant until he learned the trade from his toothless Italian mentors whose broken English was worse than his. It was easier just to work, though he kept on top of all the events going on back in the homeland including the Brezhnev years of repression, the Chornobyl explosion in 1986, the end of the Soviet Union in 1991 and Ukrainian independence. He didn't live to see the Orange Revolution of 2004. He would read his Svoboda Ukrainian daily newspaper out of Jersey City religiously as three or four of them often would arrive on the same day. So he went from respected intellectual to respected manual laborer and craftsman, though he did make pretty good money until his retirement. He proudly bought his first black Buick with cash (he didn't believe in credit) and kept it for nearly twenty years. He pronounced the name something like "Boo-ick." In emigre Ukrainian it was his *kara* (taken from the English word "car"), which in real Ukrainian meant "punishment." It wasn't a punishment of course, but rather just something to get him to church, to work, and to the store. He barely put 5000 miles a year on it and it was always waxed to a lustrous shine. He bought the first family home in Queens the same way, with money saved and not a penny wasted on frivolous things. A lot of his friends from the old country squandered their money in bars and in the Ukrainian club called Tryzub, or Trident, but not he. (The trident was the emblem of Ukraine that was banned in Soviet times. It's made a comeback since independence.) He did love to drink whisky and Rolling Rock beer, but never to excess. He'd religiously have a shot of Seagram's Seven in the morning when he woke up, at lunchtime with the Italian crew of masons, and in the evening after dinner. Like a Japanese, he couldn't pronounce the "l" in "Rolling," so it came out sounding like "Rorring." He lived to the ripe age of 77, never having been sick a day in his life in his adopted homeland. He did, however, become a bit stooped over because of the heavy hauling he had to do. The years of heavy loads of mud, as the paesano masons called it, of mortar, in wheelbarrows and lifting sixteen-inch blocks curved his back into scoliosis and made him an inch or two shorter, though he never was one to complain – except about the "lyakhy" (the pejorative Ukrainian word for Poles) and the "prokliati Moskali" (accent on the last syllables – the damned Russkies).

Mention the word "communism" or "revolution," and he would fly into a rage. He and his wife Olesya, who worked at the counter in a bakery shop in the Ukrainian neighborhood where they had settled, saved every nickel they could squirrel away to pay for the education of Nicholas's father, who graduated from high school despite having to learn English as a teenager and who got an engineering degree from Stony Brook University and along with that a well-paying job with the local planning commission as their engineering consultant. Nicholas's younger brother Yaroslav (known as Jerry by his American friends) got his accounting degree from Stony Brook, while Nicholas got his in English literature from there, too.

Nicholas took a job at Nassau Community College and learned to hate it with a passion, a hate that grew with each year. The place wasn't bad. It just was stifling him, and he didn't know why. The students were getting worse each year (or he was getting smarter – *hardly*!), and the course load was way too heavy, though the pay was pretty good. He just was suffering from burnout. His brother with the malleable bicultural name Yaroslav-Jerry, who could have never even dreamt of forgetting his Ukrainian origins as a result of that first name, married the proverbial nice Ukrainian girl next door Rostyslava (Rusty in English), whom he met at church on Sunday, and was living the hyphenated Americrainian assimilation dream with three kids and a house in Syosset. He worked as an accountant for Pathmark, and his wife became the archetypal Ukrainian *hospodynia*, or housewife, making everyone gain pound after pound each year on Ukrainian *varennyky* (potato dumplings), *holuptsi* (stuffed cabbage), and tortes of all kinds for special and even not very special occasions. Great torte making entered Ukrainian culinary life through the Austro-Hungarian occupation. Some colonial invasions have their upside. He and his wife became more and more Americanized and just as the church they attended switched to mostly English masses, their Ukrainian identity became more and more submerged and melt-ingpotted as time went on. They spoke at home in English to the kids to the disdain of the grandparents, but made them go to the summer camps at the Ukrainian Soyukivka resort in the Catskills at Kerhonkson. But that attrition of language skills will happen when foreigners come to foreign lands and have children. Oddly, Nicholas, who wasn't particularly interested in the homeland of his ancestors when he was growing up, who didn't have kids of his own, got infected with searching for his ethnic roots later in his life.

Nicholas had gotten married much too early and his "mixed marriage" (i.e., to a non-Ukrainian Sicilian girl and also the child of emigrants, the latter of whom could barely speak English even after being in the US for over thirty years). Nicholas and Gina after several years of making a go of it just came to the mutual realization that they didn't get along and couldn't iron out the differences between them. They turned out to be just totally different people than the two people who married each other. Nicholas was both introspective and outgoing, that is, he became outgoing after overcoming his early teenage shyness. He was also a Libra and even-tempered, though he didn't believe in any kind of zodiacal predetermination of personality. Gina was Aquarian, restive, fiery and even explosive, but also very introverted. Over time Nicholas constantly began to brood over his job, which bored him beyond tears. Unhappiness breeds unhappiness (Tolstoy must have said something like that, Nicholas thought, as he recalled it from one of the classes he had taken at Stony Brook with a professor of Polish extraction), and he bred a lot of it, though he and Gina thankfully neither birthed nor bred any children, though they tried. But you need the former to do the latter.

The dream to go to the homeland came a year or so after his marriage ended. There were no kids to divide Solomonically; they had two separate but equal cars of the same vintage, so they could each take one, both of them Toyotas and no longer American-made Buicks like his grandfather's; and both shared just an apartment as their abode, one that Nicholas was happy to move out of, taking with himself most of the Ukrainian trinkets he had recently accumulated in his search for his Ukrainian roots (a Kozak (aka as Cossack) *bulava*, or mace (a symbol of power); multicolored *pysanky* Easter eggs; a few embroidered shirts; inlaid enamel wooden boxes from the Carpathians; and a growing Ukrainian music and literature collection he had picked up from the Arka and Surma Ukrainian stores on Seventh Street on the Lower East Side). He particularly liked the Kvitka Cisyk folk songs he had picked up. Her voice was pure, gentle and powerful, and the instrumentation exquisite. Unfortunately, Kvitka, whose name means "flower," withered away of breast cancer in 1998. Her claim to fame in American culture was singing the "Have you driven a Ford, lately?" jingle and having had her name mangled when she appeared on the Johnny Carson show once. Gina decided to keep the embroidered tablecloths someone had given them as a wedding gift because they reminded her of the Italian ones her own mother had brought over from her mother's home town of Sciacca in Sicily.

When the dream of Mr. Viktor and the murky city had come to him, Nicholas took it quite seriously. He first decided to take an extended summer vacation and sign up for an advanced Ukrainian language class at the Harvard Ukrainian Research Summer Institute. He had started taking another class at the same time with a professor of Ukrainian literature from Yale or Princeton; he couldn't quite remember where he was from, but it was one of the Ivies. The guy was SO arrogant and had SUCH a condescending attitude that Nicholas dropped it on the first day.

Nicholas's homespeak Ukrainian was on the old-fashioned side and frozen in time circa 1943 when his grandparents had left – since they and his parents were the conveyors of his spoken language skills. He also remembered many of the Old Church Slavic words from church services such as "prysno," "vonmim" and "paky, paky." So at the summer class he had to unlearn those ingrained habits of kitchenspeak and churchspeak with his parents and grandparents, who lived in houses next door to each other in the Ukrainian neighborhood in Queens on 31st Street, to learn to speak in the way that Ukrainian was spoken now in the abandoned homeland.

Nicholas's teacher Andreya in the summer program was from the Taras Shevchenko University in Kyiv and was super. She was bright, bubbly and kindhearted, and married to an energy company executive in Ukraine. Nicholas spent some extra time with her in the afternoons working on his spoken Ukrainian and she on her spoken English in the coffee shops and ice cream parlors of Cambridge, and by the end of the summer session, he had built up enough confidence to take the plunge for a journey.

Nicholas also met the Ukrainian writer Andriy Yurkevych there, who gave a reading from his poetry and prose works. Yurkevych was doing a writer's residency in the summer at the Tufts creating writing program. He had been invited by Rurik Denysiuk, who, despite the heavy-duty Scando-Ukrainian first and inescapably Ukrainian last name was Director of the program and a poet and novelist who wrote in English. The three of them (Nicholas, Rurik and Andriy) hit it off quite well and spent a lot of time in the evenings ruminating over the meaning of the universe as well as the blessings and curses of Ukrainianness, and sipping cognac and draft beer in the establishments of Cambridge like the B-Side Lounge and John Harvard's. The Ajanta Indian restaurant on First Street was also a favorite spot for them to meet. Nicholas loved spicy Indian food, and Andriy enjoyed both that as well as the exotic flavors he had never tasted before his residency abroad. He later wrote a cycle of poems called "The Tastes of India" that must have been influenced by the meetings at the restaurant. And Nicholas invited Andriy to come visit him on Long Island for a few weeks at the end of the summer and the beginning of the academic year where they spent some time at Long Island Beaches and visiting Nicholas's good graduate school friend Sarah at her family's summer home in Sag Harbor.

With speaking skills improved after the end of the summer in Cambridge, Nicholas decided to apply for a Fulbright to teach English during the course of the next academic year – and to his surprise managed to get one on the first try. He was granted a leave of absence from his teaching position for a five-month Fulbright stay and got a placement at Ivan Franko National University in Lviv, the city of lions, a city of about 800,000 people (and a good 120,000 of them students) in what was described to him as the western cultural capital of the country. It was the biggest city closest to the villages where his grandparents and parents were from, and, in fact, nearly equidistant from both of their respective villages. It was also the city that in a purely intuitive way he somehow understood *had* to be the city of his lucid dream. Some things you just seem to know.

FLIGHT 4772 TO WARSAW

The first leg of the flight to Warsaw was mostly uneventful except for one chance meeting. Though curiously Nicholas met a rather attractive woman by the name of Lilia from Poland on the flight. Her long pitch-black and naturally curly hair flowed down her shoulders and back. Unfortunately for Nicholas, he was able to speak with her mostly only for the last two hours of the flight. By nature Nicholas was shy, and it took him a while to start up a conversation with her, and she was extremely tired and slept for several hours before awakening from a deep sleep that seemed filled with dreams.

"Do you speak English?" He mentioned to her after she groggily woke up as the plane according to the flight-position tracker screen was flying over England.

"Sure," she laughed with a nice sparkle in her warm brown eyes. "I did my Ph.D. at Harvard. I've lived in the States for five years."

"Oh… I did my Ph.D. at Stony Brook in English. I wrote on Milton and Blake. You know, the heaven and hell stuff. Paradise lost and paradise gained. What did you write on?"

"Antonych."

"Is he Polish?"

"Kind of," she laughed. "He's Lemko, but he wrote in Ukrainian. He was a poet who died in 1937," she said in her mildly accented English. "Bohdan Ihor Antonych is his full name."

"So what are you doing in Poland?"

"That's where I live. I teach Ukrainian at Jagiellion University in Krakow. But I've traveled a lot to Lviv. That's where Antonych went to school and did most of his writing. He died of pneumonia there in a hospital in 37."

"Wow!" He said. "That's quite a coincidence. I'm going over to Lviv on a Fulbright. I've been learning Ukrainian and getting back into my family roots. You might think it's a bit strange, but I had a dream about seven signs of the lion that I need to find in Lviv. It intrigued me."

"You know, Antonych has a poem called "The Sign of the Lion...," she said, and paused thoughtfully. "I have a copy of it in this book," and she pulled out a volume from her travel bag and flipped through it until she found the poem. "It's from his 1936 collection *Book of the Lion*."

"Can you help me translate it into English?"

Here is the translation that emerged from their collaboration:

THE SIGN OF THE LION

A kingdom of dead flowers – the desert sleeps
in a golden red shirt of sand.
The stripling sedge is the devilry of foliage,
the chasing of the sun's ecstasy and lightning.

Living candles above the coffin of the earth,
stiff weeds suddenly like a burning bush.
Like bushes bent over by a hand,
the bottomless abysses of faith bend aside.

And you see eternity – an opal sky
and the fluttering of the red streams of flame.
From behind mountains of centuries the Constellation
of the Lion leads, this is the sign
                    of monarchs, of warriors, of prophets.

The sun darkens in a cloud of gray birds,
the laurels of a storm crown it, brown, blue,
and thunder, like the golden signature in a book,
will endure on the pages of the desert.

The signature of thunder in the royal book of lions
written by the winds from below the Sinai,

from the slopes of the mountain that embellish the brocade
spire of sands with the garland of God's lightning.

Sinai wind, strike the open playing cards!
Without you I am an empty vessel of form.
On guard all the day over a prophetic spring,
and the night is like a bible red and black.

Nicholas thanked Lilia as they disembarked from the plane and
took down her phone number and exchanged email addresses with
her. Was the poem the first sign of the lion he was supposed to find?
He was tired at that point since he couldn't sleep on the plane, so
he'd have to mull it over another time.

ARRIVAL

Nicholas's first impression of the country after he arrived by plane from Warsaw was, to be honest, that of a third-world place. The sturdy but noisy Lot Airlines propeller plane that carried him to Lviv took about an hour and a half during a mildly bumpy ride. In looking at the name of the airline, Nicholas focused on the fact that it's strange how the same word means different things in different languages. "Lot" means "fly" in Polish, "lead weight" in Russian, "fate" in English (as in the English expression "that is my lot"), and in Ukrainian the same as in Russian. It is also the Biblical name of the single righteous man, whose family is saved by God from fiery destruction and whose wife's curiosity ends up turning her into a pillar of salt.

The cement runway looked weatherworn and pockmarked on the cloudy day. Lviv, Nicholas was to find out, was well known for its cloudy days and rain. Nicholas remembered a Natalka Bilotserkivets poem he read in his language class with Andreya that started with the line "It always rains in the cities of Lviv and Ternopil." Bilotserkivets, whose name means "white church," was actually from Sumy and not from Bila Tserkva (the town of White Church – 400 kilometers away from Sumy) in Central Ukraine, though the latter is probably where her distant relatives might have been from. Your last name in Ukrainian can often reveal where you come from. Nicholas was learning that names could be quite meaningful in Ukrainian.

The plane landed and Nicholas got off with everyone else to board a dilapidated pigeon-blue and grimy white bus that took the passengers to the gray, green and dingy terminal room. Various declaration forms were strewn all about in different languages in antediluvian holders on the walls and on very short tables that were quite uncomfortable to write on. Nicholas couldn't find a declaration form in English or Ukrainian, so he decided to do the one in Russian because he could at least understand it.

It took nearly an hour to get through the baggage check and customs at the airport. They questioned him on whether he had gifts for relatives (all his aunts and uncles had died, though he might have had some cousins left, but he didn't know them). But his name was a common one – so he could be related to half the country. Two faculty members from Ivan Franko National University greeted him at the airport – Marta and Roman, who were linguistics and history professors respectively. Roman was a bearded man of average height with long dark hair and an expert on the ancient world of Greece and Rome, and Marta was a sweet and animated comparative linguist specializing in metaphorical constructions in English as compared to the Slavic languages. They were his good and caring hosts for the duration of his visit and helped get him settled in his apartment at 13 Nechui-Levytsky Street and in learning the ways of his new land for the next five months. Their friend Marko, a photographer for the Lviv Gazette newspaper, happened to have a trusty, not very late model maroon Volkswagen, which Marko offered for picking Nicholas up. Nicholas was to find out that Nechui-Levytsky was a realist Ukrainian writer from the 19th and early 20th centuries. For Nicholas, the city of Lviv-Leopolis turned out to be far from a third-world land and more than a cold, gray, wet and stony city. It was, rather, a place of great beauty and history, and, apparently, of mystical dimensions and implications.

NO ONE EVER PUTS
CHANGE IN YOUR HANDS

Almost no one ever puts change in your hands in this country when you buy things. Very different from back home where everyone without a second thought will take the grubbiest-looking money from your hands and give you change right into your hands. They must think money is dirty by its nature here. It must have been remnants of socialism or an aversion to capitalism. Most shops and restaurants, and even food carts on the street, have a small plastic tray on the counter for money with an advertisement for beer, cola or something else emblazoned on it. You place the money on it and you get change back on the plate. They'll only put money into your hands if the plate is somehow covered with the half-loaf of bread you're about to buy or some other goods you're buying that have covered the tray.

EVERYBODY PLOWS
THROUGH YOU ON THE STREETS

Leopolis is a dangerous place for walkers, of which there are multitudes. Everyone walks here, particularly in the downtown feeder streets to the Old Town areas. People nearly knock you over every time. It's utter madness with its own rules and regulations unlike the ones you're used to back home where you usually move to the right of anyone coming in the opposite direction. It's like a gray stone billiard table with tens of thousands of human billiard balls, but no one knocks into anyone else. Expect every driver here in this city NOT to stop for you. Half of them are in big SUVs or BMWs (status symbols) and most of them are talking on a cell phone, as they are about to plow through you. They only stop when a uniformed police office sticks out a baton or a hand at them. They do also stop screechingly at the white-lined pedestrian crossings, of which there seemed to be at least a few in the city.

If Nicholas were to wait during the morning from 9-11a.m. or early evening from say 4-8 P.M. to cross Copernicus Street near his house, he'd still be there waiting. It's just a solid line of cars all the way to the light at Nechui-Levytsky Street. You learn to pick a spot to jump across the street in front of a car that had come to a stop and just started to pick up speed. When they're not gunning the engine, they'll slow down for you, or at least they won't step on the gas. There was the same problem crossing the street by the main post office near the university, but at least there were a lot of traffic lights where you could cross. There were also immense problems crossing the street at Sich Riflemen Street all the way to the center of town. Fortunately cars would turn left or right onto side streets, which gave you sufficient time to sneak across to get to the Puzata Khata (Pot-Bellied House) restaurant for your cup of coffee or cheap but tasty Ukrainian fast-food meal of the day. Varennyky, the potato dumplings with sour cream, and the borsch were Nicholas's favorites there, and worth risking your life to cross the street to get to the restaurant.

The parking is another issue. WHAT parking? There are no public parking lots or parking areas. The city wasn't built for cars. People just pull their vehicles onto the sidewalks regardless of what size they are and wherever they can. They even block narrow entryways into courtyards of buildings where people park their cars and can't get in and out. It's an unwritten rule that taxi drivers take up the corner positions on the sidewalk, sometimes on all four corners of an intersection. They sit in their cars smoking a cigarette or blasting some god-awful Russian *popsa*, pop music until you knock on the taxi window to barter for half the price they ask for. No taxi meters in the taxis in Leopolis, but Nicholas learned to dial 059, 081 and 083 for the radio taxis that charged ten hryvnas to get to the train station instead of 15-20 from the ones on the streets. He knew he'd never complain about parking in New York ever again.

Sundays were the only days of rest from the traffic. Gendarmes dressed in round hats and with billy clubs stood at the feeder streets to the Old Town with orange traffic cones blocking off all vehicles except the tramcars that had to get through on the rails and an occasional VIP car. Sunday was strolling day in Leopolis – couples young and old, families, groups of teenagers and older students. Nicholas learned to appreciate Sundays when the only vehicles on Liberty Avenue were the horse drawn carriages carrying tourists and the miniature electric cars for kids in front of the Opera House.

ALMOST NO ONE SAYS THANK YOU IF YOU DO SOMETHING NICE FOR THEM (EXCEPT YOUR FRIENDS)

That seemed to change a bit over time. Nicholas made a point of always thanking people in shops and cafés. Every once in a while he'd get a response. He held doors open for men, women and domesticated beasts, and received the politest response usually from the beasts, dogs that smiled a happy smile of gratitude. The entrance to the main building of the university was a particular problem for Nicholas. It had a single door open of its double doors with a constant flow of people coming in and out. At first Nicholas, through a lifetime of ingrained habit, would wait. But he learned that he would just keep waiting if he waited. He learned he couldn't be polite and manage to enter the doors of the university to teach his classes. You had to simultaneously plow through the door sideways as people were coming from the opposite direction to force them to turn sideways and let you in. In his first two months there, he recalled holding the door open for an older woman who smiled at him and said "spasybi," (thank you, that literally comes from the expression "praise be to God"). But she was the only one.

Your friends, of course, are a different story. Your friends here are always there for you. And always generous to beyond a fault. And always polite and caring and giving. It was one of the beautiful things he learned to love about the place. He learned that a place just isn't a place. It's the people.

THE LVIV-KYIV EXPRESS

Nicholas woke up at 4 A.M. – an hour before he had set his alarm clock. Premonition of an impending trip always made him super sensitive to time. He was on his way to a Fulbright orientation meeting in Kyiv, which was little more than six hours away on the express train. After he called the taxi at 5 A.M., he stepped out into the entryway of Building 13 on Hyphenated Writer Street as he called it, Nechui-Levytsky Street, and waited there for ten minutes till it arrived. That was one guy with two names. Nicholas's apartment was #11 in Building 13. Although he knew that fact, he had never focused on the number of the building before. Sleep depravation makes you conscious of different things. Not that it bothered him that it was building #13. He wasn't superstitious. But he was glad his apartment wasn't #13. That would have been a double-whammy. The cobblestone streets with tramcar tracks in both directions were wet with snow falling at the just below freezing air temperature and melting right as the snowflakes hit the rust-colored and black cobblestones. The streets were empty with an unearthly light cast by the haphazardly lit street lamps, one or two of which would flicker from time to time. There were only two or three people waiting at track #4 in the pre-dawn light – probably because he had arrived a little earlier than he expected. The cab took him only five minutes to get there and cost him ten hryvnas – about two dollars.

The train ride started off as a boring one – rocking, rocking, but not enough to lull you to sleep. As it rocked to and fro and occasionally screeched, and as he glanced to the right at the woman right next to him in seat number six in wagon number six, all he could think about in his sleep deprived state (he got up at 4 A.M. to catch the 6:20 A.M. train) was the way the beautiful unknown woman's stretch pants both showcased and covered her womanly shape. He could see that often enough as she leaned forward to talk to two girlfriends in the two seats in front of her. He developed a new appreciation for spandex or polyester – whatever material it was made of. Her top showed off her trim figure. A tight, ribbed sweater, hunter green in the upper third that accentuated that part of her torso, black below to match the slacks. A glittery black plastic bag with gold highlights sat in front of her on the floor. And her black leather handbag with brass zipper handles lay on her lap. Her henna-colored hair was the typical color found on every other woman in this part of the world, young or old. But on her somehow it was fashionable and not tacky. The green top of her sweater accentuated her wide shoulders. An embroidered x-pattern on the outer sides of her slacks that showed bare skin underneath drew attention to the shapeliness of her leg. A tantalizing touch of an accent. She wore two gold-colored rings on her right hand with small coral-colored stones and a dull gold-colored loose bracelet. While her physical beauty was just that – external beauty, the woman's hyperawareness of her own attractiveness somehow considerably irritated Nicholas. She constantly pulled out a small pocket mirror to check her mauve lipstick and eye shadow. She also kept looking at her short-cropped nails that suggested someone who worked a lot with her hands and not a prima donna. The nails were colored in a lustrous opalescent tan shade. He could see the beauty was fatal, but he knew it wasn't for him. Too much glitz. Right then she gave him a sly, inviting smile in a quick glance to her left. And that changed everything....

Nicholas certainly would be remiss if he didn't assure you here that nothing happened, that it was just his imagination gone a bit wild. Yet only two people can say for sure one way or another what did or didn't happen, and he was one of them.

In Kyiv, Nicholas stayed at the centrally located Soviet-style high-rise Kozatsky Hotel that was just off of Kyiv's Independence Square (*Ploshcha nezalezhnosty*). It was two metro stops away from the train station and a five-minute walk from Hrushevsky Street where the Fulbright offices were located.

The informational meetings at the Fulbright offices were largely uneventful except for the live performance of seven of the members of the a cappella Drevo Folk Ensemble. The name of the group was the old Ukrainian word for "tree." It was also the same root for the word "drevniy," meaning ancient. So whether they were ancient or a tree, or an ancient tree, the voices were exquisite in their disharmonic harmonies learned in villages from the *babtsi*, the grannies, who always wore sun- and time-faded scarves of many colors. Those elderly women, whose faces were wrinkled like the whorls on the bark of an ancient majestic oak, were the keepers of culture and wisdom and transmitters of knowledge from generation to generation. There were songs of lament, over the loss of a son or husband or child. There were songs of joy: wedding songs, songs of love and lust, songs of life. He got to meet the twenty or so other Fulbright scholars at a reception after the performance. A feminist writer there by the name of Lydia in a short-short black and white miniskirt with knee-height black leather boots and jet-black hair zoomed in on Nicholas for an inordinate amount of time. She, he would say, suggestively, invited him to come over to visit her place during his stay in Kyiv. She was so overbearing that Nicholas felt overwhelmed by her presence. So he looked for a pretext to escape her cloying orbit. At his first opportunity and gasping for air from the one-sided conversation, Nicholas shifted his attention to a reticent but attractive female singer from the Drevo group who turned out not to be very talkative. So he chatted with a few of the other singers at the reception as well as with the group's leader.

Just one other event became embedded in Nicholas's mind from that brief winter trip to the capital. As he was walking past the two uniformed hotel employees toward the elevator, they greeted him in Russian after he showed them his room key and hotel-provided ID-receipt. He answered them in Ukrainian. After going up to his sixth floor room, he made his way to the *dezhurnaya*, the older woman keeper of the hotel keys for each floor. His hotel room was spartan by any standards with just an old single bed, a dull brown and chipped formica-covered desk, an equally decrepit bland-looking chair, and, fortunately for him, a separate bathroom, but with towels that were so nearly paper thin they were more like dishcloths. As he was unpacking the one small duffel bag that he had taken with him for the trip, the antediluvian monstrously large old rotary phone began to ring loud enough to wake the dead in the lobby five floors below him. It was clattering like a lumbering Soviet tank stuck in the mud. He picked up the receiver off the rattling tank.

"Do you speak English?" A young and quite enticing female voice asked him from the other end of the line in ever so mildly accented English.

"Yes… I do…," Nicholas stuttered, unsure why someone would call him in a city where no one knew his number.

"Would you like a beautiful girl for the night?" She asked.

"That'd be great!" Nicholas laughed as he answered in a kind of afterthought, "I just don't want to pay for it!" ("Or catch any venerable diseases," he thought to himself but ended up not saying it.)

There was dead silence on the other end of the line. His phone rang two more times at fifteen-minute intervals until the maiden of the night with nearly impeccable English skills gave up the ghost with him, off to find another partner more willing to part with his Euros or dollars. That certainly was the highlight of his first stay in Kyiv.

Nicholas's trip back to Leopolis-Lviv the next day on the evening express train was mostly sleepy and uneventful.

PAN VIKTOR

Pan, or Mr. Viktor was the keeper of the mysteries and one of the first friendships Nicholas struck up in Leopolis. That's all that Nicholas knew about him. Not quite all on second thought. He knew he was known by other names: Mr. Basilisk and Mr. Bazio. Why three names? He had even more. That's just the way it was. No one could explain it to him. And no one could explain why he had eyes of different colors that would glow, especially on photographs. He did know that the "Mr." part of his name, according to time-honored local Ukrainian custom, was to call people by "Mr." (Pan) or Mrs. (Pani) or "Miss" (Panna) and their first name and in the vocative case, the case you use when you address someone. It was a sign of respect, particularly for someone older or someone to whom you had just been introduced. It had nothing to do with the Greek god of pleasure, though for the male version of the appellation it was spelled the same. The Soviets, of course, in their heyday frowned on such formalities, preferring the *tovarish*-comrade title.

Nicholas first met Mr. Viktor on an unusually warm and late January day, a globally warming 14 degrees centigrade during a winter heat wave, at the open-air Italian Courtyard Café on Rynok Square, the Medieval central market square of the city with its 44 houses that were planned in the 14th century when Lviv was under Polish rule. Each house was four-stories high and of a different color, ranging from faded yellows and light-to-dark greens and black. On all four sides the houses surrounded the faded yellow Ratusha, the City Hall building in the center of the square with its tall, angular clock and bell tower.

Mr. Viktor was sitting at a table next to a polished tall white statue of an anatomically correct Adonis, that is, with no fig leaf. Nicholas couldn't help but notice a statue of blind justice in the corner of the courtyard. Mr. Viktor's dark eyes immediately homed in on Nicholas's as if old friends were recognizing each other after a long absence, but, of course, they had never met before. Mr. Viktor motioned for him to sit down next to him, and Nicholas obliged.

Mr. Viktor was a tall man, but not too tall, with a baldpate on the top of his head with hair on the sides and back, and with a short-cropped, neatly trimmed beard. It was odd that he had half a mustache. That is to say, it was trimmed neatly from the top, halfway down his lip. So it met with his beard and formed a near-perfect oval. There were slight tinges of gray in his beard. He looked in his mid-forties, but oddly, sometimes caught in a millisecond of a blink, he would look much younger or much older – like a man seemingly of multiple ages flashing back and forth between those ages, nearly unnoticeable to the naked eye like the flickering of a computer screen.

Nicholas had seen earlier pictures of Mr. Viktor with a ponytail and getting body-painted for a rock performance in his student days. This Mr. Viktor was more staid. "Older and wiser," Mr. Viktor would say to him later.

"There are forces here at play that you just don't understand," Mr. Viktor told him at one point of their initial conversation. "I can tell you something about it, but not everything. You'll have to learn for yourself. And you'll learn better on your own path, at your own pace, and in your own time."

"Do you know anything about signs of the lion?" Nicholas asked him.

"I don't know…," Mr. Viktor answered hesitatingly. "I don't really know much about them. I just know they exist and they're extremely important. I can tell you, though, that they're somehow connected with you."

Mr. Viktor's right eye seemed to have an even brighter glow as he said what he said. It showed up in the photographs even after Nicholas had erased the red eye in his Photoshop program.

THE TASTY RUMOR CAFÉ

That is where Nicholas met Mr. Viktor on more than one occasion. One time on a cold February morning with the globally warmed temperature gone, right after ordering a coffee, a plate of *varennyky* (boiled potato dumplings) and fifty grams of Zakarpatsky (Carpathian) cognac, the lights suddenly went out. "It happens pretty often," Mr. Viktor said. "They'll bring out the candles soon. Funny, it happens a lot while I'm here." The nearly completely asymmetric café was underneath the Les Kurbas Theater where Nicholas had seen a performance of *The Good God of Manhattan* the previous week. He was hoping to meet the black-haired actress who played the role of Jennifer in a bright pink dress. Somebody told him she was from Kharkiv. But no luck so far. He might not recognize her without the shocking pink dress she wore in the play. And she wouldn't appear in the café nude as she did on stage for the last ten minutes of the play. Oddly, being a man of normal heterohormonal predisposition, it was interesting only for the first titillating minute or two, that is, while she was naked. Nicholas then intuitively had a mind to take his coat off and cover her because it was fairly cold in the unheated theater. "She's cold! She's cold! She's shivering!" He kept thinking to himself. He suppressed the impulse to give her his coat, not wanting to become the center of attention. But his friends told him afterward that the audience would have loved it and thought it was part of the play. It's experimental theater, of course.

The Tasty Rumor became the usual place for Nicholas and Mr. Viktor to meet. Although Nicholas had already gotten to know him well enough to call him just by his first name, the more formal way of address seemed to be more natural for him and stuck. The Tasty Rumor also turned out to be a self-realized appellation, for virtually every time Nicholas was seen with someone alone by someone he knew, particularly someone of the female persuasion, Nicholas would hear about it from his friends with a smile and a wagging finger in the fishbowl of what to many was known as *Selo* Lviv, or the Village of Lviv. Everyone seemed to want to live vicariously through someone else and in small or even large ways was unhappy with their own lives. Mr. Viktor explained it to him this way: "It really shows you that people care about you. If they didn't care about you, they wouldn't say anything to you at all. You'll get used to it," he smiled a knowing smile.

THE BEGGARS
AT THE DOMINICAN CATHEDRAL

Nicholas decided to go to the Dominican Cathedral to church on a snowy February Sunday. The colorful word for February in Ukrainian is "liutiy," meaning fierce or ferocious. And this Sunday morning was certainly a ferocious day in what was becoming a ferocious month. While Nicholas believed in God – he couldn't believe such a wondrous world and universe created without a supreme being – he attended church just once in a while. It had just become too routine for him and less meaningful. And he felt he could express his faith in other ways. Faith for him was something personal, something inside him, and not a social event.

The walk was fairly long from his apartment – twenty-five minutes or so. It felt long because it was so cold. The church was filled with people. It felt warm inside, almost like a living, breathing being rather than a stone edifice – or to say it more precisely, it had an inner warmth – despite the fact that there was no discernable heating system or heat source. The combined 98.6 degrees of five or six hundred worshippers bundled up in fur, leather and other winter coats seemed to heat it up considerably along with the voices of the choir and people singing to accompany the choir. The hot breath of so many voices must have risen into the arches and filtered down. Everyone stood during the service in the Baroque cathedral with statues on the sides and an iconostasis. That was the icon screen dividing the corporeal world where he was from the celestial realm behind it. The choir was exquisite and at times gave Nicholas goose bumps when they hit certain notes and harmonies that rose up and bounced down from the rafters. He sang along with parts of the liturgy – snippets of passages he remembered from childhood. Some of the melodies were familiar, others very different from what he could recall. The only point of irritation for him was the constant shuffling of people past him in and out of the church. He tried hard to concentrate on the meaning of the service – and the readings about the Prodigal Son. He felt more than a bit prodigal in coming back to this place, his ancestral land. The origin, the source. The source of your life and being in spirit and in your genes. A hidden genetic code locked up in the smallest atoms inside you – that draws you back to your origins in dreams and in imagination.

When the liturgy ended, Nicholas began to walk out the door. There were three beggars there: an unkempt and dust-covered gypsy woman holding her just as dust-covered and seemingly intentionally smudged child, a robust teenage boy who looked as healthy as anyone with no immediately evident infirmities, and a stooped over sad oval-faced elderly woman in a faded but once colorful scarf. She must have been over eighty and her coat nearly as old as she – the shabbiest and most threadbare he had ever seen on a living human being.

The gypsy woman was screaming nearly hysterically in quite expressive Ukrainian at everyone to give her money to feed her child, who looked plump and not particularly ill nourished. The boy pulled out a laser-printed sign saying he needed money for an operation. But the sad-eyed woman just stood there silently, eyes downcast, holding a tin cup. Nicholas was immediately drawn to the old woman and reached into his pocket to pull out all the coins he had. They jingled as they fell into the cup. He had the urge to pull out even more money from his wallet, but the crowd pushing out of the church forced him outside too quickly to do that and shoved his hand upward by jostling his elbow from behind. The elderly threadbare and faded woman smiled at him as he passed, and a tear of gratitude trickled out of her left eye. He hadn't given her that much money – a few *hryvnas*, a dollar or so at most, enough maybe to buy a half loaf of bread.

Might this have been his first test? A test of what though? He thought so because he felt energy pulsing in his mind and body, as though an electric current had been turned on inside him. It was as if the first sign of the lion wasn't an object to be found at all, not a physical key, not a thing, but a thought or emotion or a lesson learned. He walked home tracing the same path he took to get there, completing a circle of his journey where he began. But though the circle was complete, he was somehow changed by it in a way he couldn't yet understand.

THE LECTURE AT THE ETHNOGRAPHIC

There was to be a public lecture at the Ethnographic Museum in the downtown off of Prospekt Svobody, Liberty Avenue. The building was well known by the locals for the Statue of Liberty at the top of it that overlooked the central square in front of the Opera House. The speaker was Professor Potojbichny – accent on the next to last syllable – a renowned professor of mathematics, senior academician of the Academy of Sciences (even though he was just around 50 years old), and knower of many things beyond the realm of his field of specialization. He also was known to play guitar, make up rhyming poems at the drop of a hat, and perform at scholarly events and gatherings, often times making up songs of considerable wit on the spot. His verbal creative skills matched those of his mathematical ones, though he, renaissance man and Jack of all trades that he was, always seemed to relate everything to mathematics and its precision as an answer to everything – even the irrational.

Nicholas had gone to one of Professor Potojbichny's lectures previously. There he learned the mathematical fact of his name Nicholas or Mykola in Ukrainian (and English for that matter), being in the middle of the alphabet, was a clear mathematical marker of his in-between nature, his balanced personality (he was also a Libra, the scales of the horoscope – not that he believed in such things). He was not too hot or not too cold, not too talkative and not too reticent, not too tall and not too short, not too fat and not too thin, not too handsome and not too ugly, not too anything. He was something like the golden mean, the medium, the average when you weigh in all factors. He was every man. All, according to Potojbichny's lecture, because of the mathematical centrality of his name in the alphabet – if you give all the letters numerical values. Those earlier in the alphabet are favored because of their numerical status. The rest of the earlier lecture was mostly about numerical voting patterns that tended to exclude extremes and favor mediocrity – the average. Was Nicholas just mediocrity, the average, an Ivan Ivanovych Ivaniv? Nicholas was so impressed by the talk that he wanted to listen to this renaissance man again, who seemingly had more knowledge than anyone else had of the arts and sciences stuffed into his brain like a giant and infinitely swirling DVD ROM or computer hard drive that was organic and ever expanding.

There were about fifty people in the chilly auditorium when the lecture began. The room and building seemed right out of the Secession Period – the turn of the eighteenth and nineteenth-century Ukrainian Art Nouveau. It was all finished in a dark and aged mahogany with various bas-relief images of chubby cherubim and other decorative motifs on the walls, the ceiling and corners. The bench seating looked more like pews in a church. They creaked as everyone sat down or turned to talk to someone. With all the talking and turning, everyone's hot breath seemed to slowly warm up the room. Mr. Viktor arrived late along with Jan Shchurakiwsky, the unofficially designated guide to underworld Lviv, the beginning of whose last name comes from the root of the word "shchur," meaning "rat." The underworld, of course, was the dominion of marsupials. He had a boisterous smile on his face as usual, smirking a kind of "Heh-heh-heh."

The lecture began with the professor saying he was going to speak about the interface between the measurably scientific and the mathematical with the metaphysical. His scholarly horn-rimmed glasses conveyed more than a touch of scholarly arrogance as they slipped down to the tip of his nose. He also had a tendency to gesticulate wildly with both arms spreading away from his body to the side to make a point.

"If you read in chronicles and the accounts of the building of all the major monasteries and major cathedrals in Ukraine, you'll find that spots were chosen by men with sixth-sense abilities, with divining rods that sought out the most powerful energy fields emanating from the earth. Two of the most powerful fields are at the Kyiv-Pechersk Monastery of the Caves and at the St. Sophia Cathedral in Kyiv. The diviners felt the pull of those forces as they coursed through the rods and through their bodies. Today we can measure those fields with precision instruments and with satellite imaging and sensing techniques. Thus it is a provable and indisputable fact that they exist. Why do they exist? *That* we don't know for sure. Why do poltergeists appear most often in houses above deep limestone beds? They just do.

The two religious shrines in Kyiv are among the most powerful energy vortices in the world. Curiously, in our 750-year-old city of Leopolis, there is an astounding cluster of smaller energy fields that in concert form a mega-ring of powerful energy sources that are all invisible to the naked human eye. In infrared satellite imaging I have been able to pinpoint seven of them that together dwarf the fields of the two particularly powerful sources in Kyiv. These quote-unquote "sacred" spots, too, were divined by diviners – some of them the Molfar wizard blacksmiths from the Carpathians – before the foundations were dug and the churches built. The Boim Chapel, although it's a small church, has electromagnetic readings nearly off the scale. St. George's Cathedral at the highest point of the city has similar powerful readings. And this is not limited just to religious sites. Lysa Hora, Bald Mountain that overlooks the city was the site of the castle ordered to be built by Prince Danylo of Halych in 1256. While we can logically see the benefit of building the castle at one of the highest points in the city to observe oncoming enemies from twenty kilometers or more away, the site also has quite intense electromagnetic and other as yet immeasurable forces at play. While we posit the source of highly charged fields as being from deep in the earth's core or crust, we do not know why they are created. And they seem to be linked in some profound way to external sources of electromagnetic radiation, especially the sun and other stars. The scale is too large for us to really get a good picture of it, but I assume it forms a mathematically precise grid. There are of course problems with the earth's magnetic fields when sunspots and other cosmic events occur. These often influence the weather and even, it is felt, human behavior. It is my theory that the energy forces emanating from the hotspots in and around Lviv form a consistent pattern and grid aligned with cosmic forces, the purpose of which may be to hold other forces in balance. Remember that for every positive there must be a negative and vice versa, for every action an opposite reaction. This is the mathematical perfection of the physical universe...."

The professor's name Potojbichny came from the words "po toj bik" – beyond that side, or from the other side. If he were English, he would have been Professor Fromtheotherside.

NATIONAL IDENTITY THEFT

Four empires have had control over this land: the Polish-Lithuanian Confederation, the Austro-Hungarian Empire, the Second Polish Republic, and the Soviet Union. The city has had a nominal identity crisis and has been know by an assortment of names under its various conquerors: Leopolis, Levensburg, Lemberg, Lwow, Lvov, and finally back to the Ukrainian Lviv (pronounced as if it were spelled Lviw).

Identity, nationality, ethnicity – these are random things, genetic in some ways, happenstance in others. You're born into them by accident of fate and time and place. If you're born in this city in 1890, you're a member of the Austro-Hungarian Empire. You could be Ukrainian, Polish, Jewish, Armenian, German, or Austrian – but you're still a Hapsburgian. And besides your native tongue, you speak German – plus Ukrainian and Polish. You're not persecuted for your ethnicity or language. You have some representation in the capital of Vienna. And life isn't too bad for you. If you're born here in 1946, you're a citizen of the USSR (the CCCP in Russian). And life is about to become considerably worse, even after the depravations of the war. The poet Marina Tsvetaeva once wrote that she didn't want to be a citizen of a country whose name had no vowels. Not even a magical incantation like "open sesame" for her could make those harsh consonants stretch apart to let her squeeze back into the land of her birth – though she was to return eventually and meet death by her own hand there in a deep and unrecoverable depression. No more German was to be spoken here in the country without a vowel in its name in 1946. The Nazis had already cleared out the 40% Jewish population of the city and destroyed the main synagogue in the town – known to the locals as Golden Roza (Rose). The SS turned over the keys to the building that housed their dirty deeds to their Soviet counterparts. It must have been solidarity among the brotherhood of sadistic tormenters. Ukrainians and Jews alike were shipped out in cattle cars by the Nazis during their occupation to Krakow in Poland, splendid sister city of Leopolis. In Krakow, Jews were sent south to their obliteration. While the Ukrainians, who were considered Untermensch by the Third Reich too, could still work the plows, build the houses, and man the factories in the Rhineland as slave laborers. Nicholas's grandmother had taken that six-hour train ride to Krakow. He tried to talk to her about it a few times. She wouldn't say a word when he asked about it. "I can't," she said. "I just can't." A primordial sadness would come over her when he brought up the subject, and her face would take on the look of funereal mourning. Nicholas found out bits and pieces about what had happened back then from her in unguarded moments. Her village, just outside of Brody where a vicious battle between the Soviet army and advancing panzer divisions took place, was saved because of its name – Berlyn. Nicholas's grandmother had told the story to him once in an unguarded moment. According to her, Berlyn and not Berlin with an "i," but the Nazis, who were not known for their subtlety, were fooled by not knowing the difference between the two front vowels, one more frontal than the other. Their hearing, perhaps deafened by cannon fire and bombs exploding, must not have not been too sharp that day. They were duped into thinking that the village was named after the German capital. They probably never found out that it was the dialectal name for the hops that grew there on tall wooden racks to make the beer at various nearby and more distant breweries. They thought the residents must love Germany for naming the village after their capital. So deep into the Rhineland the cattle cars continued, and at least in Nicholas's grandmother's case, fortunately not to the mills of death.

Krakow was the transfer point for the prisoners of war – the Jews in the cars en masse along with those deemed extreme Ukrainian nationalists were transferred to Auschwitz to the camps of doom. It was random chance that brought Nicholas's mother Maria Borovykovsky to the US, USA, United States of America – a country that had vowels in all of its names. And her homeland Ukraina that was left behind had four friendly vowels in its name. Her own last name came from the word for a boletus mushroom. Her daughter (Nicholas's aunt Oksana whom he had never met) was a playmate of the daughter of a captured Polish lieutenant in the same camp. The Polish officer heard word in 1945 that Soviet troops were advancing along with the Americans. He more or less knew where the lines of demarcation would end up, so he told Nicholas's family to get as quickly as possible to the American side. So he loaded up a horse-drawn wagon with everyone in the family (grandfather, grandmother, and five children, one of them Nicholas's mother) and whatever possessions they could gather to make it to the American side and what would eventually become freedom, a new life, and the loss of a homeland. Though American propaganda teams rode through the camps telling everyone that Dyadya Joe, Uncle Joe Stalin, was ready to welcome them back with open arms, the Polish officer knew that the open arms of the country without a vowel in its name had bayonets and rifles, arms that shoot, in those welcoming hands. A significantly worse fate awaited those who returned. The Polish officer had spoken to one of the Americans from Chicago who was in one of the propaganda teams. The fellow from Chicago by the name of something like Joe Witkowski, he was at least a –ski as everyone remembered it, managed to speak broken Polish and answered the Polish officer's query about if what he said was true. "No," he said. "For God's sake, get the hell out of here. They just don't want a flood of emigrants to the US. That's why they've been sending us around. I feel sick about it. But I have to tell you the truth. You're a Polish citizen. They won't bother you. They'll let you stay in Poland."

So the Polish officer (whose name no one in Nicholas's family could remember now) drove them to what was going to become the American sector. And that saved them. Those ending up in Soviet hands were enemies of the state without a vowel in its name for allowing themselves to be captured. So you were either shot on sight without trial (as happened to Nicholas's great uncle Volodya upon his return) or sent to a labor camp in Siberia without trial for a 25-

year term (as happened to Nicholas's great uncle Mykola, whom he was named after). Mykola was released after serving ten years in the general amnesty that Khrushchev declared when he took power after Stalin's mystery-clouded death in 1953 on March 5.

So if you were born in the city of Lviv in 1946, you were a citizen of a country without a vowel, a country without kindness and compassion, a country of labor camps and informers, of the equally disemvoweled NKVD and later equally disemvoweled KGB. You also were coerced into learning Russian because that was the language of the vowelless state of the "friendship of nations and peoples." They just neglected to say it was coerced friendship. If you were Polish or Austrian, you were in a most unfriendly way expelled to the new borders of your homeland, losing rights to all your land and the property you couldn't take with you. If you were Jewish, you were already either gassed to death or hiding your identity to survive. Metropolitan Sheptytsky of the Ukrainian Greek Catholic Church, who was criticized by some for greeting the conquering army with bread and salt, the traditional Ukrainian greeting for visitors, secretly ordered that the priests under his jurisdiction hide Jews from the Nazis and give them fake baptismal certificates. That managed to save a few thousand Jews from merciless annihilation. The Soviets crushed the Greek Catholic clergy of the church when they took over the western part of the country in 1946. All of them were arrested and sent to prison camps or murdered – except for those who managed to flee. Nicholas had met one of those who had escaped – a hefty priest by the name of Nestor Byk, whose last name meant "bull." He was the realized metaphor of his name because he was built like a bull, an historian with a Ph.D., who later was to publish a lot about wartime events that he personally experienced. He lived up to his last name, because when Soviet forces arrested him (all Greek Catholic priests were enemies of the state for being Ukrainian, and therefore nationalists), he was put on a train in the Ternopil Region to be taken to Siberia. He managed to make his way to the back of the last car of the train when he made the sign of the cross, asking God for forgiveness for what he was about to do, and then slugged the Soviet guard to unconsciousness with one punch. He quickly jumped off the slow-moving train that was moving around a bend and made his way to Poland, then Germany and eventually America. He later was to become a good friend and pastor of a church that Nicholas and his parents attended. And Nicholas remembered, too, that God, of course, had never written on the tablets "thou shalt not punch a Red Army officer forcing you to go to Siberia to your imminent doom."

If you happen to be in Leopolis in 1991, you get to tear down all the statues of Lenin and can speak Ukrainian again in the open. You get to change the names of streets from Soviet heroes of the fatherland to Ukrainian heroes with names like Chuprynka and Bandera who were enemies of the Soviet state. So nationality and citizenship are temporary and malleable concepts. In researching his own lineage, Nicholas discovered his own blood could have been born of Tartar and Mongol hordes from the 12th and 13th centuries. You are what you feel you are, even if states try to steal or bury your national identity. And blood and genes become assimilated and recombined. You become what you are born into and the language or languages that you speak. Virtually anyone could be a victim of national identity theft or national identity drift.

THE SEER OF SPECTERS

The city is supposedly full of specters. You just can't see them. You're supposed to feel them sometimes in cold spots in the air as you pass on a warm day. Or an even colder spot on a cold day. There are shadows everywhere, but just not in the shade, in every corner of the *Stare Misto*, the Old City. Nicholas never believed in such things before. He wasn't sure he believed in them now. Maybe his mind would change, maybe not.

He had met the artist Ivan Vasylenko in the café at the Philharmonic on a side street off of the beginning of Academician Street. Oops! The street was now called Shevchenko Boulevard, but many of the older locals still called it Academician out of habit. Shevchenko Boulevard/Academician Street had a small square with a statue of the historian Mykhailo Hrushevsky at the other end of it. The café was a small one called "Za Kulisamy" (The Backstage Café) with only five or six tables and a small pool table in the middle of the room. It was smoky as a lot of cafés in the city are with a handful of musicians, artists, and writers taking drags on cigarettes in between sips of various alcoholic libations – mostly *horilka* (vodka), Uzhorod or Zakarpatsky cognac and beer on draft, especially the local Lviv Porter and Lviv Lager. There was another café called The Cult that had just opened to the side of the Philharmonic, but few of the locals went there. It was gaudy and pretentious, calling itself the "club for worthy Lvivians," with New York prices meant for the tourists who were flocking to the city from Poland, Germany, England, Russia, and North America in larger and larger droves in the summer. Nicholas would have gone there if it had been advertised as for *unworthy* Lvivians, since he considered himself one of those.

Nicholas and Ivan chatted about this and that at the Backstage Café. Mr. Viktor had introduced them recently. The conversation was mostly of an esoteric kind – on art, literature, and music. Ivan turned out to be a comfortable conversationalist with Nicholas, and it seemed natural that after an hour or so of interesting chat, Ivan invited him to come take a look at some of his paintings at his studio on Tershakivets Street, which was a fifteen-or-so-minute walk from the Philharmonic café . So they walked over along the spottily lit street close to a drab old Soviet-style hotel that was in the middle of being remodeled. The one thing about Ivan that Nicholas found troubling was the fact that he seemed to focus in and out of conversations, seemingly disappearing into another world, as if he were flipping between dimensions and having simultaneous conversations in both. A blank look of aphasia seemed to cover Ivan's face when he phased out of his conversation with Nicholas. "He's an artist," Nicholas thought to himself. "They're supposed to be weird."

"I just got released yesterday," Ivan nonchalantly said as he turned the key to his basement studio that was down a couple of steps and in the middle of a long unlit corridor – "from the psych ward."

"Shit! What am I getting myself into?!" Nicholas thought to himself. "He's wacko!" But instead he actually said to Ivan: "Well… That's interesting… What happened?"

"I check myself in from time to time – when it gets too much for me."

"What gets too much for you?"

"The *pryvydy*, the ghosts. The ghosts of the city. I see them everywhere."

"Why?"

"I don't know. But I know they're there. They come to me every night and haunt me. They never give me any peace."

"Are they haunting you now?"

"Not so bad now… Being with other people sometimes keeps them away. They don't like to share attention with anyone, or the noise of voices keeps them away."

"Why do they haunt you?"

"I just have the ability to see them. I've always seen them. They moved the cemetery – the old church cemetery – to build part of the city. They never should have done that. Don't disturb the dead. It gives them no peace. Where they were was where they should be."

Ivan opened the door with the second double-twist of the key. The lock clicked loudly and reverberated in the hollow of the darkened corridor that didn't have a working bulb to illuminate it. The two-room combination apartment-studio was dingy and spattered in paint on the floor and walls. There was only one painting in the studio – a giant one that took up almost an entire wall. It was about eight feet wide and six feet tall. You could see the right bottom quadrant of it needed to be finished. Ivan seemed to work from the center out as he painted a painting. The rest of the painting had the look of being complete. The upper half had a glistening deep red and darkish blue background – the red was like the burnt crimson color of old icons aged three or four centuries. It was sky in the background, but somehow not sky. Night but not night, a time in-between. The foreground had a roughly outlined, almost shimmering city block of buildings of the inner city in the middle. All over the canvas in random order were white specters of different shapes and sizes, all stirred up and somehow with faces more menacing and in horror than Munch's "Scream." But faces that seemed to be comfortable and frequent visitors to Ivan.

"This is what you see?" Nicholas asked.

"Yes, this is exactly what I see. Every day I paint them as I see them. They're everywhere. I do one or two of these big paintings a year and sell them to Polish or German galleries. That usually gives me enough money to live off of for a year or so. I give half the money to my mother and spend a little on my friends. I roll up the painted canvases to make them easier to send – and they restretch them there. I can only paint one or two of these big ones a year. It takes so much out of me… That's why I need the *horilka*… (He pointed toward the bottle of vodka.) I have the energy to paint just in the morning. Even when I close my eyes after having a few drinks, the howling never ends. And when I open my eyes – they're everywhere around me again. That's the price I pay, but they're also the source of my inspiration. They come to me from the beyond. They're my friends, just like my friends who come to visit me in this world. All my inspiration comes to me from the beyond. That's why I check myself into the psych ward. For some reason, the area where the psych ward is seems to deaden their influence – no pun intended, they're already dead. Heh-Heh… (He snickered to himself.). They don't follow me into churches either, but you can't live twenty-four hours a day in a church. The Chapel of the Boims and the Armenian Cathedral are especially good spots to get away from them for the time it takes to listen to a church service. But no more church services at the Chapel. It's just open at odd times for tourists. Zhenya, the sweet old woman in black, who always wore a dusty man's black felt hat, used to let me in whenever I needed to and never charged me. She was the tour guide of the place and was a walking encyclopedia of the history of the Chapel and the city. But she died a few years ago – and the new young girl who works there isn't as predisposed to me. She just thinks I'm crazy. Zhenya somehow knew what was tormenting me. She used to tell me about the Chapel holding a key to some forgotten mystery. When you gaze at the vaulted ceiling at the right time of day, you see something, the infinite or a sign. Enlightenment, I suppose, of a certain kind. She knew six languages fluently – Ukrainian, Russian, Polish, English, French, and German, and gave the tour of the Chapel in any one of the languages to tourists and could switch into one of the other languages at the drop of her man's dusty black felt hat that complemented her sweet and kind face. The Armenian Cathedral is only open for church services on Sundays and holy days, though they do open the courtyard more often. I've gone to church services there, but as soon as I step through the doors onto the sidewalk, there they are, waiting for me, the specters. And when I'm in there without a church service going on, I see their faces trying to get through the walls. They don't come in, but if you stare intently at the wall, especially during particular times of day, figures begin moving on it. They're not there during a church service, though.

The cemetery never should have been moved. Not even the Boims are buried in the chapel anymore. They moved them to Lychakiv Cemetery. They weren't happy about that. They told me from the beyond. Progress, the city planners must have thought, when they moved the cemetery. They moved it to reroute the Poltva River and covered it over. They *never* should have done that! It was unnatural to make a living river bathed in light a river of death and darkness. But you should never disturb the dead. Let them rest in peace, otherwise they'll give you no peace."

As local custom warrants and after his lengthy explanation, Ivan the Ghostseer offered Nicholas coffee or tea after several shots of *horilka* for himself and Moldovan five-star cognac for Nicholas, the latter of which Nicholas preferred because he liked to taste what he was drinking going down and sip it. Nicholas happened to have a small bottle in the bag he always carried around with him. You always needed to have some kind of bag with you to carry your important papers and also to pop in fresh vegetables or bread that you pick up at a market on your way home. Or in this case a small bottle of Moldovan five-star cognac.

Ivan pulled out an old wide-bottomed brass Turkish coffee pot, lit the pilot lamp of a small rusted stove in the corner of a room, and began to make the coffee. It was all done in a time-honored way. First the Ghostseer spooned just the right amount of the finely ground powdery coffee into the bottom of the pot, then he added just enough water to cover it. After that he put the pot on top of the gas flame until he heard it boil and crackle a bit. He pulled the pot off the flame right then and added more water, nearly filling the pot to the brim. Then he put it back on the flame and watched carefully to make sure it didn't boil over. He pulled it off right at the moment before it was about to overflow. The Turkish invaders of more distant times and coffee-loving Austrians more recently must have passed down the ritual in this city of four cafés on virtually every corner. That age-old brass Turkish pot seemed to contain the taste of every cup previously ever made in it. And that inherited taste was good – with just a spoonful of sugar.

There was a large half-covered window looking out on the street from inside the kitchen area that had rusted metal gratings on it. Right at that moment from inside the artist's studio the window reminded Nicholas of a psychiatric hospital or prison bars. The kitchen area (if you can call it that) was a mess. The single once white but now dingy table had all kinds of partly opened tins of fish and other foods at various stages of consumption, desiccation and rot – along with the bottle of *horilka* that Ivan had gulped down virtually without uttering a toast. That was odd because Ukrainians love to toast every drink.

Nicholas had to relieve himself and asked where the bathroom was. It turned out it was near the entrance to the corridor outside the apartment – and shared by two or three other apartments in that wing of the basement. Since the water was turned off (as it often is in the city other than at 6-9 A.M. and 6-9 P.M.), there was no way to flush. So Nicholas simply had to add to the urine stench that permeated the unlit bathroom. "So this is the life of a bohemian artist," he thought to himself. "I'm glad I'm not one," he thought to himself, although he actually had painted four or five abstract paintings so far during his stay and one more representational one of the Armenian Cathedral. He had given them all away to his friends.

After Nicholas came back into the apartment, Ivan started to doze off while sitting at the table. This was getting a bit awkward for Nicholas, so he told Ivan he had an appointment with his friend Myroslava. Ivan jolted out of his sleep and gave Nicholas the last names of three or four Myroslavas he knew, but none of them matched the one Nicholas mentioned. It was a popular name in this town and country, and all the Myroslavas Nicholas knew were especially nice. He didn't really have an appointment, but just wanted to give Ivan the time to sleep off his latest inebriation. Ivan also gave him two books of his poetry he had just gotten published. One book had a series of ghost-like faces on the front cover. Ivan tried to read a poem from memory to Nicholas, but after three or four lines, he would phase out into his other state. Nicholas usually asked for an autograph from writers who happened to give him books, but not this time. He politely said he'll read them as soon as he has a chance. He'll get the autograph later.

The brief meeting with Ivan the Ghostseer lasted a little more than an hour in the studio. Nicholas was glad he had overcome his trepidation about crossing the threshold of the apartment, and, after thinking about it, decided that living with the unseen couldn't be that bad – as long as you don't see or hear the unseen yourself. He walked down the dark and dank corridor and up the two or three steps from the basement studio into the courtyard of the building, turned right for ten paces to the apartment building door, and turned left as he exited the front entrance. He immediately felt a presence – hard to explain it in any other way – watching him. He looked across the street and saw a tan-colored stucco church. Above the doorway there was a symbol in bas-relief – an eye in a triangle – a bit like the one on the back of a dollar bill. He didn't feel threatened by it right then. It was just something noticeable, something he could feel with his sixth or seventh or eighth or who knows what other sense. Who really knows how many senses humans really have if they only use ten per cent of their brains? He continued on his way, slightly buzzed from the few shots of cognac he had sipped without having eaten anything, down *Pekarska vulytsia*, which would be known as Baker Street if it were in London.

THE UKRAINIAN TUTOR

She was redheaded Olenka, a natural looking though henna-colored redhead, not like the overkill types that were as common in the city as green grass and leaves on a sunny summer afternoon in Striysky Park. Nicholas made an arrangement with her after he had met her. They hit it off quite well at a weekly English-language conversation club meeting at the British Council office at the university. Three hours per week of Ukrainian lessons in exchange for three hours of English. They met in the late morning on Mondays, Wednesdays and Fridays. When the weather was nice, which in often gray Lviv means not raining too hard, they would go for a walk, usually in the park right next to the university. Other times they would go to one of the cafés near the university, most often to the Puzata Khata, the Pot-bellied House Restaurant right behind the university that had an expansive coffee shop in its basement. While it was an extremely popular and often crowded student hangout, at that particular time of day when they met, there was plenty of room to sit down, and it wasn't too noisy.

Olenka was married with a husband and ten-year-old twin girls. She was rather attractive and not a cookie cutter beauty, not the run of the mill kind you come across flipping through pages of fashion magazines. Flashy beauty never impressed Nicholas. Olenka's beauty, at least it seemed to him, came from inside. Plus she had a disarming smile and sparkling grayish green eyes. Smiles were rare on the streets of Leopolis where everyone was in too much of a rush.

Olenka taught in the Political Science Department at Lviv National University, mostly courses in writing and editing. She dreamt of learning English well enough to get to the US or Canada for an extended visit to polish up her English and to take graduate courses in journalism. She had been to the US to work on an editing project for a month or so, but didn't have the chance to work on her English then. During the course of the project she lived with a Ukrainian family in the Ukrainian neighborhood in Chicago not far from St. Nicholas Cathedral, and spoke Ukrainian to all the Ukrainian and Polish shopkeepers. And she spoke nothing but Ukrainian at the office where she worked on her editing project. So it was almost as if she had never left home.

Nicholas learned quite a bit about Olenka over the course of their meetings, and his Ukrainian improved dramatically. He managed to de-diasporize the Ukrainian he had learned at home from his family. Old habits die hard, especially linguistic habits. He wouldn't say what he had learned about Olenka in detail. He decided to keep that a secret.

One day he was waiting for Olenka in the Potbelly Restaurant on a drizzly Friday around eleven. She was running a little late and he was sitting there a little big hungry, earlier than usual because a rumbling tramcar had rattled him awake at 6:28 A.M. when the first one pulled up at the stop on Hyphenated Writer Boulevard, Nechui-Levytsky Street. Fortunately his apartment was on the other side of the building closer to Bohun Street. Bohun was a famous Kozak (aka Cossack) Hetman or leader – a word that came from the English phrase Head Man. Though the word "het'" with a "t" meant "away" as in "go away." And the nineteenth-century realist writer's name came from two roots. The left side of his hyphenation meant "can't hear" and the right part of his name from the word "lev" or lion. In his groggy state, Nicholas wondered why lion guy Levytsky couldn't hear. So he may have come from a line of deaf and dumb mutes, or at least deaf ones. So unhearing lion guy needed to write instead of listen. Get more sleep next time. And don't rattle and rumble so much tramcar. Names are meaningful in this land.

When Nicholas reached his turn in the caféteria-style line, he ordered some *hrechka* (buckwheat groats) and a plate of *varennyky*, boiled potato dumplings. Waiting for Olenka gave him a chance to look around the recently remodeled restaurant. The Potbelly was in rough-hewn log wood motifs – a giant artificial Ukrainian village house. Hutsul (the name of the mountain people from the

Carpathians) kilims lined the interior wall. The colors of the kilims were orange, maroon, harvest yellow, hunter green, and a touch of black. It was hard to describe the pattern. It was somewhat geometrical and somewhat of a zigzag pattern. It reminded him of American Indian designs. Something like Navajo rugs if he was keeping his tribal colors in order.

The tables in the restaurant were made of heavy oak and lacquered to a dark almost impenetrable brown with the wood grain barely showing. It was parasol city through the windows, which were arched about 15 feet high on the first floor. Wind was whipping and snapping up the tops of umbrellas. There was tolerable blaring music coming through speakers in the restaurant with flat panel video screens placed strategically throughout showing video clips of the performers.

A maroon quilt-patched hooded coat passed by the window. It must have had a person inside, but he didn't see who it was. A sandy gold and silver speckled umbrella. Then a young teenage couple with a plaid pink, light green and white umbrella. The buzz cut and not very handsome guy was trying to steal a kiss from his beloved, who wanted no part of it, particularly in front of the window to the restaurant. She pushed her hand into his face. He looked like a cretin, she looked very attractive. A typical combination that he had noticed in the city. Then Nicholas saw a leather-jacketed girl pressing the on button on her cell phone. A guy smoking a cigarette. A lot of people smoke here. An older woman hobbling along in a drab dark brown coat. A young girl in a white nylon jacket with a black umbrella for contrast. Black gratings on the soot-stained sand colored back of the main university building. A guy in an almost perfectly round dark umber leather cap with a short brim. Nicholas hadn't seen anyone in a hat like that ever before. A rainbow umbrella, another plaid one. Through the next window toward Sichovi Striltsi Street (Sich Riflemen Street), a sign that said "UVAHA" (ATTENTION) with a yellow banded ribbon circling in concentric circles. "UVAHA" underneath it too. More fine drizzle. Unaware of the clinking noise of glasses and silverware striking plates. The Ghostseer had called Nicholas that morning just before he left from home. Nicholas just remembered that. "Come visit me," he said. "I want to have a chat with you. The code at my building entrance is 680." "When will you be in?" Nicholas asked him. "I'm always in," he replied. "What's up with you?" "I just wrote a play – they might stage it." "What's it about?" "It's about sinking into the depth of yourself," Ivan answered. Yes, that's what he said, but in a single word in Ukrainian that's a bit hard to translate – *samozahlyblennja.* "And about the search for God." "That's nice," Nicholas answered, knowing he was too busy that day to stop by.

The pounding rhythm of really bad music jolted Nicholas back into his present time. You don't want to hear the words – they're just too silly. A younger guy in a leather jacket (status symbol) and a cell phone (another status symbol but also a necessity for many) – even though the average salary was 1000 hryvnas a month ($200). A cell phone cost 250 hryvnas, fifty dollars for the cheapest ones and up. Whenever anyone asks what you make here, which people often do ask, they mean per month – Nicholas refused to answer, explaining that it's impolite to ask that question where he comes from. Not that he made all that much money back home, but he always had had enough of it to get by.

Na-na-na-na-na the beat goes on in the female singer's voice, repeating na-na-na-na-na over and over again until it thankfully just ends. You look down, and a ceramic tile floor appears before you, which you never looked at closely before. It's the color of red brick with a combination of small and larger squares and rectangles. Another plaid umbrella through the window. This one stylish and classy, in subdued darker tones. It's getting late and Olenka hasn't called or let you know she'll be late. You have a meeting soon "at Taras" with a student who wants some advice on understanding James Joyce or Faulkner, not that you ever understood them yourself in the first place, even though you understand the words on the page there, just not all of them in their combinations. A tall burnt orange minibus on the street. You see the "UVAHA" sign again and decide to pack up your things in your small black nylon tote bag, the one you always carry with you, because you always know you'll pick up something here or there at a store. Today you'll be picking up a box of milk (yes, they sell milk in foil-lined hermetically sealed boxes here – in plastic bags too without an easy way to open them – you have to clip the corner with a pair of scissors!). You also know you'll need to pick up your regular fix of Svitoch chocolates too – milk chocolate for sixty cents a block of a hundred grams. Everything sells by the gram or kilo here. The filled ones are easy to find, but the milk chocolate doesn't seem to be in all the stores. Everybody tells you the Svitoch chocolates tasted better before Nestles bought out the company, but they still taste great to you. You hate Nestles back home in the States except for the crunch bars. And this Svitoch bar was better than anything you had ever tasted from Nestles, including the crunch bar.

The music is a little more palatable as you're leaving – Maria Burmaka, though you like her earlier songs and now harder-to-find music that was authentic folk before she went pop and turned into a bleach blonde. She looks terrible as a platinum blonde. Cheap somehow. But cheap and glitzy sells here to the mass market, just like it does in Europe and back home.

"Gotta go," you said to yourself and realize you had your cell phone off this whole time, so Olenka couldn't call you even if she wanted to. And you didn't have voice mail for your cell since you can't figure out how to set that up. But you realize something must have come up, probably with her twin girls. The flu had been going around. Maybe that's it. An epidemic had shut down the schools a couple weeks back, and the weather was shifting from chilly to warm and vice versa in completely unpredictable ways. This place was caught between two weather worlds that sometimes alternated in strange ways – the warmer Mediterranean south and the frigid north. So you went off to meet the student you were supposed to meet "at Taras," remembering to take your green umbrella.

IF YOU AWAKEN SLEEPING LIONS

"If you awaken sleeping lions, their spirits will devour you. They'll follow you, then they'll devour you."

That's what the crazed woman spat out on the street to Nicholas when he was walking home along Doroshenko Street to teach a class. Her hair was streaked in red and her face looked dusty, as though she had not bathed in at least a week or so. She had fiery yellowish eyes and hissed like a cornered stray wild beast when she spoke. She had heavy eye shadow caked on the lids of her eyes and painted on her face like a warrior going into battle. And her clothing seemed to be in retro 1950s style, as if she didn't belong in Nicholas's time. He immediately understood somehow that he needed to run like a bat out of hell past her and not let her slow him down. When he had created a safe enough distance from her, all he could think about was what she had said. All he could think about at that moment were lions in the city, and he began to see them everywhere.

There were images of lions in the city *everywhere* in the city – thousands of them. He was later to find out that there were 2500 of them in all. Mostly statues or bas-relief façade decorations of lions. Many of the older ones that had been gnawed away by the elements were already being restored. They usually were in pairs or multiples of two – never just one of them. The two lion statues down Copernicus Street from him on his way to the university were sitting and not sleeping. They were below an earthen embankment atop of which was a sign for the Lazarus Hospital and the Lazarus Greek Catholic Church. "Which Lazarus?" Nicholas thought. "It had to be the one who came back from the dead," he realized almost immediately. "The other Lazarus was in hell asking for a droplet of water to quench his thirst. So he couldn't have a church named after him. Or could he?"

There were lions in front of the Ratusha, the City Hall building – in fact two pairs of them: two guarding either side of the entrance to the building and another small pair to the left side of the entrance as you look directly at it. There were two of them holding up a second floor balcony at 25 Rynok Square above a perfume store, and there were four of them on second floor columns of the building at 23 Rynok Square, right on the corner where a blind guitarist usually played Ukrainian songs on the corner. A legless man, to whom Nicholas always tossed change from his pocket, sat in prone position with a blanket over his legs next to the building cattycorner from building 23 at 22 Rynok Square. And there were two resting and friendly lions at the Gun Powder Tower beyond the rampart wall of the Old Town. He had seen sleeping lions somewhere during his meandering through the city, but he just couldn't remember exactly where that was. So he, for the moment, didn't have to worry about awakening any sleeping lions just because he couldn't find them.

THE NICHE TO NOWHERE

Nicholas walked past it a hundreds of times as he walked from his apartment at Hyphenated-Writer Street toward the downtown along Copernicus Street. It was a niche hollowed out of the embankment alongside the sidewalk. It was made of dusty and darkened red bricks with green moss growing particularly on the sides and top. It had a little sand at the bottom. Workman probably left that the last time they pulled up the cobblestones in the sidewalk to even it out a bit. The cobblestones were on a bed of sand, but in wintertime some of the stones seemed to sink. What struck Nicholas most when he looked at the niche on this particular day was that it led to nowhere. It just stopped. There didn't seem to be any reason for it to be there since it had no evident function. There were hundreds of other niches around the city and three or four more on that same street, one with a reposing lion on either side of it, another bas-relief with what appeared to be a monk pouring water out of a jug. All the other niches he had seen in the city had an object inside them – a statue, a place for a potted plant, a small fountain. This one went nowhere. A niche with nothing in it. "Very odd," he thought and took a picture of it since he happened to have his camera with him. Just down the street less than a block away was the brick Citadel high up at the top of the hill. "Maybe it's something to do with that?" He reasoned. He had never gone up the hill to the Citadel. Something was drawing him there now. He examined the bricks in the niche more closely, but he couldn't see any rhyme or reason for it to be there. They happened to be older bricks, too, well weathered by rain and wind and not of recent vintage. He then decided to stand inside it and felt as if he were crossing through a barrier, a kind of porous membrane. He felt a slight draft of air and a tingling sensation as he stepped into the niche that passed quickly. When he stepped out of it, the sensation was gone. Back into it he stepped, back came the sensation. He did this a few more times and several people walking past starting giving him odd looks. The tingling sensation kept coming and going with each entrance and exit into and out of the niche.

Could it be some kind of portal? But not one to anything in this world… It might be significant, but then again, maybe not. He never looked at the niche the same after that day. He somehow knew it was to play a role in something that was going to happen. He couldn't explain it with his rational mind. It's like trying to find the fourth angle of a triangle, or what the poet Bohdan-Ihor Antonych calls "The Great Unknown." Nicholas remembered that the Fifth Angle Café was two blocks from his apartment, the angles beyond the geometry of the angle of a triangle in another dimension, the invisible, the unknown – that fifth angle of the triangle of trinity, a human being's capacity for belief in the unseen. The next time Nicholas passed the café on a walk to the train station he realized that the word "kut" in the name of the café wasn't in the meaning of "angle" at all: it was in the meaning of "corner," because there are five corners where the three roads met at that point. Mathematical perfection can explain a lot, but not everything, and especially not human fallibility in the polysemy of words. There is harmony in the movements of the spheres in clockwork regularity, but that is the harmony of matter, and not the spirit. The spirit is another thing altogether.

KNOWLEDGE IS A SPIRAL

That is what Mr. Viktor said to Nicholas in one of their more and more frequent meetings at the Tasty Rumor Café. Not a straight line. Not just a fact or a bunch of facts. But also what you feel. Transfactual. Transrational. Part of the ninety per cent or more of the human brain that humans don't use. And if you plot your experiences in a mathematical way, it's something like a spiral. To put it in a non-mathematical metaphor, it's something like a roller coaster that brings you up and down at different speeds at different times. You rise, you drop in free fall, and you linger ready to tip down at the top. And although you come back to where you began at the end of the ride, you're changed by the experience on the inside, sometimes in most mysterious ways. And sometimes you just want to puke your guts out after the ride….

CLUB PICASSO

It was on Zelena Vulytsia, Green Street. The club was a third of the way up on a hill off of Ivan Franko Street. It had gas masks on the wall and a dark orange and greenish interior with low indirect multicolored lighting – just the way you expect a dance club to be. It was just off the beaten path of the tram tracks. Nothing in it reminded you of Picasso except the name. It had a service bar at the back with several leggy waitresses in tight black hot pants serving the tables. Nicholas has been there twice. The first time was with his writer friend from Ivano-Frankivsk, Andriy Yurkevych. "Frankivsk" as the locals called it was a three-plus bumpity bump, screech, lurch and halt, dusty train ride from Leopolis. Andriy was staying at Nicholas's place in the guest bedroom that had been built in the attic. Andriy was quite a handsome guy and far more than moderately famous in his homeland and abroad. He had written a couple of "post-modernist" novels as the critics called them and was constantly being asked to go to Europe to give lectures and to be a writer in residence. "The voice and conscience of the Ukrainian people," one paper in Zurich had called him after a speech he had given at the Europarliament in Strasbourg. He traveled a lot, so his English and German had gotten quite good. Andriy was what you called in the old days a babe magnet, the protoimage of the Ukrainian playboy writer as one critic had called him in an article published in Scotland. Though Andriy resented the appellation since he had been married to the same woman all his adult life. Several beautiful young women of various ages at the club, milling about in groups of three or four, giggled when they saw him. None of them got up the gumption to approach him. Andriy took it all in stride and mostly ignored it. Nicholas couldn't help but notice it.

They took a table toward the back of the room for two for the Plach Yeremiji (Jeremiah's Cry) concert. A sociologist acquaintance from Canada showed up a half hour before the concert was about to start, an expert on crime and the Ukrainian mafia, with one of his Ukrainian cousins Vika Pylypenko from Kyiv – a pert and perky thirty-something divorcee who had a teenage son from her marriage and was working as an interpreter for evangelicals coming to evangelize Ukraine. She made good money doing that – enough to buy a new car and apartment after a few years. The two of them asked to sit at the table with Andriy and Nicholas, so they obliged. Andriy called the waitress over – the one who was wearing a tight shocking pink short-sleeve top and a short-short leather skirt. Her legs went on forever, as one song of Jethro Tull went that Andriy particularly liked and remembered. Jethro Tull had been his favorite rock band and he knew most of their lyrics by heart. The waitress dispassionately asked what they wanted to order – and Andriy told her to bring everyone half liters of Chernihiv Red Ale *rozlyvne* (draft beer). In Ukraine the rule is to go from the weaker alcoholic beverages to the stronger stuff. It took Nicholas a while to get used to that, since the tendency for him was to go in the other direction. The Canadian sociologist Jim Oshchirko-Bakenbardy, who was a heavy-set guy with a jolly laugh, bought the second round, and Nicholas the third. The ladies don't buy rounds in Ukraine. Call them sexist or whatever you want, but that's the way it is. Get used to it. Every culture is different, and you have to act like a Roman in the land of the Ukrainians, even if that meant drinking out of cups made of brain-damaging lead. The non-PC nature of the country was growing on Nicholas. He felt he could be freer in what he said here than at home in the US. No one was looking over his shoulder to condemn him for a misspoken word. Live and let live, as the saying goes. Let speak and continue to let speak. It really was a refreshing feeling of freedom.

When the stage lights went on, the rock group stepped out to a fast-paced dance tune with heavy drumbeats and electric guitar riffs running through the music. It was energizing for Nicholas to hear it. And the lead singer's voice was deep, powerful and emotional. He even sang a song or two from poems written by Mr. Viktor and

Andriy. The beat was driving and a lot of couples as well as young and old women in pairs without male partners went out on the dance floor. One dance led to another. Each song seemed to have its own inertia that kept the crowd moving and flowed into the next.

"Want to dance, Andriy?" Vika asked in a coquettish smile.

"No, I'm not dancing today. I'm just drinking. I just drink or dance. I never do both."

"How about you?" She turned to Nicholas.

"Sure, I guess," he answered. "But I'm not that good of a dancer."

"Just try to keep up with me," she said.

They took the floor while Andriy ordered a hundred grams of cognac for himself – that was about the equivalent of a double shot in the US. He sipped it slowly as he surveyed the darkness on the floor and sparkling multicolored lights from the circling globe hanging above from the ceiling.

Though Nicholas was in pretty good physical condition, the fast-paced dancing quickly did him in. Vika had barely broken a sweat and was ready for more. So she dragged him out by the hand for another dance – and another – and another. She was just too sweet for him to say "ni" (no).

Nicholas finally got her to sit down after the third song in a row. He claimed he needed a beer and some mineral water to replenish his bodily fluids. The sweat was pouring down both his cheeks and forehead, and he felt warm under his shirt. So it was good to rest.

The concert went on for about two hours. When it ended and the Canadian sociologist and his dancing cousin had left, Andriy suggested that he and Nicholas go back to meet one of the band members Mykhailo, who was an old friend. The indifferent miniskirted waitress was blocking the way to the backstage door.

"What do you want?" She asked as they approached.

"We're good friends of Mykhailo. Ask him if you'd like…."

She cut him off and flicked her hand nonchalantly to let them enter. When she saw that Mykhailo recognized Andriy and shouted out a "privit, staryj" (yo, old man) to him, she turned away to start cleaning up. Most of the place had emptied out and the miniskirted waitress with frosted blonde hair turned up some Doors music in the room to help pass the time while she cleaned up. "Waiting for the Sun" droned throughout the now empty hall.

The backstage area was Ukrainian bohemian. Mykhailo was chain-smoking with a cigarette in one hand and grabbing a young girl by the waist with the other.

"Bring me some *horilka*," he said as he stumbled a bit backward. The Ukrainian word for vodka comes from the verb "hority," to burn. One of the guys from the band brought him a bottle.

"Hey, Misko [the diminutive for Mykhailo], that's not your wife!" Andriy joked to him.

"My wife knows about her – but she knows I'll always come back to her too, so she doesn't care. Variety – you know…."

"The spice of life as they say in English," Nicholas joined in.

Mykhailo took a swig out of the bottle and passed it to Nicholas.

"Nooooo…," he said right away, "not for me! You have to remember I'm an Amerikrainicano – we try not to mix what we drink, and I've already had beer and cognac today. Start with one thing, stick with it. And Vika's dancing did me in. She had all the guys trying to cut in, especially a couple of African guys, med students from Nigeria. They love the way she jiggles her booty. Too much for them. Just too hot. But she refused them all and said she only dances with one guy when she goes dancing. Andriy, you idiot, you lost your chance to help me out with her."

So they chatted for about fifteen minutes with Mykhailo until they decided to make their way home – a good half hour walk since they wanted to sober up a bit and not take a taxi while they were under the influence.

While they were in the process of shuffling out of the club, the miniskirted waitress in the now completely illuminated cavernous club hall was dancing alone to the Doors. Andriy was especially struck by the fact that the dance was just for herself. She didn't know anyone was watching. It was liberating, loose and free, as if she were casting out her soul to explore the universe. She wasn't just another *shlondra*, a slut, in a go nowhere job. She was infused with a soul and the spirit of dance. Something mystical, something powerful that needed to be released from deep inside her. That was the last thought they were left with as they passed by the gas mask decorations hanging on the wall to exit the building. The walked home along the cobblestone streets, and the night air invigorated them. They slept it off in Nicholas's apartment without any noticeable hangover the next day.

ICON OF THE SAINT AND DEMON

It was an icon unlike any other Nicholas had ever seen before. He saw it in the apartment of one of his colleagues in the English Department at the university who had a small party at her place on Doroshenko Street. He couldn't help but stare at it. It drew him closer and closer. It was a fairly new, recently painted icon on a piece of dark brown stained pine – not the typical wood used in traditional icons where pear wood was most common. It was about seven inches wide and about nine inches tall. A haloed, white-bearded saint was holding a long-handled hatchet. The hatchet had a thin black handle and gold-colored head and blade. The blade matched the color of the saint's halo. The saint was wearing a loose white cassock with a reddish sash belt and a robe covered in white, blue and gray crosses. He was standing on a green hill with red seedlings of plants dotting it. Behind him were tall sandy-colored mountains and a bluish-gray sky. The saint held the hatchet behind his head with his eyes turned to strike an almost comical winged demon hovering in the air next to him. The demon had the long face of a goat with horns, four sharp, thin fingers on each hand, claws on his feet, and a crooked tail. He was taking a defensive position with his arms in front of him, readying to defend himself from the saint's swing. The yellowish ochre tiny wings of the demon were spattered with red, as was the saint's halo. It was as if it were not the saint's first blow. It was typical for Saint George to slay a dragon or serpent in icons with a sword pointed to the ground where the creature was slain.

Even more curious about this icon was the fact that the saint looked like a much older version of Nicholas – just with a white beard and a receding hairline. Was the icon a premonition of a battle to come? But this most likely was a different saint.

THE INVISIBLE RIVER

It's more than an urban legend – the Poltva. In Polish it goes by the name Peltew. It's always confused by typesetters and proofreaders from other parts of Ukraine, because they read the town and region of "Poltava" there, since they've never heard of the river – or seen it. It is, it exists as a river, just one you can't see, and one that Nicholas felt might be a good spot to look for one of the signs of the lion. Its source is hundreds of natural springs since Lviv lies right on the watershed boundary to Europe. It runs from the train station underneath the Opera House. Almost all great cities have rivers – the Seine, the Thames, the Hudson. This city has one too – you just can't see it unless you go into the depths of the underground passageways. The local writer Shchurakiwsky is supposed to know the way. Someone had told Nicholas that Shchurakiwsky used to give tours, and they even say he used to live there beneath the city in the underground when the KGB was after him in the bad old days of the USSR. He knew every dark tunnel and every creaky door and passageway. The KGB was never able to find him though. Gray rats blend into the color of the cobblestones and the color of much of this city. It's easy for rats to hide in the shadows.

The Poltva runs into the Western Buh (with a plosive "h" sound, but sometimes spelled Bug, sounding like "boog") River, at least that's what the keepers of the wisdom at Wikipedia said in the Ukrainian version where it is written (until someone emends it) that the Poltva "in the spring and summer lets people know about it with a specific and not very pleasant odor" and that "sometimes the Lvivians joke and say that this is their greatest current contribution to European society." So the Lvivians in their uniquely human way (including Nicholas for the past few months) were contributing to the fecundification and fertilization of their western neighbors. According to the Wikipedian author you can listen to the "underground gurgling of the sewage wastes" from the orchestra pit of the Lviv Opera House.

Mr. Viktor explained the river's importance to Nicholas at one of their meetings at the Italian Courtyard Café. He remembered what he said as something like this: "The river was covered over by the Austrians. All the city's sewage was polluting the river, and there were all kinds of epidemics – cholera, malaria, and dysentery from Giardia, myriad mosquitoes, and flies. So they placed slabs over the river to stop people's access to it in the city and saved them from contamination. Not many people know that the banks of the river were right where Prospekt Svobody, Liberty Avenue, is located. But a river *is* time; a river *is* the water of life, the principle of eros. They never should have covered the river up. People were polluting it with human waste, defiling nature, bespoiling life and its source in the water. They turned the river of life into Thanatos, a river of death, a river of doom, with their wastes. And they continue to bespoil it to this day. Instead of cleaning up the river the way they should have and revealing it to the world, they've hidden it away in an underground world. They covered up the problem, hoping it would disappear, when they should have solved it. Just because you can't see it doesn't mean it doesn't exist. This is the curse the city will have to endure. It will have problems with its water supply until they bring it back into balance with nature – until they bring back the river of life and release it into the sunlight the way it was intended to be, the way the city was founded by Prince Danylo among the hills on the banks of the Poltva in its primordial beauty. This will be the task for the next fifty years – to undo that curse and bring back the river to life."

WHERE DOES THE WATER GO?

Six to nine a.m.. Six to nine p.m. Divisible by three. It's the clockwork by which most of the city operates for water for its daily needs. Nicholas remembered seeing a map by A. Rudnytsky on the third floor of the Jewelry Museum at one of the corners of Rynok Square. Its title was "The Heart of Europe." And it had a map that showed Ukraine at the very center of Europe with two red lines meeting virtually right at Lviv. These were the lines of the watershed of two parts of the continent that met at the city of lions. That couldn't have been coincidence. It must mean something. The red line where the waters flow to the West and to the East. That was an important sign, but of what, he wasn't sure.

BARBARA THE SOUL-STEALER

Varvara, the stealer of souls. Barbara Langisz, whose coffin portrait hangs on the fourth floor of the Historical Museum on Rynok Square with her sweet, looping locks of hair. Mr. Viktor wrote about her in one of his books. It's fiction, of course, he said, it's fantasy. She's the urban version of the *niavka*, the wood nymph with a hole in her back, who finds unsuspecting young males wandering in the forest to tickle them to death and fulfill her virginal unrealized desire in the netherworld. She died at the age of eighteen before fulfilling her dreams. She experienced only Thanatos without the eros. So she returns to the earthly realm from the beyond on the last Friday of each month in Lviv to seduce and bring back an unsuspecting young male soul to her realm. Nicholas felt he *had to* visit the Museum on Rynok Square as some point to see the seventeenth-century portrait live and in person. Barbara would be waiting there for him....

KEYS TO THE IRON GATE

There are iron gates everywhere in the city to courtyards to garages. From age-old buildings in the *Stare misto* (the Old Town) and passageways into courtyards to what they call here the *New Ukrainian* or *kruti* (crooked) businessmen's homes on streets like Pryroda (Nature) Street next to the Forestry University buildings and grounds. The courtyard at the Armenian Cathedral seemed to always be locked with a key and a padlock with chains – along with a pile of rocks near the entryway to the courtyard. The rocks seemed to say something to Nicholas. Although at first glance they seemed to be just rocks, placed there randomly in a pile near the black wrought iron gate, Nicholas felt they weren't random. There were large and small keys everywhere in the Museum of Antiquities, where Barbara Langisz's portrait was, but none of them seemed to open anything that, at least, Nicholas could see with his eyes. But he was drawn to the largest key that was over a foot in length (he still wasn't thinking metrically) as well as a key with four blades at the bottom that didn't looked like a key. But the rocks and keys were telling him that objects have a voice and a history of their own and sometimes speak to us. Nicholas intuited that the key was really inside himself, somewhere there in the cobwebs of his brain. That hidden key was more important than all the metallic ones in the universe.

THE *CHUB*

It's called the *chub* in Ukrainian – a Kozak scalp lock. Something like a Mohawk haircut, with head shaved on the sides and back, and with a tuft going down just off the side of the center of your skull from the crown of your head to your brow. It was just a little shorter than a punk version of the Mohawk – the hairs were about an inch and a half in length. Nicholas had thought about getting the retro-traditional haircut after he had seen one on a tour guide of a museum of ethnographic art. A local poet by the name of Nazar also used to have one. The look appealed to him right away in his ethno-heightened state of awareness. And he needed a haircut since he was feeling *pelekhatyj* as his grandmother used to say in diasporan Ukrainian, scraggly. Someone had told him that the Kozaks had to earn the *chub* in battle and that if they died in battle, angels would pull them up into heaven by that tuft of hair. The *chub* he had seen worn by Yul Brynner in the Hollywood movie version of Gogol's *Taras Bulba* wasn't particularly authentic and was more of a ponytail in the middle on top of his head. But that particular movie was filmed in Argentina in the early 1960s with not too much authentic detail. Tony Curtis was totally miscast in the movie as Bulba's son Andriy, especially with the latter's Brooklyn accent, and the guy who played his brother Ostap looked a lot more Italian, Spanish or Puerto Rican than Ukrainian. Even though Yul was much too svelte and muscular for the part as described by Gogol in his famous tale, he established an ultracool prototype of the Kozak in Nicholas's mind with his shaved head, macho presence and foreign sounding voice. If the film had been true to the original story, Bulba should have been pudgy with a big gut, and barely able to mount his horse. He did remember that Christine Kaufman was a delicate beauty in the part of the Polish love interest in the film, for the sake of whom Andriy Bulba betrays his country despite her objections. Nicholas found out later that all Ukrainians in Ukraine who have seen it hate that movie. But he still liked Brynner's swagger and Christine Kaufman's refined features and eyes. All the Ukrainians were waiting for Gerard Depardieu to make a more authentic version of the story, though Nicholas thought everyone would find something to criticize in that – if it ever gets filmed.

As Nicholas was walking through the Old Town during a chilly late morning, on a whim he stepped into an old style *parykmakherska* (hairstyling salon) on Staroyevreiska vulytsia (Old Jewish Street) that had a sign saying it had a men's and a woman's salon. It actually was a really small room with just two shabby, rotating salon chairs and two mirrors ("one chair for men, one for women," he thought as he walked in). There also was a heavyset woman at a small table doing a pedicure for another equally heavyset woman. No, they were both just fat. It was better to be linguistically freed of euphemisms. Fat – not corpulent, just fat, Nicholas kept repeating in his mind. He could say it and think it here. And not worry about whether he could or should say it.

After Nicholas walked into the door of the salon, he was greeted by a rather dour-faced young girl who looked to be about twenty and much too young to be so disgusted with life. "Whaddya want?" She snapped. "A haircut. That's why I'm here," Nicholas snapped back and smiled despite her frown. "Wait here," she curtly answered and pointed to the rather uncomfortable looking vinyl-covered dark maroon chair by the door. He sat down and the girl walked out briskly. He could see through the window that she had stepped outside for a smoke. A minute later, a woman, whom Gogol would call "pleasingly plumpish" or something like that, in her mid-thirties walked through the door. She had bleached frizzy hair with about an inch or so of her black roots showing. She also had shiny gold molars that were still common in this part of the world. She politely asked Nicholas what kind of haircut he wanted. He was about to say "a Kozak *chub*," but he wasn't able to spit the words out of his mouth. A Kozak would have just said "do the *chub*, baby." Well, at least a contemporary Kozak might say that. But he wasn't there yet, so he just told her to cut it short on the sides and back so it would be good for a month or two before his next haircut. She turned out to be very nice and started talking to him about her little girl and her husband who's a sweet guy but who drinks too much, especially *horilka*, Ukrainian vodka. Nicholas asked how much the haircut cost when she finished, and it turned out to be eight hryvnas or about a $1.60. So he gave her a ten and told her "bez zdachy," to keep the change. The *chub* might happen down the road when he becomes a little more emboldened. He knew he wasn't quite ready to take that dramatic plunge.

RAMIFICATIONS

An American friend of Nicholas's arrived for a weeklong visit – Bill Baranovsky. So Nicholas showed him around the city that was becoming more and more familiar to him. The *baran* part of his name meant "ram." Bill looked like his name, with three days of stubble on his face and a shaved head and tattoos on both arms. He was a brawny former football player and workoutaholic, who pumped iron in the gym three times per week. The two had met at the NY Athletic Club in Port Jefferson Station in the sauna after a workout when Nicholas was doing graduate work at Stony Brook. The ram-named man got his degree in criminal justice from Stony Brook and was working as a detective doing desk duty in Brooklyn as the result of some overzealous arrests of drug dealers in East New York. He didn't know he was Ukrainian until Nicholas let him know the secret meaning of his name. It turned out his family circa 1895 had lived in a small village a half hour drive outside of Ukraine named Lyubeshko before immigrating to the US. Bill was taking some vacation time to come to visit his friend in Leopolis and to check out his roots (as well as the local "maidens of the night" that he had heard about from marriage agencies on the Internet). "Well the Ukraine girls really knock me out/They leave the west behind," as they say….

When Jan Shchurakivsky heard that Nicholas's friend was arriving at the airport, he offered to send someone with a car to pick him up. It turned out to be a surgeon friend of his Marko Pynkivsky, who arrived with the car, a metallic tan BMW that was two or three years old. Volodya Harbuziuk, the former owner of a downtown café where Shchurakivsky used to hang out called Femida, also showed up. And Nicholas's actress friend Vira Malaniuk also decided to come along for the ride since her mother was taking care of her son for the day. Nicholas has met her a week earlier after her performance at the Zankovetsky Theater in the play *Hutsulka Ksenya* (Ksenya the Hutsul girl). It was a really corny play once commissioned by an emigre playwright. So it was a full retinue that greeted Bill on his first visit to the ancestral homeland that he had never known about.

The retinue waited for about an hour after the plane landed to go up to the main terminal building. They were experienced greeters, so they sipped some Lviv Porter at a small outdoor café while they were waiting. Then they made their way to the dilapidated airport main waiting room with old Soviet glory-to-the-workers'-paradise wall mosaics still on the upper part of the walls. When Bill finally came through with a big green military issue duffel bag, Nicholas ran over to him.

"Hey, Bill, how'ya doin'?" He asked him as he gave him a bear hug.

"Rough flight… And this airport! Fuckin' damn… I thought for a minute I was arriving in the Ukrainian Congo."

Then Nicholas said to him: "Three manly kisses on the cheek, Bill. That's what these guys want to give you!" He pointed to the two guys with him, and not to Vira. One of the guys, Volodya, had had a few too many beers to drink and was teetering back and forth a bit.

"How about her?" He said, pointing to Vira. "Can't she give me the kisses?"

Bill continued to mildly protest at first, since he wasn't used to the custom, particularly when he was about to be kissed by two hefty men, but his protests turned to cultural acceptance when he overcame his macho-man Americano reservations.

"You hungry?" Nicholas asked him.

"Yeah, I'm starving. I came in on an Air France plane from Paris, and they didn't give much to eat. Too much Boursin. I need some red meat!" He bellowed.

"I know a good place to go," Marko chimed in. It's right here near the airport. Five minutes away."

So they loaded up the luggage and drove off to the restaurant, which turned out to be in the middle of nowhere with nine or ten gazebos for outdoor eating and a rock garden next to a lake. Nicholas tried to look it up later on the Internet and thought it might have been one called *Ozeryanyj Kraj*, or Land of Lakes (like the brand of American butter) or Lakeland.

They started off with a bottle of chilled *horilka* that everybody downed with gusto since it was a warm day. Thirst needed to be quenched.

Then they ordered plates of cucumbers, tomatoes, cheese, black bread, sausage, baked garlic, and more.

While Bill had pointed to Vira as a point of interest when he arrived, he didn't really talk much to her at the outdoor restaurant. Instead he seemed to bond with the two guys and started making plans of what to do with them in the next few days. Nicholas ended up chatting mostly with Vira, who looked exquisite in a long white cotton dress with eyelet holes all over it. The holes weren't revealing, but just gave her the look of being cotton cool. She looked like an angel in the outdoor rock garden of the restaurant and Nicholas took about a dozen or so pictures of her. Marko and Volodya insisted on picking up the restaurant bill despite Bill's insistence that he, as a more moneyed American, should. But he and the two guys had had far too much to drink, while Nicholas and Vira remained sober, but the guys did manage to drive everyone home in one piece. Vira lived near St. George's Cathedral at the top of the hill overlooking Lviv. After stumbling groggily from the jet lag and the *horilka* into Nicholas's apartment, Bill immediately crashed onto his pull out couch bed to wake up the next morning in his ancestral homeland.

A trip to village Lyubeshko was on for the next day. Bill and Nicholas went off to meet Marko and Volodya for the trip. Lyubeshko was not too far outside the environs of Lviv. It was mostly countryside and a dirt road off the main two-lane highway to the village, which had water and mud standing all over it from a rain that had fallen two days before.

"Let's find the *starosta* (accent on the last syllable), the village elder…," Volodya announced, and asked a few passers-by where to find him. He turned out to be walking on the grass beside the road about fifty meters away, so they approached him.

"Do you happen to know anyone by the name of Baranovsky in this village?" Volodya asked the elder, who was wearing a dark blue coat dusty woolen jacket that must have been fifty years old.

He scratched his forehead and tilted up his cap before he answered.

"Half the village is named Baranovsky…."

"Maybe you could point out some of the eldest Baranovskys around?"

The *starosta* pointed to a house where a stooped over thin gray-haired man and a short portly woman in a scarf were standing.

It turned out they were about eighty years old and remembered bits and pieces of the Baranovsky family past, and how one of the Baranovskys married someone over the mountains in Poland from Sanok in the Lemko region, then emigrated to the US. But they lost touch. They did think they were distant cousins. So Bill, happy that he met someone from his peasant proletarian past, smiled to take some pictures with the relatives lost from his family tree. Since he didn't have anything to give them as a gift, he pulled out a $100 bill to give them, which they refused to take.

One other of Bill's adventures on his weeklong stay was noteworthy – a trip to the Kolyba Restaurant with Marko and Volodya who had become fast drinking buddies with Bill. The restaurant was a fancy place for the "new" Ukrainians, the big-money *kruti* (crooked) people who earned their fortunes in less than law-abiding ways. The restaurant was a place of some renown. It had been the place where NATO generals met when visiting Ukraine during war games in the NATO tank training grounds west of the city toward the Polish border. It was also the place where Pope John-Paul II had gone to dinner with a retinue of cardinals and other churchmen during his visit to Ukraine. The owner Myroslav had a picture of himself on the wall smiling widely with the Pope.

There was a wedding going on at the same time as the three gentlemen arrived, and it was like a who's who of Lvivian Ukrainian culture in the restaurant with artists, writers, rock stars, and politicians (including the mayor).

The three guys sat down with Myroslav at a table and started exchanging anecdotes and jokes, with Marko and Voldodya translating with their broken English for Bill with his non-existent Ukrainian that seemed to improve considerably in his mind as the evening went on. Everybody understood the language of gesture and laughter. They drank chilled pepper *horilka* and popped pieces of *salo* (pork lard) and pickles after each 100-gram double-shot. Bill became a particular favorite of Myroslav's as they told salacious joke after salacious joke that in the usual way seemed to become all the more funny the more under the influence they became. Why do they never seem to be as funny when you're sober?

"Eat, we must eat!" Myroslav announced and ordered some food for everyone – *deruny* (potato pancakes), shashlik (shish kebob) on skewers, beet salads, black bread, and more.

"You know, they've tried to kill me seeks times already," Myroslav started telling an anecdote to Bill in broken English. "They shoot me in right leg few months ago – three guys," and stuck out his three middle fingers of his right hand to emphasize the point and then slapped himself with his hand on the spot where the bullet had grazed him. "I pull out my gun and keel one of them on spot in street. Then two other guys start wrestle me. I grab knife from one and stab him in gut – real deep – and son of bitch start howling like stuck pig. He vas stuck pig! Then third guy take off. I pick up gun off street and start chasing him. But my leg hurt, and I no chase him down. But I send my guys next week to make sure to keel him in front of his wife. They got what they deserved, bastards. You don't mess with old Myroslav!" And he slapped himself on his upper belly.

Bill just laughed and downed his shot of *horilka*, then looked at old Myroslav smiling in the picture with the pope.

At one point Myroslav said: "Time to bring out special stuff!" And he motioned to the waiter.

"You are my SPESHUL friend!" He said to Bill. "You get to have this. I keep it for speshul occasion. It's *samohon*, firewater, homebrew. It vill take hair off armpits in von sip." And he poured out four healthy-sized shot glasses of the clear brew.

Everyone downed the glass to the bottom, toasting all the women in the world who had made their lives so wonderful and so miserable at the same time.

Bill's eyes nearly popped out as he downed the glass. He started laughing giddily and stroked his hand across Myroslav's *puzo*, his potbelly. Suddenly two guys in dark glasses and black suits ran up to him with loaded revolvers pointed at his head.

"No, no, silly, he my friend! NO SHOOT! FRIEND!" And smacked his hand across Bill's stomach as he let out a laugh.

When Bill somehow managed to get home, he seemed to remember everything about the evening up to the guns pointed at his head by the non-alien men in black, but everything else fell into oblivion in an alcoholic haze. It took him a full two days to recover, and he decided to complete his last few days in his ancestral homeland as a more sober sightseer.

Since Nicholas wasn't there at the restaurant, he just listened in amazement to Bill describe the evening to him. Nicholas had gone to his newfound friend Vira's birthday party for her son, so he missed all the excitement first-hand.

THE WHITE RAVEN

It might have been incorrect to say that no raven appears at the crossroads. Actually, there are no crossroads. And this raven is a saying, a metaphorical one. To be a white raven in Ukrainian is to stick out like a sore thumb. Nicholas realized that he was a bit of a white raven both back home in the US and here in Leopolis. In the US his bifurcated soul made him feel out of synchronization with place. He was by nature of his first name mathematically in the middle of the alphabet, both in English and in Ukrainian. He was Nicholas and Mykola. Accent on the second syllable of his Ukrainian name. He was between two worlds and realized that he might be better off trying to be a white raven in the snow. He wanted to fit in somehow – in either one of those worlds.

THE BLUE BOTTLE CAFÉ

If you don't know where to find it, you'll never find it. You need someone to take you there. It's down a long, slightly twisting and unlit passageway off Rynok Square off of Ruska Vulytsia, Rus Street, the 19th century name for Ukrainians – deep, deep in the bowels of the building – one of the intriguing three-story buildings just off the square. You step in a shallow pothole here and there in spots as you stumble through until your eyes get used to the light. There's a tall inner courtyard above you in the very middle of the passageway with iron ladders and overhangs. No one looking down from above. A bit too cold yet for that this time of year in *ljutyj*, the "fierce" month of February. Your traveling companion is the sister of your friend Anya who's doing graduate work in the States on Milton. You're coming to meet Nadya, whose name means "hope," for the first time. You decided to meet her "at Taras" as the locals say, a common meeting spot and nearly sacred place in the city, although the statue was of fairly recent vintage. That's the tall statue of Taras Shevchenko right off of Prospekt Svobody (Liberty Avenue) that leads to the Opera House that's the gem of the city – modeled after the opera house in Vienna. Shevchenko is the great 19th century Ukrainian bard who wrote of freedom during the Tsarist Russian Empire and wanted to be buried in Washington, in a land "brave and free" as he called it? Or was it high upon a hill overlooking the Dnipro? Well, that's at least where they ended up burying him, in Kaniv overlooking the wide river that "roared and moaned" in his poetry and not in Washington. Shevchenko's dream of freedom was realized before his death after being bought out from his serfdom – and again later after a decade in exile in Kos Aral and elsewhere in the nomadic wastelands at the very wildest edge of the empire where enemies of the Russian state were punished. Now Taras had become more than just a symbol for his people who achieved their freedom in 1991; he's a landmark where it's convenient to meet your friends under his nose and caressing bronze gaze. Before deciding to go to the *Synya plyashka* (the Blue Bottle) you had to find Nadya, who told you on the phone, "I look just like my sister." You told her you don't look like your brother, whom she's never met, and will be wearing a gray winter parka with a black skier's wraparound ear band on your head. She didn't know what that was. Even though no one from here wears them, you like them because they fit easily in your pocket. "What happened to the top of your hat?" Professor Potojbichny had asked Nicholas once when he had just been introduced to him on the street through Mr. Viktor. "He's kidding," Mr. Viktor added. "I know," Nicholas smiled and nodded.

Nicholas first scanned the people around the statue. Two guys smoking cigarettes nervously pacing, evidently waiting for their dates. A slightly heavyset blonde woman in her thirties who was quite attractive, but definitely not Anya's sister. Anya had told Nicholas that Nadya looked *just* like her – just *much* more beautiful and a little older. Nicholas decided to turn his eyes away from the statue to scan the square. A few older people with the typical for this part of the world plaid red and blue square plastic bags that peddlers carry for their goods who couldn't have been Nadya. Too old and not beautiful – as least in his imagined sense of feminine beauty as Nadya's sister had described it. As his eyes moved around the square in counterclockwise motion, he caught a glimpse of the piercing eyes of beauty. His look was returned – and the moment of mutual recognition was complete. She was sitting on a wooden slat bench painted green, and as he moved toward her, she stood up. "Well, she is beautiful," he thought to himself. More beautiful than Anya? I don't know…." But she had a wonderful smile as she greeted him – and those eyes that were so zestful and filled with life. The windows to the soul – he remembered from some Faulker he had read in high school or freshman English in college. Or was it James Agee? He couldn't remember exactly. But it was one of them.

She said his name "Nicholas?" with a question mark. And he answered with "Nadya?" in the same way. "Where would you like to go?" She asked. "I'm in your hands, so take me somewhere you'd like to go." "Okay, how about *Virmenska vulytsia* (Armenian Street)? It's my favorite street in the city. I love the Armenian Cathedral courtyard. It's probably closed, but we can look inside through the iron gratings of the fence. Then go to the Dzyga Art Gallery. I used to work there, putting up exhibitions and writing catalogs for them. I'm mostly a freelance art critic now for a couple of papers and magazines. One of my friends probably has an exhibit there right now. I haven't been there for awhile, so it'll be nice to stop in."

The art gallery was pleasant and warm, and they looked at the mostly abstract paintings in some detail. It was uncanny, but her and Nicholas's taste seemed to coincide on everything. It was as if they had known each other for a hundred years; he even said that to her later. It was the truth and not a made-up comment. And she said the same to him. They ran into the director of the gallery shortly after finishing the perusal of the mostly abstract paintings on the stone walls. It was more cave than gallery in that part of the building. But with the indirect lighting it had a certain warmth to it that made its stone walls inviting. They passed by a man walking with an older woman coming out of the gallery. He turned sideways and blurted out, "I haven't seen you in a while, Nadya, I miss seeing your lovely face…. I have a fiftieth-birthday installation coming up on Friday. Make sure you come over for that if you have the chance." Nadya nodded with a smile to him that she'd try. "That's my old friend Slavko Bauman," she said to Nicholas.

"Let's walk a bit," Nadya said as they turned toward the exit. They walked out of the building, turning left onto the street that led to the Dominican Cathedral with its soot-blackened stone walls. This is where the booksellers put out their books – in that courtyard outside of the Ivan Fedorov monument. He printed the first bible in Ukraine. The prices were good on the books, but it was getting late and they already had put almost everything away. They walked down Staroyevreiska vulytsia (Old Jewish Street), which had a mixture of antiquarian shops and cafés, and a different kind of shop here and there. The various nationalities used to have their own quarters in the center of town. The Armenians back where we were, the Jews here. Then they turned back a bit toward the Ratusha, the City Hall, and there it was, the Blue Bottle. Or at least a sign for the Blue Bottle Café . Ukrainian has two words for blue, and this particular one meant "dark blue." It was a small unimposing sign that you would hardly notice unless you were really looking for it. It just happened to catch Nicholas's eye. It was just a kind of dark blue pastel colored bottle on a weatherworn dark piece of wood. An imposing piece of graffiti was just before the entrance to the café – "VAMPIRISSIMO" all in English capital letters and hand-painted in black.

"Want to go in?" Nadya asked.

"Sure, why not."

"Oh, I wanted to show you this. See this stairway? Step up on them."

He stepped up on them and they creaked.

"They're living steps," she said. "They play sounds when you walk on them – more than just creaks." Nadya seemed fascinated by small details. Nicholas immediately liked that about her.

So they moved away from the living steps and walked through the rest of the passageway to the café , bringing us to where we were at the beginning of this part of the story.

There were two ponderous slatted wooden doors at the end of the stony and faded stucco inner corridor. There was the scent of urine and mustiness here and there. Another sign that seemed to repeat the one at the entrance near the street hung over the door to the left. Nadya opened it and led Nicholas in.

"Do you want to sit a bit? Or keep walking?" She asked. "I'm fine either way."

"Sitting would be good for a while."

So they took one of the five or six tables in the small café – the one to the right side toward the back corner. There was a third blue pastel-like painting of a blue bottle on darkened wood over the doorway to a small room adjacent to the main part of the café where the bartender, cashier and service preparation area were.

"There's a picture of Kulchytsky," Nadya pointed to a spot on the wall. "He supposedly brought coffee to Vienna and Europe way back when."

"He looks a bit spooky to me," Nicholas added. "Everybody seems to talk about ghosts in this city.... He looks like he's part African? Was he?"

"Yes, he does, doesn't he," she answered.

A slight, goose bump chill of a feeling descended on Nicholas as he sat down closest to the small cylindrical pellet stove that seemed to provide the only heat for the Blue Bottle. The feeling made him wonder if one of the signs of the lion might be here. He looked around the room and saw two older teenage girls chatting. One of them kept looking over at him. Probably wondering why such a beautiful woman was with such an average-looking guy. Maybe she thought he was her pimp! No, that's impossible. She didn't look at all like a "maiden of the night" as the writer Shchurakiwsky called the local *shlondry* in his book about two such "maidens" cavorting around in Leopolis. Nadya was much too classy and elegant for anyone to even think that. Then there was another table with two couples in their late fifties or sixties who were chatting away in German, taking pictures of the interior. Polish and German tourists had been visiting the town in droves these days. The walls were filled with Secession Period pictures, drawings and paintings – from the late 19th and early 20th century. Apparently the place had been meticulously designed by Bauman – the guy they had met at the art gallery. He took painstaking detail to recreate what once was – a timepiece that takes you back to a gentler, more refined age. The picture of Kulchytsky particularly struck Nicholas. He appeared to be an African or a particularly dark-skinned individual with a thin moustache in dapper evening attire. He had a nice, friendly, inviting smile. The other pictures harkened back to the scenes of the less hectic city life of those earlier days with horse-drawn carriages.

"Nadya, what would you like to order?" Nicholas asked her.

"Oh, my favorite here is the frothy cappuccino."

"I'll have some cognac. It'll warm me up a bit from the chill. This stove in the corner is doing a good job of that too."

So Nicholas ordered the libations – the Zakarpatsky cognac, which was the least expensive one on the menu and in his opinion the best, the cappuccino and a bottle of local mineral water from the Carpathians. He and Nadya talked about this and that. He turned his eyes away from her several times. He was afraid she would catch him staring at her. He couldn't help but stare, but he did his best to disguise it and from being too obvious. It was as if he were seeing into her soul through those dark eyes that were the deepest, softest brown he had ever seen. Well, maybe it was just a fantasy he was experiencing. But fantasies are an enjoyable ride when they take you away to certain somewheres.

As he often did during his trip, Nicholas took pictures of Nadya with his digital camera that he almost always carried around with him. He was quite shocked to see that Nadya's beauty didn't translate well to digital film. It turned out she wasn't very photogenic. He couldn't figure out why, because she looked so much better in reality. So he learned that pictures don't always tell the complete story. Pictures sometimes lie. Believe your own eyes and ears and senses most of all – he was quick to learn.

THE BLIND SINGERS

Two peasant women dressed in fairly recent vintage and heavy full-length fur coats sang out to the passing crowd that rarely stopped to listen, giving each of them a coin or a small bill into their tin cup. Coins made sounds, so that was the more popular donation. The women would at least hear the donation. They were half a block away from the blind accordion player outside Hotel George. Striking about both of them was the whiteness of their eyes that seemed to roll as they sang old peasant songs they had learned from childhood in the villages. Rumor had it that these particular beggars were working for a kind of *sutenir*, a pimp for beggars. He'd take a cut of their daily earnings for giving them protection and allowing them to sing at that spot. And they were there every day – rain, snow, sleet, or hail. That's what many of the locals thought.

The women sang in two-part harmony – one low, one high, the latter stretching for notes. Each song sounded like a lament, even if it was a more joyful song. They were truly singing for their supper. There used to be a third singer with them, but she had died a year or two ago. Someone had told Nicholas that the third singer's daughter had a TV special on her a few months back. She had some kind of mental impairment and was an artist who did primitive paintings of village scenes. But she wasn't a good singer, so she didn't follow in her mother's begging and singing footsteps.

There were other beggars at different spots of the downtown. A bandura player with a big white moustache and in full Kozak parade regalia. His uniform was dark blue and dusty, just as his repertoire was. But he received a lot of contributions to the box he placed on the pavement in front of him. Then there was the blind guy on the other side of the Hotel George playing the accordion – mostly Ukrainian dance tunes. There was also the beggar who sat opposite the Ratusha at Rynok Square, huddled up against a storefront. He had had both of his feet amputated. Nicholas always contributed to his upside-down hat when he passed. You'd also see other assorted *baby* (pronounced BAH-BY, a short-voweled "i" sound and accent on the second syllable) from villages in dusty old cloth coats wearing colorful scarves that had faded with time. They usually stood in doorways on busy streets with a cup in their hands or on occasion with an outstretched palm, though that seemed to be an improper way to beg without the mediation of a collecting device. Just opposite the double amputee on the opposite corner was a guy who played guitar and sang Ukrainian and Russian songs with a hat turned upside down. And between Rynok Square and the Galician Market (a great place to buy fresh vegetables and fruits, meat, and cheeses) about a block past the Chapel of the Boims, were a fiddle player and a *sopilka* (tin whistle) player who played mostly dance tunes. And the beggars were at the entrance of every church on Sunday. There were more and more of them as the weather got warmer.

THE HALL OF SYMMETRY

Nicholas returned to the soot-black stone Ethnographic Museum for a second lecture, actually a "book presentation," as they call it here, a book launching of one of the local poets who was the member of some underground performance group in Soviet days that had come aboveground. He was supposed to meet his curly-haired friend Raya, whom he had met in the Humanities Institute at the University of Lviv. She was late and wasn't in the hall when he arrived. He, in fact, was late himself because of a sudden snowstorm that seemed to snarl traffic up a bit. After fighting his way onto a bus, he did manage to get a seat on it at the very back, but, regardless, it chugged along slowly through the bottlenecked rows of too many cars and too many buses in too small of a space on the slick narrow streets. During his previous visit to the hall for the lecture on energy forces, he focused almost exclusively on the lecture and not on the room. This time, the room captured his attention much more than the reading, even though it was an overflow standing-room-only crowd. He managed to squeeze just inside the door.

He looked at the floor first. It was a well-scuffed and worn oak parquet with bits and pieces of wood missing in spots. But the two-inch size strips of wood were all grouped together and set in such a way to counterbalance each other's movement, creating an almost perfect balance and stasis, an extraordinary symmetry in each parquet piece that was a foot wide by a foot long and a virtually perfect square. The walls of the room were lined with either dark walnut or dark oak wooden panels – Nicholas couldn't get quite close enough to tell. The room was really in two parts, the rectangular part of the room for the audience to sit on linked padded wooden bench-chairs set up like pews in a church, and a stage for speakers that formed a semi-circle behind it. The semi-circle shape seemed to beg for another semi-circle to complete it. The back wall of the recessed stage area contained about twenty wooden panels made of the same wood as the walls in the audience area. They seemed to alternate narrow eight-inch panels with wider door-size panels, all contributing to the sense of order and balance. Above the paneling on the wall behind the dais wall was a row of pudgy babies – all in a semicircle. There were eighteen of them – yes, Nicholas counted them – and they were all happily playing. Some were sitting, others standing. One was holding a shepherd's crook with his left hand and petting a friendly billy goat with his right, another was holding a lute. The sky behind them wasn't blue, but rather a pinkish copper color that reflected more light than the wooden panels below that seemed to absorb light. Nicholas noticed a name and a date on the back wall of the chubby children playing: Lewandoski 1898. There was also a crimson lamp hanging above in a small chandelier above where the poet giving the reading was standing. The crimson lamp seemed important.

The very top of the semicircular back wall was a thick dark greenish and deep gold wallpaper in a repeated geometric design that reminded Nicholas of snowflakes. The design was repeated on the three other walls of the room for about six feet above the wooden paneling. The wallpaper seemed to repeat its pattern in rows of threes, sevens and nines. In the edges between the wall and ceiling was a deep reddish marble strip about a foot wide. It was hard to discern because the ceiling was high. Nicholas also noticed the room had black onyx marble pillars running up about halfway up the wall to the ceiling in all sides of the room. The marble seemed to have brownish or gray-green streaks running through it. Again, it was hard for Nicholas to tell because there wasn't any direct illumination on the columns (for lack of a better word) – they really were more like slabs for decoration rather than an architectural feature holding up the ceiling. There seemed to be six on each side, four in front, and four in back. Again, the symmetry and balance were overwhelming when he looked closely at it. There was one large chandelier in the center of the room. It had glass flowers in an attenuating pattern in three rows. The flowers looked a lot like horns. And you could almost hear them play as you looked at them. Nicholas heard a moaning sound as he was looking at the chandelier. It didn't seem to be coming from anyone in the room but from the room itself. He heard it again a minute or two later. It was like the moaning of a wounded animal; not a shriek, but just a low-pitched moan.

Nicholas felt a slight poke in his back that startled him out of his concentrated focus on the symmetrical hall. It was Raya, who had missed quite a bit of the reading. She apologized for not having saved him a seat as she had promised. She whispered in his ear to meet for coffee tomorrow. "Sure," he said. "Just give me a ring on my *mobilnyk* (my cell phone) when you're free. I have nothing planned for tomorrow." "Catch you later, I have a lot of work to do at home," she said, and left the room as the poetry reading was ending. "I have to get home before the water shuts off at nine…."

Nicholas stopped to chat with a couple of his friends. The mustachioed and quite friendly fantasy fiction writer Bohdan Bily (whose first name means "God given" and last name pronounced "Beelee" means "white") shook hands with him as soon as he saw him. Everyone, at least all the men, shake hands with you every time they see you in this country. It's something you just get used to. It eventually becomes second nature. Just don't shake hands over the threshold of a doorway – that's bad luck. You'll end up getting into a fight with that person if you do. He noticed his friend Marko with his wife Luda: he was taking pictures of the event for the Vysoky Zamok newspaper. He wanted to ask Marko to take pictures of all the details and features of the room that he had never noticed before, but then he thought Marko might think he was silly for asking. He also noticed a really old woman in a black dress with prickly black hair. She caught sight of him, and her momentary gaze made him shudder. He turned his eyes away, and she thankfully passed. While he was chatting with Marko, he looked at a carved wooden relief to the left of the semicircle stage area on the wall. He turned to the other three corners of the room and noticed that each corner had the same wooden relief. Why didn't he notice that before? If you're not looking for something, you don't notice. This time he was looking intently, concentrating his mind and gaze to process everything he could in as much detail as he could.

The wooden sculpture, more like half a sculpture, had a leaf design with a crown at the top that looked like a castle wall. In the very middle of it was a fat spider. "Why a spider?" He thought to himself. "Why not," he replied without even thinking about it. But when he thought about it, of all the things you could put in the middle of that wooden wall sculpture, why put in a spider?

Since he had focused so much on the inside during the reading, he decided to look closer at the exterior of the building. He realized it wasn't really soot black, but just looked like that in the shade. It was a darkened sandstone on the first floor of the building on the two sides facing Prospekt Svobody and Hnatiuk Street. The lower level on each side had three large windows in the center with a window on each side – with wrought iron gratings on all the windows. The part of the building right on the corner was shaped like a cylinder with four tall marble columns at the entrance with wrought iron gratings over the door and a semi-circular balcony atop the tall entryway. The roof was green copper and lights on the cylindrical part of the building were green to imitate the copper ceiling at night. The second and third floors were a tan brick. Nicholas has passed it many times, and he just never noticed the upper floors were made of a different material than the first. You sometimes don't notice things until you really look – he kept thinking to himself. A Statue of Liberty was atop the building over the cylindrical part of it above the copper roof. And directly below at the top of the first floor of the cylindrical part of the building was the head of a roaring lion facing down. Nicholas remembered very few if any of the thousands of statues of lions on the city's building facing down or roaring. Most of them were peaceful, acting as guardians and not ready to attack, but just resting or sometimes evening smiling. The roaring lion at the Ethnographic marked this as an important spot in Nicholas's mind.

THE CHAPEL OF THE BOIMS

The chapel was one of Nicholas's favorite places in the city. It was quite small and probably could fit just a few dozen people at one time. It was built in 1609-1615 by Georgy Boim, a Hungarian businessman who had moved to the city and who had converted from Lutheranism to Catholicism. It was meant as a private chapel next to the family graveyard. The relatives of Boims buried there might have been among some of those graves that had been moved, the spirits that were troubling Ivan the Ghostseer, but Nicholas wasn't sure about that. The chapel's soot blackened bas-reliefs from the front were its most impressive feature from the outside. Something you don't normally see on a church, and there were portraits of Georgy Boim and his wife on the back outside wall of the church.

The chapel is right off of Rynok Square, within ten or meters of it, and next to the Metropolitan Roman Catholic Cathedral. Its entrance faced away from the square onto a small alley where the World of Coffee Café was now located.

Nicholas had heard many people talk about the older lady Zhenya who used to give tours of the chapel in multiple languages before she died four or five years earlier. She had a perfect memory of everything you'd ever want to know about the chapel and its history. But now that she was gone, so were those memories.

Nicholas had gone over to meet Mr. Viktor at three "at Taras."

"You're the only reliable Ukrainian I know in this city," he said to Mr. Viktor as Nicholas arrived five minutes late because one of the other American Fulbright scholars in the city had run into him and chatted for a bit at the one reliable university computer lab at Saksahansky Street.

For once on this rare occasion the chapel was open. A professional photographer was in the chapel with a hefty tripod set up to take pictures. It turned out to be a friend of Mr. Viktor's, so, after the ritual handshake and greeting, Mr. Viktor continued to chat with him. Nicholas paid the two-hryvna (40 cents) charge for each of them to a large-framed woman with a cigar box – and bought a brochure on the chapel for six hyrnvas from a man standing next to her.

"He's the official historian of the chapel," Mr. Viktor said to Nicholas as he saw him buying the brochure out of the corner of his eye. "If you want to know anything – just ask him. He doesn't charge for questions!"

Nicholas took the opportunity to ask if the Boims were buried in the chapel.

"No, they moved them to Lychakiv Cemetery long ago…," he answered and seemed to have a long pause at the end of his thought.

"That's not right," Nicholas said. "They never should have moved them. Don't disturb the dead in their place of final rest and let them sleep." Nicholas was certain that is what Zhenya would have said.

"Too late now," the keeper of the chapel's history answered. "What is done is done."

Several interior features of the chapel were particularly striking. The amber and reddish (what seemed like mahogany and walnut) inlay on two side altars – and a rose-colored or peach stucco color on two circular windows in the side left wall. The combination of the light filtering through and the stucco's color gave it a bit of an unearthly glow, as if you were in a slightly different world under a slightly different sun. And the absolutely most powerful impression in the chapel was when Nicholas looked straight up into the single rotunda. The diamond pattern and predominantly celestial blue burst upward into infinity. It was as if in this tiny chapel you could reach upward and touch the boundless universe with a single gaze. This was the realization you have when you experience the awe of absolute beauty of being. It was unlike any other feeling Nicholas had ever had about any other church he had ever visited.

He gazed with a transfiguring fixation for a good fifteen minutes up at the vault. Nicholas though Mr. Viktor might have though he had gone mad, but Mr. Viktor himself was lost in intense conversation with his photographer friend. And a group of ten or so Polish tourists with their tour guide in the interim had squeezed into the chapel. Nicholas hardly noticed them. He knew more about the chapel in that one upward transfixed gaze than thousands of books could have taught him, but it was something he couldn't explain to anyone else. It was just something he now knew that he had never known before.

Mr. Viktor tapped Nicholas on the shoulder at the end of his reverie and said "Pora?" with a question mark, which meant "Time to go?"

The outside of the chapel was just as detailed as the inside. The soot blackened bas-relief sculptures on the top front of it dominated. Nicholas had walked past the chapel hundreds of times before. He was somehow always drawn to it. There was also a practical reason he saw it so many times – it was right there at the main entrance side streets to Rynok Square. So it had a pivotal position on the close periphery of the square.

In the three or four historical articles and pieces Nicholas had read about the chapel, none of them said a word about the eight lions' heads at knee-height guarding the front of it. They were on semicircular columns. He had never noticed the lion face bas-reliefs before in the hundreds of times he had passed by. Each lion had a ring through his nose. Nicholas's dreams told him there were seven signs of the lion to be found – not eight. Maybe this was a clue? Or maybe a false clue? Or might there be an eighth lion? It was interesting that none of the descriptions mentioned them. And *that* was somehow significant. In order to truly see you must always truly look. And certain knowledge comes from beyond your five senses.

As Mr. Viktor and Nicholas walked away, Nicholas took a closer look at the sitting, pensive statue of Christ at the top of the single cupola. It reminded him of Rodin's "Thinker" (but this Christ, of course, was wearing a crown of thorns).

THE GOLDEN DUCAT

The café was in the basement of a building on the corner of Rynok Square on Ruska vulytsia (Rus Street, or Ruthenian Street). *Rus* was the ninth-century name for the land of the later-to-be Ukrainians. The café was newly remodeled but with an old history – the history of a ghost that had haunted the spot for centuries. A golden ducat from the fifteenth century had been found during excavation for the remodeling. So it wasn't named after the image in a Bohdan-Ihor Antonych poem – the golden ducat of the moon. They even had put a glass mirrored ceiling in the café with the image of a spirit above it – a reminder of the otherworldly presence that most people couldn't see. Some of the locals called the café – Café Pryvyd (Café Ghost). It really only served coffee, melted chocolate and desserts and no alcohol. No smoking, either, which Nicholas particularly appreciated since he didn't smoke in this land with few smoking prohibitions.

His first time there he had gone with his curly-haired friend Raya. She was quite short in height with a birthmark near the bottom right side of her nose that gave her face a special character. She was always a ray of sunshine whenever Nicholas met her. You needed rays of sunshine on the many cloudy days of this gray and sometimes sunless city. Raya would often help him find things such as books or old maps or souvenirs for his friends and family back home. He went alone this time, just because he felt like being alone and meditating a bit.

The café was down stone steps that led into a dimly lit, slightly damp and chilly basement. It was divided into two parts – the first was the service area where two waitresses and a waiter stood behind a bar with various exotic bags of coffee behind them on shelves on the walls. There was also a cappuccino and Turkish coffee making machine behind them, from which pleasant smells, intoxicating for coffee lovers, wafted. The main dining room area was through an open stone doorway to the left. Nicholas sat down in the corner. Darkened mirrors lined the upper half of the walls of the room as well as the ceiling. It was blackened mirrors that Nostradamus used to see the future.... Not that Nicholas would believe anything like that. He did not see the future in the smoked mirrors of the ceiling.

According to local legend the café has been haunted for 800 years. It was located at the corner of a former cemetery. But Nicholas, who had grown up in rational America, didn't, of course, believe in such things.

The menu was incredible large and it took him some time to leaf through the onionskin pages and choose what he wanted to order. He decided on the hot strudel and a cup of Kenyan coffee with milk. The locals often call the latter coffee Americano, since it was unheard of using milk with coffee in Lviv until recent times. The locals were used to taking their coffee black with a lot of sugar. Both the coffee and strudel were exquisite, orally orgasmic as Nicholas's friend Charlotte used to say back home in the US.

The café was completely empty except for Nicholas and the three servers in the other room. This allowed Nicholas time to focus a bit and look closer at the dining room. The room had seven dark oak wooden tables with matching chairs. On the right side as you enter the room were three small niches a meter or so wide. The first one was a little larger than the others and had a table in it. The other two were too small for a table. The last recessed area next to which Nicholas had sat down had a stone and aged wooden ledge. This is the one that drew Nicholas's eye the most. It had an old slightly cracked violin to the left of the niche with a single string remaining in it, a deep orange flamenco dancer's folding fan with black and gold trimming next to it in the middle, and on the right side a dark green felt hat turned upside down with several coins in it. The hat reminded Nicholas of the one Harpo Marx wore in the old Marx brothers' movies. Four pieces of sheet music lay in front of the three objects. The stone in the walls of the room were smaller in the recessed niches – none larger than eight inches by eight inches.

The stones on the other walls were somewhat larger, particularly on what must have been two load-bearing walls. A light green stucco covered the one interior wall with square and geometrically jagged cutouts to show the original stone underneath. A lot of the older buildings in the city used this technique to give a glimpse into the most ancient aspects of the architecture underneath the renovations.

The other wall, to the right of Nicholas, had a two-panel diorama of street scenes of Leopolis from an earlier age with figures of people in bowler hats, walking canes, and long wide-skirted dresses walking in front. The diorama to the left had a sunburst of a sunrise in its left upper quadrant with an aquamarine sky illuminating what looked like St. George's Cathedral. The diorama to the right had a different street scene with an eerie crimson sun and a red sky that must have been at sunset. The red sky of sailor's delight – Nicholas thought to himself. The corner of the room next to the diorama had a heavy black chain that barred entrance to the narrow stone steps going up. A large bat about eight inches wide with wings outstretched was suspended above the steps with bright yellow illumination coming from above. The ghost was in that corner – a white-sheeted figure both behind and above the steps and reflected in the ceiling. At the center of the wall next to the ghost's corner was a fireplace with a mantle. The stone mantelpiece had an inkwell with a quill pen, with a feather atop it mostly colored a burnt umber with black horizontal stripes about an inch apart running along it. There was also a black metal candle holder with three nearly burnt out orange-colored candles and a really worn book in cracked leather binding. It was the size of a large gift bible, but it obviously wasn't a bible. It was a book that Nicholas felt he would someday read or write in. Just not today.

The black mirror ceiling reflected everything below in reverse. It seemed the mirrored surface was convex and made the ceiling appear arched. Nicholas could see everything in the room reflected in the ceiling if he looked close enough – everything but himself.

THE BLUE ROSE

It was a special double-class that Nadya had arranged on Romanticism as her students were finishing up their survey of that particular –ism for what they called their international literature class. She asked Nicholas to sit in on the class and award the winning team the blue rose. The class of sixty or so students was divided into four teams, each with a captain. In the team quiz show format each team would be asked ten questions in each round, and Nicholas was supposed to ask bonus round questions on English or American Romanticism.

The group was quite rowdy when Nicholas walked in and barely noticed him in their collective self-absorbed preparation. They were mostly females with one or two guys who seemed to stick out like sore thumbs on the periphery of the large classroom. Once Nadya officially started the class, she calmed down all the students. Nadya looked quite attractive that day, the kind of beauty that comes from within and radiates like beams of light. She was wearing a kind of colorful part-paisley silky spandex top whose dominant color was a medium sky blue or the aquamarine color of the sea reflecting that kind of blue sky. She was wearing a diaphanous narrow blue scarf of almost the same color. The scarf was about a meter long and dangled down past her waist. The black polyester slacks she was wearing emphasized the other colors in her wardrobe even more. The blue color really drew out the extraordinary beauty of her round face.

The students were energized. They roared and clapped furiously when their team got the right answer. Nadya had to calm them down each time by threatening to take away points for rowdiness.

All the teams got Nicholas's first bonus question wrong. He asked them where Thoreau had written *Walden*. Two teams answered "in jail," and the other two said "in the woods." When he told them he wrote it at his home in Concord, Massachusetts after returning from a visit to the pond, they let out a collective gasp.

Nicholas thought about asking them Wordsworth's definition of poetry, but decided against it. Too specific, he thought. "Emotion recollected in tranquility" would have been the right answer – from his "Preface to Lyrical Ballads." Just one of those things that stuck in his mind. He decided on giving them a quote and asking them who wrote it instead. At least this way they could make an educated guess. The quote was: "I am a transparent eye-ball. I am nothing. I see all. The currents of the Universal Being circulate through me; I am part or particle of God." Two of the teams answered "Emily Dickinson." Wrong. It wasn't poetry, but it was poetic. The same two groups got the question right on what Emily Dickenson's favorite word was in her poetry – "I." "I" is all she had in her world of illness and isolation – and her poetry that made her life bearable. Two of the teams got it right – "Emerson." From the beginning of his book *Nature*. Again, just something that happened to have stuck in his mind.

He had to translate the quote on the spot into Ukrainian for the class, which he did without too much trouble. His Ukrainian was getting better each day, though he'd make typical American mistakes all the time, at which people would laugh from time to time. As the visiting guest in the class, Nicholas ended up presenting the blue rose and a peck on the cheek to the captain of the winning team – a teeny tiny girl in jeans with dark hair and a haircut that reminded him a little bit of a toy poodle with bangs. His thoughts were meant as a compliment. It looked really nice on her. She received some collective "oohs" from all the other mostly female students in the class when Nicholas gave her the peck and she returned it. When he left the room, Nadya asked the students to give him a good round of applause for participating, and they sent him off with a deafening roar as he waved back, more in embarrassment than in gratitude.

While Nicholas had been waiting for the students to turn in one of their answers, he scribbled a poem into his copybook that read more or less like this:

THE BLUE ROSE

A blue rose with the longest of stems in your hand
wearing a blue, black and ivory blouse
the colors intertwined in the winding spiral design
like a tall attenuated vase
and a thin cerulean gossamer scarf
that dangled below your waist –
there are flowers of magic
in the name Nadya
a flower of being
one that transforms
what can never be
in nature.
The artificial
of art
the ideal
of what
you may
or may not seek
or want
to be.

He was too embarrassed to give it to her, so he didn't. It was just
his scribbles.

HOHOL

You probably know him better as Gogol – the Russian form of his name. He was Nicholas's namesake too – Mykola, though he was better known by the Russian version of his name – Nikolai. Empires like black holes swallow up everything in their path or near them: nations, peoples, languages, lives, identities. The Russian Empire swallowed up Hohol. And he let it swallow him willingly to make a name for himself in his time.

Nicholas had read him in college in English in a Russian literature in translation class at Stony Brook taught by a Polish expatriate, who emphasized the *Ukrainianness* of Hohol in his class. Better to pronounce his name with a pharyngeal "h." A sound that harsher guttural Russian doesn't have. The horror tales of the farm near the village of Dikanka particularly etched themselves in Nicholas's imagination. Nicholas hoped to visit those villages and towns of lore near Kolomiya in the Carpathians, where, according to local mythic cosmogony, the devil's spit created the outcroppings of craggy mountains. Demons and witches, the evil that can surround us in what appears to be a placid and beautiful world of nature. And then in a later story there was the demon Viy with eyelids that drooped all the way to the ground. One glance into those eyes of evil underneath those monstrous lids was enough to take away a human soul. Nicholas's favorite work by his namesake was *Dead Souls*. It was fraught with the fear, the fallibility and the temptations of the world that eventually terrified Hohol into a premature death. The circle of human existence from birth to consciousness to death, with the only possibility of transcendence the three-horse carriage that flies off into spirit at the end of the first half of the novel, into another realm. Hohol asked for a ladder on his deathbed, a ladder to climb his way into heaven – just like Jacob.

THE GUN POWDER TOWER

Two reposing smiling and stately lions guard the entrance to the stone turret-like tower not far from Rynok Square. It was built (according to guidebooks and histories of the city) in 1554-1556. One particular guidebook had said it was horseshoe shaped, but when Nicholas went to see it, he thought it was more like an oval cut off at one end. It was something like the shape of a running track with the entrance side flattened. It only had a few windows in the middle of it and at the top as well as in the front. It was, of course, a storage tower for gunpowder, so no need for much sunlight in there.

The lions in front were so friendly and playful that they seemingly invited you to play with them. So many lions in the city were in pairs at entrances of buildings. There were two of more recent vintage at the Ratusha (City Hall) entrance. The original Ratusha had burned down in a fire in 1848 and had two lions of more recent and less interesting vintage.

THE TALL WISPY WOMAN

She was beautiful, tall raspy-voiced Tetyana – or Tanya for short, though she preferred the long version of her name. Thin, gaunt, and pale – with long flowing black hair that dropped nearly to her waist. Nicholas agreed to meet her at the Golden Ducat Café. She invited him out for coffee, something that the local Galician women don't do very often if they don't know you well and haven't yet defined personal social boundaries. She told him the café was her favorite place to go. Nicholas's professor of Ukrainian had translated a few of her poems into English. Some of the poetry was on the erotic side. He remembered that one of the poems was a vivid physical description of lovemaking in the woods with a brutishly vigorous lover. Well, this was the town where the term masochism was born, coined from the name of Count Leopold von Sacher-Masoch and his *Venus in Furs*. Why didn't they call it Sacherism or Leopoldism? Oh well, irrelevant quirks of philological history. Tanya was dressed to play the femme fatale to the hilt – even now in the middle of the day. A black pillbox hat, a sheer black fishnet veil over her forehead and eyes, a long slinky knit black dress – something right out of *Casablanca*. Or maybe she was trying to be Blok's Mystery Woman, his image of Sophia, the embodiment of Divine Wisdom, who ends up becoming something more carnal and terrestrial. She certainly looked carnal and terrestrial today. Wow! She certainly did look carnal and terrestrial. The soft brown sadness of her eyes was seductive beyond belief. She reminded Nicholas more than a bit of the famous Nachman portrait of Anna Akhmatova sitting in a chair in black and wearing a shawl. Akhmatova, of course, was her pen name. Her real name was the Ukrainian Horenko (from the word "hore" in two syllables meaning sorrow). Nicholas sensed that he would meet Tanya again at some point under different circumstances, but the feeling was fuzzy.

A PASSAGE TO NOWHERE
AT THE WHIRLYIGIG DZYGA

Dzyga means whirligig, as in a spinning top. It's a stone building that now serves as an art gallery and cultural center with a café and art store inside. The building becomes a passage to nowhere at the end of Virmenska vulytsia (Armenian Street). It operated once as a stable – Nicholas recalled someone mentioning that to him. It had been covered over a hundred years ago – no one quite remembered when, to form a tunnel with two or three long steps. The stone arch of the tunnel passage opens up at the back end to a six or seven meter high rectangular room. Large blocks of what looked like sandstone rose up on the sides and ceiling. It was a building built around a tunnel, or a tunnel built into a building that covered over the street that now went to nowhere. Actually it went to somewhere now, a large room. A dead end, or was it really? One got the impression that it was striving to go to somewhere else. Was it intentionally made that way to stop people from getting somewhere? Or was it just an accident of fate, a random idea or the joke of an architect or builder from the past? There seemed to be too much planning and too much stone in it for it to be random. It was nothing but weighty embodied thought and stone.

Nicholas enjoyed hanging out in the art center's café. At one time or other you'd run into all the artists, writers and assorted bohemians of every age and size you could ever imagine. And they'd introduce you to everyone else, except for the ones they happened to be feuding with at a given time. But most feuds were short-lived. The inside café was fairly small with room for six or seven tables, but in the summer they would set out tables on a cobblestone terrace in the street right in front of the building – with bright red umbrellas that protect you more from the eternal mists and rains in this city than from the sun.

Nicholas arrived a few minutes before 5 P.M. when the "happening" (the word was the same in English, from which it was borrowed, as it was in Ukrainian) of Slavko Bauman was to start. It was the day after his 50th birthday, which had occurred on March 2, and he had promised to do something particularly cool for the evening of the third. Nicholas had read in the Lviv Gazette newspaper that morning that Slavko had rented a white stretch limousine with a red carpet to go to the Philharmonic. The limo pulled up to the entrance before a symphony performance of the Leopolis Orchestra of classical pieces from soundtracks of Hollywood movies. He stepped out in yellow pajamas, the kind you associate with inmates from insane asylums, walked the red carpet that had been rolled out for him to the entrance, waved to the crowd, and stepped back after a minute or two into the limousine that whisked him away. The picture in the paper was one of him waving to his admirers (even though some of them didn't know who he was). To them he must have been famous, of course, or a Mafioso, since he had just arrived in the stretch limo. Some may have thought he was Boris Berezovsky looking for some love from the people, any people, even Ukrainians. Or maybe they thought it was Gerard Depardieu, who had been frequenting Ukraine for his plans to film *Taras Bulba*, Gogol's romantic tale of the Ukrainian Kozaks. Regardless, only somebody ultra famous would have driven up in that limousine.

The gathering crowd kept getting larger and larger at the entrance to Dzyga, and became the realized metaphor of a living whirligig as people swirled around to meet others they recognized. The name of the place suggested a driving force and movement, and just such events gave it the quality of a living organism. The painter-seer of the other side was there next to Mr. Viktor and someone else standing next to him whom Nicholas didn't know. Mr. Viktor introduced the fiftyish gentleman in a gray suit to Nicholas, but it happened so fast, he couldn't remember the name. Then the science fiction and fantasy writer and editor Bohdan Bily arrived a minute or two later wearing a black beret that matched Mr. Viktor's, almost making them look like twins. Ivan the Ghostseer looked at Nicholas and asked who he was. He was standing there with a mug of beer in his hand – and it seemed to have been his third or fourth or maybe even fifth one, at some point you stop counting. Nicholas then told him he had been to his studio, and as he related details about the visit, Ivan pieced the rebus together in his mind and said, "Tak, tak, tak… (Yes, yes, yes)." Ivan the Ghostseer thinks in images. He's a painter. That's what painters do. That's why it took him a minute to get focused and oriented. He also seemed to be under the influence of the beer, and that tends to steer him into his alternate realm rather quickly. Ivan was the ultimate realist painter because he realistically painted what he saw in his head. His poetry was the same way – direct, and exactly what was there in his mind. Nicholas asked to take a picture to commemorate the meeting, so with the artist in the middle and the two black bereted gentlemen writers on either side, he took a picture for posterity with his camera.

Precisely at 5 P.M. the doors to the main hall of the art gallery opened. There must have been two or three hundred people, young and old, pressed close to the entrance waiting to go in. The event was advertised mostly by word of mouth. God knows how many would have showed up if it had been in the papers or on the radio. But word gets around in this town rather quickly, the town with the café called the Tasty Rumor. And the newspaper story on his entrance at the Philharmonic must have also had some effect on the crowd, curious to see how he had come into so much wealth.

The crush of people squeezed through the doors – first into the vestibule, then into the second door into the main gallery. It was too much of an onrush of humanity for Nicholas and his friends, so they decided to wait a few minutes until things died down a bit. And Ivan the Ghostseer caught sight of a couple of his friends sitting at an outside table, even though the temperature was about 45 degrees Fahrenheit, so he sat down with them for another beer, or two or three. Since the weather had been snowy and cold the last several weeks, the 45 degrees felt like summer. Everything is always relative, especially temperature.

When the time seemed just right, Mr. Viktor exhorted: "What do you think, guys? Let's go in."

While the crowd was still fairly thick, you could get in without much trouble. It was easy to navigate through the tunnel part of the gallery, harder to get into the back room. Bauman was in a thin bright orange hunter's vest greeting people. More precisely, it looked like the kind of vest highway workers, street cleaners and tramcar ticket takers would wear. Bright orange meant official. And he was official this evening. He used to have long hair that grew straight down the middle of his back. He was one of the first hippies in Lviv in Soviet times, living in the *Andergraund* (the underground), as they called it in Ukrainian – a step or two away from the watchful eye of the KGB. He was the child of political exiles and had grown up in Karaganda in the Far East. At the first opportunity, his parents returned to Lviv with him. While he grew up speaking Ukrainian with his family for the first two decades or so of his life in the Russian-only atmosphere of Karaganda in the far reaches of the empire, he couldn't read or write it very well when he first returned to the city of his birth. That's perhaps why he became an artist. He thought in images, just like Ivan the Ghostseer, just without the influence of the spirits from the other side. He had cut his hair fairly short now because he had become director of the art center, but shaved it in a straight line on the sides and back about an inch above his ears to somehow mark in that way that he was still an artist with certain attitudes despite his respectable position as an administrator. Various people came up to Bauman to congratulate him on his birthday, and he was all smiles, as he should have been. Everyone gave him the traditional Ukrainian three kisses on alternating cheeks. You could see he appreciated that even more from the pretty girls and attractive older women who were showering him with attention on his big day. The Romanians kiss you twice in their greeting ritual, once on each cheek, the Americans just once – and usually only across gender boundaries and only if you know someone pretty well. Nicholas thought that the

American peck must have been a remnant of the emotional side of the cultural past before the calm rationality of a Puritan handshake had taken over the greeting ritual. Though Ukrainian men shake hands with you like crazy, ten times a day if they see you ten times in a day. Whether it's a handshake or a triple kiss, that's the way it is and you get used to it.

The first art piece of the installation that Nicholas came upon was an old timeworn harp with only a few of its strings intact. A branch of a tree bent into an arc with a single string tied to its two ends stood suspended next to the harp. The two pieces were arched in different directions.

The walls lining each side of the tunnel of the first part of the gallery area had tall paintings of the trunks of birch trees on two-foot wide by ten-feet tall pieces of canvas. Cut tree trunks without their branches were also placed in strategic spots on the side walls. It was the interplay of living nature and the artistic perception and transformation of it, with the wooden harp an emblem of art of music, the art that humans make from nature. Mr. Viktor surmised there must have been a combined fifty of both the real trees along with painted ones, though he didn't bother to count them. All the actual trees were dried up. The artist never would have destroyed anything living for his display. He always had a purpose and a symbolism behind his art. He was recreating the Carpathian Mountains in his artistic motifs – the Carpathian Mountains of his birth that were four hours away from Lviv by train or car. He must have in this way been returning to his origins. Sometimes you have to go back where you've been to see where you are and to find out where you'll be going. That's human nature. That's the way of the artist, too.

With people milling back and forth from the back room, Nicholas tried to navigate his way in that direction. He heard the baahing of goats and wondered if that was a taped sound effect or not. There were camera flashes all over and wandering musicians playing various sounds on their instruments out of *Shadows of Forgotten Ancestors* (the Parajanov movie made from the Kotsyubynsky novella). The first musician that Nicholas observed was a tall man in a tuxedo playing what looked like a small tuba or French horn. He walked back and forth through the crowd, muffling the sound of the instrument with his fist. When Nicholas finally reached the larger room at the back, he could see a man in an upper loft area playing a small *trembita*, which was the Hutsul instrument that was used for communicating across the rugged mountain terrain. It was used to announce Ivan's funeral in *Shadows of Forgotten Ancestors* and had a hollow, muffled sound, somewhat like the long horns that Swiss mountaineers use. The same man switched back and forth to a *sopilka*, which gave off a sound very similar to the Irish tin whistle. Below the *trembita* player was a small wooden pen with three white baby goats. The goats traded off baahing individually and seemed content to let the crowd take pictures of them in their microuniverse with water and straw to comfort them as they stood huddled together at the back of the pen.

The walls of the large room at the back of the gallery had the tallest paintings of birches that rose up almost to the height of the room. There were a lot of people milling around and encircling something in the very center of the room, but Nicholas couldn't see over their heads to see what it was.

Nicholas finally broke his way through to see it was a fiddler playing a fiddle in a particularly colorful embroidered shirt. He was lying down on a single bed with a tall wooden headboard and a smaller footboard. The bed was covered in a white linen sheet and trimmed with embroidery along the edges. It had a deep blue smaller cloth on top of that with a matching cloth folded in half over the headboard. The fiddler, who was apparently one of the best known violinists in the city, played off and on – and was covered with a pile of hay from the middle of his chest to the bottom of his feet, forming a conical mound about three feet high at the tip above him. What did it all mean? A phallic mini-mountain? Who knows. But it was fun. It was a happening. It was Bauman's birthday statement. The birthday of a good man born into the universe, who makes that universe a better place by his presence, something always worth celebrating.

WHITE GLOVES
AND THE BOOK OF SILENCE

That's what lay at the end of the exhibit by Olena Turianska in the Lviv Art Gallery just off to the right of the Opera House. A pair of white gloves on either side of a book marked with the Ukrainians word "tysha" – silence. The exhibit was one of paper cutouts by the local artist. They were painstakingly symmetrical and detailed cutouts that echoed the central theme of infinity, of the perfectly repeated and expanding pattern of creation, or what Nicholas in his mind at that moment wanted to call infin*etudes*. They were various conceptualizations of what the artist saw as the human need to mimic the infinite, to mimic perfection, that perfection that comes from the divine.

Nicholas would have missed that part of the exhibit if the baby-faced armed guard at the entrance to the museum had not told him about it. Nicholas had gone through the three other exhibition halls of the museum and had picked up his coat from the coat check lady, who also served as ticket seller to the museum.

It was a typical rainy day in Lviv and many of Nicholas's friends had left the city to visit family and friends for the long holiday weekend, especially their mothers. Since International Women's Day fell on a Thursday that March 8, the Prime Minister of the country had declared a four-day weekend to celebrate for the entire country. So more than half the country had shut down. The other half stayed open to make money off the other half of the holiday revelers who needed to go to restaurants and cafés, and to buy chocolates, perfumes, flowers, and other assorted goods for their especially loved woman in the family who was celebrating the holiday that had been made popular in Soviet times. While women still weren't in too many positions of power in the country (except for the blonde braided bombshell Yulia Tymoshenko), women were held up high on a pedestal by the old-fashioned males who were in positions of power. They, of course, all must have had mothers and daughters, though you sometimes wondered if the former were the case.

Nicholas decided to go to the museum himself. It's always hard to pace yourself with someone else in a museum. Certain art works require more attention, others less. And it's hard to get two different sensibilities and internal time rhythms synchronized. So going alone resolved that issue for him, and in the end he was glad that he did.

The museum exhibited paintings from the 14th through the early 19th century. Three of the halls were devoted to icons. The 14th through the 17th century icons were mostly in the Byzantine or folk Byzantine styles. They were particularly striking and drew most of his attention. There was something about the simplicity of emotion in them, the harmony of colors, the otherworldliness about them that drew you into the world of beauty and contemplation. The late 17th and 18th century icons were markedly different to Nicholas. Even the later images of his namesake St. Mykola (Nicholas) were much more corporeal and less mystical. They were obviously written (you "write" icons in the Slavic tradition) under the influence of secular portrait painting that had become popular in the 17th and particularly the 18th century. These later icons were also signed on the back or attributed to a particular icon painter. They were also especially "busy," too crowded with images filling the entire panel, making your eye wander and not focus. The older icons had a true simplicity to them, a symmetry and a harmony of color that made them all the more impressive for Nicholas. He was no expert, of course, but the earlier icons not attributed to a particular painter seemed to take him to a more profound place during his observation and contemplation of them.

Striking, too, was the fact that these masterpieces of art were from tiny villages with names like Ilnytsk and Zubrytsk. Some of them were from villages that were now in Poland, harkening back to the shifting borders of this borderland. Three particular icons particularly left a mark in the mind of Nicholas – "Mykyta and the Demon," "The Transfiguration," and "The Last Judgment." They all seemed to him to be variations of themes or scenarios being played out or to be played out in his life. The "St. Mytyta and the Demon" icon reminded him of the small comical one he had seen at his friend Lyuda's place, just in a much older version of it. In this one at the museum, Mykyta had skewered the tiny demon from above and behind him, and was pushing him away. Was this a battle, metaphorical or real, that Mykyta was about to undergo?

There were four different versions of "The Transfiguration," all of them sharing the same theme, but painted in slightly different ways. Two of them had a transfigured Christ suspended in the sky and encircled by a brilliant oval bubble of light with beams projecting from it. They were both modern-looking in a way, even though they were from the 14th and 15th centuries: they both looked like an alien abduction. The other two "Transfiguration" icons had Christ encircled with a differently shaped aura and with more subdued beams emanating to or from Him. Transfiguration, that notion, seemed to stick in Nicholas's mind. Was he becoming transfigured in some way by events or his experiences here? He felt the same as before but just in different circumstances. Was it pure happenstance that "The Final Judgment" was waiting for him on the final room at the end of the exhibit?

THE ORBS AT PIDHIRTSI CASTLE

Even after his visit to Ivan the Ghostseer, Nicholas had more skepticism than any real belief in the legends and myths that so many shared with him (from scientists and scholars to street cleaners and check-out girls), though it was all in fun. There was a consistency in what they said with small variations, a kind of collective mass awareness of the subject. One incident shifted him a little closer toward belief – a visit to the Castle at Pidhirtsi with his friend Vira, his actress friend from the Zankovetsky Theater. Vira had the day off and her little boy, a budding actor at age five or six, was being taken care of by his grandmother for the day. It was a typical story. Vira fell in love, got married at 18, got pregnant with a guy from Slovakia and had a child at 19, and by 22 realized her husband, who was five years older than she, wasn't able to cut loose from his carousing ways. So too many nights when he didn't come back home proved to be the tipping point for her. But she did manage to finish her training in acting and was slowly moving up the ladder to main roles at the theater. Nicholas had met her through Jan Shchurakiwsky, whose wife was friendly with her. Vira wasn't what you would call a classic beauty, but she was an original and just glowed a natural glow. She had a slightly elongated face and a dimple in her chin, high cheekbones, and thin wispy blondish auburn hair. She had a small dark birthmark on the right side of her face that gave her an extraordinarily distinctive look when you saw her up close. She was really easy to talk to, so Nicholas enjoyed doing things with her from going on walks to seeing performances at the Zankovetsky Theater next to the Opera House or one of the other theaters in town. He wasn't, he thought, romantically interested in her, though once in a while he mulled it. That fear of ruining a good thing, a good friendship always seemed to get in the way.

It was an hour's drive to the old palace through hills and fields, with the only rest stop – a roadside tree behind which one could take a bathroom break. The palace had been built by a Polish nobleman if he remembered correctly – by the name of Pototsky. No, he found out later that he was wrong. The oldest mention of it was 1440. It became the property of Polish nobleman Stanislaw Koniecpolsky in 1633 and became a well-know stopover for Polish nobility on their way to Ukrainian territory. It had been turned into a tuberculosis sanitarium during Soviet times when they just basically let it fall into ruin. The Soviets were good at that – one of their great success stories as an empire – letting historical treasures fall into ruin. The dark stone on the outside of the building was as strong as it could be. The inside was crumbling with stucco coming off the walls all over the floor, and the wood in the doors and windowsills rotting. They were in the process of remodeling the palace, with a ways to go yet.

"They say there are spirits here that haunt the place – they're supposed to be those of the patients who died," Vira said to him with a lot of conviction."

"Sure, sure, I don't really believe that," he answered as he walked through one of the first floor rooms. "There's nothing to take pictures of inside," he added, "let's look around outside."

Nicholas pulled out his Minolta camera and began to take snapshots of the palace from all four sides. It was mostly a rectangular building set on the top of a small hill that was level with the ground in the front and dropped down on its other three sides. The weather was picture-perfect. Sunshine. Not a cloud in the sky. Pasture land, fields and forests in every direction.

As he walked around the palace grounds, Nicholas felt a slight chill from time to time. "I bet it's the spirits," he thought to himself and laughed at the thought. "Just a gust of wind." He didn't dare tell Vira. She'd give him the entire song and dance about the spirits – and he just didn't want to deal with it.

A week later after he developed the roll of film at a shop on Peksarska Street, his jaw dropped. On two of the pictures there were five or six translucent orbs of different sizes. He asked the cashier what they were. "Must be drops of water on the lens," she answered matter-of-factly. "Why don't you check the negatives?"

Nicholas pulled them out and saw they were there on the negatives too. No scratches or markings of any kind on the negatives – just the images floating and transparent with the palace behind them. Water on the lens? It wasn't raining... It wasn't early morning dew... And they didn't appear in any of the other negatives except on those two.

"Maybe you took those shots pointing at the sun," the cashier added.

"No, the sun was behind me," he replied with a small bit of hesitation. "I don't believe in this kind of stuff, but everybody I meet here does," and he laughed a nervous laugh.

There are many mysteries in the world, this was just one of them waiting for an explanation.[1]

---

1 NB: In 2011 an episode of the American TV show Ghost Hunters was devoted to the castle under the title "Ghosts Of The Eastern Bloc: Ukraine And Poland."

THE PLAY AT THE ZANKOVETSKY

Nicholas has decided to go off for walk early on a rare sunny Sunday afternoon in early March. As he reached Ivan Franko Park near the university, his cell phone began to vibrate. He answered it before it started ringing, and it was his actress friend Vira. The signal was so strong, as if he were right underneath a cell tower, that he couldn't really hear what she was saying because of the distortion. There must have been some kind of magnetic boost of the signal by something in that part of the park. It was far from the television tower on High Castle Mountain that dominated the skyline. So that couldn't have been it. And he didn't see any cell phone towers in the immediate area – just the tall status of Ivan Franko overlooking the park and the university named after him. But when he was able to focus on what she was saying, it turned out she wanted to invite him for the 6 P.M. performance of *Amadeus* that day, where she was playing Mozart's beloved Stansy. "Come over to the service entrance at the theater at 5:30 P.M. or so, and I'll get you the ticket," she told him. "I really want you to see it." "Sure," he said. "That'll be *chuDOvo* (wonderful)."

After the brief conversation, Nicholas decided to go up the hill in the park along a wide brick and blacktop paved alley. He came across a large three-meter square bit of graffiti in the park that made him laugh. It was a giant smiley face with the following inscription underneath it: "HAPPY FUCKER." He took a picture of it and continued to move up the hill as he snickered to himself about the secret message embedded in it that only those who knew English would get. He also noticed a bunch of brown squirrels scurrying all over in search of food and partners of the opposite sex, chasing them when they found a suitable mate, which virtually was whatever one they had hope of catching. Nicholas mused that maybe he should take that approach during his stay.

He walked all the way up the hill to the end of the park and made a slight right turn to get to St. George's Cathedral, which was on one of he highest hills overlooking the city. The church was much too crowded to go inside, so he stood for a while just outside the entrance where a few other latecomers had gathered. He focused in and out on the last part of the service and decided to step away from the entrance after a while to watch as the churchgoers exited – to see if he happened to recognize anyone. He didn't see any familiar faces on that particular day. It was largely an older crowd, with men in their sixties and seventies wearing the same faded blue, black or dark gray suit they must have worn to church for the last forty or fifty years. Black leather jackets seemed to be the dress code of the day for people under thirty and for the last several decades for both the men and women. There were a number of women of different ages. They mostly seemed to be dressed nicely and not too gaudily, except for one or two younger teenage girls whose skirts were above the red zone on the slutometer. And a few of the middle-aged women were trying too hard to look and dress twenty years younger with tight faux leopard-spot slacks or showing too much cleavage. Nicholas tried not to pay too much attention to it, but couldn't help but notice.

The cathedral itself wasn't one of Nicholas's favorites. It had a wonderful location and beautiful views. It was covered in yellow stucco with golden-domes, one of them being remodeled. The inside, though, was overkill for him. Too many Baroque statues. Too many icons. Too much gold. He preferred simplicity to gaudiness.

After the service ended and most of the people had walked past the two professional beggars standing at the churchyard gate, Nicholas took a right to walk toward the old Roman Catholic St. Elizabeth's Cathedral that had its spires covered in scaffolding for restoration. After passing the church, he decided to take a walk through the train station market area. It was quite crowded on that sunny Sunday afternoon. There seemed to be a rhyme and reason the way things were organized in the market, but other than a sign or two pointing to certain kinds of shops like "clothing" or "household goods," Nicholas couldn't figure it out. The first three or four rows of kiosks and open air booths seemed to be all manner of food – from meats, fresh fish, cheeses, vegetables, to breads. The scents were intoxicating with the crowds filling virtually every aisle with a line at almost every spot. Then there were clothing stores and household goods and luggage and sporting goods. There were some good prices on clothing, but Nicholas didn't need anything. So he just walked through each of the aisles, finally buying just a loaf of fresh whole wheat bread to take home with him.

"Hey, Nicholas," he heard from someone in the crowd. It was an acquaintance of his Nastya whom he had met at the Polytechnic University in Lviv. She taught English there and had flirted with him the last few times she ran into him. She just wasn't his type. It was not that she wasn't attractive. She had long straight black hair and an exotic look to her. She was quite intelligent and a good conversationalist. Sometimes it just doesn't completely click and there is no logical explanation why. She was teaching colloquial expressions and sayings, and wanted Nicholas to help her out with some words she didn't understand. Nastya had just come back from the sauna with a friend, who was standing right behind her. "Hey, I'm sorry I couldn't go with you to the sauna. It sounds like it would have been fun with the two of you," Nicholas flirted with her a bit, even though he thought it was really stupid once he blurted it out.

"Yeah, no men allowed – unfortunately," she took his flirtation more seriously than Nicholas had hoped, but with a smile. "Could we have coffee in the next few days? I want to show you some of my work – and I have a few English questions to ask you."

"I'm going to Frankivsk this week to visit my writer friend Andriy for his birthday, so maybe later in the week, Friday or Saturday after I get back?" He answered.

"Yurkevych? The writer? Wow! You *know* him?"

"Sure, he visits me all the time. I have an extra bedroom at my places and he crashes there when he's in town. I met him on a reading tour in the US and we really hit it off. So he's my good friend. I help him with some of his translations from English. I worked on his Gregory Corso translation. I forget how he translated 'Penguin dust, give me penguin dust, I want penguin dust' – but it was something other than penguin dust that was wild and crazy in Ukrainian."

"Do you know how famous he is? Could you introduce him to me sometime?"

"Sure, be happy to. For me he's just a good friend."

After the meeting with Nastya he walked away from the market for the fifteen minute walk home. The heel of his right foot was hurting from all the walking he was doing, particularly on that day, so when he got home and had a bite to eat, he took a nap to stay off his feet.

At about five in the afternoon he woke up and after pulling himself together a bit, set off for the theater. It was a twenty-minute walk, which should get him there in plenty of time to pick up his ticket. When he arrived at the service entrance on the side of the theater closest to the Opera House, he opened it up and went down a dark barely lit corridor to a kiosk with a guard behind a glass window. The guard wouldn't let him pass, so he called Vira on his cell to let her know he was there. She sent out her make-up artist to bring him over to the dressing room. It was total chaos in and around the dressing room area. Various actresses in eighteenth-century wide and puffy dresses, mostly white, tan and subdued yellow with lots of frills, were running about in their stocking feet and with various amounts of makeup and occasionally with a wig already on. Nicholas kissed Vira on the cheek when entered the dressing room, then shifted to the left and right again to complete the ritual of three kisses.

"My makeup! I'm worried about messing it up!" She blurted out.

"Hey, I can leave you two alone," the makeup lady added. "Time to put on your wig," she said after that, "so you'll have to keep your hormones in check till after the performance."

Vira motioned to a friend of hers to come over.

"Could you take him over to his seat? It's the second row. Seat #1."

"Pa," she said as she raced to the seat in front of the mirror. That's Ukrainian for "bye" – particularly from women. Kind of like a French "ta-ta." Western Ukrainians often say the "Pa-pa" in reduplicated form, but just once when they're especially in a hurry.

Vira's tall friend whisked Nicholas away and down some dimly lit steps into the bowels of the theater with darkened crevasses, nooks and crannies, old props lying around from disuse, pipes, steps and doors leading in every direction. Everything happened so fast that Nicholas could have never retraced the steps that led right to the door nearest to the first row.

"Vira will be waiting for you at the door here to take you to her dressing room after that. Just wait there," the tall woman told him politely. "My husband and I will come over too. We know the way. We're sitting somewhere in the middle. She gave you the best seat today. You'll be sitting next to her pharmacist. She's a nice lady, just not very talkative."

Vira's friend was right about the pharmacist. She seemed sweet, but hardly said a word to him other than a polite "hello."

The performance began with Salieri being played by Mykhailo Bozhenko, a distinguished artist of Ukraine, which was actually his official title after being so designated by government degree. He was perfect for the role – pompous and self-absorbed as he recited his soliloquy to God.

A cell phone buzzed off in the row right behind Nicholas in the middle of the soliloquy.

"I see someone of you in the audience didn't listen to the request before the play started to turn off your cell phones," Salieri adlibbed to the audience as they laughed.

"It's for you, Salieri! It's a call from God," Nicholas blurted out in Ukrainian without thinking, then kind of sank in his chair hoping to avoid any attention the comment might have drawn to him.

The crowd and Salieri laughed even more boisterously and started clapping.

"I'll take Him on my personal line this time," Salieri retorted as the crowd clapped again as he continued his performance.

Vira was absolutely super in her role. She had just the right combination of playfulness and seriousness that the role required. The guy who played Mozart was good, too, giddy and giggly and unabashedly self-absorbed in his own artistic world. He was a little too tall, though, and apparently the other shorter guy who normally would have played Mozart was out of town on a film shoot and unavailable.

Nicholas had to admit that the simulated sex scenes between the too-tall Mozart and his friend Vira on stage found him wanting to jump right in on the fray. He restrained himself this time.

Vira just glowed on stage. She was like a brilliant star that absorbed all the light on stage and the audience's gaze. She got the loudest round of applause from the audience, which gave everyone a standing ovation at the last curtain fell.

Just as she promised, Vira was there waiting in her white frilly dress at the door marked "SERVICE ENTRANCE. ENTRY PROHIBITED." Four or five of Vira's friends where there, one with a camera trying to convince her to let him take a picture of her.

"I *hate* pictures of myself," she said, "but I want one of all of you."

"Shut up and get in the picture. One of just you first, then a group shot," a tall guy with a mustache said. He must have been the husband of the tall woman.

After three pictures, Vira shouted out a "follow me!" And she darted away like a spinning top.

This time she skirted from the dark hallway across the back of the stage to the dressing room that was just offstage on the other side.

Vira rapped on the door and asked, "You decent?"

Nicholas didn't hear the answer, but the other actress wasn't decent yet because the door was still closed. So everyone waited while Vira bubbled back and forth, giving people single pecks on the cheek. The make-up woman pulled off the curly locks of hair that were pinned on the top of Vira's head and took them away.

"Is that a wig?" The quiet pharmacist asked.

"No, it's my hair. I grew it long and cut it to use for the part."

When the dressing room door opened, Vira scurried to get everything together to entertain her friends.

A block of dark chocolate was already broken up into bite-sized pieces in its opened tinfoil package, and a mandarin orange was broken up into pieces on a plate. There was a bottle of unopened cognac, a bottle of Shabo red wine from Odessa, and a bottle of champagne. The cognac and red wine were opened immediately and poured out in shot and wine glasses. Vira and her dressing room roommate kept scurrying about putting on hot water for coffee and tea and making sure everyone had something to drink and eat.

Vira was nearly manic, probably the emotional release after the performance. Nicholas couldn't help but look at her, such a bundle of good and beautiful energy. He tried not to make it too obvious, but she noticed and gave him a lovely return look when she did.

She kept refilling the glasses for everyone until all the bottles on the table had nearly emptied. The two couples that were there, the pharmacist, and Vira's dressing roommate (who, it turned out, was born in the same year as she and had gone through acting school with her) got up around 11 P.M. to leave. One had "things to do," the others had children to attend to. Nicholas was just slightly buzzed from the three or so glasses of cognac that Vira had poured for him to the brim. She probably had downed a couple more than he had and showed no effects from it.

"I really want to see you tomorrow," she said to him. "Alone, if you can make it. Coffee? Maybe at the Svit Kavy Café (the World of Coffee)?"

"Sure," Nicholas replied without giving it a thought. "That'd be nice. Give me a ring when you're free." The café was on the same alley as the Chapel of the Boims.

"I have a rehearsal until about 2 P.M. – maybe after that?"

"Sounds great!"

It turned out that one of the couples had a car parked right outside the theater at the service entrance, so they offered to give Nicholas a ride home.

He had only the minor tingling of a small headache the next morning. But the meeting with Vira just didn't work out the next day. Her rehearsal went past 4 P.M. And he had some things to take care of and an editing job to do for the English version of an art catalog he had contracted to do. She did call him to let him know the rehearsal had gone way overtime. "Next time, soon… Okay?" She said. He wondered what was so important.

KAVA

Kava, kava, kava. Accent on the first syllable. It was more than a mantric chant. It was a way of life. The Ukrainian word for coffee. Feminine in gender in Ukrainian, talkative, communicative. Something slow and relaxed. The word was masculine in Russian (*kofe*) even though it had a neuter ending. The concept was more neutered and neutral in Russian and less essential to being. The same was true for the word in English – coffee. You can take out coffee in the US. It was a practical necessity, not an art form or life experience.

Nicholas hated Starbucks back home – the unpleasant burnt taste of it kept him from enjoying it. He preferred individualized coffee shops with a bit of character to the chain of mermaid madness and triply-overpriced lattes. As chains went, he preferred Dunkin Donuts. Maybe it was the proletarian peasant roots in him. He, of course, came from a line of true village people. A chain of being that went from farmers in Ukrainian villages to the higher education he and his brother had achieved in the US. You can take the peasant out of the village, but the village always remains in the peasant. Not that there's anything wrong with that! Salt of the earth kind of stuff.

There are no take out chains in Lviv. No take out coffee styrofoam cups. No Starbucks where you get your paper cup latte and run off to work. People, of course, do sit in Starbucks and chat. But in Lviv, people will spend a third of their salary on coffee for the month just to be with their friends to *spilkuvatysya*, to communicate. Coffee time was sacred time, a time that transcends quotidian time. And if you invite someone out for coffee, you're the one expected to pay. Even though Nicholas tried to cover the check on many occasions when someone invited him, he always backed off when pressed over the issue. He knew he made a lot more money than his friends did and just wanted to help them out. But they would always answer in an unfeigned, raised and indignant tone: "*Ya zaprosyw* (or the feminine past tense *zaprosyla*)." "I invited you." With both a masculine and feminine ending, depending on who invited him. He got used to it.

Coffee is the time you share your being, your thoughts, your intimacy. Most of Nicholas's friends like their coffee Turkish style in a small cup with lots of sugar. Mr. Viktor always took his coffee black and with sugar. Raya would always take hers strong and black with no sugar, though once in a while she would have a cappuccino, especially at the small coffee shop at the back of the *Pivdenny rynok*, the Southside Market, that was once an outdoor bazaar that had turned into an elegant shopping mall with hundreds of small stores.

Everyone also had his or her favorite place to drink coffee. With Mr. Viktor it was the Tasty Rumor Café. For Raya, it was Coffee Paradise. For Nadya it was the Blue Bottle Café or the *Smakota* (Tasty) Café on Copernicus Street right near where Nicholas lived. Olenka would always have cappuccino, especially at her favorite coffee shop Café Geneva near the university on Kostelivka Street. Ada would only have melted chocolate and never ordered coffee during the times Nicholas met her – and her place of coffee preference was the Golden Ducat.

The Tsukernya (Candy Shop) Café on Old Jewish Street was probably the most popular café for most Lvivians, especially if you wanted to impress someone. He didn't particularly like the more expensive and all-too-touristy spots like the Viennese Café on Prospekt Svobody (Liberty Avenue) and Café Veronika on Shevchenko Boulevard. They were all too prissy and Viennese for him, though he didn't have a problem going there once in a while.

Nicholas would also introduce other people to other cafés as time went along, though he would have an inner sense about which café would fit whose personality. When he met a bunch of Peace Corps volunteers one evening at the Kupil (Cupola) Restaurant on top of a hill overlooking the Stefanyk Library, his favorite restaurant in Lviv, he told them they definitely had to go to the Golden Ducat for coffee the next day and gave them directions. He just somehow intuited their preference.

While Nicholas enjoyed many of the coffee shops he went to, he enjoyed Coffee Paradise the most. Even though it was a newer place, it had a certain scent, decor and charm that drew him back to it. It was one of Raya's favorite cafés, though she had several favorites.

TRAIN 274: LVIV-FRANKIVSK

Nicholas got up at 6 A.M. to take the 7:30 train to Frankivsk, a small city at the foothills of the Carpathian Mountains. He found a shortcut that got him to the train station in exactly 19 minutes. He didn't realize that the winding road right behind his apartment building went almost to St. Elizabeth's Cathedral, just a long block from the station. The circuitous route he used to take before took him at least 25 minutes and he realized he was making an unnecessary loop. And the entire road was well lit and pretty safe. He thought about waiting for a tramcar, but he was already at the cathedral by the time one arrived. So he decided to keep walking.

A potbellied conductor was waiting at the first car to take his ticket. He certainly looked out of uniform in the cotton leisure shorts and faded crimson-colored Harvard tee shirt he was wearing. This guy obviously was not a graduate of Harvard, and he must have just stepped out in his sleeping clothes. The train originated in Kyiv and had just arrived in Lviv.

"You're in seat #1," the conductor said to him as he took the ticket. "But sit anywhere you want. There's just an old *baba* (granny) sleeping in the car."

Nicholas lumbered up the metal step board to enter the well-traveled train. This particular one was an overnighter from Kyiv, but with completely open sleeping compartments without doors. There was no privacy in the land of no privacy (sometimes) – a remnant of earlier Soviet days. It had double seats for four, kind of like a booth in an American diner – just with a small table at the end closest to the window. And it had another table on the opposite side of the wagon with two seats. The seats and table converted to a bunk bed on the bottom, with another one above it. So this train could sleep six in each open compartment.

Nicholas was hoping to be alone for the three-hour ride, but no luck. Despite the fact that only the sleeping *baba* was in the first car with the covers pulled nearly completely over her head, two guys plopped their things down on the bunk bench just opposite him. Both of them looked like working class blokes, one of them in a turtleneck and dusty jeans, the other in black corduroy slacks and a sweater that would have been out of style in the US twenty years ago. They both took their shoes off, and the corduroy-clad dude plopped himself on the bench and immediately fell asleep. The other took a bag of food they had brought with them and started eating at the table opposite the sleeping compartment. The heavy scent of garlic wafted over to Nicholas from whatever the guy was eating. Like everyone else in the country, he had a cell phone that he played with from time to time, sometimes watching and listening to a TV comedy, other times probably text messaging his girlfriend or wife. Or both! You never know, as Nicholas's former Ukrainian teacher Andreya always used to say.

After about an hour of rocking on the train, the sleeping guy was awakened by a call on his cell. It was clearly his wife checking up on him and chewing him out. "Yes dear" sounds about the same in every language of the world.

"I was sleeping till you woke me," he said to her. After responding with a few curt words, he sat up and put his shoes on.

The sun had come up and started to shine through the clouds and smudged window. The sky was a mixture of powder blue and puffy white clouds.

Nicholas noticed one other person out of the corner of his left eye in the car – a bleach blonde woman of about twenty or so wearing blue jeans and a tight white sweater top. He could see she was looking at him out of the corner of her right eye as they were seated in adjacent compartments on opposite sides of the aisle of the train car. Her compartment was one row ahead of his. This was a typical cat and mouse game that women played here with Nicholas (and probably with other men of course too). It was a kind of flirtation, but a harmless one during which no one wanted to get caught. It was a window-shopping flirtation, but when you're confronted, you answer "no, no, no, just looking. I'll let you know if I seriously want to buy."

He knew then that if he approached her or said something, she'd vehemently deny everything and close up like a clamshell. She'd do anything but admit any interest in him.

She probably thought he was from Europe or the US. And that, of course, might intrigue her. The locals can tell you're not from around these parts by the way you look, by the way you dressed, by the way you walked, the shirt you were wearing, or the style of your shoes. They were all brand crazy in this country: Nike swooshes, Ralph Lauren polo players, Levi jeans, Columbia jackets, designer everything (even if they were counterfeit). Nicholas hated all that and refused to buy anything with overt labeling. She kept looking at him from the corner of her right eye and he at her. It was fun. Damn, it was better than watching the black-corduroy-clad sleeping guy or the jeans-guy gorging himself on garlic-infused food. Nicholas's smile, too, was a clear giveaway that he wasn't from around here. No one smiles from around here on the streets. Maybe it was city life – with all the traffic that needed to be dodged, the massive seemingly interlocked rush of people and cars.

What can you see from this train to Frankivsk?

At night, darkness, and an occasional light from a desolate station. But this was during the day.

Fields, stacks of hay bundled sideways, electric wires, the scratches on the formica from too many people cutting their breakfast, lunch and dinner on the table, the smudges, spots and dirt on the window pane, trees, decidedly deciduous, with an occasional evergreen, white leafless birch trees, more fields with mounds of hay piled up high, grass wanting to turn green from an all too brief winter, a village house here and there, mostly made of brick, hills on the horizon the closer you get to the Carpathians, a fleeting glance from the blonde who wanted you to know but not to know that she liked something about you.

She started eating an apple delicately – with little bites from her front teeth.

"Eve," you thought right away. How could you not think of that? It's ingrained in cultural memory and your psyche, almost part of your genetic code. But she didn't offer you a bite. There were plenty of trees outside the windows of the train, but none of knowledge. More houses. A small village. Open space. Another cluster of houses. One with a satellite dish. Overgrown fields waiting to be plowed. A tall mound a few hundred meters wide. Nicholas was beginning to think metrically. Maybe the bones of your ancestors buried in the mound. It looked unnatural. An hour or so away from Frankivsk, formerly called Stanislaviv, meaning Stanislav's town. Too much time on your hands when you travel alone. A horse drawn cart, an old bright yellow Lada car, one of the worst vehicles ever made in the bad old Soviet of unions. Lada was a Slavic goddess – and the name of a few of your female acquaintances. The car barely ran when it was new, but somehow it kept chugging along after twenty-five or so years of rubber bands and tinkering. They repair everything in this country until it truly dies a complete death. Some new three-story houses are being built. By relatives from the US. Or they must be crooks. Three-story paradises, and your friend Andriy called them in a poem that was turned into a song by Jeremiah's Cry.

She bent over. White underwear and soft skin. Harmless glances, flirtation born of boredom. A lone tree in a broad field. Why did they leave that standing?

Black soil. A green field of grass. A layer of tan and browning fallen leaves form the bed of a forest. She bent over more to reveal a little more skin. Does she know she's doing that? Does she know the effect it has on you? You're sure she doesn't realize it, and you know you shouldn't look. You do anyway. You do have eyes. And you know it's there waiting, even when you look away….

Your compartment neighbor has taken another nap. The working class bloke in an ugly gray acrylic sweater with yellow and white diamond patterns on it that looked like it was bought at Goodwill during a going out of business sale. It had an "X" zigzag pattern across the top if it, which did well to date it even more. If you saw anyone wearing that anywhere else in the world, you'd know he wasn't from a civilized nation.

Her underwear was actually lavender. It just looked white in the low light. But it brightened a bit outside and you could see it better. There's even more of it showing now. That helps to tell. And it's bunched up at the top. The guy isn't snoring, just an occasional sniffle. His other friend at the table opposite you is reading the paper – the want ads, probably looking for a job. A different one than the one he has.

It's gotten cloudier, though a few spots of the graying sky have a backdrop of powdery blue.

She looks as bored as you do and keeps staring straight ahead, though you still see that corner of her eye. She's leaned back for a moment, taking away that glimpse of skin and lavender that she's been showing.

More hills – rolling, muddy dirt village roads. Puddles with dogs sipping out of them, too lazy to run over to a pond in the woods. A snow fence painted green. A pair of geese painted white on a green shed.

He hair comes down half way down her back. It's soft and fluffy, like the hair on Nicholas's cat back home.

It's gotten grayer and foggier. No more powder blue backdrops or spots in the sky. Fifty minutes away. A call from Andriy on your cell.

"How's it going?"

"Good, good, be there in less than an hour."

"Tak, tak, yes, yes, see you then!" He said groggily. He must have just awakened.

She looked back at you again.

A long look this time.

You caught her looking, and she didn't turn away. She even smiled. She heard you talk on the cell. She heard you're going to visit some guy Andriy, and not a girlfriend or wife.

A hazy factory with long yellow pipes.

The game will be over soon. But it passes the time.

High-tension wire rusted towers just past the factory. Or maybe it was a power plant, you can't tell from the thickening haze.

No call from Vira, but it's still early. Nine forty two.

She's chewing gum slowly, bored to a living death, but you like that oral fixation and smile to yourself.

A homemade greenhouse made of plastic sheeting. More trees blocking the view. Everything a color-deprived tree-trunk brown. The trees, the earth, the grass, the road, the roofs of the houses. Even the sky begins to look tree-trunk brown. The land is tan in spots where the dormant grasses have been lying.

Forty minutes.

She's still chewing gum s-l-o-w-l-y. You focus again on her oral fixation.

Even the water lying in places in the fields is brown, though once in a while at the proper angle it reflects the grayish white sky.

Spring will be here to add color soon, you think to yourself. Spring officially begins in Ukraine on April 1.

She's still chewing gum, but looking down now.

She looked back at you again for a long longing look as the train pulls to a stop – probably the last small station before you reach Stanislaviv.

She didn't want you to notice this time.

Thankfully a green roof on a trackside building has a corrugated green roof to add a little bit of color to this morning on this particular day of your life.

Tanker cars next to you as the train pulls away from its dead stop. Rusted gray.

She smiled at you as the conductor gave you back your ticket with a little notch clipped out of it from the top. He mentions your name. That elicited a bigger smile from her. It must have been a nice name for her. She had a super smile the few times she smiled. Maybe just the ends of long journeys bring you smiles.

Only a half hour to go. To journey's end. Your friend is a writer. A famous writer. He could have described all this better, even the way she's chewing her gum. Not as slowly anymore.

As the tram approached the Frankivsk station, she pulled out a red comb and began combing her long straight strands of wispy hair. "Wow!" You said to yourself. "That drives me even crazier…."

Nicholas could see Andriy outside waiting for him beside the track. He was happy to see him – and to tell him about the game of eye tag he just played to help him pass the time. This was a land of potent potential with many possibilities waiting to be realized.

AKULA, THE SHARK

"Whatever happened to Akula?" Nicholas asked Andriy as they were taking a cab to Andriy's apartment.

"He's dead. Dead and gone. Too much *horilka*, too many clogged arteries, too many enemies. But he supposedly died of natural causes."

Akula, accent on the second syllable and pronounced as in the word "cool," the shark, was a big man with a pot belly the size of three or four bowling balls. He used to like to wear a Nike jogging suit, light gray with a red stripe down the sides of his legs. He had been a fixture in Frankivsk till his demise.

On an earlier visit to Frankivsk Nicholas had made his acquaintance. Andriy Yurkevych and three of the local writers and artists stopped in with Nicholas at the old Soviet-style hotel restaurant at the center of town. It was 11 A.M. and the guys wanted a little drink, so they ordered a half-liter bottle of *horilka* just to get their blood coursing through their veins. Nicholas decided not to partake of the morning libations because he was taking antibiotics for a sinus infection that had just hit him a couple days before.

Akula walked in right then as they were sipping that first drink.

He had grown up with Yurkevych's cousin Romko (the diminutive form of the name Roman). When Akula the Shark caught sight of Romko, he slapped him on the back as if he were making a take down in a wrestling match.

"I'm buying you a bottle, guys, and you have to drink it down to the last drop!" Akula the Sharkman bellowed. He pulled out a wad of money to buy the biggest bottle he could find and slammed it on the table.

Everyone took a glass and raised it in honor of the Akula the Sharkman while Nicholas raised a cup of tea.

"Why aren't you drinking with us?" Sharkman asked Nicholas.

"I'm taking antibiotics… Sinus infection," Nicholas answered matter-of-factly with a sniffle.

"You know, I've killed men for less!" Sharkman bellowed. "But I'll let you live this time. Next time you'll HAVE to drink with me!"

"Next time I promise to have one with you," Nicholas smiled.

The four other guys at the table downed the entire bottle of *horilka* in toast after toast, with the third one, as usual, for the ladies. Andriy seemed to hold the liquor well and just smiled an ever-widening smile. The others didn't fare quite as well and stumbled out of the restaurant, knocking back and forth into tables and chairs.

"We have to walk this off," Andriy said with a grin as they stumbled out of the hotel restaurant.

And they walked most of it off, except for one of the local writers by the name of Vasyl Yevshan, who, from behind his coke-bottle bottom horn-rimmed glasses, hurriedly said "excuse me" and ran behind a tree to eliminate the excess gastric juices churning up from his gut to his gullet. Nicholas heard the gurgling and wrenching sound of *horilka* and stomach acids exiting from his stomach onto the dusty earth next to the tree.

Akula the Sharkman was now dead and buried, and Nicholas didn't need to repay him with his promise of a drink.

END OF FLASHBACK

THE HOUSE
ON SHEVCHENKO BOULEVARD

When you look at a collection of someone's books and CDs and works of art, it tells you a lot about them. This was Nicholas's first visit to Andriy's new place, and he was staying in their second-floor *mansard* (attic) guest room. The music collection was quite eclectic – from Coltrane and Thelonius Monk to contemporary punk and classic rock. There was Led Zeppelin, Bob Marley, Tom Waits, Sting, Nick Cave, Dave Mathews. It included traditional and contemporary Ukrainian music, but nothing you would call "popsa" here – the pop dance music for the masses that had a shelf life for a month until everyone got tired of it being overplayed over and over and over and then some in cafés and restaurants. There were hundreds of everything in two tall CD towers in the living room, another in the kitchen, and more upstairs in a study. Nicholas also liked most of what he saw there. He had even given Andriy a few CDs – some Procol Harum, he remembered, for sure.

The house took up the third and fourth floor of a low-rise apartment building. Nicholas hit his head twice going upstairs to the guest room – the ceiling jutted out from an overhang above the stairs. He managed not to bump his head for the magical third time during his stay so far, but that probably was awaiting him.

There were over a dozen plants in the well-lit living room underneath the open stairs nearest the living-room window and three more plants that needed less light closer to a sliding door that formed the interior wall of the room. There were two paintings by MANDRYK on the wall behind the couch. Mandryk was an artist who liked to go just by his last name. It was kind of like deciding that you're a Picasso before you only need a last name to be recognized.

One was of a goat sitting on what looked like a black steel hospital bed. It had a bright red background. It was a side view of a graying brown goat with his chin resting on the taller metal headboard of the bed. One of the goat's horns was a bright yellow. The painting to the left was apparently a large woman or figure in a wide green dress or tunic holding two large fish in her white or white-gloved hands. The fish were pointed in opposite directions and lying sideways in front of her. The one looking to the woman's left covered her from the waist to the neck with a bright green fin. The fish covered the figure's face completely, so you couldn't recognize its gender or who it was. The background behind the figure was a dark green with slight variations in the depth of the hue.

The third painting on the wall behind the couch was by the writer himself, who dabbled in art and music. It had a multicolored figure (light, medium and dark green, orange, pink, lavender, and white) with thin white streaks that looked like hands, a red neck and a round white face with one round white eye to its left and a red vertical stripe near the mouth area. Its left ear was yellow and its right one orange – with a medium blue outline. Seven relatively thick, straight, black hairs stuck out of its head. It seemed to be some kind of creature, whose body was wide like a butterfly with its wings spread out. Darker and lighter brown and orangey tan and small yellow shapes formed the background behind the figure, giving it some depth. Nicholas meant to ask Andriy about the painting, but decided against it. It was more fun to guess what it was. And Nicholas was sure Andriy wouldn't give him a straight answer because he was prone to mystification and carnivalization. He liked the Ukrainian art of "khokhma," of playing a joke, but always with a serious face. That's why he was a writer and not an insurance salesman.

Fish dotted the room everywhere – a wooden fish made of small chips of wood on a wooden stand, a larger fish that was meant to be a wall hanging like a pillow with shiny golden scales, deep red fins and flippers, orange lips and eyes, and a purple material alternating with silvery shiny metallic hues on its face. Andriy associated himself with the fish (even though he wasn't an Aquarian according to the signs of the zodiac).

There were eight or nine other paintings on the walls – one a particularly realistic one of a bridge over a canal in Venice, another an impressionistic kind of canal scene with buildings on both sides, two small abstract paintings, one with vertical random stripes of various lengths ("smushky," you would call them in Ukrainian), and another with mostly horizontal stripes that looked like a rolling field, a blue sky above it with white puffy clouds at the top. More "smushky." One painting was an abstracted young female figure with a small circular red mouth, short and white feather-like lines surrounding her that gave her a look of being in motion. And the most striking one was a little girl at the base of the stairway. Her large face was looking up over what looked like a blue windowsill.

Besides books everywhere, lining the writer's study, and in upper shelves in the hallways, Nicholas particularly noted a black Venetian carnival mask almost hidden away in an upstairs hallway.

CELBRATION FRANKIVSK-STYLE

Andriy came out into the kitchen where Nicholas was sitting and sipping some mineral water. He looked elegant in a black sport coat with a trim European cut and a dark maroon knit shirt with a zipper collar. Although there was no dress code, Nicholas decided he needed to put on his dark blue cotton suede sport coat on so as not to feel like a *bila vorona*, a white raven, at the Club Chimera Café, which was where the party was going to take place.

Nicholas was the only invited guest from out of town. Everyone, except for his businessman neighbor and his wife, was either a local artist, a writer, a poet, a neighbor, or a spouse of one of the above. Andriy had told him this was his artsy group of friends, that didn't mix as well with other less artsy friends he had, so he decided just to invite this particular group.

The Chimera was not too far from the central square of the town and a ten-minute or so walk from Andriy's house. So Andriy, his wife Olya, and Nicholas set off, each carrying bags filled with all manner of spirits, salads and other food. Andriy told Nicholas that he'd never get a car like everyone else in the country, who saw them as a status symbol. He could afford it, especially since he had just won a really big fifty thousand dollar European literary prize a couple months earlier.

He also said he'd never get a cell phone – even though his wife Olya had one and was fielding calls all morning from friends wishing him a happy birthday, or a Ukrainian *mnohaya lita*, many happy and healthy years. There was even a call that morning from one of the oligarchs, the name sounded like Fistachchuk, who was trying to ingratiate himself with Andriy. But Andriy refused to take the call. "Let the fucking pisshead do something for the country, dammit," Andriy said (in a rough translation of dynamic equivalence into English).

He then turned to Nicholas and added: "I need to hide from people sometimes. That's why I still live here. I have my friends. It's peaceful, out of the way. Everybody knows me. But when I need to travel, I can go. You have to have that time to concentrate. That's why I've refused a bunch of offers to take a job and move to Kyiv. Everybody would hound me day night to do this and that, appear here and there, and I'd never have any peace."

"Yeah, I could get used to the town here. Lviv is a much more hectic pace. It's a big city with something going on all the time. But people almost knock you over every time you take a walk there. Lot's of sunshine here, too. I had four days of rain and clouds when I left Lviv yesterday morning for the train. The clouds followed me till I got here."

The Chimera was the cultural hub of Frankivsk (or Stanislaviv as it used to be called and as Andriy and many of his friends still called it). All the major writers had readings in the café and lots of artists exhibited their works on the walls. The café had one large room at the main entrance where most of the writers had readings and performers played. Then it had another dining area at the end of a corridor that was set up as an art gallery with six or seven tables. Then in a side room it had a private dining area that seated about 15 people around a long series of tables with a big screen flat panel TV monitor at one end of the room. There was one more room with a smoking area in the back for meetings that had room for exactly nine people at a curved table. The Frankivsk Rotary Club was meeting that evening in the back room, though one wondered if it might be a secret Masonic society or some other such mystery organization headed by some guy called Monsignore.

It was in the room for 15 or so people that the party would take place. The table was already set for 12 with silverware, bottles of champagne, wine, *horilka*, cognac, mineral water, orange juice, salads, plates with cheese slices, plates with sliced tomatoes and cucumbers, three different kinds of bread, sliced *kovbasa* (ringed garlic sausage) and other meats, etc. etc. etc. There was a lot of etc. This was all before Olya had even opened up the bags she had hauled over with Andriy and Nicholas. There were plopped down to the side of the entrance to the room.

The room had a neo-cave design. Its walls were entirely brick that had been cleaned up, remortared, repointed, and glossily shellacked. There were pictures of women from the past of Stanislaviv from circa 1900 behind glass affiches on the side walls – these were in honor of International Women's Day on March 8, a holiday Nicholas never remembered being celebrated with much pomp in the US. Someone told him that most of the country still celebrated the old Soviet holiday – it gave them a long weekend and cause to celebrate women, which the men did with boxes of chocolate, champagne, flowers, and invitations to dining and dancing. Though they'd always expect the women do the dishes since they had more important things to do like read the paper, watch television, and have a nightcap.

Besides pictures, Nicholas also noticed some facsimiles of old Polish and Ukrainian newspapers from the same Secession time period. One of the artists present at the celebration by the name of Vasyl had done the interior design of the room. He tried to look the part, too, of a Secession period artist with a waxed moustache that curled up at both ends.

The guests arrived in small groups of two or three. The couples were mostly married. When a critical mass of ten had arrived, everyone sat down to the feast. That was around 7:30.

The champagne bottles had their corks popped first and Andriy asked everyone to make their toasts short. Whoever made the shortest toast would win the biggest prize. Gifts were also passed along to Andriy, who snickered at a few of them. Three artists gave him paintings. He had expressed his concern at his apartment that the artists would give him paintings. There was just nowhere to hang any more paintings in the house. One was a realistic though slightly impressionistic scene of Ivano-Frankivsk. Another was a still life. And the third was a mock "portrait" of Andriy that looked like Maggie Thatcher on a bad hair day with no makeup on, or a transvestite who should get his money back for a badly executed operation.

"Where the hell am I supposed to hang *that* one?" Andriy asked in bewilderment as he pointed to it.

"Well, at least it's in a nice frame," Nicholas chimed in. "You can reuse the frame…."

Nicholas sat next to Andriy's wife Olya, so he had someone he knew to talk to. He had a cognac for his first drink, but drank it slowly in sips, savoring the taste with each sip. It's the aftertaste that proves the worth of a good cognac, and this one, a Tisa from Uzhorod, had a smooth and mellow five-star aftertaste after it went down.

Everyone else was pounding the drinks down one after another and mixing and matching. The silent writer Ihor was mostly quiet at the end of the table with his equally quiet girlfriend or wife. Nicholas wasn't quite sure of the story there. He learned not to ask. A lot of people Nicholas had met were on their second or third wife or husband – not Andriy, though, who got married at 18 and was still married to the same woman for over twenty years (despite the daily temptations of groupies surrounding him everywhere he went).

Nicholas would have played a few songs on guitar for the party, but he didn't want to haul his guitar on that three-hour train ride to Frankivsk and back. He had written a couple songs and jammed with a few of the local Lviv bands from classic rock like Plach Yeremiji (Jeremiah's Cry) to up and coming local punk bands. Next time, maybe.

The shortest toast of the evening was "Za Tebe" (For You) in three syllables up to that point in the evening. The artist toast-maker, who was sitting to Nicholas's right, certainly had a warm and toasty inner feeling after five or six shots of *horilka* and a couple glasses of champagne. He stood up and announced that he was the winner of the shortest toast prize. Nicholas whispered to him that he could have said "Za Tya" in Old Church Slavic in two syllables. "Damn, that's right!" He said. "Next time!" He added but quickly forgot.

A mushroom soup disk arrived at around 8:45. And the main dish, which consisted of the choice of trout or veal with rice and potato pancakes arrived rather late at 9:15.

And so the evening went on with toast after toast after toast after toast – until around 11 P.M. when the café was supposed to close. Nicholas managed to blast half a bottle of champagne over mostly himself. The hot lights in the cave café probably had heated it up way too much over three or so hours of sitting on the table and it shot up right into the air above him. Since Nicholas was on a planet with gravity, it managed to drench him quite thoroughly. Right after eleven Andriy got particularly energized and started telling stories in rapid succession after the infamous Ukrainian "na konya" toast – the toast to the horse so he safely brings you home. He started telling anecdotes about his writer friend Volodya Irpinsky, who liked to pound down a few himself. His wife had sent him out to get a loaf of bread late in the evening. He somehow got waylaid by a friend of his and ended up drinking a bottle or two of *horilka* and got lost for two days wandering around the town and sleeping under a tree somewhere. "Where's the bread?" His wife asked when he came home the next day. "Damn," he answered. "I forgot. After buying the *horilka* I didn't have enough money left to buy the bread."

Then there was the story of his poet friend Pavlo from Kyiv, who had gotten to the airport in a really trashed state from the night before. His friend, who was flying with him to represent Ukraine at a writer's conference, told him vehemently: "No more *horilka* for you, dammit! Not until we get to Vienna!" Unfortunately, his friend had to go to the bathroom, and when he came back, he saw that Pavlo had already downed half a liter of Finnish vodka he had picked up at the duty free shop. He polished off the rest of the large bottle before he stumbled onto the plane. Then he woke up in Vienna the next morning and screamed out to his traveling companion: "What the fuck is going on?! I'm in Kyiv one minute, and now I wake up in Lviv!"

For those who may not know it, Lviv is a dustier and more crumbly version of Vienna with a spruced up Opera House based on the design of the Viennese one. Or from a different perspective, Vienna is a prissier less authentic version of Lviv. It all depends on perspective.

The favorite story that Nicholas heard that evening was about Andriy's cousin Romko, who was at the party with his wife. The two of them had left early – around 9 P.M., because they had to catch the last *marshrutka* (microbus) to make their way home in a surrounding village about 40 minutes away. Romko had sworn off alcohol for almost three years. In the bad old days of demon alcohol, everyone knew Romko was trashed when he'd stand up on the table in a restaurant or café and start reciting his poetry. This evening he remained on the wagon and was quite civil and subdued, drinking only orange juice and mineral water. But the story was from his heavy drinking days. One day he heard that his friend Bohdan's father was dying. In small villages news travels fast and rumors even faster. At about one in the morning Romko's mind became fixed on this realization about his friend's father. So he bolted out of the house and ran all the way to the priest's house over a kilometer away. He rapped on the door to awaken the priest and told him that a man was dying, and he needed to give him his last rites. The priest asked him where the dying man lived. When he told him, the priest said: "That's not my parish jurisdiction."

"A man's dying, for God's sake! He needs his last rites! You have to give him his last rites!" Romko shook the priest by his nightshirt collar as his alcohol-enthused eyes flared madly.

So the priest quickly got dressed and drove over to the dying man's place. They knocked on the door at about two in the morning to give the man his last rites. They heard some shuffling inside and the lights flickered on. The opening door showed them that Bohdan's father Petro was perfectly alive and kicking, though in slow motion because he had been aroused from sleep. When he heard why the two men were at his door at two in the morning, he grabbed his old friend Romko by the scruff of the neck and began screaming at him: "You idiot! You tryin' to bury me before my time! Get the hell out of here!"

Romko got the hell out of there for fear of his own life. In a panic and not knowing what to say to the priest, Romko said:

"Wrong house, father! It's a different guy that's dying! We'll go to him tomorrow!"

So by midnight, after hearing the various stories, the group got up and helped Andriy take away his birthday haul, that, besides, the three paintings, included numerous bottles of liquor stuffed into bags, a Tom Waits concert DVD, and a few packages yet to be opened. These all went into the trunk of Andriy's neighbor's car that was parked just outside the back door inner courtyard service entrance to the café. It seemed as if the crowd was going to disperse under the clear and cloudless Frankivsk midnight sky, with the Big and Little Dipper shining as though they were sparkly and new. Just not yet... Borya the artist who had given Andriy the painting of the local Frankivsk scene opened the trunk and pulled out one more big bottle of *horilka* and a single glass to use for everyone to warm themselves up in the now chilly night. Only Borya's wife Svitlana and Nicholas refused to partake of the libation, and Borya managed to keep the glass filled till nearly two. And Andriy's neighbor turned on the stereo of his car full blast and swung the doors open to provide some additional entertainment. It was so loud that Nicholas figured someone would complain and call the police. But no one did.

"Everything was nice up till we drank 'na konya'," Nicholas said to Andriy just before two. "That would have been enough."

"But without this it wouldn't have been *this*," Andriy added and gestured with both of his palms, right at the moment that everyone decided it was time to walk, or in Nicholas's case, to ride home in the car.

So everyone parted in a happy mood. No police came to file complaints. No one was arrested. No one vomited in public. Everything was cool. They arrived at Andriy's house at a little after two and everyone helped carry the various gifts and bags up the three flights to his apartment.

"How about some tea?" Andriy asked his wife and Nicholas. And she put on a pot. And then Andriy picked up a half-empty bottle of Ararat cognac that Nicholas had given him and said,

"Well, we ought to have a nightcap to help up get to sleep." Nicholas was ready for one and sipped it down along with the tea, while listening with Olya and Andriy to some eclectic music from Andriy's collection: Calexeco from the Tex-Mex border, Sheshory from the Carpathians, and Ocheretyanyj Kit from Vinnytsia. All of it acoustic. When the clock hit 3 A.M. everyone agreed virtually simultaneously – "*pora*, time to sleep."

This is the typical way you celebrate a birthday in Ukraine, at least a birthday in Stanislaviv style.

Everyone woke up around noon and after having coffee and a light breakfast stepped out to walk around the downtown a bit. It was a beautiful day. Sunshine. Not a cloud in the sky, which was as blue as whatever you imagine the most beautiful blue of the Mediterranean is. No hangover for Nicholas. Andriy and Olya managed not to show any permanent effects or defects from the previous evening. They stopped at the House of Beer Pub for a bit of a pick up before going over to Borya's art studio in the uppermost floor of one of the older unremodeled buildings about a block from the central square. They just managed to get back to the house to pick up Nicholas's single traveling bag, grab a taxi to the train station, and arrive there in the nick of time five minutes before the train's departure time. Nick-of-time Nicholas had had enough impressions from the last two days, so he silently leaned the back of his head against the tan colored steel wall of his compartment and dozed in and out of the bumpy three hour ride to Lviv. He had none of those anticipatory heightened emotions that he had on his way over to Frankivsk. And there was no flirtatious blonde to wile away the time to play the eyecatch game.

THE ANGEL OF CHAOS

Angels usually bring peace and order, but not this one. She had the face of an angel, with bright blue eyes and long blonde hair with the roots slightly showing that in her case looked really interesting. Her name was Adriana (one of those female Ukrainian names that Nicholas really liked). She was dressed to kill in classy Ukrainian chic (leather boots just to the bottom of her knees with sparkles and shiny diamond and emerald shapes and colors on them). She was wearing a down-to-the-mid-calf fur coat that looked really warm and accentuated her slim waist. Her dress form fit her at the top and flared out at the bottom, highlighting her full figure at the top and roundish bottom with a tiny waist. Nicholas had been asked to come to the English class to help students with figuring out the meaning of some of the words in the Shakespeare sonnets they were studying. All that went fine and Nicholas's guesses were better than any of the instructor's. Adriana just stared at him the entire "para" (the hour and twenty minutes of the class) with her chin resting on two delicately clenched hands with elbows perched on the desk.

The instructor of the class arranged for a tea afterward with all the students (about 30 females and 2 guys), and Adriana went out of her way to bring Nicholas a cup of tea and later to chat with him in the corridor out of earshot of everyone else. She really wanted to meet with him because she felt he was "a kindred literary soul" for her. When she said that, Nicholas was hoping to find out if she might like to become a kindred body too ("hey-hey-hey" as Shchurakiwsky writes in one of his darker tales). Damn, Nicholas thought he might be sunk. This may be one of those mutual I want to blankety blank your brains out deals, and then they'll get to know each other. His manhood was, ahem, intrigued. Super mutual vibes. She has a sweetness and a shape that most men would kill for – and a beautiful smile. And those light blue eyes that just made him melt. She was smart, too, but Nicholas wasn't thinking about her intelligence right at that moment since the beast in him had taken over. Sometimes men think with their brains, other times with something else below the belt. After she said that, he just slapped some proverbial cold water on his face and agreed to meet with her for "coffee" the next week. Nicholas found out from his friends that in the local custom, that really meant something more than just a casual consultation, because coffee was something intimate, particularly in the dark corner of one of the city's cafés. "You should have met her in the English Department if you wanted to keep it professional," one of his friends told him. "This way you're giving her hope. And hope is all a Galician woman needs. I'm surprised she came up to you. Galician women usually don't do that. She's either from somewhere else, a big city, or she's er-a maybe a bit on the loose side… But I guess you'll find that out!"

He didn't find out, though, since she never called him back.

SKULLWORDS

That's the title of one of Ivan the Ghostseer's collections. He wrote what he saw. And he saw death. He saw ghosts. He saw the underside of life, which was always on the knife's edge of dreamdeath. Copyright concerns do not allow publication of the author's works without his consent. The author may not truly have the capacity to consent because he may be more in the other world beyond everyone else's reality. The author may be a madman, he may even be a genius, but not one to consent. Madness is in the eye of the beholder, and the edge between madness and genius runs close to both notions. Madness demands life on the edge, genius does sometimes too. But we are permitted to describe images and things in his poems like the "nerves of existence," "despair," a "knife," "blood like a tear," all of them illuminated by the "hundreds of faces of death." Everything is about him. His "I," his self, his definition of being through the prism of what and how he sees and what we cannot. Not all knowledge is knowable by every human being. And we can only be what we know.

A SOIREE
AT THE DZYGA WHIRLYGIG CAFÉ

Nicholas received a call from Nadya on his cell phone just as he was leaving the university after an English class he had taught there. He was teaching a course on language through film and had just shown the film *My Big Fat Greek Wedding* to rousing success. The students couldn't get enough of it and wanted to see it again. While they got a lot of the physical and situational humor, they did miss quite a bit of the linguistic play, so that's what he ended up explaining to them the most.

Nadya said to him quite coyly when she reached him by cell: "A mutual friend is here who'd like to see you." He could hear her laughing, but she wouldn't tell him who it was. "We're already at Dzyga. It'll be a surprise for you."

"I'll be right over," he said, but two of the female students who had just walked out of the class stopped him to answer a few questions they had for him. So he arrived a little later than expected at the art gallery café. It took about 15 minutes to walk over from the university to the gallery. The weather had warmed up a bit and two groups of young brooding avant-garde wannabes were smoking, sipping tall mugs of beer, and ruminating at a table outside. Nadya and her friends were not outside, so he walked up the rest of cobblestoned Armenian Street into the Dzygian Whirligig passage to nowhere, the covered street that had been walled in.

Nicholas found the group sitting at a large round table on the left side of the smoky café, which only had five or six tables. The ceiling was high and arched with two rows of paintings on one side. All of them were paintings of rows of pears in subdued warm browns, earth tone reds, mellow greens, and several combinations thereof in each painting. There must have been 16-20 of the paintings in all, all of them variations on a theme, all on the same size paper or rough metal plate. It was hard to tell without touching the surface. One nearly empty bottle of champagne was already sitting on the table. There was ever-smiling Nadya, with a twinkling smile. She was elegantly but simply dressed. "All those paintings are Slavko Bauman's," she said to him as she saw him admiring them. "Even the tall one over the doorway."

The "mutual friend" turned out to be Lydia, the highly egotistical feminist writer from Kyiv, a seeker of scandals who had tried to seduce Nicholas at a wine reception when the two of them had first met. The seduction didn't work – he wasn't even mildly tempted under the influence of a hundred or so grams of cognac. She wasn't too subtle about it, and though he thought she was interesting, he didn't find her attractive in *that* way, and it just didn't feel right. He was a man of his intuitions, and he just didn't have a good feeling about it. Whether it was the chemistry or his state of mind, he just didn't know. It could have ended up as the old Woody Allen movie he was wont inexactly to quote from: "Sex without love is an empty experience. But as empty experiences go, it's not half bad." And then there was the other piece of dialog from another or maybe even the same Woody Allen movie: "Let's make mad, passionate love," Diane Keaton says to Woody. "Okay, I'll get the soy sauce." He just wasn't up for an empty experience this time. He had had enough of those back home. Anyway, it was hard to find soy sauce in Lviv, which only had one very bad Chinese restaurant.

The third person at the table was gray-haired and gray-bearded Jan Shchurakiwsky the writer. He apparently knew both Lydia and Nadya and was in the process of flirting with them mercilessly when Nicholas arrived, saying something like "divchata, divchata, divchata" (girls, girls, girls) and gesticulating with his hands. He let out a big guffaw when he saw Nicholas and pressed his hand firmly at the first opportunity. "It'll be good to see you'll be in my cage tonight," he said to Nicholas with a sly wink. "I'll even share the *divchata* with you. I'm not greedy. Two are enough for me. One more is on the way and should be here any minute." A fourth person at the table whom Nicholas had never met before was introduced to him as the artist Tolya, who was a smiling, friendly looking, and slightly stocky fellow in thick black-rimmed eyeglasses. He was also apparently a former classmate of Lydia and Nadya at the Lviv Institute of Polygraphy (it had its name changed recently to the Ukrainian Printing Academy). Tolya shook hands with Nicholas, but it turned out he wasn't very talkative. He mostly kept to himself while he sipped the champagne, occasionally whispering something into Lydia's attentive ear. Lydia was the most rambunctious and rowdy of the bunch, constantly making highly opinionated and categorical pronouncements. "I'm always psychoanalyzing," she said at one point. It was almost as if she weren't engaging in conversation with anyone else, but rather absorbed in a game of verbal fencing. Nicholas didn't want to be under her microscope this time or anywhere near her verbal parries, so he tried to stay as invisible as he could to her. Though he had to admit that when she had tried to seduce him before, he did enjoy the game. And she didn't take it all that seriously, either. A lot of women in Leopolis seemed to like to play the hot and cold game. Nicholas found that the best way to cure it was just to ignore them. That ended up getting him more attention in most cases – even when he didn't want it. His few months in the city had made him far less of an expert on Galician women that even he could imagine. So he decided it was just easier to go with the flow and not take things too seriously.

Rather than share the champagne, Nicholas decided to order a beer – the local Lviv brew on tap seemed like the best choice. He sipped slowly as the conversation went on, touching on themes such as "orgasm in literature," "prokljati Moskali" (damned Russkies), different writers like Andriy Yurkevych, art, and the mess that is Ukrainian politics. Since the three other than Shchurakiwsky were school mates, and since Lydia was in town for a rare visit after she had moved to the capital an eight or nine hour overnight train ride away, they apparently had decided to have a bit of a reunion at the art gallery where they often used to meet in earlier days. Nicholas was happy to be sitting next to Nadya since he felt most comfortable with her. Lydia was so boisterous and SO extroverted, and such a chain smoker, Nicholas just wanted to stay out from under her radar, which she quite openly directed onto Shchurakiwsky, who, she said, had served as her career "mentor." If that meant mentor in the ways of amour too, Nicholas wasn't sure. But he was happy not to be the focus of her seemingly boundless and aggressive energy.

Then at one fine moment, something that often happens in folk tales or in the poetry of Alexander Blok after drinking some bitter wine, SHE arrived after about forty-five minutes of friendly chatting following Nicholas's arrival. It was a new she, someone he had never met before. Nicholas was introduced to her right away. Her name was Ada, a femme fatale if he had ever seen one, who, also, it turned out, had studied at the university with the other three. She was an exquisite beauty, with one of the most intriguing faces he had ever seen, and Nicholas couldn't take his eyes off her as much as he tried to turn away. Something kept drawing his gaze to her as if he were a missile heat-locked onto its target. And she noticed every time he glanced or even openly stared at her. She kept casting return glances in his direction and initiated quite a few of her own. When the glances met, her eyes and lips smiled a sly smile. "Wicked thoughts," Nicholas thought to himself. "Both mine and hers. Damn, maybe I'm ready for one of those empty experiences…."

She came in wearing a thin knee-length black or dark green leather coat, it was hard to tell in the subdued light that had just been dimmed by the café staff. She also was wearing ankle-length black leather boots with medium height pointy heels. While Nicholas didn't talk to her much directly after she sat down, mostly because she was on the opposite side of the table, he overheard her say several times to Lydia that she didn't want to go home that night. She seemed to be fending off phone calls and text messages on her cell phone, probably from her live-in boyfriend. "Probably from a possessive big skulking black-leather jacketed guy," Nicholas thought to himself. "No, she's too delicate and refined," he concluded on second thought. But there was the look of distant unhappiness on her face, a look that was transparent and easy to detect, a signal he had noticed many women give off in Leopolis. She wasn't wearing a wedding band, something that Nicholas looked for immediately, but had a silver ring on each hand – one on the middle finger of her right hand and another on the pinky of her left. She wore a knee-length tight-fitting black dress that slightly flared out to the sides at the bottom and really showed off her as perfect as could be slim figure. Black sheer stockings added to her classically attenuated look. She obviously was not a *shlondra* (a slut) looking for a good time. No, she was classy bitch. Nicholas meant bitch in that nice old politically incorrect way. He noticed that he felt a lot freer with what he could think and say here than back home in the land of the free.

She had a really unique, what the traditional British and Celtic folk songs formulaically call "lily white" face and skin, accentuated by a red lipstick that made her lips look wet, luscious and totally inviting. Her hair was fairly short and fell just to the base of her neck. It was stylishly bunched in a small ponytail in back. She was an artist who specialized mostly in portraits and sometimes in nudes. Nicholas wanted to offer to pose, but with Nadya sitting next to him, decided not to offer what would have seemed like a pretty intense flirtation (even though he would have meant it as a joke – HA!). The two were school friends, of course, but nonetheless… discretion rules sometimes and you suppress thoughts even when you feel free.

Out of the blue Shchurakiwsky asked Lydia quite matter-of-factly if he could "matsaty" her – feel her up a bit. Without a second thought, she said she had no problem with that because she doesn't have any complexes. She traded places with Ada so she could cuddle up next to him. He put his hand up the inside of her black-stockinged leg about four or five inches from her knee and turned to Nicholas "Hey, want a little bit? Be my guest." Shchurakiwsky snickered, but Nicholas just smiled and didn't partake of the offer, even though Lydia seemed more than willing to oblige by opening up her thighs even wider. While all this was going on, he heard

Nadya say her hands were cold. So Nicholas took her left hand into his and said, "Yes it is. Cold hands, warm heart – as they say in English." "That's a nice saying," she answered. "I hope it's true!"

After a minute or so of rubbing the inside of Lydia's thigh with the tips of his fingers, though not going up too far toward what might be construed as a danger zone, Shchurakiwsky put his hand on each of Lydia's breasts just for a microsecond. "Oh-ho!" She giggled when he reached out because she didn't think he'd actually do it. Shchurakiwsky just smiled a wickedly delightful smile. While the original "feeling up" started with the promise of heating up sexually, it really just ended at the "Oh-ho!" stage and fizzled out. It seemed more like a game, a performance for the gathered audience of knowing friends.

"You know Jan has never actually kissed me," Lydia decided to announce to the group.

"Then you'd really be in trouble," Nicholas chimed in. "That would mean he really cares for you."

Femme fatale Ada nodded and gave Nicholas one of those knowing looks of touched truth.

"Hey, Yan," Nicholas got the writer's attention. "I hear you used to give tours of underground Lviv. Is that true?"

"Hell no," he answered. "They make up all kinds of rumors about me. I've never given any tours of anything. They say I'm a sex maniac, a pimp and a pervert. Just because I write about some of that in my books. And they say I'm a collector of souls, but not dead souls like Hohol's Chichikov. *Live* souls! How silly! They say I'm some kind of vampire with fangs, too, who comes out to take souls after midnight and hide in my underground coffin under a moss green stone slab in Lychakiv Cemetery during the day. And they think I gather witches around me for satanic rituals. Why if one of the reporters who worked for that local *Postup* rag would see these three ladies gathered around me in Dzyga, they'd think they're my retinue getting ready to prepare a witch's sabbath and there'd be an article about it the next day. I'd wink at them, of course. It's all in good fun. But it's all a pile of *himno*, of *shit*, as they say in your language. I'm just a guy having a good old time, as these three witches, er, ladies will attest, hey, hey, hey." The three ladies and Tolya, who had the wide smile of an overfed contented cat, all just nodded in agreement.

Right around 10:00 P.M., as often happens in Lviv when you're in a group in a café or restaurant, someone stands up and says, "Time to go somewhere else." That someone was mostly silent Tolya who stood up and made the pronouncement.

And everyone got up and sauntered lazily out of the café into the clear but chilly night after the bill had been divvied up. Nicholas was paired with Nadya, who grabbed him by the arm and out of the blue asked him to speak English to her. Shchurakiwsky moved off ahead of the pack with Lydia, and Tolya with his school friend the femme fatale. Everyone holding each other by the arm. Not in a loverly kind of way, just in the great tradition of the Lvivian friendship between a man and a woman.

"I understand English. I just don't speak it very vell," Nadya said to Nicholas.

"Your English is perfectly fine. You hardly make any grammatical mistakes. It's really good," he assured her.

"Vell, I just vanted to hear you speak in za langvage you ver born into – to hear khow you neturally zound. I love the vay you speak English. You know I can't say zat 'TH' sound – it's so hard for me. Zere's nozing like it in Ukrainian."

"Well, I've had a lot more practice with English than you," he smiled at her in the dark and chilly night air.

Right near the multitude of *marshrutka* (minivan) bus stops by the Halytsky Bazaar, Shchurakiwsky announced that he was going to go his own way. He had to be home before midnight, he said, to keep his vampire legend intact. True to form, he didn't give Lydia a kiss, but he did give her a pat on the back with both hands and a hug. "We'll have sex in public next time," he winked at her. "Sure, Yan, sure," she answered and gave him a big-eyed you're-bullshitting-me look with a smile.

The group had, as groups of people in nighttime Lviv tend to have, a kind of wandering inertia as it continued the process of what they call "vodyty kozu" in the local parlance, of leading the goat to water. They meandered through the underground passageway under Prospekt Svobody near Hotel George over to Shevchenko Boulevard. At one point Nadya and Nicholas lost the rest of the pack. Nadya called her friends on the cell phone and found out they had ducked into an Internet café for femme fatale Ada to check her email.

"Want to go in?" Nadya asked Nicholas. "No, not really. I can check my email at home. I've learned not to be a slave to the Internet here."

They popped into the crowded Internet café where about a dozen computers and monitors were hooked up in small booths like in an old language lab. It was stuffy and noisy in there, so Nicholas and Nadya decided to move outside. Everyone else followed in a minute and stepped into a pizza parlor. Nicholas sat down next to femme fatale Ada who hardly said anything to him for a couple of minutes. She kept staring at him. Lydia and Nadya had moved off to the counter to order a pizza and beers. It was an odd chaser to champagne, Nicholas thought, but since he was drinking beer before at Dzyga, another Chernihiv Weiss Beer on draught seemed to fit right in for him. The waitress called out that the pizza was ready and Nicholas brought it back to the table. It was pretty much like an American pizza, though it didn't have much tomato sauce and had corn on it. But it tasted fine – except for the odd taste of the corn.

"It's getting late," femme fatalochka said. "Maybe you can all come over to my place tomorrow to look at my latest paintings?"

Nadya and Tolya readily agreed, though Tolya seemed to be more and more under the influence and could have been coerced into just about anything quicker than you could say zombie.

So they all sauntered over to the main bus stop on Prospekt Svobody to wait for the right numbered bus or microbus to take them home. Lviv is a city of small, narrow streets, so there are a lot of microbuses, the *marshrutky* as they call them. Normal-sized buses can't safely navigate many of the winding streets. Everyone lived more or less in the same direction except for Nicholas who was going to walk home. "It's fifteen minutes for me," he said. "Maybe twenty," Nadya added with a smile. "But it's a nice night. So as the three of them edged their way onto the bus lazily, Nicholas bade his farewells and walked away. "Tolya has such a zombie smile on his face," he thought to himself as he waved. "At least he'll go down happy if he's the witches' ritual sacrifice tonight."

The walk home was uneventful. Copernicus Street was dotted only with occasional couples walking arm in arm, sometimes stumbling and a little bit tipsy.

The next day Nicholas got a surprise call from Ada the femme fatale, who sounded frightened or shy or a combination of the two. She wanted him to help him with something. The first thing she said on the phone was, "This is Ada from yesterday. Do you remember me?" He certainly remembered her and was more than happy to meet with her sometime soon. "How do I get in touch with you," he asked. "I'll send you an email with my coordinates," she answered. "That's strange," he thought. "It doesn't take much to write down a phone number or an email address...."

HIGH CASTLE MOUNTAIN

It's more than a hill, not quite a mountain, 413 meters high. It's really just called "High Castle," but that wouldn't mean much in English. It's the highest point in the city and a place of pilgrimage for nearly everyone who visits. The view on a clear day when fog doesn't lie low in the city stretches across furrowed fields and the outlying dotted "three-story paradises," as the writer Andriy Yurkevych calls them, the big gaudy houses on tiny plots of the neo-wealthy (usually by nefarious or at best questionable means) New Ukrainians. "Nobody's lily white in this country," a businessman once told Nicholas. "The best you can hope for is a tinge of gray."

You can see for 20 kilometers or more on clear days. It's name "Vysoky zamok" means "tall" or "high castle" because a castle once stood on top of the tall hill, though in a different spot than most people now think. Prince Danylo of Halych, where the name of the region of Halychyna (accent on the last syllable) or Galicia comes from, had the castle built sometime around 1256, at least that's what the Galycian-Volynian Chronicle says. The original castle didn't sit at the very peak of the hill, but rather at a small ridge just below. You can still see ruins of part of the rampart wall. It was made of a dark brownish black stone. The Galycian-Volynian Chronicle notes that when Prince Danylo was riding past the picturesque Poltva River and looked up at the high hill, he told his son Lev, after whom the city is named, this will be a wonderful place to build a great city in your honor and a castle high on that hill to which he was pointing.

The trek up the hill was really in two parts. You could either take a winding road that wrapped around the hill or more straight up along a sometimes stone sometimes wooden step path where at times the steps ended, just leaving a beaten dirt path through the sparse forest and brambles. The path was well worn. The goal to reach the circular vantage point at the top was for both locals and tourists alike. It's the first thing that Nicholas's newfound friends told him he absolutely HAD to do before he did anything else after he arrived. The locals such as Mr. Viktor would celebrate birthdays by making a pilgrimage to the top with a bottle of this or that libation, usually champagne, to be shared with friends – and just about any time of the year. The visitors ranged from children alone or with their parents, tourists, teenage and older couples, sharing a kiss at the top as their reward for the climb, to boisterous and rowdy leather-jacketed hooligans taking a break from their hooligan ways to get some exercise. And, of course, there were many people just like you or me or Nicholas, who was just your average everyday man with an ethnic identity crisis he was wont to overcome.

On this day Nicholas decided to take the straighter path instead of the looping ring road. Though it was vertical, it was quicker and more of a challenge. He was in decent physical condition, so it wasn't too much of a problem. The only problem was the fact that it had rained the night before and parts of the ground were still a bit wet and slippery. But Nicholas looked carefully at the mossy green and dirt path below and just ahead of him, at times latching onto a heavy bramble or branch.

Some journeys you take with others, some you take alone. Somehow he felt that one of the signs of the lion might be revealed to him at the top of that mountain. So this journey he had to take alone. This was a place like most of the churches in the city, a sacred spot where the spirits of the city dare not go, that's what Mr. Viktor had told him. Ivan the ghost-seeing painter had told him the spirits COULD NOT go there. A hidden barrier kept them earthbound and further away from the sky – while the top of the hill was in that interstitial place between earth and the heavens, a place where those forces were balanced.

The journey up was easy at first even though the steps were a meter or so long and far apart. As the climb became more vertical and the steps shorter, the harder it became. Really worn spots of earth tended to be just beyond roots of trees that jutted out of the ground. The visible roots served as a kind of stirrup that would keep your foot from slipping back. It was late morning and the sun was heating up the moist earth as it filtered through the trees in places, ridding the dense air ever so slowly of remnants of a morning fog that had already turned into a wispy mist. Slight beads of perspiration dotted Nicholas's forehead and he wiped them off with his forefinger that he dried off on his jeans. He could see a few people ahead of him and a few behind at different stages of the trek. By far most people had decided to take the ring road, which he could see would intersect in a few minutes, fifty or so meters above and ahead of him. When he slowly but steadily reached the spot, he stopped to look back from where he had come. Every journey has its rewards, and his was beyond just a sense of accomplishment. His spirit was already lifted high even though he had not reached the peak. Two-thirds of the path lay behind him. He took out of bottle of Carpathian mineral water from his blue nylon knapsack and downed a few wet swigs before he continued on his journey. The last part of the path zigzagged up the hill, reaching a paved blacktop access road, which he followed for just a minute or so until he reached the last part of the hill. Then he could see there was one more small hill to climb – about 20 meters high – to reach the best vantage point with a blue and yellow Ukrainian flag marking the point above him. This part of the path circled around the final hill with a metal railing in spots.

The wind whips the flag on High Castle Mountain. Pigeons flap their wings above your head from time to time entering into a restful glide when no one bothers to feed them. There was an endless circle of people, mostly young teenage couples. You realize it's after 5 P.M. on a school day. They climb up the uneven incline of cobblestones. Bits of broken glass from bottles and bottle caps dot the crevasses between the cobblestones. Too many humans have passed this way on the ritual climb. The railings are intact – even painted black except where Olya, Vova, Vasya, Andriy, and Vitaly have scribbled their names on the black circles in the middle of the railing.

You imagine what this place looked like before the blackened Soviet-style apartment buildings were built on the wings of the city at the base of the hills. Only one straight road leads from the city. All the others wind in different directions.

You took the trek up High Castle Mountain on the spur of the moment. The weather was beautiful and almost even warm – 13 or so degrees centigrade.

Nadya had wanted to go up the hill the night before with her friends, pick up a bottle of something, and go up. But her two girlfriends had high heels on and couldn't make the trek at night. Nadya was wearing more comfortable low-heeled boots.

You know the way down will be easier. But you feel free at the top.

You hear Ukrainian words, some broken English of a really beautiful long-haired girl trying to communicate with what seemed to be her fairly unattractive, some might even say ugly, boyfriend from some non-English speaking country. She was speaking in the common language they both know, and he could, of course, be her ticket out of the country to someplace more comfortable and Western. Too many guys were smoking cigarettes with smoke blowing right at you in the whipping wind. At least the girls with lollipops weren't emitting noxious smoke.

You're glad you came up the mountain alone today. Sometimes you need to be alone. Today is one of those days. Ada called you earlier that morning – the femme fatale from the night before. You had given her your business card, but never expected her to call. She sounded shy on the phone and it seemed like a transparent pretext. But you didn't know the answer to her question and couldn't help her.

What were you supposed to say? "I think you're hot – and I want to do you! Do you want to do me?" But that's your visceral part of your brain talking. You didn't, of course, say anything of the like. You're too polite to be that way. But you did ask her how to contact her if you happened to come across the answer for her. She said she'd send you an email with her coordinates. She sounded nervous, really nervous, and shy. But you need her to be a little more direct with a hint or two – just a "let's have coffee sometime" – but that in the unwritten rules of the city and place almost always means a date."

The trees and the low ridges of the mountains are in the distance. A friend of yours mentioned he wanted you to take a ride with him outside the city tomorrow – about an hour away by car. He has a little bit of business to take care of, but he wanted to show you some of the countryside. It'll be nice to get away for a bit beyond the gray cobblestone streets and houses, you think to yourself. You get up off the cold metal bench and get ready to start the trek down to the rumbling of a train passing far below.

A MORNING AT STEFANYK LIBRARY

Raya had agreed to take Nicholas to Lychakiv Cemetery the next day if her sister decided not to visit their mother that day. She called at 9 A.M. to let him know she was free and could. He also wanted to get a library card at Stefanyk Library off of Copernicus Street so he could check out some books in the library. Nicholas decided to kill two rabbits with one shot as they say in Ukrainian. He met Raya at the freshly painted light yellow stucco building at 10:45. Actually, he was five minutes late because he forgot his cell phone when he left his apartment in a hurry and had to run back to get it.

Raya was there waiting for him at the turn from Copernicus Street onto Stefanyk Street, intuiting which direction he would be coming from, and went through the process of getting a library card and looking up a few things in books in the main reading room that basically had one wall lined with books on shelves and the rest of the room filled with lacquered oak desks and chairs. The library had been spruced up rather nicely through the donations of the Antonovych family from the US, and the floors were nicely lacquered in a dark stain. The walls both inside and out had been freshly painted. The outside stucco walls were a subdued yellow color that made the building stand out amid more drab gray surroundings.

Nicholas wanted also to take a look at some old manuscripts in the manuscript reading room too. He had heard some unique things were there, but that particular reading room was closed that day, so it would have to wait for another time. The entire process of getting the library card took only about ten minutes. So there was hope that the remnants of the old Soviet bureaucracy were dead and gone.

"Want to go to the Skrypka concert?" Nicholas asked Raya as they stepped outside the building. "I noticed a poster on my way over here. We can stop by at the Opera House on our way to Lychakivka." When she realized the date would work for her, they stopped by the box office, which was about a fifteen-minute walk from the library.

The tickets for the lead singer of the supergroup VV (the initials in translation stood for the Wails of the Aquarian – *Vopli vodopliasova*) were expensive by Ukrainian standards. Two-hundred *hryvnas* or forty dollars for the best seats. Raya insisted that Nicholas not buy them. A week's salary for one ticket was the thought that probably was in her mind. So she told him she was quite happy with the balcony seats for eighty hryvnas each. Then they walked over to the beginning of Lychakiv Street to catch the tram to the cemetery, an obligatory stop for visitors to this city of spirits.

AN AFTERNOON
AT LYCHAKIV CEMETERY

"Don't take her to movies, but to cemeteries," Nicholas recalled from the American poetry course he had taken at Stony Brook. "Sit her up against a crooked tombstone and woo her the constellations of the sky."

In Nicholas's case, it was she (Raya) who took him to the cemetery, but not at night and not for wooing. Visiting the cemetery was the thing to do for a sunny afternoon in Lviv. You take the #7 tram down Lychakiv Street till you get to the corner of the cemetery. Then another five minute walk to the main gate. If you have a relative or friend buried in the cemetery, you don't have to pay an entrance fee. Otherwise it would be a ten-*hryvna* charge.

As they were walking Raya saw an open service gate and told Nicholas to run into it after her. He followed obediently without questioning. He had learned to trust her and follow without question.

"It won't be open for long. If they leave it open, that's an invitation for us to go in," she said with a pixie-like grin and a glint in her eye. "The cemetery's in a lot better shape now than it used to be in Soviet days. They've paved most of it with bricks instead of the old dirt paths, and people are cleaning up the weeds around their family graves for the holidays."

There was peace and quiet in the hilly cemetery with people wandering around in various spots. There was nothing ominous or otherworldly about it. Raya pointed out a lot of the older Polish graves at first with some of the most unique but now weatherworn sculptures. Every marble and stone monument and every name told a story.

There was a proud white lion at one of the graves marked with the name ORDON. The base of the monument was cracked and crumbling, but the lion continued to stand proudly as it roared into the sky. Might this be a sign of the lion in the city of so many lions? One of courage in the face of death? Nicholas wasn't sure. He didn't feel anything with his extra senses. He was struck by the fact that there were many sculptures and bas-reliefs of angels weeping throughout the cemetery. Why would angels be weeping if the spirits of the deceased have been joined with them in heaven? It was for those left behind in the mortal world to weep for their loved ones. Then there were the personal stories. Artur Grottger who had died at the age of 30 in 1867. His beloved wouldn't marry him in this life, and he died of a broken heart. Then she had a statue of herself sculpted on top of his grave so she could be with him in stone spirit. Unrequited love was requited at least symbolically. He looked upward at her statue from two meters below. "Love when you can in this life, otherwise you're left with just the cold stone of memories," Nicholas thought to himself as he looked at Raya in her bright pink coat. There were fresh flowers planted at the base of the grave by someone who must have appreciated the story.

There were graves of the famous and not so famous, though every soul, every life must be somewhat significant somehow in some way to someone. The poet and civic leader Ivan Franko had the biggest larger than life statue that didn't elicit much of a reaction from Nicholas. Whether it was socialist realist, nationalist realist, it didn't seem to make much difference in some cases. Then there was the statue of Volodymyr Ivasiuk as a young boy, whose grave had both fresh and artificial flowers brought every day to pay homage to him for his murder by the KGB. His "crime" was writing extraordinarily popular songs like "Chervona Ruta" (Red Roue). His true "crime" was writing them in Ukrainian instead of Russian. There were graves of musicians, artists, actors, actresses, dancers, politicians, priests, nuns, archbishops, bishops, generals, colonels, grunts in the Afghan war, mafia hit men, men hit by the mafia, Austrians and Hungarians, Poles, Ukrainians, Russians, Soviets, non-Soviets, priests, Orthodox, Polish Catholic, Greek Catholic, non-Catholic, maybe even Baptists, and even a non-believer here and there with the wishful thinking of a cross placed as an afterthought for an afterlife. Heroes of the Great Patriotic War, heroes of the Ukrainian underground and resistance armies, heroes of Polish wars, heroes of wars against the Poles, and lots and lots of less than significant non-heroes. Individual and family crypts, statues, simple crosses, simple slabs with a cross chiseled on them or in bas-relief, geometric slabs with no religious symbols as the sign of Soviet times. Cyrillic script, Latin script, Polish script, German script all etched on the tombstones. Urns, candles, fresh and potted flowers, time and weather worn wooden and concrete slab benches, gray and red cobblestone pathways, some pathways still just dusty paths, chapels and chaplets with and without cupolas in various states of repair and disrepair. And the all-seeing golden eye in a golden triangle on a white background on the gray gravestone of Polish nuns marked "GROBOWIEC SIOSTR OPATRZNOSCI." It had golden lines shooting in every direction from the golden eye. The sky was blue with high puffs of occasional clouds, the perfect day to visit a cemetery in Leopolis with pink-coated blue-eyed Raya.

NADYA'S INDECIPHERABLE EMAIL

An email came addressed to Nicholas from Nadya. Unfortunately, it looked like this and was indecipherable for him:

Ï›èâ"ò, Ìàeêëå!

Äÿêófl çà äÿêófl .

Â"›ø ñóïå› (äîâîäèëîñÿ, ï›àâäà, ÷èòàòè ç" ñëîâíèêîì). Ó òåáá âèøóêàíá " äîá"›íà ïîàç"ÿ, ìåòàôî›èêà ïå›åäîâñ"ì. Ùå ›àç äÿêófl çà Ê›àñó ïå›åäàíî¿ ìèò". Ùîäî âå÷î›à, òî ìåí", ç"çíàflñÿ, áóëî í"ÿêîâî ç ï›èâîäó ê"ëüêîõ ìîìåíò"â, àëå ìåíøå ç òèì. Íå çàáóâàe çà íåä"ëfl: òè çàï›îøåíè äî íàñ íà Ïàñõó! Ç"äçâîíèìîñü, ïà-ïà.

Ìàøà

It got garbled in the process of transfer, or his computer just couldn't translate the font she had used. Nearly forgot to mention that he sent her the poem he had written for her. Actually the poem kind of wrote itself. He had no control over it and it and he just was the Muse's messenger. He didn't write many poems, but just happened to write one on that day he was sitting in as a guest in her Romanticism class.

He called her about 6 P.M. on April 1 to let her know he couldn't read the email except for a winking yellow smiley face that seemed to get translated without a problem. She was busy with other plans she had already made, but said she'd call back the next day and meet with him for coffee if she could.

He got a text message that evening on his cell phone from her at 8:20 P.M. He had to decipher her text messaging shorthand in transliterated Ukrainian since it popped on his screen that way. The original said (more or less): "za zaprosynu na kavu, daruj, mala inshi zaplanovani spravy, na zhal. Lysta ja tobi perewlu v attachi: u tb nejmovirne 4uttja KRASY!"

That translates something like (in expanded form): "for the invitation for coffee, pardon. had other plans, unfortunately. I'll send you a letter in an attachment: you have an incredible sense of BEAUTY!"

The next message from her was: "To perenesemo kavu na zavtra? Ja i svoju poeziju prynesu, ok?" In English that is: "Let's have coffee tomorrow then? I'll bring my poetry, ok?"

Since Nicholas wasn't particularly good at text messaging, he wrote back a simple "ok." He wasn't even sure how to make an exclamation point on his triband cell phone! So he didn't even try. He did learn how to do that later – it was the button on the left just below the "yes" button.

CITY OF DREAMS OR WHAT?

Nicholas was understanding more and more with each passing day that this was a city of dreams, one that stimulated him in many ways, one that focused his creativity and made him more responsive to it and more emotional. It was a place of powerful creative forces. Perhaps it was those powerful electromagnetic forces that Potojbichny had discussed in his lecture – or something else altogether. The professor thought you could measure it, but Nicholas doubted that. At least not with any measuring devices he knew of.

It was a city of many fascinations, of recreations, of intriguing people, of mesmerizing architecture and buildings, a place that every day you will find something new and interesting (but only if you look). But it was also a city of unrealized dreams, a city of lives gone awry, of history gone mad, of sorrow. It was a city of both sunshine and of a gray drizzling day. It was a city unlike any other city. It *was* the city of dreams.

THE OLD APOTHECARY

It was a museum now. The way an apothecary used to look in the city in the nineteenth century. The first floor was a working drug store with buxom elderly ladies in white smocks behind the service counter and the walls lined with apothecary jars from the distant past, but you could pick up just about whatever medicine you needed in Nicholas's time present. The olde apothecary was authentic. Authentic period ceramic jars, flasks, flagons, scales, snub-nosed bottles, vials, dark secret underground musty brick and stucco passageways in various states of repair, and poisons… yes, *poisons*. And the antidote for poisons and a nineteenth-century prescription of choice that served as a panacea – theriac, which was made of the flesh of a viper, opium, and dozens of other ingredients. It was one of the chemist's main concoctions back then. The poisons must have been tasteless but deadly, artful but quick back then. At least that is what Nicholas imagined.

As usual, Raya wouldn't let Nicholas pay the small entrance fee to the museum. "*I* invited you!" Was her usual answer, and always with a smile.

Raya had been to the apothecary many times before. She loved showing *her* city to visitors from all over the country and the world. She led him without even thinking through the passageways, pointed out every detail in every nook. One of her gifts was the ability to see detail and what other people often failed to notice.

Nicholas was particularly struck by a stuffed grayish-white owl perched high up on a wall near the ceiling of one of the rooms. Its gaze made it look nearly alive – as though it were ready to dive from its perch to find its prey. Nicholas didn't feel threatened or frightened by it. Just the opposite – it seemed to emanate a positive energy that he felt bathed him with its gaze. He felt the two dark eyes follow him as he walked past, not spying, but just observing and maybe even protecting him. He felt that protective gaze from Raya sometimes.

"Look in there!" Raya blurted out to Nicholas as they were meandering down a dark salmon-colored stucco passageway.

Nicholas quickly looked into the dimly lit room and started back – it was a bearded longhaired man, somewhat crazed and pirate-like, staring at him.

"I hope I scared you," Raya smiled slyly with her eyes. "He's made of wax."

"Well, the unknown, the unexpected always makes you afraid until you know it," he let his thoughts become utterance as he pondered her mischievous prank.

The rest of the museum consisted of black wrought iron candelabras, arched doorways, worn wooden steps. There was nothing more ominous than the wax figure just inside the darkened doorway that lost its ability to frighten once he knew what it was.

The short trip to the apothecary was a journey to another time. The objects there emanated their own asynchronous presence – the past and present together simultaneously in the duration of his stay. "That's what makes the future," Nicholas completed a puzzling thought for himself, but he didn't utter it aloud this time, even though he thought Raya understood that anyway.

Asynchronous time, the stuffed owl, the theriac. Antidotes for symptoms. Our small human minds are left with impressions and only significant or insignificant details, unless you happen to have a photographic memory. Remembering too much, though, might create a blurry white noise that keeps you from understanding what is most important.

SHADOW SPIRITS ON THE CEILING

Nicholas lay down on his bed for a minute with the ceiling light on. After he shut his eyes for a minute, he saw a small shadowy figure thorough his eyelids, yes, *through* his eyelids. It moved high above him along the ceiling toward the wall to his right. The closer it got to the wall, the more rapidly it moved away from him and disappeared. It seemed unnoticeably to have made its way from a tall old green ceramic coal stove in the corner of the room past the ceiling light, then to the side wall. It was hard for him to describe it. It had a dark outline on the outside with a lighter shade of gray on the inside. It looked something like a bent forefinger, or a shrimp in its general shape and was about four inches long. Nicholas shut his eyes six or seven times and the "creature" or shade or shadow or whatever it was shot across the ceiling – as if it was trying to pass through somewhere else without him knowing it. It didn't frighten him. They didn't seem to want him to know they were there. But somehow, and Nicholas couldn't figure out why, he could intuit what they were: time scatterers, who were shifting between times and dimensions, holding them together like living stitches. Somehow he had the ability to see them scurrying about now when they didn't want him to. Whether that was a gift or a curse only time itself would tell. Sometimes you see only with your eyes closed.

THE METROPOLITAN CATHEDRAL

It was a tall tan-colored Roman Catholic Gothic church from the outside with statues at its entrance and the back. It was dedicated to the Blessed Virgin and had a bas-relief image of John Paul II on its outside front entrance wall, commemorating his visit there a few years earlier in the city to a crowd of over a million. Inside it was decorated in pinkish mauve motifs on the stucco sidewalls and in pale blue on the four columns holding up the central vault of the church. Particularly striking to Nicholas was the symmetrical floor. Black squares interlaced with octagonal tiles on both sides of the church where the tall darkened oak pews were. The larger tiles were a muted dark green. Down the central aisle were rows of completely symmetrical flowers and leaves. Alternating rows of five-petaled flowers in threes all the way from the back of the church to the slightly elevated altar area – with rows of leaves in fours – for a total of seven. Each leaf of the five-petaled flower (a circle in the center with four leaves surrounding it) had another flower within a flower/leaf. This seemed to be an infinitely repeating pattern in the finite space and microuniverse of the church. Three sunburst hosts lined both the sidewalls above the cruciform side wings of the cathedral. Green marble columns were on either side in front, with a large amphora bas-relief to the left and a statue to the right. The church had no misty odor to it even though it was drizzling and gray outside. It had a particularly sweet smell to it – even though it was cold. It was not the odor from scented candles, but something else that Nicholas could not pinpoint.

At the top of the area behind the altar were stained glass windows – the central one of the Mother and Child – both of them wearing golden crowns. There was another window below that with what looked like three angels right beneath them.

TIME IS NO LABYRINTH

[Just the title remains for this chapter. Apparently there once was something written here, but it was either deleted or moved somewhere else.]

THE STATUES IN THE ITALIAN GARDEN

"Do you have time to meet today?"

"Sure, what's good for you, Mr. Viktor?"

"I have to turn in an article around 2 P.M. at POST-POSTUP. I want to get paid before the paper folds again. So how about three? It's a nice day, so why don't we meet at Taras and decide where to go from there?"

"*Domovylys* (agreed)," Nicholas said in the formulaic one-word answer in Ukrainian.

THE DEJAVIEW AND THE INVISIBLE CAFÉ

Nicholas ran into curly-headed Raya by chance on the street as he was walking from an English tutoring session with a couple of students from the sociology department. They were getting ready for a trip to London and asked him to help them with their spoken English. They ended up talking to him more in Ukrainian about London, where Nicholas had previously been four or five times, with various questions about things to see and do there. Pubs, the British Museum, Big Ben, the Tower Bridge, the Thames, Hyde Park, Cambridge, and more about pubs covered most of his answers.

Raya was supposed to help him get to see some really old manuscripts at the Stefanyk Library later that day. She knew the chief archivist. And if you know the chief of anything in Ukraine, you can pretty much get anything done with a speeded-up process without going though the usual red tape with fifteen different signatures of people who were never in their offices or said come back the next day (when, of course, they're not there). But, alas, today was "Cleaning Day" at the library – or in a more direct translation from Ukrainian, "Sanitation Day." The chief archivist wasn't in either. "Tomorrow morning, we can come over tomorrow morning from 10 to 2. They're open on Saturday," she said as he came out of the library's administrative office.

"Would you like to go for coffee?" Nicholas asked. He owed her one since she had taken him out for coffee on Monday, as was her habit. When in Ukraine always take a friend out for coffee on a Monday to start off the week well. While Raya tried to tell him she wanted to treat him, he reminded her that he made the invitation, so it was his prerogative this time. She didn't fight the unassailable Galician logic and said: "I have to take you somewhere you haven't been then – and it has to be someplace interesting. I hate these new shiny places. The ones that smell of old Lviv are the ones I like – and the ones that try to recreate that past." So he followed her – first to the right of the library on Stefanyk Street, then to the left on Tchaikovsky Street, and then to a street with no sign to the right and another to the left past a bright yellow stucco church with two large icons painted on the outside front entrance. The café, which was remodeled in turn of the nineteenth-century style, was right on a corner just past the church and in a similar yellow stucco color. It was called the Dejavu, pronounced Dejaview in Ukrainian. And while the main room was a little bit smoked up from a pair of German-speaking guys having a beer, they were about to leave. So Nicholas sat down at a table with Raya by the window and the light. Most of the tables in the café were in darker spots. Rough hewn wood beams were on the ceiling and arches. Metal sewing machine bases provided the legs of the tables, and glass tabletops had century-old pictures, objects and clippings underneath. "You have to see the bathroom!" Raya insisted. "When it's time, I will," he replied with a wink and slight laugh. When he did go to the bathroom several minutes later, he looked around at the various century-old objects such as a drum and old wooden bowls.

"This is a nice place, Raya." He said to her as she sipped her Turkish coffee. He ordered a coffee with milk and, as usual, they gave him cream.

"Why do they do that?" He asked. But when he thought better of it said, "Yeh, yeh, even in the States I always have to tell them to give me milk and *not* cream. They're both white, that's why they mix it up."

"Yeah, it means the same for them. So you should do the same here." She added.

Nicholas tried to explain Yogi Berra to her. "Dejavu all over again" was Yogi's famous quote. But baseball seemed to be lost on her, but she did appreciate the humor of Yogi's redundant logic.

"Do you know about the café that no longer is?" She asked him. "It's been gone for a while but everyone talks about it. It's a couple of blocks away from here on Saksahansky Street."

"I'd like to see it," he was enthused about the idea. "Maybe it's an interdimensional one! One that exists in another time or place or dimension." He hoped.

THE ARKUBEET

The name came to Nicholas in a dream. Another one of those lucid ones that this time left him in a cold sweat and made him shudder into wakefulness. It was a creature – one from elsewhere, not of this earth, but on this earth, something that wanted to bring more of its kind here.

The creature was a hideous obese creature, with rolls of lard-like substance flopping around its gut, sides and back. It was dreadful to look at with flaming eyes that alternatingly flashed red and black as a pit with a pointed tongue like a viper.

Nicholas approached it in his dream – and it noticed his presence and opened its mouth to reveal three razor-like rows of pointy golden and silver teeth one behind another. There were prepared like a buzz saw to devour anything in their path. With eyes flashing red and black and teeth buzzing like a saw, the creature wanted to do nothing but destroy. It wanted flesh, it wanted blood, it wanted death, death, death. Nothing but death! Nicholas grew tense in the dream, not knowing how to deal with it. He heard a voice say, "I'm here." Then he immediately woke up. No one was physically present, but he felt a comforting presence. But the dream didn't reveal to him who it was.

A MOLFAR BY ANY OTHER NAME

Nicholas was fascinated by the Molfar, the village wizard, from the Parajanov film *Shadows of Forgotten Ancestors*. Professor Potojbichny had mentioned a Molfar in his lecture too. The name reminded Nicholas of the word "malefactor" for whatever reason. Molfars were reshapers of reality. Nicholas learned from his friends that there were Molfars still practicing today in the untamed Carpathians, the home of vampires and legends like Vlad the Impaler from Wallachia who turned into Dracula in the collective imagination. Nicholas's friends spoke of two such Molfars, though they could only remember the name of one of them – Nechai, whose name probably means something like "Non-despair."

"Chur, chur, chur," the Molfar chanted in the Parajanov movie to turn away a powerful oncoming mountain storm. Then he fell to the earth in exhaustion in the arms of the all too corporeal and lusty Palahna as the dark clouds turned away. Blacksmiths were usually Molfars. Nicholas remembered that blacksmiths were wizards too in the Celtic and Olde English traditions. The village blacksmith was the keeper of the devilishly hot burning hearth, the one everyone needed to superheat the metal to transform it into shoes for their horses and to make the plows to sow the fields. So they were the most indispensable of people, even if you might associate them with dark powers. They were transformers of matter necessary for life. Alchemic transmutationists.

In a conversation with the poet Volodya Drymbaryk, who himself was from the Carpathians, and a fellow Nicholas had met through Mr. Viktor during a recent trip to Kyiv, Nicholas found out that the Molfar doesn't really usually turn away bad weather as the one does in the Kotsiubynsky story and in the movie made from it, since the weather is a part of nature that everyone in the Carpathians accepts. The Molfar really was there to cure cows from not giving milk, to make barren women fecund by making them run naked at daybreak through the morning dew (which happens in the Parajanov movie – only in the case of the film with the Molfar observing voyeuristically as Palahna fleshily runs past him), to removing curses from women who can't seem to find a husband, or from men who can't seem to find a wife.

Nicholas's Ukrainian tutor Olenka knew where one such Molfar lived, so Nicholas decided to take the trip out with her by a route of three *marshrutka* minibuses and a long walk through a path in the woods to a town that Nicholas would never have found on his own. Nicholas expected a log hut isolated on the side of a treed mountain with black smoke billowing from the chimney and goats and chickens and all manner of other beast grazing all around the homestead. Instead he found a small ordinary white stucco house in an ordinary town.

What do you say to a wizard? Nicholas didn't come to the Molfar for a specific reason other than cultural curiosity, though maybe the curse of his first marriage might have to be removed. He, however, had done a pretty clean job of that within the confines of the American legal system.

The Molfar looked like an ordinary human: bald, with a tan shirt, and a mismatched gray suit. He looked to be in his seventies and wore square glasses with semi-transparent wide rims. The house looked like a normal house. There were no chicken or crow's feet hanging on the walls, but various Hutsul paraphernalia. And their conversation was just a regular conversation about the kinds of things Molfars do. There was nothing voodooistic about it. He said, among other things, that he was "put on this earth to serve people" and that "all the energy he directs at healing people is returned to him from the universe. If a Molfar violates the laws of Nature or uses his powers for personal gain, those powers will be taken away from him. I'm the very last of my kind." He concluded by saying that "a Molfar can end up doing good or evil."

"Be careful what you wish for," Nicholas added from the American saying, "you might just get it."

"I sense a dark aura about you," the Molfar motioned to Nicholas. "Do you want it removed?"

"Well, I kind of like the way things are going at the moment, so if the aura is bad, I'd rather keep it for fear of getting one that's worse," he laughed.

"Have it as you wish," the Molfar explained. "I only tell you what I see and what I can do."

"And how much it costs?" Nicholas thought to himself. But he's not supposed to make material gain from his craft….

Olenka was fascinated by the Molfar, or at least by the image of a Molfar if not this specific one. She didn't know what to do as she and Nicholas were leaving after their brief encounter, so on a pure whim she decided to kiss the Molfar's hand. At that point Nicholas was already moving through the front door. The Molfar quickly grabbed Olenka right after she kissed his hand and pulled the door shut after dragging her inside the house.

He started to kiss her on both hands intently, uttering charms that made no sense in human language, or at least not in any one of the four languages that Olenka knew. Red hair was the sign of a witch, so he might have thought her to be one. He kept trying to kiss her hands back and convince her with incantations to stay with him. He even quickly changed into a red Hutsul kiptar coat with tassels and a colorful round wide-brimmed hat with all kinds of sequins and buttons. Olenka finally succeeded in fending him off and make her way outside through the front door.

"I'll never do that again!" She said. "That was close! I don't know what got into him."

THE LABORATORY
OF PARANORMAL ACTIVITIES

It was located at the Brothers from Rohatyn Street, house number 26, in the oldest part of town. Twenty-six is two times thirteen, Nicholas thought to himself. The building was made of stucco with a new cobalt blue coat of paint on the first floor that made it stick out amid the unrestored buildings all around it except for the Classic Café with its newer ochre-colored stucco and neo-old Viennese look. "The building was trying to imitate a darkening evening sky," Nicholas thought to himself as he passed it for the first time.

"Don't go there," Mr. Viktor later said to Nicholas. "They're just in it for the money. They don't have a clue what they're doing, but I know it will cost you a pretty penny if you don't watch out."

THE FOUR STATUES AT RYNOK SQUARE

There are four statues at Rynok Square that create an almost perfect square around the rectangular Ratusha, the City Hall at the very heart of the Old City. While looking at the two lions guarding the front entrance, the goddess Diana the huntress was to the right with her two hunting dogs. A muscular Neptune was to the left with a trident. Amphitrite with her left hand raised was to the back of the Ratusha to the left, and Adonis with a spear and a slain boar was to the right in the back. Each statue had a fountain surrounding it that would be turned on in the summer and shut off during the winter. Each statue faced away from the building and was centered in a fountain. Symmetry. Geometry. A rectangle. A square.

THE MANSARDS TO NOWHERE

These were fake windows in buildings meant to entrap ghosts from bothering the occupants. They were dead ends for the dead, particularly those who have too much time on their hands.

NO CATS ALLOWED

That was the sign on the wooden café door on Armenian Street. Strange, we expect no dogs allowed. Why no cats? Lions are cats. Cats seemed to be attracted to Nicholas in this town and all over the country for that matter. He had a big, puffy, fluffy cat at home by the name of Lada. She was a Norwegian forest cat with a Ukrainian goddess's name. She used to cuddle up to his right leg at home on his bed. He missed her a lot while he was away but left her with a friend who was taking good care of her. He kept a picture of her on his laptop screen.

TOURISTS IN THE OLD TOWN

On a sunny Saturday on the first of April, Nicholas had visitors. Halya an English language teacher from Donetsk with two of her friends from Kharkiv along with her cousin Zhenya, who had moved to Lviv from Kyiv six months ago and had never even taken a walk through the Old Town yet. Since they were on holiday in the Carpathians, and the train back home went through Lviv, they decided to stop there to take a look at the city they had never seen before and meet up with Halya's cousin.

They arrived in the late afternoon around 4 P.M. So Nicholas decided to walk downtown and show them around Rynok Square first – and they wanted to take pictures near two of the fountains (the statue of Neptune with private parts hidden and the one of Diana the huntress with her two hunting dogs). Everyone wanted to see the inside of the Metropolitan Cathedral after that, which was open for visitors, particularly because it was *Verbova nedilya*, Pussy Willow Sunday, or at it is known in the West – Palm Sunday. The church had seven or eight worshippers praying in different random spots in the cathedral. Nicholas focused on a side altar while the visitors went toward the front of the church as close as they were allowed to get toward the altar. There were three chairs with signs in Polish and Ukrainian saying: "Worshippers only beyond this point." Since they weren't particularly worshipping and just admiring the inside of the church, they remained at that point for about ten minutes, speaking in hushed whispers to each other. When they left the church, Nicholas directed them to walk out toward the left and to take another left up the street toward the Chapel of the Boims.

"This is the best coffee in town – and the most expensive," he said as he pointed to the World of Coffee Café with all of its outdoor tables filled, mostly with Poles and German tourists with a spattering of Russians. They continued up the narrow street to the Chapel of the Boims, but, unfortunately, it was closed with a padlock on the front door. The sign said that it was open until 4 P.M. – and they had arrived after closing time. Given the good weather, lots of sunshine and blue skies, they would have had hundreds of more visitors paying the two-*hryvna* entrance fee, but not today, and not after closing time.

After about an hour of walking, the four visitors wanted to take a rest and stop at a café. Nicholas recommended the Dzyga Art Gallery Café or the Italian Courtyard, but said they absolutely first had to look at the ruins of the ramparts first. So despite some protests, he dragged them over to the stone and brick fortification wall with a small moat and a bridge over it. It was about three blocks away from where they were standing near the Kornyakt Bell Tower and the Arsenal. When they saw the eight-century-old stone and brick wall, they insisted on taking pictures in front of the rampart wall with rectangular slots for firing weapons – and also by the bridge over the moat. Then he showed them the back of the Arsenal, which was a museum of ancient to modern period weapons.

Before going to the Dzyga Café, they also made a stop at the Dominican Cathedral where a single priest with a deacon and a handful of worshippers were singing vespers in a melodious chant that echoed and reverberated from the rafters. It was interesting to see the church empty, which gave a better indication of its size. It looked much larger on the inside than from the outside. The Cathedral had originally been a Latin Rite church but had been turned over to the Greek Catholic Ukrainian Church at the end of Soviet rule or right after Ukrainian independence in 1991. While the four visitors looked around at various Baroque statues, Nicholas took a look at a stained-glass window to the right that he had never seen before. Just as he was looking at the window a young woman took a picture of the altar with the flash on. "NOT DURING THE CHURCH SERVICE!" A man snapped at her as he bolted toward her wagging his finger, and she apologized and put the camera away. The man returned closer to where the priest was chanting the evening vespers. Nicholas decided to take a picture of the stained-glass window since it was in a small alcove and out of sight of the guardian of the flash cameras. He snapped it quickly without the flash on, and, fortunately, the guardian didn't notice.

The window really drew Nicholas into it, but it was hard to physically describe it. It primarily consisted of eight squares that formed the rectangle of the window. The squares had thin black, what seemed to be wrought iron, crosses dividing each square into four additional squares. And each larger square had an identical pattern of interlaced circles that were tan and dull gold in color on a background of celestial twilight blue with a red square in the middle. The window was framed on the outside in an even darker blue than found on the inside of the squares with ones at the top looking like doves with outstretched wings and three golden butterflies and two golden birds on each side. The window, with indirect light shining on it from outside, was infinity embodied. The winding, symmetrical circles took a path that led back to themselves.

Following the visit to the Dominican, the group walked over to the Dzyga Café and decided to sit outside where they all ordered a glass of hot red wine. Nicholas tasted it, and it was a little too fruit-flavored for him. Halya was particularly impressed by a small strange bronze fish sculpture on a short pedestal just outside the entrance to the gallery. Nicholas asked her to kiss it for a picture, and she obliged.

ACUITY

Nicholas was feeling more and more in touch with his feelings the longer he stayed in the city. He couldn't figure out what it was that was making this happen. He just developed more and more of an acuity, an openness to everything. It was just a beautiful awareness of being totally alive – and listening and really seeing everything around you. Was acuity one of the signs of the lion he needed to develop? If so, he was there. He could see detail where before he would see only the general outline or shape of things.

THE MUSEUM OF ANTIQUITIES

Nicholas had wanted to go to the Historical Museum of Antiquities on Rynok Square on several occasions. He had tried to go there twice before with Mr. Viktor. One time it was closed for "Sanitation Day" with a hastily scrawled sign on cardboard put up at the wooden door at the entrance; and the other time, it was just before closing time and he managed just hurriedly to glance at the exhibits on the second floor without really seeing them. He had promised his friend Halya that he would show her cousin Zhenya around the city, and was hoping to go with her, but she was busy this particular day. Nicholas found out that she had moved to Lviv six months earlier from Dnipropetrovsk to take a job as a computer supervisor for the Ukrtelekom Company. She had to work from 8:30 A.M. until 11 P.M. almost every night to figure out other people's programming mistakes. So Nicholas decided to go alone. Since everyone he knew except for Mr. Viktor had full-time jobs, and sometimes two or three of them, Nicholas had gotten used to going to things by himself and rather liked having the time to concentrate on what he was seeing rather than rushing through at the pace of someone else's perusal clock.

The two-*hryvna* entrance fee was the lowest he had come across for a museum in town – 40 cents. There was a money exchange on the first floor, so he exchanged a hundred dollars for 504 hryvnas. Now he had enough Ukrainian money for 252 tickets to the museum, but he decided just to buy one. At first he was the only visitor in the museum although what looked to be a Polish mother and daughter came in about a half hour after him.

The museum exhibition started on the second floor. And the three or four older women who acted as hosts on each floor made sure that you entered each room in sequential numerical order because the museum exhibits were set up in chronological order. Nicholas found that out later when he tried to enter a room out of sequence and one of the women jumped up and pointed to another room rather vigorously, urging him to go in that direction.

The first hall on the second floor had arrow heads, metal fish hooks, iron hatchet heads, blades from a scythe, nails, clay pottery from various local towns, rings, a tiny bronze icon, metal latches to boxes, all in glass cases. There was also clay pottery from different local towns and villages. All the objects were from everyday life. The parquet floor in the museum rooms was quite interesting – it consisted of oak squares in a crisscrossing geometrical pattern with a lighter wood, perhaps beech, inside the oak slats, creating four triangles within each square.

One object in the room completely stole Nicholas's attention. It was a ten-foot high white stone *bovvan* on a wood pedestal painted black. It was described as an old Slavic idol from the tenth century that had been discovered in the town of Zbruch in 1848. Since ancient Rus accepted Christianity in 988AD according to chronicle accounts, that made it from the same century. Grand Prince Volodymyr had all the idols thrown into the Pochaina River when he accepted Byzantine Christianity, but Zbruch was quite a ways away from Kyiv and the Pochaina.

The idol represented the structure of the universe in three parts: 1) the highest with the sky and the gods; 2) the middle the earth populated with people; and 3) the lower – hell, inhabited by evil spirits suffering in their punishment.

The top part of the idol had a single round-brimmed and conically-shaped hat that looked a bit like a small sombrero with four faces underneath it on each side of the square pillar. Just below that were pairs of hands with the right pointed upward across the front of the chest of each figure and the left pointed across the body and down. So the two arms were parallel to each other with the hands pointed in opposite directions of earth and sky. Symmetry and balance in the world of the highest realm. There was the figure of a horse just below that of the parallel arms.

Below that was the nearly full body figure (only the feet were missing) of four different people on each side of the idol with arms extended. The arms were outstretched about belt-high, with fingers pointed slightly down. The faces were fairly flat at the top with just slightly arched slits for the eyes and mouth with a small square nose. In this realm of life in tenth-century Ukrainian cosmogony, it wasn't a face of happiness or sadness, but something in between.

The very bottom row of hell was a frowning face on three sides – but not on the right side. These faces, which were all slightly different, had deep sunken eye sockets, flattened square noses, and a deep frown. The tenth-century conception of hell obviously didn't think of it as a particularly pleasant place. Not much probably has changed in that conception of it over a millennium.

Nicholas examined the white stone idol for quite a bit of time. He knew that because he lost his sense of time.

The rest of the room included everyday household objects like handmade wooden combs; wooden, gold, and semiprecious stone necklaces; bronze and other metal crosses, inside of which were the relics of saints; amulets made of teeth, the horns of a wild boar, red and green clay, human and animal bones. There were relics of the religion of the One God side by side with the religions of many gods.

There were black metal spear tips, arrowheads, a rusted iron sword, ax heads, chain mail that looked like it was a head covering.

The Berest Hramoty, birch bark documents from the 12th century from the village of Zvenihorod, were the most eye-catching exhibit in the case. There were two of them – one six centimeters high and twenty centimeters wide, and another two centimeters high and twenty centimeters wide. They were written in Old Church Slavic lettering. While Nicholas couldn't read meaning into the words, he was able to decipher a number of the ancient letters: IGHAJEX on one, and DOKJECHCH IXTO on another. The objects had a certain power and aura about them. The message seemed to be important, even though they just as well could have been a recipe for potato salad.

As he was about to exit the room, Nicholas took note of a grinding wheel from the 12th and 13th centuries, and on the other side of the entrance a stone baptismal font. He moved on to the next room

That next room had old maps, some new ones, and facsimiles. There was an ancient black iron pair of scissors that looked so unwieldy and dull bladed, that Nicholas couldn't imagine it to be able of cutting water.

In that first case in the second room Nicholas was drawn to a series of keys under the glass – particularly #9 to #11. They seemed to be keys to nowhere, and two of them hardly looked like what anyone born in the last few centuries would call a key. They were long with a ring at the top. The bottom of the one key had a square shape in the middle and triangles attached and pointing inward on the four corners of the square bottom.

There was a watercolor of St. Mykolai Church (St. Nicholas Church) in the room – with a note saying in was the oldest working church in Lviv and was from the XIIIth century. It was a church that Nicholas had not seen before, so he decided that he would go there to check it out on Good Friday, which in Ukrainian is called Passion Friday.

The Poltva River looked like an inviting blue line on one of the city plans from the XIIIth century. In the case opposite the city plan were stamps of various princes: from Polish Kazimir III (1333-1370) to Lithuanian and Ukrainian princes, most of them sitting on a throne and oddly looking more like a Hindu god than a local prince.

Then there was a book of laws passed by the Polish Seym way back when.

More military things were predominant in that part of the country.

The second 15th century room was filled with various kinds of armor. There was a full chainmail tunic, a helmet with dangling chainmail to cover the face and neck, a bronze shield, various maces, a sword, spears, a battle whip, battle axes, a quite dangerous looking long-poled ax, two iron face shields for horses, another shorter poleax. There were two full dress suits of armor, and curiously, they were for someone exactly Nicholas's size, as if they were made to order for him. In the corner nearest the door there was a stunningly beautiful coat of arms of the Lviv lands. It had a deep azure blue color in the middle of it as well as on the left and top with a black lion wearing a crown as it climbed up a mountain.

The third room transitioned from implements of war to implements of peace. There was a plow from the 18th century that looked like it could still work with a strong enough horse or a tractor to pull it. The word for plow in Ukrainian was the plosive "pluh," which probably has the same origin as the British English spelling of the word "plough." There were all manner of implements for tilling and farming. A wooden pitchfork with metal-tipped ends, a wooden spade with a metal blade, oaken implements for grinding grain, a salt-trader's wagon from 1723 that still looked like it could carry a heavy load, a mannequin of a woman in an embroidered linen shirt working at a wooden weaving loom. She was barefoot and working the pedals below with her feet.

The third floor of the museum comprised a jump in time. The first room to the right of the stairs had dozens of steel broadswords, a large round wooden coat of arms of the city about five feet in diameter. It contained a black painted lion standing sideways at a city gate with the gate raised and with three towers with onion domes above it. There was a gilded iron lion from the 17th century that looked like the one on the spire at the top of the Ratusha.

There was a copper coat of arms of the city with a lion looking to his right with his tongue sticking out at the open city gate – with the castle towers above him. There were four stone cannon balls ranging from twelve to over twenty-four centimeters in diameter, all of them from the 17th century. There were three iron artillery grenades from the 18th century. There was a hook that was quite dangerous looking and with a three-foot long spear tip and a curious volume in German called *The Book of Magdeburg Law* from 1581.

A room to the side of the first room had a bronze and iron treasure box from the 18th century. The tall Polish woman was talking in whispers with her mother and casting sideways glances at Nicholas, hoping he wouldn't notice her looking at him. Nicholas caught her staring at him on one occasion, and she immediately turned away. It was probably one of the codices in the Magdeburg Law book to turn away when your glance is caught. But that's just human nature, of course, unless you want to be caught.

There was a black box with bronze highlights and relief work consisting of a symmetrical lute or harp in the middle of it. There were two giant keys in a glass case – these were used as the outdoor advertisement for a locksmith's shop. There were signet impressions of several Lviv artisans, two bells, a small blackened bronze cannon, and three heavy metallic buckets. Most striking was a pen and ink illustration on paper of "The Punishment of the Baker Brakorob." In 1552 a square pillar had been erected in Lviv with a pulley system to hang bakers by their armpits for "poorly baked bread."

Lying on the ground was a wooden box from the meat-cutter's guild with a bronze image on top of a horned bull with two crossed axes underneath. On the wall above it was a large flag dated 1759 of the tailor and furrier guild with a Blessed Mother and Child on a cloud on it to the right, a three-hilled green mountain below them, and a star on top. It had a hideous looking lion with a crown next to it with its big maroon tongue sticking out and with eyes of the same color. There was also a human figure with outstretched arms to the left of center looking up at the Madonna.

In one glass display case there were bronze and tin plates, cups, grogs, and pitchers. There was another case of weapons: a rifle, swords and sheaths, a black weathervane rooster, more keys, crosses of various sizes, and three clocks.

On the opposite wall was a case of things from the East: four mother-of-pearl and amber inlaid boxes were the most impressive. One of them was about twenty-four centimeters tall, twenty-four centimeters deep, and forty centimeters wide with magnificent geometric designs all over it. There was also a coffee-making pot, a case with forty coins dated from 1310 to1698, a thick glass case with silks, silverware, a hand-held fan, cups, and a small ivory box.

In the room opposite on the same floor, Nicholas found ornately carved wooden rifles and flintlocks, a pistol, a steel ax. One of the flintlock rifles was exquisitely inlaid with ivory. There were bows and arrows decorated with ornate leather and bronze, a yataghan from the 17th century with elaborate detailed work on its sheath, more portraits of Hetmen (Kozak leaders), including the Ukrainian lover of Catherine the Not So Great (from a Ukrainian perspective) – Kyrylo Rozumovsky (1728-1803). A portrait of Hetman Ivan Samiylevych (d. 1690) looked quite African with his dark skin and large brown eyes.

There was an ornate leather saddle with a regal red, tan and gray cloth covering it. The cloth contained patterns of flowers with two birds looking at each other on the top of it. There was another full set of chain mail in the room. There was also the portrait of Ivan Bohun (d. 1664), who fought in the Kozak wars of independence. Hetman Bohdan Khmelnytsky punished him for opposing the Pereyaslav Agreement in 1654 that led eventually to the Ukrainian lands being seized by Russia. Bohun was eventually executed by firing squad by the Poles. Nicholas was living next to Bohun Street. The room also had a tiny cannon about twenty-four centimeters in length, more weapons in a case, six different *bulavas* (maces), rifles, and two small cannons. There was also a giant kettledrum made of blackened copper with clamps to hold the animal skin tightly on top. It was about a meter in diameter. There were more muskets and long rifles in cases.

The fourth floor had portraits, paintings and musical instruments. Immediately after you walk into the first long narrow room, there it is on the left, the 1635 coffin portrait of Barbara Langisz. She was a sad, long-faced girl with dark eyes. Wearing a short string of pearls wrapped tightly around her neck with matching pearl earrings, she had curly hair and wore red lipstick. Her portrait was in a gold-colored oval frame. The portrait had been commissioned to M. Petrakhevych and, according to the blurb right below it, it was considered the best extant seventeenth-century secular Ukrainian portrait. Beneath Barbara's visage was the Gospel of Luke in a glass case written in Old Church Slavic, the first age-old written language of the church, with curlicue letters, some of which Nicholas couldn't recognize.

The portrait didn't strike Nicholas as being all that good or alive in a way that, say the best portraits of Ivan Trush, the great impressionist painter who had a small museum near Nicholas's neighborhood, made people come alive. So he didn't know what the big clamor was about her. Why did Mr. Viktor find it important to write about her? Why did Nicholas's friend Andriy Yurkevych write poems about her – albeit while he was under the influence? Her portrait was just nothing striking to Nicholas. But he did think about the fact that it was a "natrunnyj portret" (a casket portrait), and it didn't belong here in a museum. It belonged on her casket.

As he moved away from the spot where Barbara, or rather the coffin *portrait* of Barbara, was, Nicholas felt an intense feeling of pressure in his head and on his chest on that fourth floor of the museum. It was as if someone or some thing was trying to break into his consciousness through his body. He felt a weakness in his legs and found himself gasping slightly for breath. He could sense the beating of his heart rapidly increase. But he fought it and gathered his strength to combat the feeling of mild nausea. Maybe it was from looking at the exhibits of the museum in too much detail and all the dust and mold that must be there on the ancient objects. It couldn't have anything to do with the portrait of Barbara, he thought rationally. But the further he moved away from the portrait, the better he felt. Was it the last Friday of the month? He wasn't sure. She might be looking for a new betrothed....

On the wall opposite the portrait were *tsymbaly*,[2] kind of like a hammer dulcimer on four legs, and an orange lacquered multi-stringed *bandura* from the 19th century. Nicholas had never seen one that color before. There was a *trembita*[3] on the top of the wall about

---

2 http://home.att.net/~bandura.ca/VMfolkBook/

3 http://home.att.net/~bandura.ca/VMfolkBook/

twelve feet in length, an old wooden *lira*[4] made of aged blackened oak, a *torban*,[5] a *hudok*[6] with a stringed bow, a drum, an *Irmologion*[7] church song book with notes, and an exquisitely embroidered blouse and skirt with red flowers.

The last room of the museum had a large Viennese clock stopped at 12:26. Was it a.m. or p.m.? It had a gilded carved leaf design around it. There were also a few hunting rifles, one with mother of pearl inlay all over it. There was a pair of dueling pistols and a hunter's horn hanging on the wall.

The most impressive object in the room was a Polish organ in an ornate box with elaborate paintings all over it. It was mostly red with gold leaf in the design of a vine with leaves in relief. There were four figures on the four corners of the organ box wearing turbans and Indian garb as well as two small carved nude female figures about eight centimeters high on the back of it where you could count twenty-one steel pipes of various sizes. There was also a large gold-framed mirror from the Pidhirtsi Castle that was carved in a gold-leaf pattern about twelve centimeters wide on the frame. The rest of the room had a double-sized case of embroidered clothing and kitchen items along with more portraits of relatively obscure people on the walls and carved chairs.

Nicholas's tour of the museum took him from the ninth century or so nearly to his present. It was filled with history, with the labors of people from his patria's past, with weapons of all kinds used to defend the land. While he looked closely at the various displays, each object had a story to tell. He was left with the feeling that something or some things there in that museum of antiquities would be invaluable to him in his quest. He just needed to keep himself open to the messages the objects might provide for him in the telegraphic language of musty time.

---

4 http://home.att.net/~bandura.ca/VMfolkBook/

5 http://home.att.net/~bandura.ca/VMfolkBook/

6 http://home.att.net/~bandura.ca/VMfolkBook/

7 http://orthodoxy.org.ua/uk/krasa_pravoslav_ya/2007/10/25/11128.html

THE BROKEN STONE STAIRWAY

There is a crooked broken stone stairway that takes you up the hill toward the Church of Lazarus. Lviv is a hilly place, hilly like Rome. He wasn't sure if there were seven hills, but there were many of them. And the Church of Lazarus lay at the top of the hill – very close to the niche to nowhere.

THE CHURCH OF ST. MYKOLAI

It was the simplest and oldest church in the city and it was located about a five-minute walk from behind the Opera House. It was Orthodox. There were only a handful of people inside when he arrived in the late morning. He was immediately struck by the zigzag geometric designs of the tiles on the floor. That infinitely repeating symmetricality seemed to be in all the churches in the city. It was fairly dim inside with only cloudy light filtering through a few tall windows and the candles lit inside by worshippers.

The cave of Christ's burial was recreated to the right side of the church. It looked just like a cave, but had dozens of bouquets of fresh flowers, some cut, some in clay pots. There was Old Church Slavic writing on the ceiling that Nicholas couldn't decipher very well. The main cupola in the center of the church was painted cerulean blue on the inside, the color of the heavens. Behind the altar on the back wall of the church was a beautiful small stained glass window, which had the image of a darker greenish-brown cross in the center of it, surrounded by a lighter ivory color. A chalice was impressed on the cross with a light green circle peacefully surrounding it. The top left side of the cross was regal blood red, the right side ivory white, and the bottom red.

The church was one of the most peaceful Nicholas had been it, perfect for silent meditation in the subdued light and subtle colors. The icons in the church were also in restrained colors. The image of the Blessed Virgin was in the center cupola surrounded by the apostles. There was a Blessed Virgin with raised hands behind the altar, and a second altar on the left side of the church, which had a darker red-robed Mother and Child. Tall thin beeswax candles were being lit before the icon for the health and memory of relatives, friends and loved ones. Nicholas lit candles for his family back home. He also lit a special candle for Raya and said a prayer for her health and well-being.

The dome behind the altar was painted a muted yellow. Numerous saints and religious figures were painted on the walls and ceiling. The subdued light made it all seem not gaudy, but completely natural. The left altar area where Nicholas had lit the candles had two pews with six embroidered gonfalons on poles: one of Christ, one of the Blessed Virgin, and the others of different saints. As with almost all the Orthodox and Greek Catholic churches in Ukraine there were no pews and everyone stood. You'd have to go to the Polish churches to find them.

There were gold highlights throughout the church – a ring surrounding the bottom of the cupola above the altar, around the Holy Doors that formed the entrance to the realm of God at the altar, and around the frames of icons on the iconostasis and side altars. St. Mykolai, the patron saint of the church, was represented by an icon in red and gold to the right of the iconostasis. The other three main icons from left to right on the iconostasis were the Archangel Michael, the Blessed Virgin with a green icon lamp lit in front of her, and Christ holding a chalice with a halo that looked orange. A red icon lamp hung in front of the icon.

Quiet meditative silence dominated in the church even while many were whispering to each other and whispering prayers. The painted burial shroud of Christ, the *plashchanytsia,* was to the right side of the church. It was being guarded by a young girl and would be guarded all night in turn until just before daybreak on Easter Sunday morning.

After Nicholas stepped outside and started off on his way home, he looked back at the church from across the street. It had one of the simplest designs in the city – just an off-white stucco with a green copper roof and two domes. For the first time Nicholas noticed there were white cherry blossoms bursting into bloom in a courtyard behind it.

SHEVCHENKIV HAI FOR THE BLESSING OF THE EASTER BASKETS

It was a cold and windy April Saturday when Nicholas walked over to his friend Marko and Luda's place to take a #7 tram with them over to Shevcheniv Hai, the outdoor park that contained two centuries of Ukrainian wooden architecture that had been brought there from all over the country. It included three or four churches along with homes from virtually every region in Ukraine. There were hundreds of people outside of the wooden St. Michael the Archangel Church where the blessing of the baskets was taking place every twenty minutes or so in the enclosed yard next to the church. The various people formed an oval with their Easter baskets set in front of them with the priest, deacons and altar boys at the center of the oval with a small bucket of holy water. Each basket had a lit beeswax candle and included *kovbasa* (ringed garlic sausage), ham, *krashanky* (single-color boiled and dyed eggs), *pysanky* (intricately designed Easter eggs), *paska* (round Easter bread), butter formed in the shape of a lamb, and a *rushnyk* (an embroidered cloth). This was all symbolic of the bounty to be shared on Easter Sunday morning after forty days of fasting.

AN SMS

Nicholas hadn't seen or heard from Ada in over a week, so he nearly had forgotten about her. He chalked it up to just one of those fleeting male fantasies. Shortly after returning from Shevchenko Meadow and whipping himself up a bowl of pasta with tomato sauce, something Ukrainians usually don't eat, he heard a buzzing coming from his phone in the study. But the phone wasn't ringing even though it was set to ring as well as buzz. So he wondered what it was. The phone continued to buzz as he picked it up with a message asking him if wanted to read an incoming text message. He pressed the green "yes" button and lo and behold, it was from the nearly forgotten femme fatale Ada, who signed it with her complete name. The message said: "Good evening, Nicholas, if you have the time and inclination we can meet tomorrow. Ada [we can get together at Dzyga]."

What was he to do? His overwhelming previous desire had chilled, and he didn't like any cat and mouse games. He was already going for the morning Easter meal with his friend Raya and her family. That would start around 9 A.M. and last three or four hours. He'd be back home by two. Would Dzyga be open on Easter Sunday? It seemed odd that it would. But what's the harm? He's a big boy and can handle himself. Now in a sober state and under completely different circumstances he probably wouldn't see her in the same way as he saw her before. So… He decided to send her back an SMS text message: "I'm free after three – Nicholas."

Oddly, instead of the message from Ada, one came in from Zhenya from Dnipropetrovsk, where she was visiting her mother. She wrote it in Ukrainian:

Xaj v koshek Vam ljazhut' i baranchyk i paska, shmatok shynky, zapashna kovbaska, i pysanok kil'ka i z korinchykom xronu… Xaj plyne dostatok do VASHOHO DOMU!!!"

It roughly translates (without the poetic colorful play of the formulaic original) as: "May in your Easter basket lie a tiny lamb and Easter bread, a piece of ham, pungent garlic sausage, several pysanky Easter eggs with some horseradish root… May abundance flow to YOUR HOME!!!"

"Wow, that was sweet," Nicholas thought and now felt guilty about arranging a meeting with Ada after Zhenya had sent him such a nice message. But it was too late now. He had started the ball rolling down on his Sisyphus self and had to push it back up the hill.

The tiny lamb is made of butter, the paska is the sweet Easter bread that's basted with butter and dark brown, the ham is ham, the kovbasa is usually sausage brimming with garlic, the pysanky are the elaborately designed Ukrainian Easter eggs, and the incredibly spicy horseradish root was usually mixed with grated beets and mixed together. Just add a couple of hardboiled eggs, a rushnyk or embroidered cloth to cover it, and a candle for the blessing of the basket, and you have it. This is exactly the way the basket looked that his friends Marko and Luda had made for him to take to Shevchenko Meadow to be blessed. And Raya had loaned him the basket to make sure it was completely traditional.

There were no more text messages from Ada or Zhenya. He was a free bird here, so he shouldn't have felt guilty. But he still did – a little bit.

EASTER DAY IN LEOPOLIS

Nicholas spent a relaxing Easter morning with Raya and her extended family at their apartment in a mid-rise building on the edge of town. She lived on the ninth floor in a corner apartment that was bright and airy, filled with sunlight just like Raya. Nicholas met her at the Easter mass about nine in the morning, just as the three-hour Easter service that began just before daybreak was winding down. She was with her niece outside in the still chilly air and saw him at the moment he arrived. The church was so packed that several hundred people were standing on the church steps all the way to the street. Nicholas remembered the melody to the "Khrystos Voskres" (Christ is Risen) hymn that was sung three times at the end of the service. It was both simple and powerful, and he felt a powerful positive energy fill him as he sang it with the crowd.

Easter dinner was also filled with an incredible positive energy. Besides Raya's family, there were several guests from Italy who were filming documentaries on spirituality in Ukraine. Raya enjoyed sharing her bounties with others and loved meeting people from other countries. The feast was magnificent and just like the ones Nicholas remembered from home with his own family. The *khrin*, the horseradish root mixed with beets, was his favorite. It gave him a powerful endorphin high as with both pleasure and pain it seemed to burn a hole through his sinuses to his brain.

After the foreign guests departed, Raya asked Nicholas if he wanted to go to Shevchenko Meadow for a walk and to see the *haivky*, the young girls singing and dancing in the meadow.

"I thought you'd be busy with your family," Nicholas said.

"No, no, everybody else has things to do. They're going to the family grave in the village. I already did that."

So they took a not very crowded *marshrutka* (minibus) and transferred to another one get to Shevchenko Meadow. There were large crowds of people, young and old and in between, milling around everywhere. Girls in colorful embroidered costumes were arm in arm and hand in hand doing springtime dances and songs of joy and fertility. The boys were performing feats of strength and agility, forming pyramids and showing their youthful virility. There were horses bedecked in colorful saddles with Kozak-costumed riders. It turned out to be just a wonderful, pleasant peaceful sunny day. Nicholas felt like he was in heaven with his paradisiacally-named Raya.

THE GOLDEN DUCAT
IS HER FAVORITE PLACE

After spending a really wonderful and relaxing day with Raya, Nicholas arrived home on Marshrutka #50 from Halytsky Bazaar at around 6 P.M. He usually walked, but seven hours of strolling through the city and Shevchenko Meadow had taken its toll on his legs that Easter Sunday. It was the first time he had taken city transport home from the downtown instead of walking. An hour after he arrived home his cell phone buzzed with a text message. It was Ada. He really was tired and didn't feel like going back downtown, so he hoped she didn't want to meet for coffee (as she had been hinting at for quite a while). After a few weeks of alternating curt with friendly emails and text messages, she sent him the following: "19:30 de vam krashche, bilia opery, korolia Danyla, chy Fedorova?" – which translates as: "7:30 P.M. where is better for you, next to the opera, King Danylo, or Fedorov?" Since he knew where the Opera House and the monument to Ivan Fedorov were, those were the best choices for him. He wasn't sure where the King Danylo was at that moment, suffering a disorientation in locality. It just wasn't one he went to a lot or one that he noticed. She was also the only person he met here who didn't want to meet "at Taras" or at "the big Franko." So he sent back a text message "opera at 7:30." He was 15 minutes away, so he decided to start walking right away even though he wanted to rest. Just a block or two from home his cell phone started buzzing. It was Ada, this time calling on the phone. She asked if he could make it 7:45 P.M. He said sure. She asked where? He said the Opera or Fedorov. "*Domovylys* (agreed)," she said.

Since he had already started walking, he decided to go downtown and take a look at the festivities going on. For some reason he walked toward the Laboratory for Paranormal Phenomena at 26 Brothers Rohatyn Street two blocks from Rynok Square. The dark blue building had a bas-relief of a white elephant on the side of it facing the Brothers Rohatyn Street and another on the other side of it. Nicholas looked up at the very top of the building directly on the corner, and there was a much more subdued in color bas-relief of an elephant. As he stood across the street from the building, he noticed on the corner just opposite to it a crumbly not very well cared for building he had never noticed before with five windows on the side street walled up. These must have been the windows to nowhere that were used to fool spirits to keep them from entering the house. It clearly wasn't a later decision to wall up the windows because the stucco and paint looked exactly the same age as the rest of the building. The spot where the Laboratory stood then was probably an appropriate spot to study the paranormal. Mr. Viktor had told him the place was a scam – and even Jan Shchurakiwsky had written an article berating the outfit as a bunch of charlatans squeezing money out of people to give them hope to communicate with the beyond. He admitted, though, that they picked a good spot for their storefront operation. It was near where a lot of strange phenomena had been reported.

After mulling his thoughts for a few minutes, Nicholas walked over to the back of the Ratusha where he heard boisterous live music playing and a joyful crowd of several hundred people with many of them dancing. He had about 20 minutes to kill before he was supposed to meet Ada, so he decided to check it out closer. The place was rocking to the Haidamaky fusion band. The lead singer was a guy dressed in black by the name of Oleksander Jarmola. He also went by the name DJ Jarmola. Their music was a combination of traditional Ukrainian folk and Hutsul mountain music with a *sopilka* (similar to a tin whistle) and a squeezebox accordion: it was fused with rock, punk and even a bit of Kozak rap. Their latest album was called *Perverzija* (Perverzion). You can check out a few pictures and get some information on them here and elsewhere on the Internet:

http://www.umka.com.ua/eng/catalogue/1945/

http://www.pisni.org.ua/persons/469.html

DJ Jarmola had a shaved head and wore a loose black linen shirt and black *sharovary*, baggy Kozak riding pants, very similar to the style that MC Hammer wore in the "Don't Touch This" video. MC must have seen some Kozaks in his day. He also brandished a silver Hutsul woodman's axe that he used on occasion as a dance prop and for syncopation.

Nicholas just caught the middle of a Hutsul dance tune "KarpatenSKA" from the Carpathians in SKA style with DJ Jarmola gyrating all over the stage and playing the *sopilka*, and the crowd responding from tiny kids to old men with canes, both groups of which could barely walk, showing the beginning and end points of a life, and filled with joy and passion from beginning to the last breath. A nearly toothless white-haired man in his 80s rocked back and forth with a smile on his face and his head swaying side to side with the beat. Nicholas caught just two more songs – "Bohuslab" and "Pisnya lyubovy" (love song). The crowd quite passionately requested the second one. Nicholas didn't want to leave at that moment, but he decided to be on time for his meeting with the femme fatale. He was really just two minutes away from the monument to Ivan Fedorov, a hefty tall black bronze statue honoring the printer of the first Bible in Ukraine.

As Nicholas passed around the corner of the Dominican Cathedral and began to walk up toward the Fedorov monument, Ada noticed him from a distance and began to walk in his direction. Just as the previous evening, she was impeccably dressed in a different black contour-fitting woven dress. She had the same black leather three-quarter-length coat and black high-heeled shoes that were more of a small boot. A slight tinge of red lipstick accentuated her refined smile of recognition. She really looked happy to see him, and that, of course, made Nicholas happy and relaxed. That nervous energy she had when he first met her wasn't there.

"Khrystos Voskres," she said, which means "Christ is Risen." And he answered with the traditional "Voistynu Voskres" (Truly He has Risen).

"Where would you like to go for coffee?" She asked after politely shaking his hand.

"Anywhere you'd like."

"I have a favorite spot… The Golden Ducat. No smoking there, and I like its charm."

"That's fine with me," he answered. "I've been there a few times and really like it – both the coffee and the atmosphere."

So they moved off in the direction of the café, which was only about two blocks away.

"It might be crowded because of the holiday," she added when they reached the street corner where it was located. "But let's go down and check – somebody might be getting up from a table."

Luck had it that someone had just gotten up, and the waitress told them just to wait a minute to clear it. It turned out to be a really small table that barely squeezed the two of them in right inside the seating area in a small alcove. Even a cramped space was better than none. It was fairly noisy and boisterous inside, much noisier than when Nicholas had been there last on a Sunday morning alone.

"Thank you for suggesting to go out for coffee," Nicholas said right away after sitting down. "At Dzyga I didn't have a chance to talk to you much, just because we were sitting at opposite sides of the table."

"I wasn't very talkative that night anyway. I was observing. It was interesting. I observe a lot before I begin to speak."

"Well, Jan and Lydia put on a show."

"Yeah," she smiled a smile as she remembered the evening. "I don't take it seriously. That's the way Lydia is."

"Well, I can't take it in large doses or every day…."

"But it's always interesting… I've known her for a long time. It's her way of playing."

"So why do you like this place?"

"Why do *you*?" She seemed distressed and put on edge by the question, as if her reason for liking it was a mystery.

"I just like it. The coffee's good. The atmosphere's nice."

"I like the ambience. I feel at home here."

"With the bat in the corner, the darkness and the mirrored ceiling?"

"That's all part of it. What about the place do you like so much that brings you back?"

"I really like the way they paid attention to detail in restoring it. And the way the objects are set up. Very intriguing. Have you noticed the violin, the felt hat and the hand-held fan in the corner alcove?"

"Yes, it's nice."

"I'm glad you invited me, ah, I said that already… But I've noticed sometimes people get a bad first impression of me. And when that happens, I don't fight it."

"I think it's your eyes – they're really dark…."

"That's because, as my father says, the Bilanchuks are filled with fecal matter up to here," he made a sign right above his eyes with the four fingers of his right hand.

"They're nice eyes, just dark, and they might seem impenetrable to some. Want to see some pictures of me? I just had them printed."

"Sure, I'd love to."

"I hate having my picture taken, but I love looking at pictures of other people. A picture captures someone's *bachennja*, their vision of someone else at that moment in time."

Ada pulled the pictures out of her black patent leather bag and began showing them to Nicholas. He wasn't particularly impressed with the three black and white pictures that he saw. But then she showed him a color shot in profile of the right side of her face that really wowed him.

"That's BEAUTIFUL," he blurted out.

"It's not professionally made…."

"That doesn't matter, it really captures something, it's a really beautiful shot. Could you make me a copy?"

"Why?"

"It's just really beautiful, and I'd like to have it. It's a different you, too. A brighter sunlit version you."

"Maybe," she said. "I just don't see why you would want it. Are you some kind of collector?"

"No, it's just nice, but I understand if you don't want to give it to me. Do you mind if I take a picture of you now? I'd like one here in your favorite place. I'd like one *na pamjatku*, as a memento."

"Maybe next time?..." She answered timidly with the rising intonation of a question.

"Actually, I'd like one of you in natural light too. In natural light the colors come out so much more true."

"Sure, but just later. I've never thought of myself as very attractive. That's why I don't like having my picture taken."

Nicholas found that hard to believe, just because he found her so incredibly attractive. But he didn't push it.

The room continued to be noisy with couples and families with kids coming and going. They spent nearly two hours in the café and found it quite easy to talk to each other without a single pregnant pause. As quiet and timid as she was at the Dzyga, she turned out to be an engaging conversationalist, though Nicholas didn't quite know whether he was expressing himself as well as he could in his slowly improving Ukrainian. While Nicholas still found Ada incredibly attractive, he didn't have that moth drawn to a flame attraction he had at the soiree at the Dzyga. He could see beyond her physical beauty, that was as beautiful as one could ever imagine, but he could now at least see a little bit into her soul. And what he saw beyond the surface, he liked, though he did sense a deeper sadness that she didn't want to talk about.

At one point Nicholas observed her playing with a piece of paper, folding and unfolding it with her fingers.

"That's a habit I have sometimes," Nicholas called her attention to it.

"I'm sorry," she said, but continued to fold the paper and alternately looked at him directly into his eyes or down at her fingers and the paper on the table. She looked into his eyes quite a bit and smiled quite a bit, both with her rosy lips and her eyes.

"Some people think that's a sign of nervousness or of feeling uncomfortable," Nicholas decided to say to her.

"Oh, no! Don't think that! Not at all! I feel very comfortable with you."

"I didn't mean to make you uncomfortable by saying that. I just meant to tell you that we're a bit alike in that we share the same habit. It's not nervousness with me. It's almost always a way of focusing for me. I'll take a bit of a paper napkin and roll it up, then pick off tiny pieces of the end. I did that a little bit today. See?" He pointed to the small bits of torn off white paper napkin. "I guess it's my way of meditating in company."

Ada looked at her watch and quietly said: "You know, cell phone signals don't reach down here."

"That's great sometimes."

"Sometimes I like to turn off my cell phone for two or three days at a time. So many calls are just people who need things to be done."

"Yeah, we become slaves to them."

"Can we switch to *ty*?" Nicholas asked her. (That's like the *tu* form in French, or the familiar form of address.)

"If *vy* (like the French *vous* form), I mean *ty*, are comfortable with it."

"I am."

"I should be going," she added with hesitating decisiveness, as though she didn't really want to leave his now comfortable presence or the refuge of the café of the ghosts.

"Sure, I'll ask for a check."

"No, better just to go up to them."

So they got up out of their chairs and moved to the other room that had the intoxicating fragrances of fresh ground coffee and chocolate.

"What did you have?" The waiter asked.

"Melted chocolate and coffee with milk," Ada answered.

"That'll be 12 hryvnas," he pushed out the check on the counter toward Nicholas. That comes out to $2.20. He pulled out a 20-hryvna bill from his wallet and pushed it along the counter toward the girl at the cash register. "Just give me back five," he added. That was a pretty big tip for Leopolis, but Nicholas preferred overtipping, even when tipping was optional. It was a remnant of the American left in him.

As they moved up the steps, Ada asked him: "Do you know the time?"

"Yes, I know time. I mean, I have the time. It's 9:30."

The two of them walked a block over toward Rynok Square, then took a left in front of the Ratusha along the tram tracks imbedded in the cobblestones. Strangely, Nicholas didn't know where they were going and didn't want to ask. He was content as a cat perched in its favorite spot and would follow Ada anywhere she might lead him that night. Just at that moment and thought, her cell phone began to buzz. Nicholas tried to walk away from her a bit to give her some privacy to answer. He assumed it might have been a boyfriend. They didn't talk about personal things much. He did find out that her mother lived in Lviv, her father lived in Athens, they were divorced and her father remarried a Greek woman he had been working for, she got up at 10 A.M. that Easter morning because she had stayed up the night before till 2 A.M. reading, and she had been a little under the weather the last week, which was the reason she hadn't called him back earlier. She was feeling better now.

Nicholas couldn't help but hear snippets from her side of the conversation as much as he tried to block it out. It was something like "the cell phone must have been out of range," "I never turn it off," "I've been busy," "nothing special," "want to come over? I can be home in twenty minutes," "I'm downtown," "where are you now?," "at Shevchenko?," "I'm a little tired," "Give me five minutes." She seemed unhappy and nervous about the conversation. Whether it was the conversation or the fact that Nicholas was nearby while she was on the phone, he didn't know.

When she had put away the cell phone in her pocketbook, she looked at Nicholas and with a slightly restrained heaving sigh said, " I have to go now."

"Sure, I understand."

"Do you like going up High Castle Mountain?"

"I've been up there once. But I enjoy going up. It's good exercise for me. I just don't like it when all the teenagers are up there. It gets noisy."

"Would you go up there with me sometime soon? I go up there a lot and write. I feel free on the mountain."

"Sure, be happy to do that with you."

"I'll let you know at least a day in advance."

"You can even be spontaneous. If you just feel like it, give me a call and if I'm free at that moment, I'll go meet you."

"I might have to go to Krakow this Thursday on business for a day or two."

"I'd love to go to Krakow with you sometime. If you were going Friday, I'd go with you," Nicholas added spontaneously.

"You'd go with me? Unfortunately, I really have to leave Thursday this time."

Nicholas realized that he might just have propositioned Ada for a weekend fling. But since she didn't seem to mind and took it in stride, he didn't think twice about it. He really meant it as a sightseeing trip with a newfound traveling companion he now felt comfortable with. Though on thinking about it more, he certainly wouldn't object to staying in the same room with her for the weekend and explore other aspects of her company. As they say in Ukrainian: "Tse b ne bulo pohanno" (that wouldn't be such a bad thing) or "Ja b ne buv proty" (I wouldn't have any objections). But the stars did not seem to be aligned for that yet – if at all....

Just as they were passing the street next to the statue of Taras, Ada turned to Nicholas and said: "It's been really nice with *vy*-vous (formal you), I mean *ty*-tu (informal you), bye...." She held out her hand, which was cold from the windy and now chilly evening, and he shook it gently and bade his farewell to her. He didn't look in the direction of the statue of Taras just because he didn't want to know what her friend on the other end of the cell phone line looked like – and wanted to leave her her personal space. He was just grateful for a really pleasant evening and walked home the twenty minutes in a somewhat elated mood along Copernicus Street, past Hyphenated Writer Street, and up Bohun Street to his apartment.

At precisely 10:07 P.M. his cell phone buzzed.

It was a message from Ada: "Djakuju za vechir." (Thanks for the [nice] evening.).

He replied to her: "Djakuju Tobi." (Thanks to *Ty*-Tu [informal You] with a capital letter.).

About a half hour later he had the impulse to say something else to her, so he picked up his cell phone and typed out: "Bazhaju Tobi teplyx, harnyx sniv." (I wish You warm, nice dreams.).

And at 10:52 her response arrived: "Djakuju tobi. tezh troshky zmerzla. zalazhu zaraz pid teplu kovdru ta chytatymu Shultsa abo Krystevu-sova, shcho porobysh)." That translates something like: "Thank you. I'm a little chilled too. I'm going to lie down under a warm blanket and read a little Schulz or Kristeva – I'm a night owl, what can you do).

From someone who was, at first impression, like a cat – ready to take flight at the first sign of commotion, Ada turned out to be a lot more conventional and human than just a femme fatale. She was interesting. There were hundreds of interesting people that Nicholas already knew, and hundreds more to meet. The meeting with her mysterious cell phone caller must have lasted just for a few minutes since that happened a little after 9:30 P.M. Unless he was there cuddled up under the blanket with her.... But he highly doubted that. He decided not to send her any more text messages that night. As the clock drew closer toward midnight, Nicholas decided to pour himself a shot of Desna cognac, which eased him into sleep.

VV

Well, it wasn't really VV. It was VV's lead singer Oleh Skrypka, whose last name meant violin or fiddle. While he didn't play the fiddle, he did play guitar and squeezebox accordion. During the concert this particular Sunday evening on April 16, he appeared onstage with background vocals performed by four young women dressed in colorful orange and red Hutsul garb. They were members of some larger vocal group on loan for the night. And behind the shaggy white-haired singer who had made his name in Paris as a chanson singer with his band were: a tall blind drummer who had to be led on stage to his Tama drum set, a traditional *tsymbaly* player, who played an instrument something like a hammer dulcimer, an older trumpet-player from the Opera House orchestra, and a tall younger flautist.

Nicholas had one minor unpleasantness when he entered the theater with Raya. The woman seating them wouldn't let Nicholas enter the seating area of the theater with his light spring jacket on. She insisted that he take his jacket to the coat check.

"Why?" He asked.

"This is the OPERA Theater," she answered haughtily.

"This is a friggin' rock concert," Nicholas thought to himself, but didn't say it out loud except later to Raya after they had been seated. He decided not to fight what he thought was the woman's provincial silliness. He didn't want to check the jacket just because he wanted to escape quickly with Raya after the performance and not wait in line.

The woman also proceeded to insist that Raya check what wasn't actually an overcoat, but a ¾ length flared red suit coat. Raya snapped back at her and said: "This ISN'T an overcoat! Can't you see that?!"

Nicholas applauded Raya's insistence.

They sat in their seats and Nicholas said to Raya: "You know, I've been to opera houses in Paris, London, and New York, and nobody's every questioned my less than black tie dress."

"Yes, she's going to teach you," Raya continued to fume. "I hate that kind of pettiness. But we're not going to let her spoil the evening for us!"

Right at that moment Skrypka walked out on stage dressed in a loose flaxen white peasant shirt. The packed house started whistling, waving and screaming. He started the concert with two love songs. He played acoustic guitar and a flautist accompanied him. He had been just eliminated from the Ukrainian version of the Dancing with the Stars TV show the day before, so the crowd cut loose with their support for him. The communists from the eastern part of the country were holding demonstrations at the Maidan, at Independence Square, in Kyiv and he cracked a joke, saying: "Well, I was back at the Maidan yesterday, and it looks like it's Maidan 1977 all over again with hammers and sickles everywhere...." The crowd responded with hysterical laughter. He, of course, was one of the many singers who played for the crowds sitting out in the cold during the Orange Revolution in 2004.

The previously insistent usher in the middle of the second number decided to seat a mother and daughter right in the row past Nicholas and Raya. Both of them were wearing overcoats....

"Now that's rude," Nicholas said to Raya. "Couldn't she have waited until after the song?"

"Tochno!" She answered. "Precisely! She's going to teach you manners and acts like that."

"No, no, don't worry about it. I'm just laughing out loud about it. Must be post-colonial inferiority complex."

After the two slow love songs, Skrypka picked up his box accordion and got the crowd screaming, clapping, stomping, and swaying. He threw in a French song here and there. After every number young girls or boys dressed in embroidered blouses and costumes walked out onstage to give him flowers or gift bags. The gift that got the biggest reaction was a bright orange-colored tee shirt that in Ukrainian had the message: "Thank God I'm not a Moskal (a Russkie)!"

The concert lasted about an hour and twenty minutes at the end of which Skrypka gave a sweeping wave first with his left and then with his right hand to say good-bye. The crowd erupted into calls for more with scattered "bravos" everywhere. Skrypka came out and did another two songs, then another three times following ovations until the lights went out on stage. The crowd, including Nicholas and Raya, Nicholas's tutor Olenka and her husband, and several of his students and colleagues from the university, stomped and screamed wildly for another five minutes until Skrypka came out, saying this *had* to be the last time. He played the song "Halyu prykhod" (Halya, Come Here), which I later found in a cool live performance on YouTube from French TV: https://www.youtube. com/watch?v=O-TlZEJV9A8.

It was just a super evening and Nicholas had forgotten about the rude woman. But Raya didn't as she let the usher know what she thought about her rudeness while Nicholas waited in line for his jacket.

Nicholas overheard Raya's feisty parting words to the usher: "Where on the ticket does it say you have to check your coat?"

Nicholas just smiled and thanked Raya for being the way she was.

The two of them walked together over to the Halytsky Bazaar to pick up the *marshrutka* #50 that would drop him off at his place on Hyphenated Writer Boulevard and then take Raya home to her apartment on the outskirts of the city. The line for the minibus had about 15 or 20 people, but they managed to squeeze in.

"*Dobranich*," (goodnight) she said to him as he got out at his stop. He replied in kind and waved his hand to her as he stepped out onto the pavement.

IN SEARCH OF THE HIDDEN RIVER

It was a rare Saturday that Raya had half a day off, so she met Nicholas at his apartment at 13/11 Hyphenated Writer Street. "Thirteen plus eleven divided by three equals eight," he thought to himself for a second when she came over in mulling over the address where he was staying. He had previously told her that he'd love to see the Poltva River with his own eyes if he could. So she volunteered to take him. "I know where it is," she said. She was free from noon to 4 P.M. So was he, since he had a meeting with Zhenya at 4 P.M. to go up High Castle Mountain. Zhenya had lived in the city for nearly a year and had never gone up the mountain.

Raya arrived at about 12:30 even though she had said noon. But time is malleable when you agree to meet someone in Leopolis. If he were meeting her at the Shevchenko monument and not at home, he would have waited till 12:30. But since he was just sitting at home listening to his new Haidamaky Carpathian SKA music, playing the song "Love Song" he had heard at their live concert behind the Ratusha and the lively "Na tomu botsi" (On the Other Side) over and over trying to memorize the words, he just waited patiently.

"Can you help me with a word, Raya?" Her face as usual was beaming under her short curly black hair.

"Sure, Nicholas, be happy to."

He pointed out the word "lem" in the lyrics.

"If only," she answered.

"Is it a Lemko word?" The Lemkos were a tribe of Ukrainians who now lived across the Polish border. Nicholas remembered the exotic woman he had met on his flight over was a Lemko.

"Yes, he's saying if only he can get to the other side," in the song.

"Thanks so much! You're a sweetheart!" He was excited about understanding the word in the context of the song. The word reminded him of the sci-fi writer Stanislaw Lem, who had been born in the city of Lviv when it was called Lwow.

Each of the three stanzas of the song ended with the "if only he could get to the other side" formula with three different follow-up collocations: in the first no one will recognize him, in the second someone will fall in love with him, and in the third no one will catch him! All three had exclamation points.

After the song ended, they set off toward the downtown on foot. First to the left on Nechui-Levytsky Street, then to the right across Bandera Street and the quite hideous nearly Social Realist monument to the victims of KGB terror. They took a left a block or so down at a nicely restored building so they could walk next to Ivan Franko Park, in which all the trees were beginning to blossom including magnolias (Raya's favorite), cherry trees, apple blossoms, and forsythia. Though she didn't know the name for forsythia in Ukrainian (named after William Forsyth he was to learn later).

"Let's take a look at the Solomea Krushelnytska Museum…." She pulled Nicholas by the arm to show him the way. They had been there the day before but it was closed.

"We don't have to," was his first response.

"MUsysh," she said, accent on the first syllable. That meant "You HAVE to."

"You lead and I'll follow," Nicholas said to her. "You've never led me to the house of a stupid man," was the rough translation of the Ukrainian saying he said to her.

"There's always a first time," she answered and smiled with her sky-blue-on-a-sunny-day eyes. The sky happened to be blue and sunny that day.

After going up a circular stairway to the second floor, Raya rang the doorbell since the door was locked.

They were preparing for a lecture in one of the rooms of the museum that particular day, but with her usual friendly persuasion Raya convinced the woman who was museum director to let them look through the other rooms, which included a number of period pictures of the opera star who had been famous in France and Italy. He looked her up on the Internet later here:

http://www.orpheusandlyra.com/Krushelnytska.html

http://www.marstonrecords.com/krushelnytska/krushelnytska_liner.htm

After the brief visit to the museum, Raya and Nicholas started off on the trek to find the underground river. They walked over to a spot behind the Opera House to pick up a *marshrutka*. Nicholas forgot which number it was and, as usual, there wasn't much room in it, so Nicholas gave a seat to Raya and stood next to her for the ten minutes or so they traveled toward the outskirts of town. Raya kept looking out the window and finally tugged at Nicholas's arm to exit the dingy microbus near a traffic circle.

Raya walked up to four or five different people on the street asking them where to find the Poltva.

A woman with a plastic shopping bag answered, "Why would you want to find it? The water's the color of liquid excrement."

Another elderly man in wire-rimmed glasses said, "It's there, you just can't see it."

A man wearing an old dusty black leather jacket responded, "There used to be a river here. I don't know where it's gone."

A fourth one, who also didn't know where it was, said: "There are awful black streams of water there." (*Strashni chorni potoky vody*)

And finally a group of three or four people responded, "It's way up the street now. You have to go a few kilometers to find it."

"I'm sorry, Nicholas," Raya said. "The best I can do is show you where it used to be."

So they walked across the street to the other side of the unkempt grass traffic circle to a dusty rock-strewn area where a giant rusted tin pipe nearly a meter in diameter angled into a dilapidated small wooden building. Nothing flowed through it, no water, no liquid excrement.

"I'm sorry, Nicholas." Raya said to him as he looked into the building.

"I'm not," he answered. "Thanks! It was great to come out to look for it with you. It's more interesting *not* to find an invisible river."

So they walked over to the *marshrutka* stop across the traffic circle to take it to *Pidzamche*, the neighborhood at the base of High Castle Mountain. Since Nicholas still had some time before his next meeting, they walked to take a look at a Catholic church where a wedding ceremony was about to take place and after that to an Orthodox church closer to High Castle Mountain. Nicholas took a picture of the Orthodox church reflected in a window.

HIGH CASTLE MOUNTAIN, BALD MOUNTAIN, AND SHEVCHENKIV HAI WITH ZHENYA

Nicholas met Zhenya right at 6 P.M. In fact, at 3:55, Nicholas got a call on his cell phone. "I'm five minutes away," he said. He was still passing time with Raya at the *kitschok*, the outdoor bazaar that sold kitchy things next to the Zankovetsky Theater. Raya was looking for a birthday gift for one of her young nephews.

Nicholas was still somewhat annoyed with Zhenya for not showing up the day before for a 6 P.M. time they were supposed to go up the mountain. Some emergency had come up with the software at the Ukretelekom offices and she had to iron it out. She also had a supervisor from Kyiv come to town, so she had to entertain him. It was part of the job description. Nicholas had text-messaged her at 5:40 to check if she was going to meet him. She said, quite telegraphically when she called him back, "Give me till seven. Meet you at the Opera House. I'll call to verify." But she never called to verify and she never showed up.

Before that Nicholas had a latte with Mr. Viktor at the Italian Courtyard Café until about 5 P.M., and as they were walking out of the building, ran into Jan Shchurakiwsky who said, "Let's go for a beer." Mr. Viktor had to leave, so Shchurakiwsky and Nicholas went to the Dzyga Café where it turned out to be closed "na remont" (for remodeling). So they moseyed down the street to the Armenian Ararat Café where they both ordered a pint of beer on tap. Nicholas was a little bit hungry, so he ordered his favorite snack food – "deruny" with sour cream, fried potato pancakes. Shchurakiwsky was not in a particularly talkative mood that day. Something was preoccupying him. When the check arrived,

Nicholas picked it up and said "I'll take care of this one." Jan said "You sure?" And Nicholas said it was a little one and pulled out a twenty-hryvna note to pay for the fifteen-hryvna bill (about three dollars). He had told Jan he needed to meet someone at seven at the Opera House, so they parted ways.

Nicholas went over to the Opera House and walked around for about half an hour, looking at the old men playing chess or checkers with crowds of 4-5 other old white-haired men looking over their shoulders. There were kids playing and every once in a while renting a small electric car to ride around the plaza in front of the Opera House. There were young couples on the dark green wooden benches, occasionally stealing a kiss. But Zhenya didn't show up, didn't call, and Nicholas decided that it was up to her explain things. He was doing her a favor. So he walked home and tried not to think about her not calling or letting him know. It was just rude. "Maybe she has an explanation," he thought. But there was no call or text message all evening. So Nicholas just went to sleep and tried not to think about it. He also tried not to think about it the next morning and just read and puttered around the house. Precisely at 10 A.M. his cell phone rang. It was Zhenya. "I'll be there in five minutes if that's okay? I need to talk to you...." "Sure, it's okay," he answered reluctantly. He hadn't shaved, hadn't showered, so he ran to the bathroom and took what in the good old politically incorrect American days they used to call a whore's bath – quickly slapping soap and water under his armpits and wherever else he could easily reach, drying it off and throwing on a pair of jeans and tee shirt. He was in the middle of throwing on the tee shirt when she knocked at the door.

"Can we meet at four today?"

Nicholas was irritated about yesterday's non-meeting but tried not to let it show. It showed anyway in his faux indifference.

"Are you really free today?"

"Yes!"

"For how long?"

"All evening. I told them I can only work till 4 P.M. today no matter what happens."

"Okay," he answers. "Where?"

"In front of the Opera House. I'll be there with a driver from the company."

"Why do you need a driver?"

"To take us up the Mountain."

"No, no, no, Zhenya, that's not how it works. You WALK up the hill to have *povnyj kaif* (total bliss), to get the totality of the experience. I'm not going up it in a car until I'm in a wheelchair."

"Okay, okay, I'll be there at four. I wasn't sure how far it was away."

"It's a five minute walk to the base of the metal steps from the Opera House. Is that close enough for you?"

"Close enough. Gotta run. The driver is waiting for me. I have to fix up some glitches in the software."

While Nicholas was somewhat in a better mood after Zhenya had made the new arrangement to meet with him, he still tried to stay at a respectable distance from her. But she went out of her way to make sure to give him a warm peck on the cheek. The peck must have been the apology that she didn't say in words.

Back to 4 P.M.

He met her right next to the empty circular flowerbed in front of the Opera House that was waiting to be planted. She ran over to him when she recognized him and said, "lead the way."

He pointed across the street to the left and she put her left arm under his arm. The gesture was a warm one and Nicholas could see that she was trying to make up for yesterday – still without an explanation, which would have been the simple American way. But he was a stranger in an alien land that even though it was becoming familiar to him, still had many mysteries.

So they walked up a series of well-worn and cracked cement steps across the street from what looked like a firehouse with a remodeled red roof. Then they followed the road to the left.

"Can you make it up the mountain here in those shoes?" Nicholas asked her. She was wearing mid-size heels, but at least they weren't the pointy stiletto ones that were so popular with all the women in town. "Otherwise we can go along the road around the bend to the bottom of the metal steps."

"Yes, I can make it. These are pretty comfortable." And they moved along the dusty and rocky path, taking foothold on roots that were sticking an inch or two out of the ground.

"It's a pretty long way up. I'm not used to exercising like this," Zhenya mentioned to him as she huffed and puffed a bit.

"Almost there," Nicholas answered. "Then we walk up the concrete and metal steps to the radio station."

"Then there's more climbing?" She asked.

"Yes-yes, you need to circle around the last hill to get to the observation point.

Lots of different names were etched mostly in white on the steps – mostly in Ukrainian, a few in Russian. There were also more than a few of the "Volodya loves Vika" type and vice versa and in many other combinations. Zhenya was fascinated by an ancient stone wall past the radio station and asked Nicholas to take a few pictures there by it. This really wasn't the place where Prince Danylo's castle was built. It was a garrison constructed by the Poles on High Castle Mountain. The real original castle was on a nearby hill, but it had been carted away stone by stone and brick by brick and used in the old stone wall of the Bernadine Monastery at the edge of the Old Town where Lychakiv Street begins.

The last part of the trek to the top was along a stone path circling the last hill. The metal railing was gone in spots and it had a flagpole in the middle of it with the Ukrainian flag flapping above it. At the base of the flagpole there was a bronze marker marking the four directions. A young girl who looked to be about 18 overheard Nicholas say that it looks like it's in German – the "S" means Sud (south in English too) and the O means Ost or east. He knew that because his family members were Ostarbeiters (workers from the east) when the Nazis captured them. The young girl argued with him at first saying they were in English. But she quickly realized the O couldn't have been east in English and acquiesced to Nicholas's explanation.

High winds were really snapping the flag that particular day. The stone observation deck on top of the mountain and the paths to it were strewn with bottle caps, empty bottles carelessly tossed this way and that, and broken bits of glass everywhere from bottles of various libations. You could hear Polish, Russian, Ukrainian, German and Italian being spoken at the highest point in Leopolis. There was a teenage girl sitting with the top of her crack exposed with a bunch of her teenage friends looking out over the city. Nicholas laughed and almost took a picture of her with the zoom lens of his camera. He restrained himself.

Zhenya wanted a picture of herself with the view showing behind her. Nicholas obliged with a few shots.

"Who is that man over there on the other mountain?" She asked him from behind her dark glasses.

"Looks like he's taking pictures," Nicholas muttered back.

"Can we get there?"

"I'm not sure. I've never been up there before, but I think Mr. Viktor said you can get up there if you take the cement steps down and follow the road to the left. We can try that if you'd like."

After breathing in the crisp fresh air and sunshine and taking pictures in every direction, Nicholas and Zhenya started to walk down the stone steps. While they were coming down the concrete steps Zhenya asked Nicholas to take a picture of her near a patch of lavender wildflowers. Right after taking the picture, a girl about age 20 or so with a bottle of Lviv Brewery 1715 Premium Lager stumbled tipsily past Nicholas.

"How about one of me?" She flashed a smile and pulled her hands apart in the air to reveal her partly unbuttoned blouse with revealing cleavage underneath. She was obviously proud of her endowments.

Nicholas obliged and she flashed him a big smile and a wink. She was with four other young guys behind her. One of them said out loud, "That's not fair. They always take the pictures of the girls and not us guys!"

"Hey, *khloptsi* (guys)," Nicholas said to them. "She asked very nicely. If you ask me politely I'd be happy to take your picture too!"

"No, no, no," they answered laughing and kept moving on their way.

When Zhenya came over to him Nicholas remarked to her with a smile, "Well, if I had been on my toes I would have asked her for her phone number."

"You seem to forget you're with *me* today," she smiled as she interrupted him. "I would have killed you."

"I think this road leads to the other mountain," Nicholas chose to ignore her comments. "I'm pretty sure we can get there."

So they moved in the direction of the other mountain, looking at flowers, mostly bright yellow forsythia, on the way.

There was a visibly worn path up the side of bald mountain opposite to where they were, so they decided to climb up it. This was *Lysa hora*, Bald Mountain, a sacred place of witchery and the gathering of demonic agencies. Barrenness was the sign of evil. Mussorgsky composed his "St. John's Eve on Bald Mountain" for *Pictures at an Exhibition*. That was a different bald mountain near Kyiv. And St. John's Eve near the summer solstice in June was a night of magic and witchery.

There are many bald mountains in Ukraine, especially in the Carpathians, places for nocturnal netherworldly creatures. A witches' sabbath was taking place at the base of this particular bald mountain on the east side. A group of younger people, mostly in their twenties and dressed in black, were dancing in a circle, chanting and singing. Nicholas decided not to approach any closer to the revelers since sunset would soon be descending. He remembered "A Night on Bald Mountain" from *Fantasia* from his childhood. He recalled, too, for whatever reason, that the animator for that was Volodymyr "Bill" Tytla, a child, like Nicholas, of Ukrainian emigrants.

At the top of the mountain where no grass or lichen or tree grew, there was a nicely built wooden observation platform. There was also a quite plain gray cross with a plaque to honor the Ukrainian victims of the Afghan War. Over fifty per cent of the soldiers from the Soviet army sent to the Afghanistan war were Ukrainians, including Nicholas's friend Andriy Yurkevych. At the top of the mountain there was a good clear view of High Castle Mountain with more tourists at the spot where he and Zhenya just had been.

As Nicholas decided to look down a nearly vertical path up the side of the mountain, he saw the inebriated girl whose picture he had taken earlier with another fuller bottle of Lviv Brewery 1715 Premium Lager in her hand. She was stumbling and teetering a bit backward on the sandy white path just as she was about to step onto the wooden observation deck. Nicholas had his camera in his hands and snapped a picture of her, then he held out his hand to keep her from falling backward.

"Thank you," she said with a sheepish smile.

"Where are you from?" Nicholas asked her.

"Donetsk," she answered. "I'm here visiting my friends from Lviv. Those guys." And she pointed to them coming up the mountain path behind her and walked away toward them bottle still in hand.

Nicholas expected to feel a sense of evil or at least some kind of foreboding on this the first bald mountain he had ever climbed. Myths and legends are what you make of them in your mind.

After taking a descent down along a more level path on the backside of the mountain, Nicholas suggested to Zhenya that they take a walk through "Znesinnya" Park. The name came from "Voznesinnya," meaning Ascension. The part was thinning out in the early evening as they walked along a wooded path.

"The meadow's great," Nicholas mentioned to Zhenya. "I just don't know if it's open this late."

"It's worth a try. I'm not in a rush."

When they reached the entrance, a soldier was guarding it, announcing to Nicholas that it's closed.

"Can't we just look around a bit?" Zhenya asked him with one of those coy smiles that Ukrainian or any other military or uniformed guy can never refuse.

"For two-fifty," this particular military guy said, as he turned his face away from her.

Nicholas pulled out a five-hryvna note and the guard slipped it into his pocket.

It was still light enough to walk around the paths to see the various wooden houses and churches that were built without a single nail. During the walk back to the park entrance, Nicholas heard the melodic sounds of evening vespers emanating from St. Michael the Archangel Church. Strange that Nicholas had not made good friends with anyone named Mykhailo here – Michael, though he had met a fellow Fulbrighter named Michael at the first orientation he went to in Kyiv.

As he and Zhenya listened to the service, he remembered Old Church Slavic words from liturgies he had attended in his younger days. An incredibly thin elderly nun gave both him and Zhenya a beeswax candle to hold during the service. It was strange that they also chanted the Greek "Kyrie Eleison" in the Old Church Slavic service.

Nicholas, though he didn't have a particularly good voice, or so he thought, chanted along with the priest, the deacon, and the ten or so people gathered in the vestibule of the small chapel. The service lasted about half an hour and Nicholas felt his spirit uplifted.

Nicholas didn't see Zhenya again after the day spent in exploration of a Lviv she lived in but hadn't really seen in six months of physically being there. She just got too busy at work. Zhenya at one point did ask Nicholas to spend a week with her in Sharm El Sheikh, Egypt on her upcoming vacation. Nicholas at first thought it might be exotic and fun since he had never been there. Separate rooms, of course. Egypt and the Turkish coast had become the main tourist destinations for the new breed of Ukrainians with disposable cash, and Zhenya had disposable cash. But after mulling it over and after hemming and hawing, Nicholas decided to say "no." He called it his non-flight to Egypt. He decided instead to spend as much time as he could with Raya, who was always there for him, as well as with his other friends.

A CALL FROM A DISAPEARING
AND REAPPEARING WOMAN

"Allo," with accent on the second syllable, Nicholas answered the phone in Ukrainian. He recognized the voice and he felt his heart quiver or palpitate or whatever hearts do sometimes when they are surprised to hear from someone as beautiful as she. It was of course SHE again, the unknown woman. She sounded nervous.

"How are you?"

"I'm doing fine. I had a lot of exercise yesterday walking around the city with a friend. We walked around Znesinnya Park and over to Shevchenkiv Hai. And I spent about three hours looking for the Poltva before that. So I'm just sipping a coffee and resting at home. And how have things been with You?" He said.

"We're on *ty* terms, remember?" He probably slipped into the formal form because he hadn't heard from her in a while – so there was a bit more distance from the previous nice conversation he had had with her at The Golden Ducat Café. Plus he was still feeling the fluster of the initial surprise. But he managed to settle himself down.

"Sorry! How have things been with *you*?" He answered in the correct familiar form with emphasis on the last word.

"Oh, some things are going smoothly, some things not so smoothly, some things even worse," she sighed ever so slightly.

"That just about sums up life," he said, unable to think of anything that might cheer her up.

"That definitely is *my* life." There was a darker tone in her voice for the length of the sentence. After a short pause, she continued, "I'm calling because I wanted to see if you'd like to meet Tuesday or Wednesday for coffee or anything, that is, if you really so *desire*. I'm free then." She put extra stress on the word *desire* and seemed to be hemming and hawing shyly, as if she were not sure of how he would answer. He focused on the word *bazhannya* that she used, which you could translate as "feel like," "wish" or "desire."

"Sure, I'd love to chat with you a bit. I have to teach a class for a friend of mine on Wednesday. And I'm meeting Mr. Viktor for coffee on Tuesday at eleven. We're planning on going to Kyiv together on Friday."

"What's a good time for you?"

"Well, you tend to be a night owl…."

"I'm trying to convert myself into a day person," she interrupted him.

"I'm really free all day Wednesday except for that class that goes from 4:30 to 6 on Wednesday. So just pick a time."

"How about six-thirty? Where would you like to meet?"

"The class is right behind the Post Office."

"So we can meet at the entrance to the Post Office on Doroshenko Street?"

"Well, it's not on Doroshenko Street," Nicholas hypercorrected her. "The main entrance is on that little side street that comes off Doroshenko Street – I forget the name of it."

"Yeah, that's what I meant. I don't know the name of that either."

"See you then."

"Do zustrichi," she answered, which means "till we meet again." She added the Ukrainian single "pa" (ta-ta).

When Nicholas hung up the phone he was energized about meeting her. "Damn, that's only ten minutes away from my apartment," a mildly wicked thought crept into his mind, and he smiled a pleasant smile as his dark brown eyes gleamed. Deep inside, in that inaccessible part of the mind where intuition resides, he also felt danger here – and compassion as well. He felt as if she wanted to say something to him really important, but couldn't. It was strange that his thoughts of her had gone from being nearly dumbstruck by her beauty at his first meeting with her, to a sense of wanting to help her somehow. He'll find out on Wednesday if she plans to share that inner secret with him. It was strange for him to alternate back and forth between feelings of yearning and compassion.

THE WAY TO PARADISE

The way to paradise is through friendship. The green-painted old Soviet-style Café Druzhba, the Friendship Café, is on the left side of Horbachevsky Street as you walk up from Sakharov Street. At the very top of the hill is a dark reddish-brown brick Orthodox Church on General Chuprynka Street. But before you get to the church on the left side is Paradise, Kavovyj Rai, the Coffee Paradise Café, with a bright yellow exterior on the mostly drab street.

Raya called at 9:30 A.M. to invite Nicholas for coffee since she was going to be teaching a class in a university building on General Chuprynka Street at eleven.

"Can you meet me for coffee?" she asked.

"Where?"

"In *Rai*, in Paradise."

"Be happy to meet you in Paradise any time. Just tell me how to get there."

She laughed.

He laughed.

"Meet me in half an hour?"

"Meet you in Paradise. In half an hour." And he smiled a wide smile to himself as he set the receiver down. He was going to meet Raya in *Rai*. Since Paradise was very close to him, he decided to walk over. That's when he learned that you reach Paradise only after you pass through Friendship.

Raya was waiting for him at a small table in a private alcove and had already ordered two cappuccinos and was sipping hers as she was marking up a student's paper.

"You look great today," he said to her when he saw her. "You're sunshine for me even on cloudy days." Wow, he thought to himself. That was dumb, but good she doesn't know the words to "My Girl." It must have been a case of intercultural interference.

"Sure, sure," she said, "but today's a sunny day, so you might not need any more." She seemed to be slightly embarrassed by the attention and touched her curly hair on the side with her left hand and then her right. Nicholas noticed that she almost always made that gesture after he complimented her over something. It was either nervousness or a spontaneous reaction to the compliment.

The interior of Paradise had light green minty walls with palm tree motifs in bas-relief on the walls and a curved white ceiling. They were bamboo stalks cut in half forming trees with palm branches in dried green and deep maroon colors on top. The main room of the café was filled with light from a picture window on the eastern sunny side. Three round glass-covered tables were in the main dining area along with two or three bamboo chairs at each table, and two round bamboo tables for two in an alcove off to the side. Tan stone accents decorated the bottom of the walls and in spots in corners. The coffee bar and counter where an elegant and *potuzhnyj* (powerful) Mercedes Benz of a stainless steel coffee-making machine stood had a tan cork covering with a marbleized black pattern. There were rows of large glass jars of coffee and tea on shelves behind the quite friendly woman operating the coffee maker. She, just like Raya, had a golden smile. "The Golden Ducat is bathed in darkness and Coffee Paradise in bathed in sunlight," the thought occurred to Nicholas.

Raya had precisely one hour for the visit to Paradise because she had to run to a *zustrich*, a meeting. Raya told him that, "You have to see the museum in Brukhovychi! *MUsysh*! You HAVE to."

"When's a good time?"

"Sunday."

"I have to go to Kyiv on Friday and come back Saturday morning, but that should work for me."

"I already arranged for a car. I'll give you a call tonight to let you know what time exactly."

When Nicholas heard that *MUsysh* from Raya, he knew, as usual, that he had no choice.

So he gave her a little pat on the hand as she rushed off to her next appointment with her elfin smile with clear blue eyes.

JOURNEY TO BABYLON AND BACK

Raya sent Nicholas a text message about two hours into his trip to Kyiv with Mr. Viktor on the 6:10 A.M. express train. "Have fun in Babylon with both the he-Babylonians and the she-Babylonians." He couldn't help but smile and showed it to Mr. Viktor who also smiled.Mr. Viktor asked Nicholas to accompany him on a reading of his poetry at the Shevchenko Museum where Nicholas read a few translations of Mr. Viktor's poems into English.

THE PALACE
OF CULTURE BOOK PRESENTATION

The Hnat Khotkevych Palace of Culture in Lviv is a tall red brick building that takes up nearly an entire city block off of Chornovil Street near one of the more crumbling, industrial parts of town. It was about a kilometer away behind the Opera House and past the Lviv Hotel. It would take Nicholas 10 minutes to walk there from downtown. The large building is right next to the main rail line coming into Lviv, and the entire building rocks to a deafening roar when a train passes it. Nicholas realized that his train that passed by it obviously had shaken it on the way to and from Kyiv.

Andriy Yurkevych had just released his latest book and was on the fourth stop in Lviv of his Ukrainian book-signing tour. He asked if he could stay over at Nicholas's place. Nicholas was more than happy to oblige since he had plenty of extra space. The book signing was going to be in the Palace of Culture auditorium along with a concert by the Dead Rooster rock band. While it had a 6 P.M. starting time for the sold out event (tickets cost 15 hryvnas or $3 – a high price for a book signing albeit with a classic rock band), it really started closer to 6:45. Nicholas had complimentary 12th row seats with Vira that Mr. Viktor was kind enough to provide since he knew the Director of the Palace. Mr. Viktor was going to be master of ceremonies of the event and was able to wrangle out five or six tickets.

The novel was about a series of interviews with some enigmatic German guy who disappeared. A lot of people seemed to disappear in Yurkevych's novels. Andriy had arrived at 10 A.M. that morning on the midnight train from Kyiv. After unsuccessfully waiting in line for tickets at the train station for a half hour for his next stop in Uzhorod, he decided to pick up the tickets later and arrived at Nicholas's place at 11.

Following a customary hug and handshake with Nicholas, Andriy asked: "If you don't think it's rude of me, would you mind if I took a quick shower since I couldn't take one on the train?"

"Well, I think we can forgive you for that one," Nicholas answered and pointed to the shower, giving him a towel.

"I have my own towel. Thanks!"

"Yeah, I always love to take a shower after those overnight train rides – to shake the dust of the road off me."

While Andriy was taking his shower, Luda, Nicholas's faculty sponsor from the university, arrived to go over the points she wanted him to cover in a workshop on the American grading and educational system that Nicholas was supposed to give the next day.

"You have 5 *baliv*, a five-point grading system, we have 4, that's the main difference," Nicholas said.

When Andriy stepped out of the shower and exchanged a greeting with Luda, Nicholas asked if he could make him a cup of coffee and breakfast.

"Eating something would be good," Andriy answered. "I'm off caffeine, doctor's orders, so if you have some *travychka*, some herbal tea, that'd be great."

"Want some *nalysnyky*?" Those were cheese-filled rolled pancakes, something like crepes or blintzes.

"Oooh, that sounds great!"

"How many?"

"Two for me."

"And how about you, Luda?"

"One's fine for me."

So Nicholas lit the burner on the gas stove, set the water to boil, and steam-heated the *nalysnyky* in another larger pot.

"These are terrific!" Andriy announced as he bit into the sweet cheese ones flavored with raisins.

"I usually fry mine," Luda added. "Who made these for you? It looks like somebody's been taking good care of you."

"Uhhh, Ulyana," Nicholas stumbled a bit in making up a name as quickly as he could.

"Do I know Ulyana?" She asked.

"Maybe… maybe not," Nicholas answered.

"Sounds like a pseudonym to me," Andriy chipped in.

"Well, a lot of my friends here feed me and take care of me."

He just didn't want to tell her since that was the way tasty rumors start. His Ukrainian tutor Olenka had already started a rumor about him and Raya when she saw them walking together as she was riding a tramcar to work. And it was Raya who had made the tasty *nalysnyky* for him, even though she almost never had time to cook because she was always so busy.

After the raspberry tea and Turkish pot-brewed coffee, Andriy disappeared off into the streets of Lviv where people constantly recognized him, shook his hands and told him how wonderful he was. He was always polite about the attention and never reacted with annoyance. But just like the heroes of his novels, he disappeared until the evening book presentation.

Nicholas had not gone to the Palace of Culture before, so he decided to set off early to find it. It turned out to be really easy according to Raya's hand-written map and directions. Follow the road past the left side of the Opera House until you reach a bridge, right past the bridge turn right at the Jewish monument, and it'll be right there. Nicholas ended up arriving at 4 P.M. and saw Andriy chatting away with the Dead Roosters. All the Dead Roosters were smoking, Andriy had just gone cold turkey a few months earlier and was partaking only of lively conversation.

Nicholas asked Vira to go with him to the reading and concert. She was thrilled to go, but needed to pick up her son from daycare and drop him off with her mother. She said she'd be a few minutes late, so Nicholas waited, and waited, and waited. Several of his other friends arrived, some of them late, and chatted with him for a minute or two including Ada, who had overslept, and Nadya, who was there to meet Ada. The two of them ended up sitting in the balcony because the downstairs seats were sold out. Vira ended up arriving about 45 minutes late. She had told Nicholas she'd be late, but he didn't think it would be 45 minutes. When she arrived by cab, she apologized profusely: "I'm so-so sorry! I couldn't flag down a *marshrutka* or a cab. I finally got this one."

The two of them entered the building and walked into the darkened auditorium that was already echoing with bursts of laughter from parts of Andriy's reading. He was describing his days at the university in the dorms, which seemed to strike a chord with the young audience. Then he started answering questions passed up on pieces of paper from the audience. Mr. Viktor was moderating, and censoring a question or two for too much explicit content. That went on for close to half an hour when Andriy declared he was answering just three final questions, after which he announced a ten-minute break until the concert with Dead Rooster.

Several people seemed to recognize Vira in the lobby and one or two asked for her autograph. One slightly inebriated portly gentleman fawned all over her. "He seems to REALLY like you," Nicholas said to Vira with a smile.

The concert started in precisely ten minutes as Andriy had announced. The first song had the memorable refrain: "then everybody fucks you" about a classified ad for a secretary who'll make $100 a month. It was based on one of Andriy's poems from his last collection of poetry.

"Well, it's not hard to remember the words to that one," Nicholas whispered to Vira as the song finished.

"That's for sure!" She smiled back.

The lead singer was lean and tall with long blondish hair and a Tom Waits-like voice. The band had a definite intense electric guitar sound with a lead guitar, two base guitars, an acoustic guitar, and a drummer. David-Byrne like dance choreography was also the order of the day.

When the concert was over, Nicholas stepped outside with Vira to chat and wait for Andriy, but after an hour of waiting, decided to go inside to check how things were going. The line was still quite long for autographs from the author, so Nicholas stepped up to Andriy and said, "This is my friend Vira. She's an actress. Maybe I'll walk her back home to her apartment. It's not far from Yura (the nickname for St George's Cathedral). Then I can meet you guys later."

Andriy answered that they'd be at Club Kult, since it was the only place in Lviv that late at night you could get something to eat other than at McDonald's.

The night had gotten chillier after the nice sunny day. Nicholas and Vira talked about movies, Nicholas about how a scene from Hitchcock's *39 Steps* was more erotic than anything explicit you'd see on screen. Vira talked about how her boy was learning to read, about how he loved to watch Johnny Depp movies, especially *Pirates of the Caribbean*. When they reached her street, Vira was worried about Nicholas walking over to the club alone.

"Don't worry! I'm a veteran late-night walker in the town. When I see a drunk, I go to the opposite side of the street. I avoid the shadows and only take well-lit streets."

"Still, you're not from here…."

"I'll be fine," and he gave her a goodnight peck on the cheek.

The Club Kult where the band was eating and having drinks with Andriy was filled with pictures of famous and nearly famous Lvivians on the walls in small frames and plaques. The band's picture was right above the table where they were sitting on the wall where there were pictures of the singer Viktor Morozov, the politician Vyacheslav Chornovil who died in a mysterious car crash, the anti-Soviet guerilla leader in WWII Stepan Bandera, the Rector of the Catholic University of Lviv, the historian Mykhailo Hrushevsky, etc.

The service in the bar was slow (which was usual in Lviv) and the bathroom nice (in regal and bright red) with a red neon light inside it. By the time Nicholas arrived from Vira's, everybody had ordered meals plus 100 grams of Uzhorod cognac or a pint of imported beer.

There was a text message from Zhenya to Nicholas about 11 P.M.: "Just got back from Kyiv. I'm tired. Are you in bed?" "No, not in bed. At Club Kult. Come on over," Nicholas answered. She cordially declined his invitation.

"How about 50 grams of the Uzhorod cognac 'na konya' (to the horse)," Andriy announced. Nicholas decided to have a small Lviv light beer instead and also ended up not paying because someone had picked up his check.

"That's too little for you to have to pay," Andriy announced, and ended up paying for most of the bill. "Are you cool with that?"

"Very cool," Nicholas answered. "My turn next time."

"Very cool," Andriy followed up.

After visiting the red neon bathroom, a somewhat inebriated artist offered to drive Nicholas and Andriy back to their place. "It's right in my neighborhood," he said.

"I think we'd rather walk and live," Andriy mentioned to Nicholas out of the inebriated driver's earshot. But the driver was persistent and convinced the two of them to go along with him.

The artist driver stepped on the gas on the curvy winding streets along an art museum, somehow finally coming out on Ivan Franko Street. Nicholas couldn't figure out how that happened since he was taking the curves at breakneck speed.

"Is it possible for you to go any faster on these winding streets?" Andriy sardonically asked the driver as the car lurched to the right, throwing him toward the window on a particularly sharp curve.

"Why slow down?" He answered, and pointed to his art studio in a building on the right side of the street.

"Yeah, that would be too safe," Nicholas added with a smile as he grabbed a handle above the window of the car to try to stabilize himself a little bit.

"How about come over to my place for a drink?" The driver asked.

"How about we do that *next time!*" Andriy answered. "If I live through this ride tonight," he whispered to Nicholas.

But they managed to navigate the winding streets to not quite as winding but still curving Ivan Franko Street that turned into Vitovsky Street, made the left onto Sakharov Street and the final right onto Bohun, which served at the back entrance to Nicholas's apartment.

"I'm getting too old for this," Andriy said to Nicholas after they entered the apartment. "I mean all this drinking and staying up late."

"I know what you mean," Nicholas answered, "And I only had two beers."

They decided on no additional nightcap "na konya" (to the horse) tonight, and the two of them folded out their convertible sleeper couch beds to rest up for the next day. Nicholas had to prepare a little bit for his workshop that he had the next day at noon, so he stayed up another half hour till 3 A.M. writing up a few notes. He was going to wing it, but just wanted to give himself some direction.

IN SEARCH OF CHORTOVA SKELYA, THE DEVIL'S CLIFF

Chortovi skeli, the filmmaker said in Ivan the Ghostseer's underground lair, the Devil's Cliffs. "Take the #2 tram to the end of the line and ask there," he said. "Anybody will tell you how to find them." That's what the dark-haired man said during Nicholas's return visit to Ivan the Ghostseer.

"You're a genius," the guy said to Ivan. "Your poetry, your paintings are genius. People just don't understand genius. Genius is different. People don't want to understand difference."

"Can I read you my latest poem?"

"Of course," he said. And he read it. Nicholas focused on the *potobichnyj* imagery, the other side of life that haunted Ivan. The skulls, the blood, the bones, the body, the self, always coming back to the self and those dark visions. But Nicholas had to run because he was running late for a dinner at his Ukrainian tutor Olenka's house. He took a right turn up Saksahansky Street, when he should have made a left to get to Ivan's house along a different street – Levytsky Street, he found out the name of it later. It was as if some force were confusing him, one external to him but inside his brain. He figured out his mistake in time, but it cost him a good half hour or more. When he finally arrived at Ivan's place much later than he had promised, the filmmaker was there chatting with him. He wanted to make a film about Ivan, and Ivan was deciding whether to let him.

"I didn't like what you did with the last piece of mine you filmed," Ivan said to him. "The singing wasn't right."

"You saw a rehearsal, Ivan. You should have seen the final version. It was *spectacular*."

The image of the Devil's Cliffs intrigued Nicholas. It was something he *had* to see. When he arrived at Olenka's place, he asked her about the Devil's Cliffs.

"You'll never find it," she said. "You have to go with someone. It's a fantastic spot, but it's a good hike. My husband and I will take you there. That guy was wrong when he said the #2 tram will take you there. It's a good hour's walk after that if you know where you're going. You're better off taking a *marshrutka* bus to Vynnyky. If you go by yourself some drunks in the woods will hear your slightly foreign accent when you ask them directions and knock you over the head for the American bucks in your wallet. Better for you to go with us. It's not easy to find."

"You'll protect me?"

"Yes! They'll be afraid of me!" She answered with a big flashing smile. "They're afraid of their own."

The dinner at Olenka's was terrific with lots of homemade wine to wash it down and five or six different salads before the exquisite *nalysnyky* arrived – something like rolled pancakes stuffed with a sugary sweet soft cheese. Jewish culinarians might call them blintzes, but they were softer on the outside, but of the same basic genre.

Olenka's apartment had been remodeled and was really nice – at the very end of Chuprynka Street past the Forestry University with its large treed green plot of land in the middle of it. Some *kruti* types, accent on the last syllable, Mafiosi had moved into the first floor apartment in the building. "Nobody bothers us anymore after they moved in," Olenka said to Nicholas. "It's peaceful and quiet here now. Though they disappear for a couple days at a time when there's a killing in Lviv…. They always get blamed for it. They're decent neighbors, though I get in their face all the time about Ukrainian politics. They're Yanukovych supporters even though they're Ukrainian."

"And they don't bother you about it?"

"No, not at all. They're used to me. I'm *pomarancheva* (orange) through and through." She was a tried and true Orange Revolutionary.

THE DEVIL'S CLIFF OR BUST

Names can be deceiving. That's something Nicholas had learned long ago in his life. Nick Cool Ass – that's what his homonymic nickname was his first year in college according to the always drunken idiots in his college dorm. He learned to accept it with a sense of humor until it wore out its wit and disappeared from common usage. It was, of course, silly and, in his mind, a misnomer. He wasn't a cool ass or a bad ass or any kind of ass except every once in a while as anyone can be when they're drunk or whatever. But he did learn that labels are sometimes more important than the truth.

Chortova skelya, The Devil's Cliff, which was actually used in the singular on maps of the city, conjured up wild associations of a hellish precipice in his mind. *Chort* was the Ukrainian word for devil. It turned out that his tutor Olenka wasn't able to get away from work and family to take him there as she had promised earlier. And when he tried to take the film-maker's advice he had met at Ivan the Ghostseer's to get there on his own, and take the #2 tram to its final stop, no one of the dozen or so people he met on the street or in a park near the tram stop had heard anything about any such cliffs.

Raya, who was more and more becoming his constant guide and companion, eventually showed him the way. And that turned out to be quite ironic. Her name comes from the word "rai" (meaning "paradise" or "of paradise"). It might have been more suitable for Ada (whose name suggested *Ad*, "Hades" or "hell" in Ukrainian) to show Nicholas the devil's ominous-sounding lair on the outskirts of Lviv, a city surrounded by forests. But that never happened for reasons of circumstance or fate.

It turned out that Raya had friends with a car who lived on Trakt Hlynyansky, which was once the main clay road into Lviv in medieval times, not too far away from a path through the woods that led to the ominous sounding cliffs. Raya, who was godmother to her friend Luba's three children, decided to turn the outing into a picnic. Luba and her husband Vadym took backpacks filled with wine and food for the afternoon trek.

It was a hot day as Ivan dropped off the first carload of hikers crammed into the car at the foot of the path to the Cliffs. The quite jovial and talkative Vadym came back with a second carload that included a few of his friends who had decided to make a day of it too.

Last year's leaves and the broken stubble of dried branches lined the forest floor as the trail snaked through along a gentle upward slope. Shards of sunlight broke through the foliage of the tall trees above in random spots on the forest floor. The higher up they walked, the more small rocky crags jutted up at the edge of ravines. Raya, in her light blue denim sun cap, was busy chatting mostly with her friends, and Nicholas decided to divert his attention to their seven-year old daughter Larysochka, who took a particular liking to him.

"Aren't you afraid of going to the Devil's Cliffs?" He asked her.

"Not when I'm with you," she said brightly. "Those are just words."

"Just words," he thought to himself. "Just words… Words have meanings though…."

Larysochka had beautiful sky blue eyes that reminded Nicholas of Raya's. She insisted that Nicholas hold her hand as they walked. "Well, I sure don't have any problems attracting the little ones!" He thought to himself. "Now if I could just translate that into the bigger ones, then I'd really be in trouble!" He continued his thoughts. "But maybe I'm untranslatable."

Larysochka was a pure joy and a bundle of energy, dragging him to the tops of every jutting rock formation they came near and to the edge of every precipice. Nicholas chased after her every time, making sure she was safe. She was totally fearless, dragging him to the very top of even the most precarious spots. His adult fear of heights along with a sense of responsibility for her safety kept restraining him. In this very short time over the course of the morning Nicholas had learned to love this child and with his entire being he wanted to shield her from harm. It didn't matter what happened to him, as long as she was safe. She climbed the highest hills and descended to the base of an outcropping to find a cave. Nicholas sensed something precarious beyond the mouth of the cave and drew her inquisitive mind away from it. There was something there, something dark, something that might cause her harm. A child's curiosity, the ability to be a child again without the deep-rooted fear of decades of life experience, and the insatiable drive to protect life were good lessons, but ones that required a precarious inner sense of balance.

When they finally reached the actual spot of the Devil's Cliffs, Nicholas failed to see anything demonic about them at all. They were more beautiful than devilish, just a tall outcropping of rocks, supposedly where the devil once had spat in folk belief, where people ranging from expert mountain climbers ready to practice their sport not too far from the city to picnickers and young lovers gathering. The remainder of the day was spent enjoying good conversation along with the food and libations that were brought for the journey. After they had all hiked back to the edge of the forest where civilization began, little Larysochka began to cry when she realized that Nicholas had to leave with Raya. "My mom and dad like you. You can live at our house," she said in tears as her father Vadym carried her away.

One thing Nicholas noticed after he returned home and looked at the pictures he had taken was that there were two caves at the Devil's Cliffs. One was at the spot that Larysochka had discovered, the cave of darkness, the cave that instilled in him a premonition of dread and that pushed him way like a mountain climber repelling against a rock mountain. The other was a cave of light on the side of the Cliffs whose entrance formed a triangle. Nicholas didn't walk through the portal that was bathed in sunlight then, but in retrospect he knew it was there. Today he learned not to fear a name alone. Not all words can harm you.

THE LION AT THE GOLDEN DUCAT

There was a spate of email messages from Ada on a cloudy Friday at the end of April. The town would be clearing out for a long May Day holiday weekend the next day. Old Soviet holidays never die, especially when you have a few extra days to imbibe libations. But Ada was being persistent.

"What's you're mood like?" (Ada)

"As usual good. And Yours?" (Nicholas)

"A working one, trying not to open the blinds, to work a little longer and not get distracted by spring." (Ada)

"I wish you fruitful work." (Nicholas) It didn't sound as stilted in the original Ukrainian as it does in English.

"Do you have time today for melted chocolate in the evening?" (Ada)

"I'll know around two. I'm waiting for a call. I'm free all day tomorrow." (Nicholas)

"Make it tomorrow. I'll SMS you." (Ada)

"Okay." (Nicholas)

Nicholas received an SMS the next day that startled him from a brief early afternoon nap. It said:

"RU free tday?"

"Sure," he typed in groggily.

"18:30 by the king?"

"By an Elvis Presley statue" was the first thought that came to Nicholas's mind since the words "the king" elicited that particular knee-jerk association from him as a child of American pop culture. "Ah, she must have in mind the Prince Danylo statue," was his second thought.

"By the Galician Bazaar?" (Nicholas)

"Yes."

"Sounds good."

"Can we make it 19:00?"

"Sure. Till then"

Nicholas got a little work done at home before he set off. He noticed on his clock that he was running a little late. He had 13 minutes to get there, but he knew it would take him 15 or so even with the best shortcuts he knew. He decided not to take a *marshrutka* minibus, just because they were so crowded and unpleasant to ride in.

Nicholas was running a little late – just by a few minutes – but he hated to be late, so he picked up his pace. He did manage to arrive at 7:02 P.M. as he crossed the street to the monument where Ada was standing.

She seemed like any other woman waiting at a monument to meet someone for coffee or a drink. She didn't look particularly femme fatalish and had a nice smile of recognition when she saw him.

"Where'd you like to go?" She asked.

"I'm fine with anywhere you'd like."

"Why don't you choose?"

"I'm mellow. Really, I just want to go where you'd like to go."

"Then let's go to the Ducat. I like it there."

"Fine with me, unless you want to try the Blue Bottle."

"No, let's go to the Ducat."

So they walked over the two blocks toward Ruska Street. Along the way Nicholas pulled out close to a hundred kopecks in change to give to a particularly bedraggled old woman beggar in a scarf. He just pulled the money out of his pocket and dropped it into her cup.

THE REST OF THE STORY WAS REMEMBERED THE SAME WAY BY BOTH NICHOLAS AND A CERTAIN NARRATIVE CONSCIOUSNESS

Ada was very bubbly and happy this evening, which was still warm but turning crisp. She was wearing a black leather coat this time.

"You're walking very fast," she said to him. "Are you in a rush to go somewhere?"

"No, no, not at all. I'm sorry about that. I was rushing over to meet you so as not to be too late. Inertia, you know. I'll slow down to whatever pace you like." He had spent so much time with Raya that he automatically walked at Raya's quicker pace, which was always as if she were rushing through a museum to see everything before it closed.

Ada's pace was slower, a mosey on a lazy evening. Ada descended first down the steps and asked if there were any tables available. There were actually three open, so they sat down at the one in the middle of the three tables on the right side.

"This one's not as cramped as the first one," Nicholas mentioned to her.

"It's a little wobbly though? Do you think we can fix the wobble?" Ada asked as she sat down and placed her two hands on the table.

"We'd need to find something to put under one of the legs – or move to another table."

"No, no, let's just stay here. It'll be fine. I'll just be careful. I'm glad you were free."

"Yeah, I'm going tomorrow to Kamianets-Podilsky to see the castle."

"I've never been there. Who're you going with?"

"Oh, a couple friends. My friend Raya arranged it all with a friend of hers Ivan, who has a car and travels a lot. And we've invited a Polish art historian to come along for the ride by the name of Renata."

"Sounds great. I'll be going to Lithuania for two days for a conference early next week, so I'll be out of town. I'm trying to get a lot of work done. I have three articles to finish, and each one is taking me forever. I've been working from 10 A.M. till 10 P.M. the last couple of days. So there's a lot of stuff to look up on the Internet and in the library. This is my first break. How did you like the Yurkevych book presentation?"

"It was really great, what I caught of it. The friend I was waiting for was about 45 minutes late. So I only caught the end of the reading and the question and answer session. And we stayed for the concert afterward."

"I think Yurkevych doesn't understand women," Ada's lips pursed nervously as if she had bit into a lemon.

"Who does?" Nicholas answered. "I mean to say, any man who claims to understand women doesn't have a clue. I sure don't pretend to. I know Andriy really well. He's been married to the same woman all his life. He hasn't fooled around any time I've been around him – despite a lot of temptations. Women are all over him like groupies at a rock concert trying to grab a piece of Mick Jagger's shirt and tear it off for a souvenir."

"I don't think you understand me."

"That's my point! You're a woman! And I don't understand you!" Nicholas smiled widely to make sure she understood he was kidding.

"You might understand a little more than you think you do…. Do you think you need to be a woman to understand a woman?"

"Emotions are emotions, people are people," Nicholas said. "And there are all different kinds of people."

They seemed to be talking a bit at cross-purposes, but in a friendly way. Ada continued to play with her folded up napkin as if it were a piece or origami that she was crafting and uncrafting, and alternatingly looking down at the folded napkin and up into Nicholas's eyes.

"Don't you psychologically analyze people ever?" She asked.

"Maybe just for fun…. I try to avoid it though…."

The waitress arrived right at that moment and Ada ordered melted chocolate with cherries and Nicholas the apple strudel and a Columbian coffee with milk.

While they were waiting for their order, Nicholas noticed a demonic-looking lion in the center alcove of the wall of the Ducat. He had never noticed it before on his previous visits.

The strudel wasn't as tasty as he had his previous time at the café, but the coffee was superb.

"I've been here several times, and for whatever reason, I've never looked closely at that lion's face before."

"It's always been there," Ada responded and looked closely at it herself. "It really looks nasty or evil," she said to him, "not that I believe in evil."

"Yeah, it has a certain look to it – as if it's listening to us or watching us. I'll have to see how it came out on pictures I took before in the Ducat. The ones I took without a flash came out great."

"The flash evens out the lighting and takes away the variations of light."

The conversation went on for a while in a quite amiable way without any of the tension Nicholas felt the previous time there with Ada. Ada seemed much more relaxed with him, more comfortable. And she seemed more human to him and off the previous mythic pedestal he had put her on in his mind. There were no telephone calls to her cell, though she did look at it once to check the time. About nine thirty she said it was time to go. She had to meet someone at the Post Office.

"We can walk over together? You live in that direction."

"Sounds good."

Nicholas paid the small seventeen-hryvna bill and walked up the steps with her out of the basement café onto the cobblestone street. He made a special effort to walk slowly with her this time, down Doroshenko Street, then making a left in front of the Central Post Office.

"Would you like to go to the theater with me sometime?" She asked him. "I'll check what's playing at the Kurbas Theater."

"That'd be great," he said. "I've been to the theater once for *The Good God of Manhattan*. The guys who played the two squirrels in the play nearly ruined it for me with their firecrackers, wisecracks and antics. But the lady in pink was terrific in that. Though when she got naked, I ended up realizing that I preferred the mystery of her when she was wearing pink."

"I'll check on tickets and see what's playing. They usually have shows on Friday, Saturday and Sunday."

"I just have to go to the Valley of the Narcissuses next Sunday. There's a busload of us going."

They stopped right in front of the entrance to the Post Office and chatted for a minute or two. Then Ada pulled out her cell phone and made a call. Nicholas moved away from her a bit to give her some privacy.

"No need to move away," she said.

"It's habit. Just wanted to give you some space to make your call. You know, in case you needed to say something personal."

"No, no, don't need to do that. If I need privacy I'll walk away myself."

In a minute or so a dark red, recent vintage car pulled up and stopped. A solidly-built guy with close-cropped hair stepped out of the driver's side. Nicholas said "good-bye" to Ada and shook hands in a friendly handshake. He wasn't sure if it was her brother, boyfriend, or bodyguard, but decided he didn't want to find out. Happy that the evening had turned out well, he moved toward Copernicus Street and made a right turn to follow the tramcar tracks that would guide him home.

Nicholas would only see Ada one more time during his stay. She left the country to visit her father in Greece and would return just before his departure. He did manage to take a picture in The Golden Ducat of Ada's hands holding a glass candleholder with a glowing orange flame. She wouldn't let him take a picture of her face.

WAITING ON LIBERTY AVENUE

Waiting on Liberty Avenue is a special art. It's always hard to find a spot on a park bench when the weather is sunny as it was today. You don't want to impinge on young lovers or the old men playing chess, checkers or cards. You finally find a place next to an older heavyset woman who is built like a bouncer at a nightclub, but she's really quiet and nice. You just sit there and let the sun bounce off you with its warmth. Pigeons come up to you until they realize you have nothing to give them today. Then they move away just like all the other beggar species. Lots of people walk by in both directions toward and away from the Opera House. Guys who look like they're *kruti* (bad asses) in black leather coats. Lots of students in blue jeans, girls still in just-below-the-knee leather boots, women in heels, three girls walking arm-in-arm and smiling, a couple of thirtyish-looking short-haired women in sensible and comfortable *krossovky*, running shoes, a hunched over older lady in a dirty old tan raincoat and wearing a faded blue scarf.

You can see the History Museum from where you're sitting, a couple of outdoor cafés covered with awnings, the more ritzy yellow stucco Viennese Café in the distance, a platinum blonde leather-clad lady in tight leather slacks and a black soft leather jacket with studs, a girl sneezing with less of a hard-ass leather look.

The wind picks up a bit and it's getting colder. Time to move on. Raya said she'd be free at three, but it's quarter to four already. She probably got caught up rushing from one place to another as usual, but you hadn't really made concrete plans, even though you did really want to see her. Especially today.

Then you see a Yankee baseball cap on a guy who probably doesn't know what the Yankees are, then a guy in a black leather jacket who could have passed for an Elvis impersonator in Elvis's more corpulent stage. The sun now hides behind a cloud and it's time to move. This is how time passes slowly sometimes, waiting for something to happen, or someone. When it doesn't happen it doesn't. But that's good. Sometimes you need that. You learn to wait patiently in the city of Leopolis.

THE *KHALEPA*

Nicholas liked the word (accent on the second syllable). Kha-LEP-a… It just rolls off your tongue. It is one of those intrinsically fascinating Ukrainian words that has profound meaning in the very shape of the sound of its three syllables. You can *potrapytysya* or *popasty v khalepu*, which the dictionary defines as "to come to grief," "to get into trouble (into a scrape)," "to get into a pretty mess." To get into a fine mess was the definition that Nicholas felt fit the best.

Nicholas felt the sense of a *khaLEPa* awaiting him. It wasn't something he could rationally explain with his five senses or logically in any way. It was like the black clouds you see approaching in the distance on an otherwise sunny day. The cosmic winds are blowing in your direction, and the *khaLEPa* is inevitable.

KAMIANETS-PODILSKY

When Raya had told Nicholas that *ty MUsysh*, that he just HAD to see Kamianets-Podilsky, he knew that there was no choice and no reason to roll the stone of a negative response up the hill. "You're always right!" He said to her. "You've never led me to anything bad. But as they say in English, there's always a first time." She smiled with her eyes and pursed lips that had a touch of pink lipstick when he said that to her. She told him to be ready at 6:40 A.M. at the tram stop across Sakharov Street for the car that would take them. Or she'd come by in a taxi and drive over to the car they were going to use for the trip. She had arranged for Ivan, the husband of her good friend Valya from Kolomiya, to take them on the three-hour drive.

The drive to Kamianets-Podilsky was a bumpy one. The highway was one-lane in each direction with hundreds if not thousands of potholes. The sky was cloudy and gray, and a drizzle alternating with a slightly heavier rain was falling. Ivan was a sure and steady driver who passed every truck and slow-moving vehicle he could with care. He sat in front with Raya and Nicholas in the back seat with Renata.

Both Nicholas and Renata were on the sleepy side and not particularly talkative in the early morning hours. They dozed off for more than forty winks at a time off and on, chatting a bit in between winks when their sleep and waking cycles coincided with a jarring bump in the road.

They passed by village after village that looked appleblossomy, as the poet Pavlo Tychna once wrote. Everything certainly was intensely appleblossomy. The white blossoms covered the roadsides, particularly in the clusters of villages on the way. After about a hundred or so kilometers, they arrived at a traffic circle in the road that took them through Ternopil (Thornyopolis or Thorny

Field Town in English), which was a large city with a tremendous amount of new building of mid-rise apartment houses going up. Ten or twelve high rises were being built on the outskirts of the city. Ternopil, in fact, was the regional center from which Nicholas's father's family had come. They were going to come close to his father's family's native village near Zalishchyky, the place beyond the forests, but they took a right turn toward Kamianets-Podilsky before they got there. Everyone in Nicholas's family had left or had died, so since there was no one to visit except at the graveyard, Nicholas decided not to ask Ivan to drive out of his way to the ancestral village.

The gray drizzle seemed to dull the colors of blossoming spring into a monotonous gray. Fields seemed dark and distant because of the rain. There were lots of gas stations with minimarkets, so the roadside services looked a lot like those in rural America or on Interstates. Several of the names of villages on signs particularly intrigued Nicholas. Sukhostav (Dry Pond) was one of the first ones that struck his fancy. If the pond were dry, why would they call it a pond anymore? It's just a hole…. And then there was Vyhoda (Comfort) and Druzhba (Friendship). Two demonic names really struck him – Chortkiv (The Village of Little Devils) and Sataniv (Satan's Village). That's what the names really were! Nicholas even remembered reading an article on a Ukrainian writer who was born in Sataniv, The Village of Satans – Vasyl Barka. Barka, whose real name was Otcheret, actually became a religious writer who wrote a novel *The Yellow Prince* about the Holodomor, the starving of over six million Ukrainians by Stalin in the 1930s. So after Barka left Satan's village he took a different path.

There was a sign on the roadside by the forest that read in big letters: "THE FORESTS ARE THE LUNGS OF THE EARTH." The elevation seemed to go up past Ternopil as they passed furrowed hills, deciduous forests, and small villages, each one with a tan, white or gray stucco church with a silver or occasionally golden cupola. The churches all seemed to occupy a central position in each village or be right there at the roadside. The village houses were built close to the road with white wet apply blossoms bursting on the trees and in orchards all over along the roadside.

In the village of Orishkivtsi there was a large roadside bright white Madonna of recent vintage with arms open and two kneeling angels with a tall niche behind her. The forests were decidedly deciduous with the apple blossoms by the village houses and in orchards near the road giving way to walnut trees the higher the car seemed to climb up the gentle slope. Where there weren't thick forests along the roadside, there seemed to be a lot of trees planted to provide a wind and snow barrier. The literally dozes of tiny roadside chapels were more plentiful than McDonalds in the US, but some as small as a telephone booth....

Nicholas had been in a semi-dream-state when the car stopped in Kamianets-Podilsky. The first part of the first word of the city's name meant stone, and when Ivan stopped the car to park by the entrance to the stone castle, Nicholas could see why. The whole town, built on the sides of a giant ravine and a small river or stream, seemed to be gray, grayish tan, and stony. There weren't many people there at that moment by the castle, probably because of the rain, but Nicholas rushed to pay for the entrance fee for everyone. He managed to pull out a twenty-hryvna note quicker than anyone else.

The castle itself was in a state of being slowly restored, probably much in the way it must have originally been.

"What are all the wooden carts doing in the castle courtyard?" Nicholas asked.

Raya ran up to a workman who was near the carts and asked. When she came back she said: "Next month they're going to film *Taras Bulba* here. Jerzy Hoffman is going to be the director."

"I heard from somebody it was supposed to be done by the Russian director who did *The Master and Margarita*."

"No, he definitely said Hoffman."

"That's great!" Nicholas added. I loved his *With Fire and Sword*. Hoffman at least knows something about the period and the Ukrainian perspective on things. It should be interesting."

There was a light drizzle and the clouds were gray, and since Nicholas had a hood on his jacket, he offered his umbrella to Raya.

"No, no thanks!" She said. "You use it."

"I have a hood! I don't need it."

"I can get wet," she added.

"And you can also stay dry," he insisted until she took it. It was also a windy day, so everyone had to keep from having their umbrellas flipped inside out.

They first went into a room on the right that had a small nondescript museum in it. There was nothing particularly impressive there – some old cannons, weapons, and even an orange-colored Orange Revolution tent with a "Yushchenko, tak!" (Yushchenko, yes!) banner on it. The next room they entered was some kind of mill in a large circular turret with wooden ladders going straight up into other rooms above. They passed a giant well in the middle of the castle courtyard encased in a stone room with a roof. Then they moved into an unremodeled cavernous underground room that had absolutely no lighting in it. Nicholas lit the way with the light from his cell phone as he pressed one of the keypad keys. The room itself had nothing but rocks and empty plastic bottles strewn about it. There were no skulls or bones of enemy prisoners. The last step was a steep one, and Nicholas almost fell as he stepped down it. "Damn," he said as his knee buckled as he stumbled onto the dirt floor. Getting out was easier since the light at the top seemed to illuminate things better than when they had walked down it.

Going up a long wooden stairway they made their way up to a small chapel that had an iconostasis in it.

"Probably right where you're standing," Raya said to Nicholas, "Bohdan Khmelnytsky once knelt down and prayed before going into battle."

"He probably was closer to the altar," Nicholas added. "But it's cool to know that."

There were more tourists on the wooden ramparts since they were under cover and out of the rain.

The ramparts on the other side of the castle were a bit more interesting in terms of the view. There was a deep green ravine and gully on the other side of the castle with a giant stone cylindrical wheel lying flat on top of a hill. It looked like a pagan place of worship with stone objects surrounding it. The rain and warmer weather had made the grass a rich and lush green. While the castle had five or six turrets, you could only go up three or four of them since steps hadn't been built for the other ones. One of the castle rooms had dummies in various Kozak and Turkish fighting garb.

The walk up the hill from the castle was impressive across a bridge overlooking the narrow river and gully. You could see a white church high atop a hill on one side at the highest point in the town, and another wooden church at the bottom of the ravine on the opposite side and closer to the river.

The cobblestone street up into the town led to the town hall and to the right of that a 14th-century yellow stucco church that was filled with worshippers for a Sunday service.

"I won't go in," Raya said to Nicholas. "One of the *babtsyas* (older ladies in scarves) will yell at me for not having a scarf on my head and for wearing slacks."

So instead she walked around the church to look at a bas-relief that seemed to be part of the original design of the building.

Another Polish Catholic church a few blocks away from the yellow church seemed to be in an almost complete state of *remont*, of remodeling – and as a result had lost a bit of its ancient character.

Most interesting to Nicholas was a *bovvan* and other stone idols in the outdoor museum not too far away from the old yellow stucco church. There was a weatherworn idol just like the one he had seen in the Museum of Antiquities in Lviv, so he decided to take a picture of it. This one had bas-reliefs on all four sides of it instead of just three, but almost the exact same cosmogony of the universe. There were also even older stone idols – three of increasing height from right to left on one side of the outdoor museum, and three more in another part of the garden but shorter in stature. Everyone else had left the museum while Nicholas was taking the pictures, and Raya came back to get him.

"Nobody yelled at you?" She asked.

"No."

"They usually yell at you for taking pictures."

"I HAD to have a picture of the idol," he said. "They don't let you take pictures of them in the museum in Lviv. And I didn't see any signs here."

"The idols are pretty common."

"Ninth century," according to what was written in the historical museum.

"I don't know about that," Raya added, "but I'm glad they didn't yell at you. There isn't a culture of friendliness in my country yet. I hope that will happen in time. A lot of people still bark at you instead of being polite. It doesn't take much effort to be polite."

After a cup of Turkish-style coffee at the café under the Kamianets-Podilsky Ratusha (Town Hall Building) in a stone cave-style room off to the side of the first floor of the building and packed with teenagers on a day trip, everyone got into the car to set off for the fortress at Khotyn, which was 24 kilometers away according to the road sign.

After paying the parking fee to an older *babtsia* (grannie) wearing a colorful paisley scarf, Ivan parked the car in the parking lot. "I have to use the facilities," Nicholas said as he stepped out of the car. "Gotta get rid of the coffee I borrowed in stone town." And he ran off to the white shack marked with the international sign of the male (a head with a triangle, with the sharpest point pointing down). International males must have broad shoulders and pointy triangular hips. The bathroom turned out to be just a hole in a wooden floor. Fortunately it wasn't too disgusting (just minor missed streams of urine and one part of a fecal deposit left on the moist wood at the edge of the hole). When he exited the clapboard hut of a bathroom, Nicholas couldn't see anyone else and decided to move down the hill toward the fortress and river below the parking lot. Everyone turned out to have gone to a booth to buy entrance tickets to the grounds. Raya had bought him one and refused to take any money from him as usual.

When you walked through a gate with a stone fence on both sides at the entrance and down a hundred meter or so cobblestone road, the view was just mind-numbing. The river was wide and muddy from the steady drizzle that had been falling all day. The castle lay in a niche in the earth that actually wasn't at the highest spot on the river bank, but nestled a bit below. Lush green hills circled the castle on three sides with dandelions blooming everywhere. They consider them flowers in this country instead of weeds. To the left was what looked like an old sentry post, a separate building with a crumbling outer wall leading up to it. The castle had three outer turrets on the corners and one at the entrance, plus a larger covered roof on the far corner closest to the river. The countryside was similar across the river, and houses were built fairly close to the shore.

"Welcome to Bulgaria," Raya said. "That's it on the other side of the Dnister." She was actually kidding, though Nicholas took her seriously for a second or two. Renata pointed out that Bulgaria was some 200 kilometers away in that direction across the river to the west. The view was impressive, even in the misty gray drizzle of a cloudy day. You still had great visibility. There was also a peacefulness, a placidness to the setting. The castle itself was a tan-colored stone with darker variations on the outside of it in spots, especially the upper parts of it that may have been restored later.

Once they had crossed the wooden bridge through the castle gate, Nicholas could see a covered building at the center of the castle courtyard with a well inside it. A wooden stairway was being built to take you to the left turret, and one of the other turrets on the opposite side near the river had a wooden stairway to take you up it. The view from the parapet was beautiful in all directions. The fortress was there to protect, but it also had a powerful inner energy and beauty that went beyond pure aesthetics. Many a bloody battle had taken place at or near this spot high atop the river bank, many lives cut short, many civilizations conquered and subjugated. That spirit, that mixture of blood and beauty and courage and sacrifice, was the making of legends.

On exiting the castle after wandering around inside it for about forty-five minutes, Nicholas noticed a hole in an old crumbling but recognizable stone wall to the left that looked almost like a portal to an elsewhere. The wall of weathered stone considerably seemed to predate the rest of the castle stones by hundreds of years if not more. You could see the river through the jagged hole and part of the greening branches of a tree, but Nicholas knew somehow not to go any closer to it. He sensed danger. Not just the danger of falling down the cliff by the river, but another even greater danger linked to that passageway. He sensed a pulsing energy from it that drew him toward it: the closer he got to it, the harder it was for him to breathe, even though he was outside in the open air, but he knew he couldn't let it pull him into it like a vacuum sucking up bits of dust from a carpet. So he backed away from it when he felt the intensity of the physical pressure and moved on with the others who had gone toward a small white building that served as a café for tourists.

In the restaurant, which was kind of a combination of an old Soviet tourist trap and a Ukrainian *shynkar* or country tavern, Raya said that she only wanted to order *mamalyga* (accent over the "lyg" syllable) at the restaurant. The word sounded great to Nicholas. The *mamalyga* turned out to be a much more tasty version of corn meal that was hot, moist and succulent with a dusty powder on top of it.

"Are you happy you came to see this?" Raya asked Nicholas while they were waiting for their meal.

"It's great! You've never led me astray. Thanks so much!..."

The road back was almost as sleepy for Nicholas as the road there, but after taking the 24 kilometer ride from Khotyn back to Kamianets-Podilsky, the sun burst out along with busloads of tourists, most of them Poles coming in from Chernivtsi by the Romanian border after they had breakfast at their hotels. Kamianets-Podilsky had many settlers during the Polish occupation in the past and several working Polish Catholic churches, so Polish tourists were quite common in the town.

The countryside toward Ternopil was the inverse of the trip in, so lots of apple blossoms, villages, and greening fields and some getting ready to be planted – just on the right side this time instead of the left. The fields in the sunshine took on an emerald, lustrous appearance. They call Ireland the Emerald Isle, but this was an emerald country if Nicholas had ever seen one. There were also many fields bursting in a sea of yellow flowers.

"That's *ripak*," Raya explained to Nicholas and Renata.

"What's that have to do with turnips?" He asked.

"No, not *ripa*, but *ripak* with a "k" at the end of it."

When he got home that night he looked up the word in his Ukrainian dictionary. It turned out to be rapeseed in English, colza in French, and canola in Canadian English. The word came from the Olde English word for "turnip." So the one consonant difference from "turnip" to "rape grass" did make a big difference and indicated the similarity of these words in these now nearly mutually incomprehensible Indo-European languages with totally different alphabets (other than the 15 letters that happened to coincide when Saints Cyril and Methodius originally fashioned the alphabet in the ninth century).

In the sunlight the colors of the green fields just glowed, particularly after the turn in Ternopil toward Lviv. The effect was caused mostly by the burst of sun that took away the previous grayness. About 60 kilometers from Lviv, soft bright green treed hills began to accompany the highway to the left. An emerald land, an emerald land, an emerald land, each glance to the left or right intensified the thought and image. The ridges were tree topped with small villages and individual houses nestled in valleys. Fields were furrowed and planted in grains at various stages of growth on both sides of the highway. Some still brown-colored soil, some sprouts of barely greening fields mixing with the fertile brown-black earth. When you looked to the right, you could see two or three kilometers. The soft ridge to the left was like green cotton candy in the sunlight. A few fields between the ridge and the road were dormant after the winter and just recently plowed. The tops of the treed ridges were bathed in sunlight, the bottoms in shadow. The sky was powder blue with marbled billowy white and gray clouds. The ridge seemed to keep moving toward and back from the road, and seemed to be further away the closer the car chugged toward Lviv. Those same bursting white apple blossoms were everywhere with a long pond to the left side of the road and with village houses to the Lviv side of it.

Nicholas wasn't sure of north or south or east or west or up or down. That was not true, of course, since he knew he was right side up with the earth below him and the wheels turning at about 80 km per hour according to earth eurostandard measurements of speed.

When the car pulled into Lviv, the stony gray city seemed to be much colder than the natural lush world surrounding it. To save Ivan some time from dropping everyone off, Raya told him to let her and Nicholas off at the turn in the road toward where Ivan lived. Renata was living in a university dormitory for visitors about two blocks from the turnoff. When Nicholas and Renata tried to give some money to Ivan for gas, Ivan refused saying that he had worked everything out with Raya and he couldn't take a penny. Nicholas learned long ago that it was impossible to argue with a Galician woman over such things, so he figured he would repay her hospitality in other ways. So the two of them walked off along Lychakiv Street toward the Old Town, which was a twenty-minute walk. When they reached the Galician Market, they both got onto the #50 *marshrutka* that went up along Ivan Franko Street that ran into Vitovsky Street, then turned left onto Sakharov Street, and after dropping Nicholas off at the corner right after the turn, finally took Raya home to the street that was at the end of the tram tracks. The walk with Raya down Lychakiv was quiet, but it was intimate and soulful for him in ways he didn't want to admit. He tried to bury stronger feelings that were coming to the surface, just because he thought she may not want him to have them. Friendship is always easier.

THE NEXT DAY

Nicholas met with Raya the next day "at Taras" at 4:30 P.M. to go over some manuscripts he wanted to check. He had taken on a translating job for a local art gallery for their catalog and just wanted to make sure he had everything right. He also wanted to go to the small Armenian Café on Armenian Street. He forgot the name of it because the sign for it was written in a script that was hard to read. He walked over to check the name. Rilikiya at 13 Armenian Street was the name. While he was waiting there for Raya "at Taras," he noticed a group of about 9 or 10 teenagers all using sign language sitting on a bench in the square opposite the statue. They were gesturing animatedly, one young girl in a red coat in particular. Though Nicholas had never learned sign language, he seemed to feel as though he understood what they were saying without them uttering anything, as though their minds or signs were talking out loud. And that seemed really odd to him. He had never felt anything like that before. Could he translate it into English or Ukrainian words? No, but on some level he really understood precisely what they were saying. Was he developing some kind of uncanny ability to understand? He wasn't sure... But something was happening to him.

Raya was five minutes late to meet him and called precisely at 4:30 to let him know she'd be late.

"I'm sorry," she said as she walked up to him.

"No need to call to let me know," he answered. "You get at least a half hour of late time from me without letting me know. That's how long I'd wait for you – at least. For you even an hour."

"I'd never make you wait an hour. I know you'd wait for me. But I like to keep my word."

"You and Mr. Viktor are the only two people in Lviv who are *nadijnyj*, that is, reliable that way."

"Thank you," she said and smiled a wide elfin smile. Then they walked off in the direction of the café.

The Rilikiya Café was somewhat disappointing. It had four or five tables outside, but it was a bit too windy and cold to sit there, so they decided to go inside. There were two free tables, so they took one in the center of the main dining room. The menu wasn't particularly inviting and the decor not very appealing. But the waitress had on a nice Armenian costume with a red, black and dark blue vest that gave it a bit of an Armenian atmosphere. She had dark black hair and a dark complexion, so she could have passed for an Armenian, though she probably wasn't. The service was on the slow side. Waiters and waiters in this town seemed to have one-track minds and never checked on other tables unless you went out of your way to get their attention. It seemed to be a universal aspect of service or lack thereof in the cafés.

Nicholas convinced Raya to have fifty grams with him of what was described in the menu as "kliukvena nastoika," or "cranberry-flavored liqueur." It sounded nice. It turned out to be more like cranberry-flavored vodka than a liqueur. Raya winced at the burning taste of alcohol when she took a sip.

"Twenty grams of this is all I'll be able to drink. Otherwise I'll be out of it. Can you help me with the rest?"

Nicholas, who had already sipped two thirds of his glass, simply switched glasses with her.

"Here, sip from the other side," she said.

"Your germs are fine with me," Nicholas answered her with a smile. "I'm sure they might even be tasty...."

And they spent the rest of the time working on the manuscript and waiting for their light dinner to arrive – salads and a cheese plate along with some black bread. The eighty grams of "liqueur" didn't have much of an effect on Nicholas. The twenty grams made Raya a little giddy.

"Don't worry, I can always carry you home," Nicholas assured her as they left the café.

THE ROOM
AT THE EDGE OF TOMORROW

It was a room where time stands still. You enter it through a loose closet board or old tall green ceramic corner coal heater that long since had not been in use and has been used just for decoration. It was in the corner of Nicholas's bedroom at 13/11 Hyphenated Writer Street, the one who couldn't hear with a leonine second part to his last name. Actually the bedroom and study were a single room divided by a bookcase.

The tall glazed dull green ceramic stove must have been standing in the corner for decades if not a century. It was dirty, cracked and chipped in spots with two iron cleanout bins at the bottom on the left side of it.

When is a heater more than a heater? When it's this one. When it's also a threshold, a portal, on the edge of something else, something unknown.

THE VALLEY OF THE NARCISSI
AND THE CASTLE AT MUKACHEVO

Most striking about the trip was what happened during the rainy ride back from the castle at Mukachevo, which stands high atop a hill overlooking a city that looked like a mishmash of Soviet-style buildings and tackily remodeled painted stucco stores. The two styles were at odds with each other, authenticity battling against inauthenticity, Olde Europe battling against K-mart. And to walk up to the castle, which seemed to have been built piecemeal at different times, you had to go up Soviet-named Tank Driver Street with the road sign in Russian.

But digressions notwithstanding, even though they are part of the same narrative in diachronicity, one moment of a terrible realization shocked everyone on the bus, one moment became the focus of a day that was largely uneventful and understated except for ONE BIG EVENT. A steady rain had accompanied the bus from after a dinner stop in a resort restaurant in Mukachevo that looked like it belonged more in Soviet times with its gaudy plastic interior than in the present. The road was black and slick underneath and in front of the bus with the big windshield wipers clearing away the droplets on the front windows in slow but regular time. A thick lightning bolt or two snapped in the distance in the mountains as the bus drove through the darkness, but nothing particularly seemed to be that close to the path of the bus. While still about 120 kilometers away from Lviv and next to a village whose name no one could see or could remember, Nicholas noticed an orange glow in the sky up over a hill on the right side of the road.

"Is that a town or something?" He asked Raya. "It almost looks like one of those projectors they shoot up in the sky to advertise a store opening back home."

"No-o," she answered hesitating. "There aren't any big towns here until we get to Striy, and that's not even a very big one. And they don't have any lights for store openings here."

The bus continued circling around the hill banking to the right a bit, and the glow suddenly became a bright fireball.

"My God!" Three or four people gasped immediately. Everyone screamed as they saw what it was. "It's a church!" The entire church was a fireball in flames – the ENTIRE church, not parts of it, with the flames devouring the cupola and cross on top of it. The steady rain seemed to be fanning the flames, as if it were gasoline, not dampening them. Two or three of the other people in the bus pulled out their digital cameras to take pictures. Nicholas couldn't get his out in time.

"It had to have been a lightning bolt," someone from the back of the bus mentioned.

"Or somebody stole the icons in the church to sell on the black market… And they're covering up their tracks by torching the church… Nobody's going to ask about icons from a burned down church." Another voice called out.

There was silence for a full minute or two as the bus continued on its way. A fire engine suddenly came into view coming from the opposite side of the road.

"Way too late," someone said.

"It's SO sad!" Another voice echoed.

"A sign from God!" A third added.

"A sign meaning just what?" Nicholas thought to himself.

Nicholas and Raya were stunned and didn't say a word to each other for several minutes and just looked straight ahead at the wipers flapping the steady rain off the front windshield of the bus. It's what happens in moments right after you witness a disaster. There's a silence that no human utterance can fill, and you just gasp.

Two days later Nicholas found out from Vasyl, Olenka's husband, that the church was only eight years old and not an old one. It had been struck by lightning, hitting a homemade lightning rod that couldn't withstand the charge. The people in the village apparently couldn't afford a professionally installed one. The village's name turned out to be Tukholka. The verb *tukhnuty* in Ukrainian meant to become rotten or putrefied or to go out or die out as in a flame. The church certainly realized the metaphor as it died out after a giant ball of flame.

Shifting back in chronology before the devastation of the church happened, the trip by bus to the Valley of Narcissi was long, nearly five hours, but the time seemed to be attenuated, mostly because Nicholas spent most of his chatting with Raya. While there was a pause or two when he closed his eyes for a few seconds of rest, the conversation was virtually continuous, with Raya shifting over every once in a while to other friends on the bus who had, at a particular moment, an empty seat next to them. While Nicholas knew five or six people on the trip, he kept to himself on the bus just because on that day he felt comfortable just being with Raya.

The southwest road to Mukachevo consisted only of two lanes, but they were virtually new and pothole-free the entire way to Mukachevo. "The Macedonians built it," Nicholas heard someone say, "that's why it's so nice." The hills and mountains were covered in greening leafy trees, with recently plowed fields at various stages of growth. More yellow rapeseed fields. Green stalks of other crops. And recently plowed fields waiting to burst into color. Streams, small rivers, twisting and turning, each village with a church right in the center of it – at the highest point.

You hit the forest just outside of Lviv in Vynnyky. And it seemed to go on forever all the way to Mukachevo. There were mountain ridges getting taller and taller the further away you get from Lviv that turn into blue ridge shadow outlines in the distance at the Valley of the Narcissi. The romantic sound of the name of the place alone intrigued Nicholas enough to take the trip. The name in fact captivated a lot of people who paid the fifteen hryvnas to sign up for the bus. "All of Europe comes to see the Valley!" Was the watchword.

Just outside of Mukachevo Olenka's husband Vasyl told the bus driver to stop along the roadside. There were several stands of people selling homemade wine. Nicholas jumped out of the bus to stand in line to buy some sweet red wine from the particular guy Vasyl had recommended to him. Nicholas had had some of that wine when he had gone over to their place a few weeks earlier.

There were rows of plastic formerly mineral water and soda bottles filled with white and red wine on the homemade stand. The wine seller spoke in the local Mukachevo dialect of Ukrainian. While Nicholas understood him, he had to strain to keep on top of what he was saying. He was giving a taste test of each bottle before selling it. Since the line was long, Nicholas asked Raya to pick up a bottle for him while he walked over the ridge to make a small rest stop. There are not many bathrooms on the road from Lviv to Mukachevo. The bus driver had stopped next to a wooded and bushy area earlier. By some shared genetic or chromosomal intuition, all the women moved to the left and the men, who were actually very few on the bus, to the right at the impromptu rest stop. Nicholas didn't need to go then. But he did now.

When Nicholas returned from the bush to which he had walked over, between the road and a local cemetery, Raya managed to buy a bottle of red wine for him and refused to accept any money for it. "Just buy me coffee sometime," she said. She would have given her last *hryvna* for the bottle – just to show her Galician hospitality. Meanwhile, back on the bus, Vasyl opened up a bottle and started passing around drinks in plastic cups to everyone. Nicholas ended up having three small glasses, which gave him a warm cozy feeling. The wine was probably a lot stronger than a normal store-bought one.

The turn to the left to the Valley of the Narcissi led to a much bumpier road. It was another 70 or so kilometers. When they hit the town of Khust, the bus had to crawl though the town because the local farmers were driving a herd of milk cows and calves through the town center. The traffic was stopped or barely moving in both directions, and it took nearly twenty minutes to get through. The cows seemed oblivious to the vehicles and in no hurry to cooperate with the tourists who wanted to get to the Valley.

Once at the Valley, things were largely disappointing from the pre-trip hype. There were patches of wild white narcissi throughout the park-like setting with a dirt road going through the middle of it and some wooden observation points, but nothing of any cosmic proportions that would have warranted the trip. But Nicholas walked through to look at the fields on the cloudy day that gave way to sunshine about two-thirty in the afternoon. The sunshine was nice, but with the ground and grass wet, it was very humid. But the trip was worth it for every second Nicholas was able to spend with Raya.

DROHOBYCH

The town was named after Yuri Drohobych, a scholar from the area who became renowned in Italy in the mid-fourteenth century. There's a big statue of him in his Italian scholar's cap just off the town square. The square was like an updated version of Rynok Square in Lviv, with a large cream-colored Ratusha (town hall) with a clock tower in the center of it, surrounded on four sides with buildings that just weren't anywhere near as old as the ones in Lviv. It was about an hour-and-a-half drive to get there in the rain that alternatingly seemed to let up and stop and return again. Additionally two lanes of the highway were being rebuilt by those Macedonian road builders, so it just was one bumpy lane in each direction with a lot of trucks and an occasional really slow tractor. So it was difficult to pass – with long lines of cars that made it difficult to make much progress. But they finally did make it. Nicholas's friend Marko, who was driving, pulled up onto the curb off the main street as they entered the town right across from a large brick building next to a church.

"I have to show you something," Marko said. "See that plaque?"

Nicholas nodded.

"That plaque commemorates this spot. This is the *kativnya*, the torture building the Nazis used. It's a building of the Drohobych Pedagogical University now."

Nicholas just kept silent as he listened.

"This is the spot where they tortured and executed a thousand of our people. They tortured them from 10 P.M. till 6 A.M. on the second floor, then they killed them in the basement. There were excavations in the basement later, and the bones they found there were given a proper Christian burial."

Nicholas couldn't speak, just because there was nothing you could say. He took out his camera to take a picture of the plaque but somehow his hands were paralyzed and the camera nearly fell out of his grip to the ground. It was as if the evil that had occurred there had left traces of that negative energy and snatched it right out of his hands. When they had walked away from the building, Nicholas looked at the trees and greenery surrounding the building and couldn't begin to understand how anyone could despoil such a beautiful and peaceful spot.

After walking around the city square a bit, Raya kept running ahead and asking people directions to somewhere. Since Nicholas didn't know what she was asking about, he just followed slowly.

"Go back and get the car," she firmly commanded to Marko. "We'll meet you at the church. It's just up that road," and she pointed to it.

The road turned out to be a dead end and Raya wanted to turn left to get to the church, which she could see in the distance.

"Let's wait for Marko," Nicholas said. "Here's a spot to sit," he said, pointing to a table in an outdoor café that didn't seem to have any customers.

They waited for a few minutes until he showed up in his older model but quite sturdy Volkswagen.

They pulled up to St. George's Church and parked not too far from it. Raya jumped out of the car and ran inside a house next to the church, which seemed to be the home of the caretaker. After a few minutes of apparent negotiations Raya came out with a woman in her forties with short-cropped henna-colored hair. In the meanwhile Marko and Nicholas walked up to the gate and looked at the wooden church that seemed to be made of hewn-cut wood and without nails. It had three towers and a bell tower next to it.

The henna-haired woman was a little cranky at first.

"This is a day off, you know, a national holiday," she frowned. "I'm doing you a big favor."

"We're terribly sorry, but it's the only chance our American friend might have to see it," Raya told her. "I'm outside already and I've sold you the tickets, so I'll show it to you."

The woman turned out to be incredibly knowledgeable about the church. It had been built in the village of Nadiiv (Nadya's village – or the village of hope) and transported to the spot where it has stood ever since in 1657. Tartars had destroyed the original church in 1499. The church was really three churches. An area at the entrance in the back of the church where the women stood during services, the church proper with its icons, including the one of Yura (St. George), being restored, and a second floor tiny chapel above the entrance that you could access only by way of a homemade wooden ladder that had aged into the same color as the walls of the church. The time-faded primitive folk-style paintings painted directly on the interior walls depicted various biblical scenes. The Garden of Eden, heaven, and hell were the most prominent. You could see tiny holes about a half-inch in diameter throughout the church.

"Bullet holes from Nazis?" Nicholas thought to himself.

"Those are ventilation holes," the henna-haired guide pointed out as she saw Nicholas looking at them from close up. "It maintains a steady humidity in the church and is one of the reasons that the frescoes on the inner walls remain intact. Natural air conditioning."

Nicholas felt a strong and warm bond with the church. It was *ridnyj* (kindred or near and dear) to him, as they say in Ukrainian, a place of comfort, a haven of warmth and natural light. He seemed to have an affinity for these locations that exuded a palpable, authentic presence and not gaudiness. He felt refreshed and awed by the experience of visiting the shrine.

After the tour of the church Raya and Marko took Nicholas to see another wooden church just a few minutes away. That one was locked up, but Nicholas managed to see the interior through a wide crack in the second floor wallboards. It was in even greater disrepair than St. George's.

The rest of the tour of the town included a stop at the bronze plaque where the Polish writer Bruno Schulz had been murdered by the Nazis. The sun was behind Nicholas when he took a picture of it, casting his shadow over the spot as if it were the spirit of Schulz.

The pinkish stucco-covered ruins of what was once the largest synagogue in Europe was about a ten-minute walk away from the Schulz memorial. The imposing stone edifice was completely gutted on the inside, with virtually all its windows broken. The exterior had a crumbling façade with large patches of unpatched stucco turning darker and darker from the elements. They did manage to raise enough money to repair the leaky roof. Raya had to ask several of the local inhabitants to try and find the cinnamon shops that Shultz wrote about when he lived there in Drohobych. After the fourth or fifth try, she was able to find the spot in an inner courtyard not far from the main square. It was all nothing but broken pieces of stone, brick, wood, and glass. You'd hardly recognize that it was once any kind of shop at all now.

Nicholas treated Marko and Raya to coffee and a bite to eat at a local coffee shop before they drove home. While it was a newer place, more western in layout, the coffee was good and the atmosphere pleasant. The place reminded him of a retro ice cream soda shop back home on Long Island. Nicholas had fifty grams of cognac to shake the chill from his bones on the windy day.

A RECEPTION
AT THE ITALIAN COURTYARD

It was a warm, sunny day, a welcome relief from previous windy and chilly days. Nicholas was invited to go to a reception for one of the city council members, Vasyl Tarasiuk, at the Italian Courtyard who was a close friend of Raya's. The place was packed when he entered with people milling around chatting with each other. Nicholas knew four or five people there and said "hello." He went up to Vasyl, the birthday boy, and gave him a handshake to congratulate him. Raya was sitting with some friends of hers, so he greeted her and asked if she wanted some champagne. She politely said "no," so he just got a glass for himself. She looked unbelievably beautiful. Like the brightest flower in the most beautiful garden he could ever imagine.

"Damn, shit, fuck, and several other expletives," he said to himself. "I didn't want this to happen...." A powerful feeling overwhelmed him, something he had not felt in a long time, maybe fifteen years ago, and a deep sadness overcame him. He knew he would be leaving in three weeks. He had to get back to teach a summer class – and he already had the plane ticket set for June 2. That realization overwhelmed him and he felt a primordial sadness over his immanent departure – and all this he had experienced over these months would disappear like a dream and become fuzzy and hazy except for the pictures that he took that would jar his memory and remind him of the emotions he was feeling now.

He knew he had to get away from the crowd of people. It was just a feeling of being totally alone in a sea of people. He tried to be as pleasant as possible to those he met and sipped the champagne. Vasyl was a real good guy, and Nicholas didn't want to call any attention to himself. But he knew he wouldn't be able to hold back tears that had nothing to do with the joyful party going on and he would have to get out of there at the first moment he could.

There was something about her when he looked at her – he didn't want to feel those feelings because he was sure she didn't want him to feel them. So he did his best to keep it inside. But his head was bursting, and the feeling was getting worse as his eyes became puffy.

After the champagne reception was over and Vasyl had given a small speech to the gathered group, Nicholas followed everyone upstairs to where a banquet table had been set up with food and wine. He thought about leaving and not telling anyone, but that would have been a coward's solution. He might not be any kind of hero, but he wasn't a coward. So he went upstairs, took a few pictures in the elegantly styled room with a feast about to happen at an opulent table, and walked over to Raya.

"I need to go home," he said to her.

"You should eat," she told him. "*MUsysh* (you have to)," she said in her inimitable way with her bright blue eyes. He didn't listen to her this time. It was probably the only time he refused to listen to her since he had known her.

"I don't have to do anything," he answered softly, hoping she wouldn't hear his thought, which he casually uttered out loud and almost unintentionally. "I just know I have to go home."

"Okay, but I'm worried about you. I'll call you tomorrow," she looked at him intently to figure out what was going on.

WHAT FOLLOWS IS A DIALOG THAT NICHOLAS IMAGINED

"I need to be alone, sometimes." (Nicholas)

"Did I do something or say something?" (Raya)

"Not at all." (N)

"Then why do you need to go?" (R)

"I just need to go." (N)

"I'm sorry if I've said or done something…." (R)

"You haven't said or done anything. It's my problem. It's an issue for me. It has nothing to do with you. I need to work it out." (N)

"Can I help?" (R)

"No, no you can't. Bye…." (N)

That dialog only happened in Nicholas's head, but Raya seemed to understand the unsaid in her single glance. It wasn't that different than what had happened in reality, just nonverbal words.

The walk home was difficult for Nicholas – across Rynok Square with dozens of happy, smiling teenagers playing and chatting by the two fountains he could see. He just was in a vile mood, and he couldn't figure out what it was. Actually, he could figure it out, he just didn't want to admit it.

"I didn't want this to happen… I didn't want this to happen… I didn't want this to happen." Say it three times and it will disappear. The feeling will be gone.

Was it the champagne? Was it the crowd of people? What made him feel the way he was feeling? He didn't want to complicate Raya's life. He didn't want to tell her what he felt. He just wanted to find his way back to his place. He kept pulling out his handkerchief to wipe away the moistness that welled underneath his eyes. Why this person and not that one? What makes you lose yourself? When you lose yourself, you unleash torrential emotion. It was that gushing emotion he couldn't control. And he needed to restore that balance inside him. That had never occurred before during his stay here – it had only happened to him so long ago that it was already once upon a time in his memory. It was as if this place, these age-old buildings, all the past experiences of everyone who had lived and loved and lost here were like an immense sounding board in a musical instrument or a tuning fork that would pick up emotions like vibrations and intensify them. The problem was that he wasn't in control. He did manage to waddle his way home slowly in the chilly air – and that helped. He just didn't want anyone else to notice his deteriorating emotional condition that was draining him. So getting into the haven of his apartment was the best place to be. He expected that Raya would give him a call to find out how he was later that night. But she didn't. She probably got back home later than she expected, he reasoned, and she thought it was too late to call. Or else she understood what he what feeling and didn't want to deal with it. But either way, he felt better in what had become his home. He felt better alone. It was a time when he knew he needed that. Maybe a good night's sleep will help him get over it. He fidgeted all the rest of the evening, making himself a cup of cherry tea from the Carpathians, taking a glass of *Dobra Voda* (Good Water) mineral water a half hour later, hoping the name of the water would help like the fairytale water of life, milling back and forth between his laptop and the TV in the kitchen, flicking channels with the remote from CNN International to the music channel that showed clip after clip of the same pop music of Ukrainian or Euro extraction. He finally went to bed around midnight.

But the night wasn't one of sleep. He felt a heavy intense pressure in his chest regardless of whether he lay on his side or back. He tossed and turned. At 4 A.M. or so he stepped out of bed and poured himself a glass of mineral water after going to the bathroom. He was trying not to think any thoughts, just relax, just feel clear and calm. He wanted to resolve the intensity of the emotion that he had inside himself and couldn't control. It seemed to come and go. He did though fall asleep this time till 8:04 A.M. when he heard the phone ring in the kitchen.

It was Raya.

"Are you okay?"

"I'm fine," he lied, but he wanted to mean it.

"I can't say anything to her," her said to himself.

"Are you sure? I was really worried about you last night. I didn't want to call. I didn't want to wake you if you were sleeping." She said to him.

"I'm really okay. It's just something that happens to me every fifteen years or so."

"Is it a problem with your heart?"

"It's not a heart condition."

"But it is with my heart," he wanted to say to her, but didn't.

"I'll be okay," he said.

"Can we meet today for coffee at noon? I have to go to a lecture, but I'll be free at noon."

"And I have to meet somebody coming in from Frankivsk at 1 P.M., so that will work for me. Where should I meet you, at Taras?"

"At Taras, is that a new café?"

"Raya! at TARAS, the statue, the one everyone meets at."

"Oh, I got confused for a second…," she mumbled as if it was as if she were thinking about something completely different. "I should know better. I heard the weather forecast might be rain –maybe meet at the Ethnographic? There's an overhang on the corner you can wait under if it rains."

"Sure, meet you then, *pa*."

"Pa-pa," she said.

Nicholas left at about 10:30 for their meeting because he wanted to cash some traveler's checks. The Fulbright orientation in DC before he left had suggested that it was better not to use credit cards or bank machines in the country, just because there were a lot of problems with stolen numbers. So Nicholas had brought a few thousand dollars in traveler's checks with him. He had four or five hundred dollars left, but wanted to cash the checks for his last few weeks in the country.

The first bank, which was the usual one he went to on Sich Rifleman Street, wasn't open that particular Saturday. Most banks in town were open Saturdays for the hordes of Polish tourists, but not this one on this particular day. He proceeded to go to six more banks on Doroshenko Street and Copernicus Street. None of them were able to cash his checks. "The woman who does that will be in on Monday," one of them said. Another answered, "We don't do that at this branch, but the one on Copernicus Street does." The one on Copernicus answered: "We don't have that much money on hand today, try the UkrEximBank around the corner." The UkrExcr(ement) Bank (as he was soon to call it) lady said she'd be happy to cash the checks, if he can show her the receipt for buying them. No one previously had asked for a receipt, just a passport, the latter of which he had brought with him. Since it was nearly ten minutes before noon, he was about ready to give up, but then realized he could take out dollars from the bank machine outside the Nadra Bank where he had been on Copernicus Street. But he looked in his wallet and saw he only had his credit card and no bank check card, and it would take too long to run home and meet Raya on time. He had been here so long that he couldn't remember the pin number of his Visa credit card, but he did remember the one on his check card. So he finally did give up the ghost after mulling all this over, even though there wasn't any ghost there and he hadn't heard anything about ghosts since the orbs at Pidhirtsi Castle, and he hadn't heard from Ivan the Ghostseer in a while. It seemed like when things were going wrong, they would go wrong in droves.

He waited on the corner of the Ethnographic Museum till a few minutes past five. Figuring that Raya had forgotten about telling him to meet him there, he decided to go to Taras, where she was sitting at a bench opposite the statue.

"I was waiting for you at the Ethnographic," he said casually.

"*Tak, tak*, yes, yes," she said. "I forgot that's what I told you. Sorry!"

"It's only a block away, *dorohenka* (dear), not a problem."

"Here, sit down next to me," she showed him a spot and brushed it with her hand.

He sat down but noticed an older gentleman had just lit up a cigarette and asked if they could move to get away from the smoke.

"I hate smoke blowing in my face," he said as they walked out of earshot.

"Are you feeling better today?" She looked up at him.

"I'm fine," he hesitated. "I'm fine." Then she told him the story of trying to cash the traveler's checks. She interrupted him for a moment before he finished, and he gently put his two fingers on her lips. She gave him a look, but he apologized right away. "I'm kidding, but just let me finish the story."

"Welcome to Ukraine," she said with a smile after he finished the story. "You need to go for a coffee. Forget about cashing the checks today. It'll all wait till Monday."

"I know," he answered as they walked off. "Here's a lucky kopeck for you. I found it on the street after my seven failures at getting my checks cashed. If I can't find one bank in seven to cash my traveler's checks, how am I supposed to find seven signs of the lion?"

"Thank you," she said as he proffered her the coin and put it into her pocket with a smile. "Want to try the Blue Bottle?"

"I haven't had much luck. But we can try." So they walked the three blocks over to the café, but all the tables were taken. Nicholas could see that Raya wanted to ask someone if they would share a table, as people often do ask here, but he immediately told her "*inshym razom*, some other time."

"Have you been to the Classic Café?" She asked. "It's right next to that blue building you like so much with the white elephant on it."

"Sure, why not?"

" I always thought it was a really expensive place, but it turns out it's not. My friend Vika told me it's really good."

So they took a table under the tent in front of the very polished well-appointed Viennese-style café. They both ordered the frothy cappuccino with cinnamon on top, and Nicholas decided to get the apple strudel with whipped cream (and two forks, though the waitress couldn't quite understand the unique diminutive form "videlochky" (little forks) he used and Raya had to repeat it in a way so she could figure it out). Most Ukrainians eat sweets with a spoon anyway, so he probably had asked for the wrong utensil.

"I'm so sorry about yesterday," he said to her after they ordered. "I thought about just taking off. I felt so *alone*, so *disconnected*, even though I knew several people at the party."

"I felt that way at a party where I didn't know anyone once...."

"It's not that," he interrupted her. "It's not that at all."

"Then what is it?"

"I'm leaving, I'll be gone, and it hit me right in the gut. I got so emotional I welled up. I didn't want to be with people. I needed to be alone. That's why I'm keeping my sunglasses on. Something happened to me that's put me on an emotional hair-trigger. I can't control it. It's a chaos that I've only experienced once before in my life."

"When was that?"

"Oh, it was about 15 years ago. And I don't want to go there again. I'll get over it."

He didn't tell her what the circumstance was that caused it back then. It would have simply told her too much and not what he thought she wanted to hear. So he didn't elaborate.

"I'll be fine," he continued. "I just have to get through it. Damn! I hate feeling this way! But really, the thought of leaving, of not being with my friends, my friends, *you* especially...."

"You have to go home. You'll get used to it. We'll...I'll miss you. We'll...I'll...We'll see each other again. You'll be back."

"I'm not sure of that," he answered darkly. "I just don't know. Something is telling me... I'm, I'm not sure what it's telling me, but it's telling me something I don't want to hear."

"Let me know what I can do to help you."

Nicholas wanted to tell her not to see him anymore while he was there, just because it was getting too painful for him. But he didn't. Instead he said:

"If you can handle me in my current state, fine, but if it gets too hard for you...."

"I'll just ignore that part of you when you're in that state, and I'll deal with the real you I've gotten to know when I see you."

The deal seemed to have been struck with nothing openly said about what Nicholas was truly feeling in the deepest part of him. It's possible he didn't really know that himself.

THE MAGIC MAN OF KOSSIV

The trip to Kossiv in the Carpathians took about an hour and a half. Raya convinced her friend Marko to take a day trip and Nicholas offered to fill up the gas tank on the outskirts of Lviv. The two-lane highway wasn't particularly crowded on that Sunday morning, and the road was decent all the way to the town. The town itself wasn't particularly interesting at first glance. There was a small stream running through part of it. Potholes and dusty streets seemed to be the predominant first impression for Nicholas. Marko had to navigate slowly turning left and right and left again to avoid the bigger holes in the road. They finally ended up on a street with a row of souvenir shops. All three of them entered the first of the five or six shops together, but then seemed to go through them at a different pace. Marko was done in five minutes with a bag of gifts. Raya was the slowest, most careful shopper and took the longest.

Each store had basically the same trinkets and souvenirs except for one shop where a younger guy made hand-made metal crosses. Raya took his cell phone number down for a future order and to promote his handicraft with other of her friends. Nicholas bought a carved pipe, wooden bracelets, *herdany* (intricate beadwork necklaces and bracelets), an encrusted inlaid box, and a handmade wooden handbag). One woman cheated him out of two hryvnas. He distinctly heard her say "three hryvnas" when he asked her the price, then told him it was five when she put it in her bag. "She cheated me out of two hryvnas," he announced to Raya. "I don't care," he said. "But it's irritating they feel they have to do that."

"Buy this *drymba!*" One hard-selling hawker said to him as he entered the next to last store. Nicholas politely said "no thanks" and left the store. The *drymba* is a jaw's harp or Jew's harp in English.

The next stop was the local magic man's private museum of handicrafts. Finding it was not a particularly easy task. Marko crossed a bridge in the car to a treed area and looked like he was lost. He asked three people where the museum was, but they said they were from out of town and didn't know. He finally rolled down the window and shouted out to a middle-aged mother with her little girl who was walking along the road, evidently coming back from church:

"*Bud' laska* (be so kind). Can you tell me how to get to the private museum?" "Turn back," she said. "Follow that road past the bridge, and ask somebody there. It's in that direction," she waved her hand in the general direction.

So Marko slowly navigated through the dusty street of many potholes but still couldn't see any signs. "Roll down the window and ask that woman in black," he said to Raya. Raya did, and the young, very elegantly dressed woman said: "You're right there. Just park and you'll see it ahead." "A real village *lady*," Raya remarked, impressed by the way she was dressed, and Marko parked the car. The museum turned out to be two doors down at 28 Hohol/Gogol Street. There was a house in front at 26, and the museum, a sky-blue colored wooden building was building number 28 behind it. The blue sign with yellow letters at the road, which was hidden partly by the leaves of trees when you drive up toward it, said: "MUSEUM of the Korneliuk Family. Free admission."

While they were walking past the side door entrance of the house at number 26, a young man of about twenty stepped out the door. "Is the museum open today?" Raya asked him. "Yes, just knock on the door in the house in back." As they walked back toward the blue house, a giant German Shepherd began barking. "Is he tied up?" Raya asked. "Yes, don't worry about him," the young man answered.

A short A-shaped woman saw them as they walked toward the museum and immediately said: "Wait here." And the three of them sat on a bench of the bright blue house. Then within a couple of minutes they heard a voice:

"Khrystos Voskres!" (Christ is Risen) A tall, somewhat portly man called out.

"Voistinu Voskres!" (Truly He is Risen) Raya and the others responded after a moment of hesitation. This must be Mykola Korneliuk.

"He's a Molfar!" Raya whispered to Nicholas as they walked to the porch of the building. "We'll see," he smiled back to her. He seemed to eye all three of them quite closely, as if he were measuring them and wondering if they were worthy of seeing his museum. His black hair was slicked back and well trimmed and he had a

white beard with a round darker circle patch in the front. The dark circle spot on gray, or the gray spot on dark hair turned out to be a visible sign of his gift of magic. His beard was meticulously trimmed and about four inches long, and he wore large square-shaped glasses. He was a portly full-figured mountain of a man, wearing a pale yellow open-collar shirt and a tan wool blazer over it with the buttons open. He walked around with a wood-carved Hutsul cane that he used both as a walking stick and as a pointer to point at different objects in his private museum.

"Do you read the Bible?" He asked.

"Yes, yes, of course," Raya answered. "We're all Greek Catholics." "All the answers are in the Bible. And you need to read it all the time." And he continued to lead them to the interior porch where he showed them his historical collection of money from the region.

Then he took them to the center room of the museum that had scores of Hutsul wedding hats, mostly for men, hanging on strings from the ceiling. The hats were festooned in bright colors: with multicolored sequins, buttons, piping, colored string, and bits of cloth, all in the brightest colors imaginable, and dominated by bright and maroon reds, greens, pink, and yellow. One hat particularly caught Nicholas's attention: it was a combination of a king's crown and jester's hat with the reds, oranges, greens and bright Hutsul colors all over it. The central room also had green and yellow plates with native designs on the walls, wooden Hutsul handmade holders for various types of food (one for butter, one for *holutpsi* [stuffed cabbage], one for meat, one for lard, etc.). "You keep one item in each wooden jar," he said to Marko. "That way the flavors don't get mixed up." There was also a hand-carved *skrynya*, or a box on legs that served as a storage place for food inside it and, when the lid was closed, as the dining table for a Hutsul family. There were also brown and maroon *kiptary*, or woolen winter coats lying in a pile in the room. And there were also brightly colored symmetrical paintings on the wall that looked like giant birds of paradise in bright blue, orange, yellow, red, and white colors.

The second room of the museum also had a number of hats hanging on strings from the ceiling. There was a pile of puffy pillows with cheerful large red flowers on them, various Hutsul woolen kilims that looked like Navajo designs, and on one table at the end of the room small icons of the Blessed Virgin that one of the Molfar's friends makes. As soon as Mr. Korneliuk pointed at one of the icons of the Blessed Virgin with his walking stick, he uttered: "Naichesnisha, naikrashchnisha, naimylisha, nasha, vasha, tvoja i moja" (which not as colorfully especially without the rhymes literally translates as: "The most sincere, the most beautiful, the most sweet, our, your (vous-form), your (tu-form), and mine"). He repeated the formula several times during the remainder of his guided tour of the museum. As they all walked out of the second room, Mr. Korneliuk pointed to a wall with seven or eight hand-carved walking sticks, larger ones for men, smaller ones for women.

The third room needed to be unlocked and was apparently Mr. Korneliuk's treasure house of crafts. It had scores of beaten metal icons with the face of the Blessed Virgin painted on them on a table and hanging on a wall to the right side. A central table had a complete set of dolls dressed in Hutsul wedding attire. They included the bride and groom, the parents of both, the best man and maid of honor, three bridesmaids and ushers, and three musicians. The left side of the room had wooden carved objects on shelves – cups, grogs, boxes of various sizes, etc. On a bench beneath it were various men's embroidered shirts, some of them seemed quite old and faded and antiques – some were wrapped in plastic.

The back right wall of the long room had about twenty hats lined up on shelves on it. These particular ones were quite intricate and old, especially the women's versions. The right wall of the room had various examples of Hutsul clothing.

"Can I take a picture?" Nicholas asked Mr. Korneliuk as he showed him his camera.

"Later," he said matter-of-factly, but then barked: "Did you take a picture?"

"No," Nicholas answered right away and put away the camera.

"Not in this room. If you want pictures, we'll take them in the next room."

Mr. Korneliuk was particularly proud of a 1994 picture he showed of Viktor Yushchenko in his museum. "I told him he would be president then," Korneliuk beamed. "I knew it, but he didn't believe me. I just wish he wouldn't have messed up the way he's messed up." And then he proceeded to give a five-minute lecture on the state of Ukrainian politics. But he was preaching to the converted.

Marko bought a handmade tie for his son. And Korneliuk took pictures with everyone. He paid special attention to Raya and went back to the antique room where he had banned picture-taking and brought out an elegant wedding bonnet in deep reds, oranges, and mint greens with scores of sequins on it for her. It looked incredibly regal on Raya. Nicholas wanted to give Raya a Hutsul hatchet to hold for the picture with the Molfar, but he protested vehemently. "No, no, not for women!" And Raya held it behind her back for the picture, knowing it was violation of the Hutsul order of things.

"Wow! That was amazing!" Nicholas said to Raya as they left the museum. "Thanks so much!"

"You should always listen to me," she said and smiled back at him.

The German Shepherd started barking in a crazed way as they walked past his cage. Nicholas decided to talk to him, and just said to him in Ukrainian: "Be quiet. Calm down. We're not going to hurt you." And it was like Daniel in the Lion's Den. The dog immediately stopped barking and sat down, just looking up at him and at the others. They walked past a long-haired cat sitting in a patch of sun by a bench next to the house. Nicholas took a picture of her but didn't disturb her. She was somehow a kindred spirit to him, and he knew she needed her rest.

The drive back through the mountains and forests was amazing. There were clusters of villages, snow-capped mountains in the distance even in the middle of May. There were hills and mountain ridges with the tall *smereky*, the silver fir trees, on the backdrop of the blue sky smattered with wisps of high clouds. There was the Cheremosh River that seemed to start off as a small, insignificant stream, but then widened up into a swift-flowing river that meandered through the mountains, ravines and down toward the lowlands. There were entire hillsides filled with dandelions and with horses and cattle grazing. There were goats and chickens nibbling on grass and fodder by the roadside. Nicholas took a lot of pictures of it all, but nothing could compare to seeing the grandeur of it with his own eyes.

THE GUY IN IVAN FRANKO PARK

Raya called Nicholas in the early morning on his cell.

"Got time for coffee?" He asked before she had a chance to ask him.

"Before one. I'll call you when I'm free," she said. "Where are you?"

"In the center." (Of town she meant.)

"Okay. *Domovylys* (agreed). See you then."

Since Nicholas had some time to kill, he decided to take care of some errands first. It finally was a completely warm and sunny day in Lviv – quite summery on a May 14. You could tell something had happened because the students lost all sense of any desire to be educated. The girls started wearing miniskirts shorter than their… Okay, that's a bad metaphor. Better not go there. And besides the miniskirts, there were the girls with completely diaphanous gauze tops over their black or white bras. EVERYTHING was visible. It certainly must have been cool under the gauze with the wind blowing through the holes to the skin. Havest you no shame, young women of Lviv! Well, it wasn't every one of the girls of Lviv. Just a few. But it was enough for Nicholas to notice and create a stereotype in his mind. The young women either dressed quite tackily or very elegantly, again, not too much in between, and none of the student grunge look that was standard dress at universities in the US.

Even though Nicholas noticed, his thoughts were still single-mindedly about meeting Raya. He taught his morning class – then went off to change some of his travelers' checks at the bank where he was used to doing those kinds of transactions. Everything worked flawlessly this time in the place where the bank teller had gotten to know him. The *blatna* (crony) system was still at work. It's still almost always who you know in the land of the guelder rose and sunflower.

No call from Raya yet, so he decided to go to Franko Park and sit and wait. There was only one spot open on a green bench. There was an older gentleman sitting on one side of the bench in a blue pinstripe suit of older vintage, so Nicholas sat down and began to correct papers.

No call from Raya yet….

Two of the papers he was reading had almost the exact same phrasing – so he knew he'd have to explain Internet plagiarism to the students. It was something he'd explained before.

After a few minutes the older gentleman got up slowly and walked away. Nicholas was perfectly happy sitting there by himself.

Still no call from Raya yet….

Just as Nicholas was finishing the last of the pile of two-page papers, an extremely thin guy around thirty sat down next to him after asking, "Is the spot free?" Since he asked only in one word ("svobodno?"), Nicholas didn't understand him at first because he wasn't focused on the question. When he understood, he answered: "Sure…."

The guy must have seen the English on the papers Nicholas was correcting and thought it was German – or saw something in Nicholas's face, or expression, or clothes that screamed "foreigner."

"Do you think I could get a job in Germany?" He asked Nicholas.

"You know it's kind of hard to get visas now to the European Union – unless you're a prostitute or caregiver," Nicholas answered. "They need cheap caregivers. And the prostitutes figure out a way to get there."

"I'm an orphan," the guy said as he fiddled with his dark alien-eye bubble sunglasses. "Lost my father to alcoholism five years ago. I just lost my mother to a stroke a few months back. I'm an orphan, an only child with no family left. I was with her when she died. I sat with her from two to four in the morning. She was really young, too."

"I'm sorry to hear that," Nicholas sympathized with him, even though he was not in the mood for this guy striking up a conversation with him out of the blue.

"I'm Russian, but I'm living here. I tried to move to Kyiv, but the apartments are so expensive there. I couldn't do it. I have a good job here and an apartment. I'm not married though. All my friends who got married complain. They have to stop smoking and drinking, can't go out with their friends. It's not worth it! I'm not getting married," he said.

"Good for you," Nicholas nodded to him and smiled. "There are a lot of beautiful women here, so it'll be hard to stay single."

"That's for sure. Where are you from?"

"The US. New York."

"Is it expensive to live there?"

"Yeah, but everything is relative. I live pretty well here. I'm waiting for my friend Raya to call."

"Ah, I see," the guy said with a smile. "Hey, mind if I smoke?"

"Not at all," Nicholas answered, "the wind's blowing the other way away from me."

So he smoked his cigarette, seemed to relax, and immediately got up.

"Do you have sixty kopecks?"

Nicholas fiddled in his pocket and pulled out the money to give him.

"See you," the guy said, and moved along.

Just as Nicholas rose up himself a minute or two later, the phone rang and it was Raya calling. "Meet you at the café where we first met," she said. "I'll be there in fifteen minutes." While she was a tiny bit off in her estimate, she did arrive twenty minutes later.

Nicholas told the story to her about the guy in the park and questioned why he asked for sixty kopecks and not a hryvna.

"He needed sixty more kopecks to buy a bottle," she said without even thinking about it. "Want to go here for coffee?"

"That's fine with me. Wherever you'd like."

"Maybe the Blue Bottle?"

"Yeah, why not, and if that's filled, we can go over to the Café Classic."

The Blue Bottle had four empty tables since it was a weekday, and the Polish tourists weren't inundating the place yet. They took the table in the corner by the stove, that this time wasn't heating the small room. The door, in fact, was left open to let in a bit of a breeze. "That stove is called a *burzhuika* (a bourgeois)," Raya mentioned to him as they sat down.

Nicholas also noticed that there was an Austro-Hungarian Empire border post at the inside entrance of the café. He didn't notice that his previous time there. He also didn't notice a few other details in the café that he focused on this time. There were portraits of guys with beards and curled and waxed moustaches on the wall right next to their table along with a map of Galicia. There was also a cuckoo clock on the wall with the clock hands stopped at 1:00. One a.m. or one p.m.? He asked himself. With the natural light from the open door you could see more of the inside of the café in natural colors. The brick walls inside were burnt orange. On the back wall there was an arch over a wall painted deep blue. There were two flags on either side of the back wall – one yellowish, and the other a red castle with the city's lion emblem on a blue background.

The menu was quite interesting this time too – just so detailed that Nicholas couldn't focus. The different coffees had names like the "von Sacher-Masoch" or the "Bruno Schulz." Far too many to remember. And the descriptions of their contents were detailed. Nicholas had the same problem in the Golden Ducat Café, where it would take you half an hour just to read the menu. He always just ordered "a tasty non-flavored coffee with milk" (and it would always turn out well).

"What would you like?" Raya asked Nicholas with a smile.

"Pick for me," Nicholas said. "I'm sure you'll pick something good."

She chose a coffee with cognac, even though she very rarely had cognac, and when she did, just 25 grams of it.

The coffee was good. The company was good. Nicholas tried not to get emotional about leaving. A single tear came down his left cheek, but he managed to wipe it away while Raya was turned away.

VYNNYKY BY THE LAKE

Nicholas accepted an invitation from Jan Shchurakivsky to visit him and his wife and their two-year-old son on a sunny Sunday afternoon at his home in Vynnyky, which was both a small suburban town Ukrainian style with a lot of individual homes and with a heavily wooded area outside of town with a lake. The lake had a lot of Sunday picnickers because of the warm weather. It wasn't too far from the Devil's Cliff on the map. Nicholas arrived in fifteen or so minutes after picking up a *marshrutka* bus on Lychakiv Street. He forgot the number. He had hoped to go with Nadya, but she was out of town in Kyiv for a conference. So he went on his own with a certain amount of apprehension.

Jan's wife picked him up with her car at the last stop of the *marshrutka*. She was what we call in the US dirty blonde, very sweet and about half Jan's age. She was on maternity leave from the Department of Journalism at the University of Lviv to raise her son until he was old enough for daycare.

When they pulled up to the older three-story home, there was a large German Shepherd tied up on a chain in the yard that barked until he saw Nicholas being friendly with his mistress Zoryanna and her rambunctious boy who was a non-stop bundle of energy. Zoryanna spent most of the evening chasing after him.

The house was lovely, with quite artistic and colorful drawings directly drawn on the walls of the house at the entrance hallway and in the living room.

"Who made those?" Nicholas asked.

"Those are Jan's," she smiled. "He's very talented."

Jan greeted Nicholas with a big bear hug when he saw him. He was bare-chested and wearing short pants and sandals. He was busy in the kitchen frying his specialty dish – *deruny*, potato pancakes, with a special wild mushroom sauce.

"Jan does all the cooking," Zoryanna pointed out to Nicholas. "He's so domestic. Everybody thinks he's some kind of murderous vampire because of his books. Or a sex maniac. But his favorite pastime is gourmet cooking."

The dinner prepared by Jan was scrumptious. A doctor friend of his and his wife and two daughters also came over a bit later. The first stage of the feast was presented in the house with the succulent potato pancakes and various salads (a spinach and mushroom one, a beet one, one with tomatoes and scallions, and a few others). The main course was presented in the back yard of the house as Shchurakiwsky set up a barbecue pit for pieces of lamb and vegetable *shashlyk* (shish kebob) on skewers. While the main course was being smoked on the spit, Nicholas stopped counting after the fourth bottle of champagne.

So first impressions for Nicholas had been wrong. Shchurakiwsky the writer cultivated a certain image for his reading public. The private Shchurakiwsky wasn't a rat at all, but a jovial and talkative epicure who enjoyed the company of others, someone who was a storyteller who told fascinating and lively stories, and who was an attentive listener too.

Nicholas managed to catch a late *marshrutka* bus back to the center of town about 11 P.M. It had a stop by the lake, so it picked up a packed busload of revelers who had spent the entire day with nature, food, friends, and various libations. Though none of them were wealthy in terms of money, their wealth in spirit shone in their love of life.

When he arrived home, Nicholas uploaded the digital pictures he had taken during the day. He was particularly struck by the fact that Jan, the rat-named man, actually looked more like a lion with his white beard and moustache along with his scraggly mane of white hair. Might he have something to do with the signs of the lion?

FONDLY FAREWELLING
TO THE CARPATHIANS

Nicholas took one final trip to the Carpathians at the invitation of Nadya and her family (her father and mother, the in-laws of her sister, whom Nicholas knew from the States, her sisters's husband Rostyslav, and Rostyslav's older brother and his wife). The destination was Slavske, which is a ski resort town 120 kilometers from Lviv. It normally is a two-hour drive on the two-lane highway from Lviv, but Nadya's father, who was an official in the Lviv city government, had a personal driver Stefan, who managed to weave around enough cars at breakneck speed to make it in a little more than an hour. Nicholas spoke non-stop with Nadya in the back seat about all manner of interesting topics that made the time pass quickly without a single dull moment. It was as if they had known each other all their lives.

To get to the base of the ski lift for Mt. Trostian, which is 1232 meters above sea level, you have to take what looked like a really beat-up dark green Soviet-period military transport vehicle with bench seating. It looked like a VW bus from the 1960s to Nicholas. The incredibly bumpy ride in the vehicle that seemed to use its passengers as its only shock absorbers jolted everyone in the vehicle as it hit every pothole and slid through the mud and puddles left from a recent rain. Nicholas nearly became intimate with Nadya on a few thunderous jolts as their two bodies crashed into each other. Both of them just laughed when it happened and just enjoyed the joyful ride.

When they reached the disembarkation point for the ski lift after ten minutes or so, Nadya's father said to Nicholas: "Just jump on and keep moving, pull in the folding metal crossbar, and look forward! Don't look down! You know, we should have had a shot or two of cognac before we got on the lift. That always helps. But it's too late now...."

Nicholas tried to follow his advice, and everything was fine at the beginning. But when three meters of open air beneath him turned into twenty-five meters or so, his panic mode seemed to take over. But he bit his lip and managed to maintain his cool. He didn't want to admit that he had never been on a ski lift before.

Nadya, who was in the seat five meters behind him, kept shouting to him and pointing in different directions. "Bilanchuk, look at the beautiful view! Look at those trees! Look at those clouds! Look at that house!" Nadya's sister's mother-in-law, who was in front of Nicholas, just kept shrieking the higher the steel cable pulled them up the mountain. "Calm down, calm down," her husband kept trying to allay her fears.

As his blue-painted metal and wood chair started to approach a wooden platform that looked like the end of the ride after ten or fifteen minutes, Nicholas calmed down considerably. But the lift didn't stop and just kept moving forward up a higher second mountain. "Shit!" He screamed as the lift took him higher and the chasm beneath him kept growing deeper.

"So you liked that, Bilanchuk!" Nadya blurted out to him with her more than rudimentary knowledge of English.

"Yes, I *especially* loved that!" He answered and tried to focus his gaze on the forests of fir trees and meadows on the surrounding mountains and hillsides in every direction.

The top of the tallest mountain looming above Nicholas came soon enough in fifteen or so minutes. When everyone was accounted for at the top, Nadya's father announced a walk around the crest of the mountain.

"I've gone skiing here with my boyfriend Sasha," Nadya said. "So I know the trails." She was in a particularly joyous mood and wrestled with her father and mother playfully, hugging them, jumping into her father's arms, taking dozens of pictures at every spot. "I like pictures with people in them along with nature," she announced at one point. She was experiencing "povnyj kaif" (total bliss) from the views and just being there with family and friends in a spot where she felt free, and the feeling that she had was infectious, because

Nicholas felt it too. It was a bit misty and cloudy in certain spots on the surrounding mountains, but you could see that the weather would be clearing up and turning sunny.

When everyone had worked up an appetite from the hike, they walked back to the base camp near the ski lift. There were ten or more various little ramshackle clapboard restaurants with outdoor seating and souvenir stands. The nicest indoor one was a restaurant called "Beneath the Clouds" with a green and yellow sign, a red tile roof and a stovepipe coming out of its roof with white smoke puffing into the air toward the clouds that seemed so close you could touch them. Nadya's father entered one of the huts and negotiated a price for *deruny* (potato pancakes), *shashlyk* (shish kebob), and beer for everyone. He and his in-laws also opened up backpacks filled with cognac, mineral water, tomatoes, cucumbers, pickles, and other treats. And so the feast began with a friendly mongrel dog that belonged to one of the restaurant owners getting fed scraps from the table.

The trip down the mountain after the feast (and the beer and the cognac) was easier than the trip up. There was no screaming from anyone or fear, just the feeling of freedom and the pure joy of existence on a beautiful day with beautiful people.

One more treat awaited Nicholas – a brief stop at a waterfall on the way back to Lviv. And after the rocky waterfall in a wooded park, Nadya's father pointed toward an open gazebo in a meadow where a second early evening feast and a bonfire next to it were set. Nadya pulled out a volleyball and everyone played in a circle to work up a sweat and build up an appetite. Nicholas hadn't played since high school, but did a good job in keeping the ball alive and passing it. All the food and libations left over from the mountain luncheon in Slavske was set out on a picnic table in the gazebo along with several more dishes bought at a small kiosk restaurant not too far from the waterfall in the park. At dusk, the driver Stefan sped just as madly on the way home, and Nicholas continued to enjoy the best of conversation with Nadya and her mother in the back seat.

THE PANICKED CALL

"Allo," Nicholas said groggily as he had just woken up.

"Nicholas! You HAVE to get registered in the OVIR, the Department of Immigration and Registration! It's past ninety days! I just found out about it from my friend Myron. I'll meet you tomorrow at the university. Otherwise it's a $400 fine!"

"Okay," Nicholas said. "What time?"

"Eleven?"

"Eleven, sure, see you then."

So they met the next day at the International Registration Office at the university. A young bleached blond secretary with chewing gum eyes was sitting at the desk of the office at the university.

"This is a visiting Fulbright scholar from the US," Raya said to the girl, who was in her early twenties. "He needs to be registered. Otherwise he'll have trouble when he leaves the country."

The blonde girl didn't have much of a reaction to Raya's words. She just sat there curling and uncurling her hair with her right forefinger.

"Anna Pavlivna isn't here today," she answered. "I can't do anything unless she tells me to."

"Then what should he do? This is important! Can't you find out something!"

"Come back tomorrow at eleven. She'll tell me how to take care of it."

"Thank you!" Raya responded huffily, and then turned to Nicholas after they walked out of the office. "*This* is the future of the country," she said, hesitating after the word "this." "She's young, she should know better. She won't lift a finger unless somebody tells her. She can't pick up the phone and find out for you what you need to do. She's too busy curling her hair with her finger!"

"Calm down, Raya, it's not a problem. We have people just like that back home. It takes all kinds."

"But I don't want you to get fined! Or you to get in trouble!"

"So I guess I'm an illegal in your country!" Nicholas laughed.

"Yeah," she managed a laugh.

"I'll take care of it tomorrow. And even if I have to pay a fine, it's not a problem."

In the meanwhile Nicholas sent off an email to the Fulbright office in Kyiv and got an almost immediate call that said he needed to register within ninety days of being in the country only if he didn't have a visa. But since he had a visa, it was valid for six months. So he didn't need to do anything. Despite the newfound knowledge of his situation, he decided to go back to the International Registration Office the next day since he had agreed to do so.

The girl with chewing gum eyes was there again along with her supervisor Anna Pavlivna, who was an older and very pleasant woman.

Nicholas explained the situation and showed a printed email document from the Fulbright office to Anna Pavlivna, who still said he should go to the OVIR to make sure and directed the gum-chewing secretary to take him. Nicholas looked a little closer at her this time. Her hair was frosted blonde with the roots showing about an inch. She continued to twist her hair with her right finger as Nicholas waited for her to collect her things. Obviously she spent a lot of time polishing her impeccable nails, putting on her dark blue eye shadow and pale pink lipstick.

In her northern regions she was wearing a tight-fitting white knit blouse with blue, white and pink sequins on it. To the south she had on a black almost skin-tight pair of jeans with a shiny vinyl "P" emblazoned on her left back pocket and the letter "J" over the right. Nicholas didn't have to go out of his way to spot this. He noticed it because he had to walk behind her from time to time because the sidewalk was narrow on the tapered side street off Shevchenko Boulevard, and he had to squeeze over when someone was walking in the opposite direction. Her spotlessly polished black shoes had incredibly high heels with a stiletto point and a giant square pilgrim's silver buckle over the top of them that looked quite out of place. The shoes came to what looked like a painfully narrow point.

Nicholas didn't have much to say to her because she wasn't very talkative. After a long pregnant pause of four or five minutes and two blocks of walking, he said in trying to make conversation: "Sorry I'm not awake yet. Haven't had my second cup of coffee."

"I have to have my one cup in the morning too," she answered. "You shouldn't drink a lot of coffee. It's bad for you."

"Two or three cups a day for me," he answered.

Mostly pregnant pauses accompanied Nicholas the rest of the way to the OVIR Office. It was actually called the DCIR Office in post-Soviet times, but everyone remembered the old name since its old acronym neatly comprised a meaningless word that at least looked like a Ukrainian word.

The main office directed Nicholas to another office next door that dealt with those types of matters. Of the three guys sitting behind a single desk in the next-door office, two of them had the look of old Soviet *mordy* or the diminutive form *mordochky* (kissers or mugs). It's hard to find a true equivalent for the word in English. A *mordochka* is a word you normally would use for an animal's snout or face, but it's used for people, too, either for ironic or just the opposite effect. Nicholas, for example, could have said to his good friends Raya or Nadya or Vira: "You have a beautiful *mordochka* today!" And that, of course, would be a compliment of the highest order.

The two guys in the office had the blank-faced looks of card-carrying bureaucrats. The third guy who responded to hair-twirling-oversized-buckle-shoed bleached blonde's question seemed pretty normal, but harried.

"What's his status?"

"*Stazhuvannya*," she answered. It is a hard word to translate. The latest Ukrainian dictionary translates it as "training" or "probation time." It, of course, had nothing to do with probation from jail, but a probationary time or on the job training.

"He's not a student," the guy shot back.

"He's teaching."

"Ah, so you're getting paid," he turned to Nicholas.

"No… I'm not getting paid. I get my expenses paid by the US government. I'm working for free here."

"Yes, it's voluntary teaching," the blonde with Nicholas answered.

"Then what capacity are you here on?" He asked Nicholas.

"Fulbright scholar."

"What's that mean?"

"I teach classes without getting paid for it."

"Why the hell don't you designate a status for these kinds of people," he said to the girl, and then turned to Nicholas, "Then you're a C-2 visa."

"No, a C-3."

"Then that's a business visa."

"No," Nicholas answered, "the category is wider than that on the Ukrainian Embassy website. It's for individuals doing charity work and volunteer jobs."

"Does he need to register?" The girl interrupted.

"His visa's good until July 21. But what if he stays longer?"

"I'm leaving on June 2," Nicholas answered. "I won't be staying longer."

"Then what's the problem?"

"None, I guess…."

"Then he doesn't need to register?" The girl asked again.

"Only if he wants to stay beyond the twenty-first."

"Thank you, bye," she said, and pulled Nicholas out of the office past three or four people waiting in line out onto the street.

"You have the leftovers of the old Soviet bureaucracy in your country," Nicholas said to the girl, who seemed insulted by it.

"Changes don't happen overnight," she answered curtly.

"It's been sixteen years…," was Nicholas's reply.

It's the same problem in the university. And the communists were in control of this part of the country for just fifty years. They had a lot longer to mess up things in the Eastern part."

"That's for sure," the girl answered, who must have been four or five years old when the bad old Soviet of unions collapsed.

THREE WEEKS GONE

"Just got back from Warsaw. Art exhibit. Lying in bed. Enjoying morning sun and spring through window. You?"

The message was from Ada.

"Just working," Nicholas answered. "Taking it easy."

"All cool with you? Can you meet for coffee tomorrow? Where and when?"

"Sure, be happy to."

"20:15 good for you? King Danylo?"

"Sure. See you then."

Nicholas was free then and knew Raya wasn't, and he enjoyed his last visit with Ada, who seemed no longer to have any magic charm or power over him as when they had first met. When he saw her, he said hello with a smile. He also told Raya she was going to meet Ada for coffee. He just wanted her to know – and in that way assure her that, well, he didn't really need to assure her about anything because he never managed to tell her, well, he hemmed and hawed, and never got around to telling her, you know, true feelings, what you have deep inside yourself, when you're afraid how the other person is going to react, when you think your entire physical and emotional fate hinges on a single word.

"Where'd you like to go this time?" She asked right away with a smile.

"The Blue Bottle?" He said to her, but knew it wasn't the right place for her.

"Let's just walk," she said, "but could you walk slower? You walk really fast for me."

"I'm sorry. But thanks for letting me know. Your heels aren't that high," he added.

"No, they're not too high. I like to wear them though."

"You're very tall to begin with," he said. "You don't need to wear them."

"Most of my boyfriends have been my height or shorter than me," she said.

"Well, one of my barely five-foot tall friends from college, whose boyfriend was a really tall basketball player, said to him in the elevator once in my presence: 'My mother always told me that height doesn't mean anything horizontally.'"

Ada smiled.

"We're at the Ducat," she said. "Is that okay?"

"Sure," Nicholas said, noticing that he liked to say "sure" a lot.

After they sat down, Ada ordered a cup of tea instead of her usual melted dark chocolate, and Nicholas ordered melted chocolate and cream with cherries. It was like an American sundae without the ice cream.

"You know, I've been thinking about numbers lately," he said to Ada. "I noticed eight old iron keys hanging on the wall in the Puzata Khata (Potbelly House) Restaurant by the university. And another eight parts make up the blue and red stained glass window at the Dominican Cathedral. And eight lion's heads on the lower part of the Chapel of the Boims...."

"What's it all mean?" She asked.

"Seven is a sacred number, like three. Eight is infinity. A never-ending path returning to the beginning. The snake that swallows itself in ancient beliefs."

"I've never been much for numbers," she said.

"Numbers hold the universe together," he answered, without really knowing why he answered that way or why he said the following. "But there are infinite ones and infinitesimal ones. Some are mystic revelations." It was as if someone else were saying the words through him. Maybe it was Professor Potojbichny's influence?

After about an hour in the Ducat, Ada politely announced: "I have to get going. I have a painting on commission I'm doing – have to get it done this week. Will you walk me over to my *marshrutka* stop? I can take one from near where you live."

So Nicholas walked her over slowly across Liberty Avenue to Copernicus Street to Bandera Street where she picked up her *marshrutka* minibus to go home. It looked like a #36 on the minibus, but he wasn't sure since it was dark. They parted with mutual smiles as she got on the bus, and Nicholas walked the two blocks he needed to go to get home. When he arrived home and crossed the threshold of his house, a message popped onto his buzzing phone:

"Thanks one more time for a really nice evening. Sorry you're leaving. It's too bad."

"That was fine, that was nice," he thought to himself. "I'm glad those feelings I felt when I first met her aren't there. They seemed deadly when I look back at it… Something or someone seems to be protecting me from that now."

He wrote back: "Thanks. Sweet dreams to you." The words weren't as flirtatious in Ukrainian as they might sound in English. He wasn't trying to be flirtatious.

GREEN SUNDAY

Green Sunday falls on the fiftieth day after Easter Sunday. It marks the church holiday of the Descent of the Holy Spirit. It's a special holiday, particularly in Western Ukraine, where everyone adorns their homes and shops (even banks!) with leafy branches and with green growing things. It's celebrated in much the same way in Poland too. Raya dropped by at Nicholas's house on Green Sunday eve to make sure he had those living green things adorning his abode. She tied a branch to his door and scattered stalks of what looked like palms on the floor. "There, you'll be safe now," she said to him, and whisked on her way to catch the *marshrutka* quickly enough to take a shower before they shut off the water at 9 P.M. Green is, of course, the color of life.

SEVEN ANGELS, A TRIANGLE
AND A FIRE IN THE BROW

It was a painting named "The Holy Trinity" in The Assembly Hall of the Lviv Polytechnic University. It was one of eleven oil paintings designed by Polish painter Jan Matejko in the 1880s and executed by his students. The Polytechnic, as the locals called it, was only three blocks or so away from where Nicholas lived and only one block away from where he had dropped off Ada the night before. Nicholas never had any occasion to go there prior to today. He was at the Polytechnic once to meet someone, but the Assembly Hall was closed since it's only open for special occasions, and he never had a chance to see the painting before. Perhaps that was meant to be, because he seemed to understand it better. When Nicholas gazed up at painting during the installation ceremony for the new rector of the university, that one fiery yellow painting seemed totally to overwhelm his being and illuminate him in a powerful way. It had a bright yellow inverted sunny triangle on the background of a patched white cloudy and blue sky. With Christ in profile to the left holding a crown of thorns in his right hand and the white-bearded God the Father to the right in profile, the image of the Holy Spirit is foregrounded and central to the painting: it is embodied in the image of a young man with a burning torch in his brow. The man accepting the spirit of wisdom from above had both his hands outstretched and in front of him, as if he were unsure of whether he would accept the divine gift or the crown of thorns. He seemed to be both on the verge of pushing it away and accepting his fate. And there were seven childlike angels that seemed to transfer that heavenly fire entering his mind and entire being down to the earth below in magnified shafts of expanding light. Those shafts of light seemed to be transferring that wisdom attained from above and life to the world below. It all seemed to emanate from the power of the flaming yellow triangle.

THE LAZARUS STEPS

The Lazarus Steps lead up to the Lazarus Hospital at the top of the embankment along the middle part of Copernicus Street. Nicholas had passed them at least once every day on his way downtown. Nicholas felt something really draw him on this particularly warm and sunny day.

He walked up the steps knowing he was walking into somewhere else. He was becoming something other than he was the last five months, but he still couldn't understand what that was or what it meant. He didn't rationally feel like he had learned all that much during his stay. He found the people who became his close to him and the city to be so welcoming and wonderful. He felt much more in touch with his feelings and his true self. But he also felt a burden hanging over him, the profoundest of imperfections in his own self, and a deep sorrow about having to leave and go home to the mundane life he was living before. The Lazarus Steps both go up and down. The path is stony and crooked and hard sometimes to get the right footing.

THE ZODIAC CAFÉ

The interior didn't look like it had much to with anything like a zodiac. But it was nicely done in neo-Secession revival artwork. It was only three blocks away from Nicholas's apartment, but he had never been to the place before or ever passed it. It was at the end of Ryleev Street and on the corner with Ustianovych Street.

Raya only had a half hour before a class she had to teach, so she asked Nicholas to meet her at the Tiveria Café by Ivan Franko University, which was the first place where they had gone out for coffee, just because it was near the university.

"You look WOW today!" Nicholas told her. She was dressed in a darker blue jean vest and a longer blue jean skirt. The material really brought out the blueness of her eyes into a celestial depth. Blue was her color. "You must get tired of me complimenting you," he added.

"No, never," she smiled coyly as she looked up at him.

"Where do you need to go?"

"Actually up your way near your apartment. I have to meet my friend Ulyana there in an hour."

"Why don't we walk in that direction then?"

"That'll be fine."

"What's that?" He asked as he noticed a small pin on her collar.

"It's a ladybug," she said. Nicholas didn't understand the word she used for it in Ukrainian, but when he looked closer he saw that it was painted ladybug pin in her collar. He was stunned for a second, but didn't tell her why. He had had a dream over twenty years ago of a woman with the childlike silly nickname of Ladybug. It was a beautiful dream. One of the most beautiful he had ever had. One about climbing a mountain for a thousand years and a day, but with a woman companion named that odd name, who made the journey's difficulties easy. He hadn't thought about ladybugs for two decades – and here out of the celestial blue of the sky and her eyes was the ladybug pinned on her collar – three of them, in fact, when he looked closer. He later remembered what his grandparents used to call ladybugs – "bozhja korovka" (literally: "God's tiny cow").

That dream he had so many years ago seemed to be coming true. The word his grandparents used turned out to have been a Russian one, as Raya later explained to him. In Ukrainian the word was "zozulya" or the diminutive "zozul'ka" – the same word used in Ukrainian for a cuckoo.

THE GATHERING OF LIVING
AND DEAD SOULS

The time and date was set in late May in the Ethnographic Museum. It was Nicholas's farewell to the city he had come to love. It was not just the city, but the people, because a city that is just buildings isn't a living city, for it would just be a cold concrete and stone thing even though it would still have stories to tell, archeological ones at least, about the hundreds of thousands who once lived there, loved there and died.

The talk was arranged by the America-Ukraine Friendship Council, which had asked Mr. Viktor to be the "presenter" of Nicholas, since for years he had often organized a monthly cultural program at the Museum. In the five months Nicholas had spent in the city he found that almost at every step he took along the *brukivka*, the gray cobblestones, he would find a place with a narrative waiting to be told. It was like the feeling he had after his now distant dream of shards of a stained-glass window. He had been collecting the pieces and could see more and more of the stained-glass picture, even though it wasn't quite complete. He had come to the conclusion that he was a collector like Hohol's-Gogol's Chichikov, though not one of dead souls like the hero of the novel by the great Ukrainian author was, but of *living* souls. *Living* souls working together for a purpose, a mysterious, yet to be understood one.

Nicholas focused his lecture completely on the positive, on the beautiful things he had experienced in Leopolis. And he talked a lot about the people from all walks of life he had met, starting with the saleslady at the storefront stand across from the main Post Office who sold the tastiest *pirizhky* in the city and who with a gold-toothed smile when she would see him would always pull out two baked pastries for him filled with potatoes. He talked about the beautiful buildings, the wonderful students he had met in his classes and at lectures.

He talked about his friends, all of whom were in the audience on the uncomfortable wooden benches that looked more like wooden pews in a cathedral. He talked about how each of those he met in his or her own way showed him and taught him so much about the city and about life, had helped him come to love every corner of this gray cobblestone place of mystery and discovery. Those who come to this city and just see drabness don't really have eyes; they don't have that inner vision that looks beyond surfaces. Nicholas had come to understand that this city of lions was a gathering ground and a meeting place of intersecting worlds, a nexus of temporality with the infinite, a place of transcendence with its many intricate designs and carvings acting as hieroglyphs for the initiated to read. This very room with its remarkable symbolic signs was an open door to the other side of elsewheres.

While Nicholas was delivering his lecture in one plane of existence, he could feel more than one foot of himself in another. He was simultaneously feeling the presence of multiple dimensions, other realms of existence, worlds visible and invisible from the vantage point of his world. In each place there were similar faces in the audience, the same, yet a palpably different place. With that second sight becoming stronger and stronger inside him, Nicholas could see beyond the outer skin, beyond the shell of everyone gathered.

Did that all-seeing eye, the one he felt always following his presence, hold a key to understanding what he couldn't yet understand? What were the seven signs of the lion he had come here to find? Had he seen and found them already without really knowing? The Chapel of the Boims? High Castle Mountain? The Dominican Cathedral? The Devil's Cliffs? The Armenian Cathedral? Bald Mountain? The Citadel? The Lazarus Steps? The Dziga-Whirlygig passage to nowhere? Lychakiv Cemetery? The niche to nowhere? Nowhere is somewhere if you know where it is. But he didn't know where it was despite his zigzag spiral of accumulated knowledge.

There was something about the city of Leopolis that sharpened his senses, his intensity and capacity to feel that heightened his perceptions in ways he had never known before.

What was his task? Why was he called here?

As he stood at the podium in his jacket and tie, he felt as if his clothing and skin were being removed by some unknown force. It wasn't an altogether unpleasant feeling. It was almost sensual, as though cool tongues of a flame that did not burn were licking off the outer shell of his body.

He felt lines of unseen energy flash to him in lightning-bolt fashion from different spots in the room. It was as if ropes of energy were being tossed out to him and tied to life preservers of innermost thought. Instead of reeling him in, the lifelines of energy seemed to stretch back and forth to people in the audience. He couldn't yet tell to whom they were linked, but he sensed a surge within himself. He also sensed fiery glowing ravenous red eyes in the audience getting more and more disturbed by the glow. He could barely see what now appeared to be illuminated lines of blue light linking with him. Suddenly, almost miraculously, and without thinking about it, but just feeling it, he FINALLY understood. It was the voice of the collective energy of the blue lines linking to his mind, giving him the final key to the puzzle that had taken him months to solve.

The shattered stained glass began to formulate a whole picture for him in his mind as if a reconstructing magnet had pulled all the shards of it together back into their proper place. He closed his eyes and could now see through his lids as if they were just a filter, blocking out harmful light to let him see unencumbered. He could now see that he was at the center of the celestial blue stained-glass window – and that there were seven signs of the lion encircling him in perfect harmony. THE SIGNS WEREN'T SYMBOLS! THE SIGNS WEREN'T THINGS! THE SIGNS WEREN'T PLACES OR BUILDINGS! The places were important, but they only were important in the way they interacted with the seven gathered living souls, in the assemblage before him, whose blue celestial light of their inner souls linked with him, the eighth sign of the lion, to restore infinite elemental blue, to restore balance in the world, to restore life. He, a man who considered himself average at best, had stumbled into the struggle between chaos and life.

Nicholas understood that the sacred places in the city he had discovered were powerful points of transformation to aid him in the preparation of the seven other signs for the journey to an interface between worlds, his world and the one of the Arkubeet that he had seen in nightmares – on the other side of the tunnel descending elsewhere.

While Nicholas knew that he had been chosen by some force unknown to him, he could now hear the raven's caw and felt nothing but doubts well inside him. The road to happiness, he thought, right at that moment, would have been to forget about all these idiotic signs of the lion and the fool's gold of prophetic dreams. He should tell Raya he was crazy about her (which happened to be true) and ask her to marry him, settle down and have children. The road to riches for him seemed to be just to say his goodbyes and forget about her, get on that United flight, and go home. He could just fall into a personal oblivion and go on with his current life's path, which, at that moment, seemed to be the easiest. Despite his doubts and insecurities, he decided to take the most dangerous path – the road that might lead to *death*. It wasn't fear of death that concerned him, but apprehension for those he had learned to love the most. Wittingly or unwittingly, he was about to make a sacrifice, which might cost everything that was dear to him in this life. To save this city he had come to love so dearly, he might never be able to see it again. To save Raya and his other friends, he may have to deny the deepest feelings he had for her and would be unable to share with her his innermost secret. And at that very moment when he knew he had chosen to be chosen, he felt the thoughts of Mr. Viktor come to him and say: "Your hour has come. But be careful. One of the signs may betray you...."

SHAKESPEARE NOT THE BARD

It was not the bard, but a restaurant. It was in the direction of the city out toward the airport. You can take the #95 *marshrutka*, whose final stop is the airport, to get there.

"I'd like to go somewhere special with you this week," Nicholas mentioned to Raya. "How about the Shakespeare Restaurant?"

"Ohhh, nooo, that's too expensive!" She answered right away, but relented after his third request. "It's a special night, maybe my last one here," he said. "My last supper," he laughed to himself as he said it, understanding his cross-lingual pun. It's actually "taina vecherya" in Ukrainian, if you mean the subject of the da Vinci painting, which in English translation literally means "mysterious supper."

The restaurant turned out not to be very expensive even by local standards. One hundred and twenty hryvnas ($25) for dinner for two. It was clean and done in retromodern natural wood chic.

There was only one other table of customers that evening with two older men sitting in the corner seemingly talking business.

The waiter was wearing green tartan kilts and about the most attentive one Nicholas had observed in any restaurant he had been to during his visit to Ukraine. And the food was outstanding, almost as good as at the Kupil Restaurant near the Stefanyk Library.

The evening with Raya was extremely pleasant, more so than Nicholas could ever have imagined. Conversation with her was always just like a gentle breeze with never a pregnant pause or awkward moment. Nicholas felt so comfortable with her. He had never felt that way with anyone else in his life. Her eyes that evening as always were like pools of azure blue light that touched his soul.

Nicholas reminisced about the past several months and how much he would miss everyone (especially meaning *her* when he said *everyone*), with Raya telling him he wasn't going away forever, that he'd be back, and soon.

Nicholas tried to keep from getting emotional and stayed under control the entire time in the restaurant. When they left, Raya asked if wanted to take a *marshrutka* or walk.

"I'd rather walk," he said. And that was a mistake. He couldn't hold his emotions back and kept wiping away tears as they walked closer and closer to her apartment building.

"It'll be okay," Raya assured him.

"You don't understand, Raya," he answered as he wiped away a tear. "I'm sorry I'm this way. I hate having you see me this way. I just can't control it."

He walked her over to her apartment building in twenty minutes or so, gave her a big hug and kiss on the cheek, and started to walk away.

"Can I say 'goodbye' to you tomorrow?" She asked as he was walking away from her.

"No, I don't think I can handle that…."

"Okay," she answered, "I'll do whatever you want."

"You know I want to see you…."

"And I want to see you…. But I'll do whatever you want. I'll be downtown in the morning."

"Just call me in the morning. Or just stop over. A lot of people will be seeing me off, so I'd just like to spend some time with you."

"We can go for coffee… Maybe to the Golden Ducat…"

"Yes, er, no," he answered. "The Ducat's not our place. It's not you. You're bright. You're light. The Ducat's dark."

"Okay, I'll call you in the morning."

And Nicholas walked away toward the tramcar that was going to take him from the last stop along Sakharov Street to Hyphenated Writer Street for the last time.

WHAT WOULD HAVE HAPPENED IF NICHOLAS HAD GOTTEN ON THAT PLANE?

First, Nicholas would have had a morning filled with partings. Everyone he had gotten to know would have met him, tried to meet him, or called him to say "goodbye." The hardest goodbyes would have been to Raya and Nadya. He would have given Raya a big hug and kiss after shutting the door in his apartment so his other friends couldn't see it. He would have met earlier with Raya for an hour or so at the Café Fresca just off Rynok Square. He would have given Raya mixed signals. First he would have said to her on the phone: "I don't think I can handle saying goodbye to you. It's just too emotional for me." And she would have answered: "I'll do whatever you want." And after their hour-long and thoroughly enjoyable chat at the Café (readers shouldn't always be privy to everything characters say in private), Nicholas would have said to her: "Thanks for not listening to me. I'm glad we met. It was great." And on the walk back to his apartment, about two blocks away he would have turned to her, grabbed her with both arms in a hug, and would have kissed her once sweetly, saying afterward in Ukrainian: "Sorry for twisting your arm…." The verb *zgvaltuvaty* literally means forcing or even raping, but in friendly conversations it always means twisting someone's arm mildly to do something against their will that they really end up enjoying. And Raya would have answered: "No, it was nice. Really nice…." And she would have smiled back at Nicholas with her blue eyes that always reminded him of a clear summer sky. And one block closer to his apartment on Hyphenated Writer Street, Nicholas and Raya would have run into Nadya wearing a blue dress and would have walked together to the apartment. Nicholas's host from the university Marta would have been waiting at the door of the apartment with a bottle of cognac to say goodbye. "We're all going to miss you," she would have said to him as she gave him a friendly parting hug.

Vira would have been out of the city taking her son to stay with her mother in Kolomiya so he could spend some time in the country, but she would have called Nicholas on his cell phone to say goodbye and to apologize for not being able to meet with him. Nadya would have also given him a hug and a kiss outside his apartment as she was leaving and would have said something like: "Bilanchuk! I'm really going to miss you! This platonic stuff isn't easy when you really get to know someone like this. I don't know how I'm going to live without you here. I've gotten so used to you." And she would have waved and turned away before Nicholas would have seen the tears trickling down her face as she walked toward Bandera Street to catch the *marshrutka* minibus to take her home.

Nicholas would have made a call to Mr. Viktor on his cell phone on his way to the airport in the car driven by Raya's photographer friend Marko to say "goodbye." Mr. Viktor wouldn't have been able to meet him because of family commitments but would have been really grateful for the call and for being remembered. His red-headed Ukrainian tutor Olenka would have met him just outside the steps to the airport building entrance and would have given him a great big bear hug and kiss. She would have also given him a parting gift of a box of Stozhary chocolates that were one of Nicholas's favorites.

After Marko had helped him move all his luggage into the check in line inside the airport, Nicholas would have had to pay a $100 bribe to get his luggage, books and assorted gifts, including eight bottles of cognac, onto the plane. The guy taking him to another room to pay the bribe would have told him something like this: "Look, United Airlines and customs will charge you $300 or more bucks to do this officially for the overweight baggage and fines. This way, give me a hundred-dollar bill, and the check-in girl gets a little of it, I get a cut, the guy in the other room gets a cut…. I have a family to feed, you know, and everybody is happy."

Nicholas would have nodded and pulled out the hundred dollar bill and slipped it to him mindlessly. Despite paying the bribe at the check in counter, Nicholas would have run into a nasty customs guy who would have given him all kinds of trouble for having too many books, especially dictionaries, no export licenses, too many bottles of cognac, and DVD and CD disks that might contain state secrets that had not been cleared by customs. He would have asked Nicholas how much money he had left, and Nicholas would have told him $600 – $100 less than before the bribe. And the guy would have told him that the fine for his violations would be ten times that plus a possible prison term. The customs guy finally would have relented once he saw that Nicholas was playing dumb and wasn't about to give him another bribe. He would have waved him through to the waiting room in frustration.

The flight back would have been totally uneventful with no turbulence and an utterly silent and rather unpleasant dour-faced Polish woman sitting next to him in the last seat in the right aisle at the very back of the cramped 767. Despite that unpleasant traveling companion, a tiny rainbow would have accompanied Nicholas on the entire trip home outside the window of his plane, a rainbow that he knew was prayed for and sent by Raya to keep him safe.

But none of this ever happened since he never got on that plane. Fate always comprises several paths, several possibilities that you take or don't take with different destinations. This one on this day was not his.

POSTSCRIPTUM

I have to admit that I found these pages scribbled in several block copybooks and on a flash drive left in an apartment at 13/11 Nechui-Levytsky Street in Lviv that I rented for the summer in 2007. I met Nicholas during a Fulbright orientation in Kyiv and found out about the apartment from him by email. I found a DVD disk with over two thousand pictures on it, too, in the apartment. I copied the flash files, the DVD picture files, and retyped the handwritten pages into my computer as best I could. Since I'm not really a writer, I didn't know what to do with them. That's why I left them like this.

I also read a story in the English version of the Lviv Gazette dated June 7, 2007 that American Fulbright visiting scholar Nicholas Bilanchuk never appeared for his flight on June 2, 2007 to Warsaw and then to Newark Airport. The story mentioned a rumor that two husky-looking guys in black leather jackets may have ransacked his apartment when they didn't find him home. The whole story had something to do with a Mafioso who apparently was under the impression that his girlfriend had met Nicholas on the Kyiv Express train and had a fling with him. He purportedly sent two ambassadors of revenge to visit him. I can't attest to the veracity of that story, but it was just a rumor and sounds quite out of character with the Nicholas I met in Kyiv.

Oddly, I found out, on that very same day that Nicholas disappeared, seven other people vanished from the city of Leopolis without a trace. Who were they really? If I can find another flash drive under the bed or in a forgotten nook of the apartment, I would be able tell you the rest of the story.

CONTENTS

Dear Reader,

Thank you for purchasing this book.

We at Glagoslav Publications are glad to welcome you, and hope that you find our books to be a source of knowledge and inspiration. We want to show the beauty and depth of the Slavic region to everyone looking to expand their horizon and learn something new about different cultures and different people, and we believe that with this book we have managed to do just that.

Now that you've gotten to know us, we want to get to know you. We value communication with our readers and want to hear from you! We offer several options:

– Join our Book Club on Goodreads, Library Thing and Shelfari, and receive special offers and information about our giveaways;

– Share your opinion about our books on Amazon, Barnes & Noble, Waterstones and other bookstores;

– Join us on Facebook and Twitter for updates on our publications and news about our authors;

– Visit our site www.glagoslav.com to check out our Catalogue and subscribe to our Newsletter.

Glagoslav Publications is getting ready to release a new collection and planning some interesting surprises — stay with us to find out more!

Glagoslav Publications
Office 36, 88-90 Hatton Garden
EC1N 8PN London, UK
Tel: + 44 (0) 20 32 86 99 82
Email: contact@glagoslav.com

Glagoslav Publications Catalogue

- The Time of Women by Elena Chizhova
- Sin by Zakhar Prilepin
- Hardly Ever Otherwise by Maria Matios
- Khatyn by Ales Adamovich
- Christened with Crosses by Eduard Kochergin
- The Vital Needs of the Dead by Igor Sakhnovsky
- A Poet and Bin Laden by Hamid Ismailov
- Kobzar by Taras Shevchenko
- White Shanghai by Elvira Baryakina
- The Stone Bridge by Alexander Terekhov
- King Stakh's Wild Hunt by Uladzimir Karatkevich
- Depeche Mode by Serhii Zhadan
- Herstories, An Anthology of New Ukrainian Women Prose Writers
- The Battle of the Sexes Russian Style by Nadezhda Ptushkina
- A Book Without Photographs by Sergey Shargunov
- Sankya by Zakhar Prilepin
- Wolf Messing by Tatiana Lungin
- Good Stalin by Victor Erofeyev
- Solar Plexus by Rustam Ibragimbekov
- Don't Call me a Victim! by Dina Yafasova
- A History of Belarus by Lubov Bazan
- Children's Fashion of the Russian Empire by Alexander Vasiliev
- Boris Yeltsin - The Decade that Shook the World by Boris Minaev
- A Man Of Change - A study of the political life of Boris Yeltsin
- Gnedich by Maria Rybakova
- Marina Tsvetaeva - The Essential Poetry
- Multiple Personalities by Tatyana Shcherbina
- The Investigator by Margarita Khemlin
- Leo Tolstoy – Flight from paradise by Pavel Basinsky
- Moscow in the 1930 by Natalia Gromova
- Prisoner by Anna Nemzer
- Alpine Ballad by Vasil Bykau
- The Complete Correspondence of Hryhory
- The Tale of Aypi by Ak Welsapar
- Selected Poems by Lydia Grigorieva
- The Fantastic Worlds of Yuri Vynnychuk
- The Garden of Divine Songs and Collected Poetry of Hryhory Skovoroda
- Adventures in the Slavic Kitchen: A Book of Essays with Recipes

  More coming soon…

www.ingramcontent.com/pod-product-compliance
Lightning Source LLC
Chambersburg PA
CBHW051631180726
48284CB00006B/1688